The Murder Trial
of the
Last Lakota Warrior

To Sarah

I appreciate your help
in writers group

Also by Steve Linstrom

The Last Ram (2013)

The Murder Trial
of the
Last Lakota Warrior

Steve Linstrom

NORTH STAR PRESS OF ST. CLOUD, INC.
St. Cloud, Minnesota

Cover Design: Liz Dwyer

ISBN: 978-0-87839-722-8

First Edition: June 2014

Printed in the United States of America

Published by
North Star Press of St. Cloud, Inc.
P.O. Box 451
St. Cloud, MN 56302

www.northstarpress.com

Acknowledgements

The endeavor of writing a novel requires the commitment of the author's family and friends as much as the author. I'm fortunate to have a wonderful group of people supporting and encouraging me, even when they don't like what I've written. My wife, Stephanie, demonstrated incredible patience in dealing with the mood swings I go through when constructing a novel. She also acted as my first editor and helped me with the character development of Laura, in particular. My thanks also goes out to Saara Myrene Raappana for her editing help. And of course, a special thank you goes to Corinne and Curtis at North Star Press for putting the whole thing together.

Chapter One

THE STRONGHOLD WAS LITTERED with the remnants of cattle: heads, horns and half butchered carcasses. Coyotes and ravens were feasting on the remains among the discarded lodge poles and black fire rings, some still smoking. Rifle pits faced the neck of land that connected the plateau, newly dug dirt already covered in a glaze of frost. There were no spent cartridges on the ground around them as they hadn't been used. Toward the middle of the plateau, a structure of medicine poles stood over food offerings left for the Great Spirit. The poles shuddered a little in the cold Dakota wind.

Lieutenant Edward Casey, his 200 Cheyenne scouts, and observer Frederic Remington paused at the entrance of what had been a Lakota camp. Without waiting for orders, the scouts dismounted and picked through the remains of what was left of the Ghost Dance camp. Casey thought it was all that was left of the Ghost Dance movement. It was clear the Lakota had abandoned the camp in a rush. Just a few days before, the gunfire from the conflict at Wounded Knee would have been heard by the Ghost Dancers on the top of the plateau. It would have alerted them of trouble well before the messengers arrived and spread the news of the massacre of Big Foot's band. They didn't wait for the army to come for them next. They left The Stronghold. They left the promise of the Ghost Dance.

Remington emerged from a pile of discarded rubbish carrying something. He waved at Casey and, wrinkling his nose at the stench of rotting meat, made his way across the abandoned camp. Casey didn't attempt to stop the scouts from sifting through the remains. He knew collecting the spoils of war was one of the prime motivators for his Cheyenne scouts to be with him here in South Dakota. Since the shooting was probably over, he gave them some time to scavenge what the Lakota had left. But the image of Remington waddling toward him with Lakota souvenirs in his fat fingers made Casey angry. He reminded himself that he couldn't afford to offend General Miles's pet.

Remington held up a stone pipe and a rawhide stirrup he had picked out of the rubbish. "These will be perfect props for me to use in my paintings," he said, waving them. Even in the cold January weather, beads of sweat crossed his forehead, and the walk to the edge of camp had him breathing hard. Casey hoped they wouldn't run into any trouble that would require Remington to move more quickly than a waddle.

"Very nice," he said. "They must have packed up in a hurry to have left that pipe."

"It's hard to believe this was the center of the Ghost Dance," Remington said, sweeping his arm across the plateau top. The medicine poles stood at odd angles in the middle of camp, bouncing in the wind. "It was the hope of the Sioux Nation and now it's all gone."

Casey knew that the name "Sioux" was generic for several bands stretching all the way to the Great Lakes, linked by a common language. He also knew the group in this part of the country preferred being known by the name of their dialect: "Lakota." "Sioux" was a term the white man called them. Casey always said "Lakota," but he didn't want to argue with the artist at this point.

"This place probably looked quite different with several hundred Lakota warriors up here dancing in a frenzy," Casey said as he kicked a frozen dirt clod across the ground and over the edge of the plateau. He paused for a moment, listening for the satisfying thump of it hitting the ground several hundred feet below. "I suppose they heard the gunfire from Wounded Knee the other day and got the hell outta here."

Remington wrinkled his nose again. "They certainly must not have been starving. Look at all the meat they left up here to rot."

"They were probably planning on more people showing up. This is where Big Foot was headed. It looks like they were planning on staying awhile." Casey squatted down and examined the rifle pits overlooking the narrow bridge that connected the plateau to the ridge. "Look at these pits. A few well-armed warriors could have held off the whole damned army."

"It would have taken a siege or a huge battle to run them off," Remington said, his breath coming out in small puffs. "God, it would have been glorious. I wish I could have seen it."

Casey sighed a prayer of thanks that the Lakota had abandoned The Stronghold. The battle would have been a cold, frustrating waiting game. On the other hand, an assault on a well-defended position would have provided opportunity for a brave officer to distinguish himself. And with General Miles's favorite artist and writer in attendance and just begging for a hero, maybe he could have . . .

"Lieutenant!" a voice carried across the top of the plateau. One of his top scouts, White Moon, stood at the edge of the east side drop-off and pointed across the plains of the Badlands. A few dark smudges on the plains marked a patrol of Lakota. They'd spotted the army on top of The Stronghold. Three puffs of smoke rose from the Indians in the distance, followed a second later by a hollow sounding "pop." They were clearly well out of range to be of any danger but were firing out of frustration.

The scouts rushed to catch their ponies. The company leaders were already shouting commands to organize the pursuit of the Lakota patrol. They didn't want to go all the way back to Fort Keogh in Montana without the opportunity to gain some Sioux horses as war booty. Even Remington was awkwardly running across the remains of the camp to his wagon, holding his souvenir stone pipe over his head.

Casey recalled his orders. The captain had been explicit. "Do not engage the Sioux in battle! The Seventh has killed hundreds at Wounded Knee . . . many women and children. General Miles does not want a full-fledged Indian War on his hands. Just go out there and find out if it's true they've left The Stronghold." Casey desperately wanted to chase the retreating Lakota patrol, but he knew there would be hell to pay at camp and his career didn't need any more setbacks. Miles's new plan for limited warfare would play out with the humanitarians and politicians on the East Coast, but it was going to be difficult to convince his scouts.

Lieutenant Casey stood in the middle of the bridge to The Stronghold, sealing his Cheyenne scouts to the top of the plateau. "You will halt this instant! Sergeant, call the men into formation." The scouts reined in their horses and shouted at him. "We don't want to go back to Montana poor, carrying only camp garbage. We came to Pine Ridge to fight!"

"We're going down and set up a bivouac out of the wind. We are not going to chase the Lakota patrol . . . We are not!" Casey shouted. "Now form up!"

The scouts grumbled but formed up their column. The Cheyenne didn't accept orders like a regular army command, but Casey had trained them well and earned their respect. They may not like it, but they would follow orders—his orders. The command slowly made its way across the neck to the ridge and then, via a washed-out gully, down to the plains below. At the foot of the plateau, they made camp. White tents and cooking fires sprang up quickly. It wasn't particularly cold for a January day in South Dakota, but night would be coming on quickly. "Make sure the horses are herded into that little boxed canyon" Casey ordered. "The Lakota would like nothing better than to steal them."

"Lieutenant," White Moon shouted across their little camp. "Sioux!"

Casey walked out in front of the camp toward where White Moon sat mounted on a large army horse. Two hundred yards away, a group of sixty to seventy Sioux warriors appeared as if emerging from the ground.

The level of tension immediately rose throughout the camp. Behind him, Casey heard his scouts scrambling to catch their ponies and the distinctive clicks of rifles being loaded. Without looking back, he walked slowly out of the camp toward the Lakota warriors and stopped fifty feet past the last tent with his hands on his hips, hovering over his army revolver. He felt rather than heard his scouts advancing several feet behind him on horseback, poised for battle. Without turning his face from the Lakota patrol, he extended his hand out to the side, palm facing his scouts and said quietly but firmly, "Stand down, Sergeant. Don't come any closer."

A group of five Lakota men emerged from the patrol and made their way slowly toward Casey. They were led by an old man covered in blankets. Three strong-looking warriors and a slender man, who was younger than the rest, followed. A murmuring from behind him caused him to slowly turn his upper body to face his scouts, hand on his revolver. "I will shoot through the head the first man who falls out of ranks. Sergeant Mason, you are responsible for keeping these men under control."

"Yes, sir," the grizzled sergeant said. "You heard the lieutenant. Stand down!"

Casey turned back toward the advancing Indians. "We are here in peace," he called.

Behind him and to his right, White Moon translated.

The old man at the head of the little group spoke in the Lakota dialect and pointed toward the top of The Stronghold plateau. White Moon translated, "I am Two Strike, chief of the Brule Lakota. Why is the army destroying our symbols? Is it not enough that you have murdered hundreds of Lakota at Wounded Knee?"

Casey replied, "We were only investigating. Bear Coat Miles has said he wants no more bloodshed." Bear Coat was the name the Lakota had for General Nelson Miles.

The murmurs from the Lakota at the mention of Miles's name made Casey wonder if he had done the right thing mentioning him.

"Someone should have told the soldiers there was to be no bloodshed before they fired on Big Foot's band, before they rode down women and children and murdered them," Two Strike said. The old man spoke quietly but firmly.

Casey felt the angry tension from the warriors in front of him, which matched the energy of the Cheyenne scouts at his back.

Two Strike raised his dark eyes to the ranks of Cheyenne warriors in blue army coats behind the lieutenant. His voice carried across the Badlands, "The Cheyenne and Lakota have been allies for many years. We shared hunting grounds, and we fought common enemies. My friend Spotted Tail avenged the Cheyenne when the army murdered Black Kettle's people at Sand Creek. Now, after the bluecoats attacked the Lakota at Wounded Knee, you stand with them? The Lakota fought together with your fathers. You are no Cheyenne. You are just the white man's dogs." He spit off to the side.

Casey didn't need White Moon's interpretation to know that Two Strike had insulted his scouts. Several of them yelled, one man saying in Lakota, "Come over here and fight, Sioux cowards. We'll show you who's a dog." The grizzled sergeant barked a command and the Cheyenne fell back into ranks, still grumbling.

White Moon attempted to translate the insult, but Casey held his hand out and interrupted him. Two Strike's words were clearly incendiary, but the old man's eyes didn't look like his heart was in it. Casey thought the words were probably more of a concession to the angry young warriors at his side than his own thoughts.

Casey pointed to the sky, "It will be dark soon. There's been enough killing. We didn't come here to fight." He made a hand gesture to one of the white sergeants behind him. "Tollifson, bring that side of bacon up."

When the sergeant came forward with the bundle of meat in his hands, Casey took it and handed it up to one of the mounted men next to Two Strike. He extended a hand to the old chief, "It's cold and getting dark, and enough people have died. Take this food and leave us in peace."

Casey had left the chief a way to leave the scene without battle and still save face. Two Strike said nothing, but Casey thought he caught a look of relief in his eyes. The old chief lightly touched Casey's hand and wheeled his horse away. The rest of the Lakota warriors shouted in victory and rode off into the Badlands. They had not killed the bluecoats in battle, but they'd won a face-saving confrontation.

Casey turned to his scouts with his hand resting on the butt of his revolver. "There will be no more bloodshed. We will post double watch tonight and make sure the horses are secure. You are dismissed."

The grumbling from the scouts was unmistakable. They had been insulted to their faces and were unable to respond. The training Casey had instilled in them in the last five years had made it clear that orders from a superior officer were to be followed in the army. Most of them had been too young to have been warriors and fought alongside the Lakota in the Indian Wars. A warrior, whether he be Cheyenne or Lakota, would never have endured the insult Two Strike had thrown at them, but they were soldiers now, not warriors.

Casey walked resolutely toward his tent. His knees were shaking so badly that he felt his entire body would collapse. Every one of the Lakota warriors and every one of the Cheyenne scouts had their fingers twitching against the triggers of their weapons. If even one of them on either side had pulled the trigger, whether it was aimed at anyone or not, both he and Two Strike would be dead by now. He knew his scouts and even his white officers were disappointed and probably thought him a coward, but he had successfully obeyed his orders and kept the peace.

The light in his tent was inviting. While his men slept in four-foot-high tents with barely enough room for two men to lie down, he and Remington had larger tents with two-foot higher walls that could even support a small table beside a bunk. For once, he was thankful for the extra equipment and luxury his observer had required. Five more steps and he could collapse out of sight from the prying eyes of his command.

From behind his tent a portly figure emerged. The last person in the world he wanted to see right now was Fredrick Remington. For an instant, he imagined what a painting of a U.S. Army Officer meekly handing over a present in submission to a fierce Lakota warrior might look like. He hoped at least that Remington would not make his face recognizable.

"That, Lieutenant Casey, was truly remarkable. General Miles will be favorably impressed by the courage you showed, facing down both the hostile Lakota and your own Cheyenne troops." The fact that Remington chose to deliver this message in a hushed tone rather than in his usual overblown, pompous voice acknowledged that he recognized how frustrated the soldiers were with their leader.

Casey also kept is voice low. "I'm afraid I don't feel very courageous."

"Nonsense," Remington said. "Please come join me in my tent for a libation before dinner call."

Casey looked longingly at the warm glow of his tent, then followed the portly man to the other tent pitched beside the wooden wagon.

"Come in, come in, my boy, and warm yourself," Remington held the flap of his Sibley tent open. It irked Casey that he was being called "boy" when he was at least as old as or even older than the portly man. However, he was too tired to make any issue tonight. Remington took the only chair in the room and pointed Casey over to the wide bunk. One of the reasons the patrol included a wooden wagon was so they could transport this extra wide reinforced "bunk."

Remington produced a bottle and two glasses. He poured each of them two-thirds full and handed one to Casey, who knew he should decline, but it had been one hell of a day. He responded to Remington's silent toast and took a sip. The big man had drained his glass in a gulp and was pouring another.

"Yes, sir, Lieutenant Casey . . . err . . . may I call you Edward . . . or Ed? Standing off Indians both ahead of and behind you was truly amazing," he said, draining half of his refilled glass.

"Ned is fine," Casey said. "After that fiasco at Wounded Knee, we didn't need any more bloodshed."

Remington paused, and a small smile passed across his face. "'Fiasco' you call it. Well, Lieutenant Casey, I would beg to differ," he said, swirling the whiskey remaining in his glass. "I'd call it a significant victory for our brave troops assigned to keep peace in a violent land."

Casey remained silent. When he and his fellow officers had heard of the Lakota civilian casualties, they'd been appalled. Soldiers were supposed to kill soldiers, not women and children. The Seventh Cavalry had killed over three hundred Lakota, over half of them women and children. It was hard for Casey to view the slaughter as a victory.

"You see, Lieutenant Casey, as you will read in my article in the next issue of *Harper's Weekly*, the action the troops took at Wounded Knee was absolutely necessary. The fact that some civilians got in the way was unfortunate, but it's the fault of the Sioux warriors who chose to bring the noncombatants to the battlefield."

"A soldier does not kill women and childr—"

"A soldier . . ." Remington interrupted holding up a finger. "A soldier does what his commander orders."

Casey set his glass on the table and started to rise. He didn't need to be lectured on military protocol by this overweight civilian painter. "Oh, sit down, Ned." Remington put a hand on his arm. "If you want to get ahead in this man's army, you need to start understanding politics."

Casey sat back on the bunk. Remington refilled Casey's glass and poured another for himself. He sat back and took another gulp. "Do you know why I'm here? Why I'm out in these godforsaken plains in the middle of winter? Do you know why I spent the month with you and your scouts in Montana last fall?"

Casey had wondered that himself. Of all the army installations in the country, why had Remington been assigned to his little command? "I suppose to get material for your paintings?"

"Pishaw . . . I can find broken-down cowboys and Indians any-where," Remington said with a wave of his hand. "I was in Montana and am here now because General Nelson A. Miles, the major general of the entire army and your supreme commander . . . wants me here."

Remington had shown up at Fort Keough in Montana with the general on an inspection trip. Miles had recently been named to replace General Crook as the Major General of the army. Most of the troops thought Miles only came out to Montana to remind the troops and the public that he was the one who had driven Sitting Bull and Crazy Horse into surrender fifteen years earlier. He had ended the Indian Wars in the field, although Crook got the credit at the negotiating table.

"The general is now the most powerful soldier in the United States Army. So why do you think he would want to have an overweight painter like me in the field?" Remington pounded on the table with his fat fist. "Think, man."

Casey took a sip of his whiskey and shook his head. He'd wondered why he'd been saddled with the care of the pompous painter himself. "He likes your paintings?"

Remington shook his head, finished his drink and poured himself another. He motioned to Casey, who shook his head. "For one thing, Nelson Miles doesn't know the first thing about art. Secondly, even if he did, do you think I'd be out here on the plains just to keep an admirer happy?" The big man's words were starting to slur.

"Nelson Miles is a very ambitious man. He already has the highest rank in the army. What do you think is next? What would be the next step?"

Casey shook his head. The world of generals and painters was not his concern. He just wanted to go to his nice warm tent and forget how close he had just come to being killed.

"I'm here, Lieutenant Casey, to get the honorable Major General Nelson A. Miles elected as the president of these United States." He made the proclamation and waited for Casey to respond. When he only got a blank stare, he continued. "Making a president is far different than it was in the old days. Instead of winning in dark, smoke-filled rooms, today's president needs to win in newspapers and magazines. It's 1891, boy! Today's voters read, and they vote for who they read about."

Remington was on a roll. He stood in the cramped tent, stretched his arms and leaned over the back his chair. "And, Lieutenant Casey, do you know what voters see in those newspapers and magazines?" He thumped his massive chest. "It's me . . . my drawings . . . my words. I will make the next president of the United States. That's why I'm here."

Casey took a sip of his drink. "How do pictures of Indians and soldiers get General Miles elected president?"

"A lot you know about politics, my boy." Remington moved his considerable girth between the chair and table, nearly knocking it over. "The next president needs to appeal to the adventurous streak in the American public. The conservatives need to remember it was he who tamed the Indians in Dakota, Montana, and in Arizona. It was General Miles who made the West a safe place to live and for commerce to thrive! The public also needs to know there is still evil out here, and only a man like General Miles can deal with these heathen savages. General Miles knows how to put them in their place, like he did at Wounded Knee, and how to negotiate to keep them there.

"You see," Remington pointed across the table at Casey, "you see, it isn't just conservatives, Westerners, 'want-to-be' adventurers, and ex-soldiers who vote. It's also the liberals, the humanitarians, and my New York neighbors. They need to be frightened enough of these savages that they want to keep a strong military, but they need to know that the general can also deal with the Indians humanly. That's why Wounded Knee was a glorious victory and why the general will now do everything he can to create peace."

"This whole Ghost Dance uprising was a result of Crook's mismanagement of military and Indian affairs. Now, in just a few short months, General Miles has put an end to it and restored peace by effectively combining words and guns."

Casey shook his head. The world of politics was confusing. He wanted no part of it.

Remington pointed at him. "That's why, Lieutenant Casey, your orders specifically stated, in no uncertain terms, that there would be no further armed conflicts."

Casey unconsciously put his hand to his chest where he kept his orders.

"Yes, yes, of course I know what your orders are. Do you think I'd be put into the field blind?" Remington said. "By backing those savages down, you fulfilled your role to the letter."

"I was afraid giving the Lakota a present of the side of bacon to leave with would be perceived as weak." Casey's words were starting to slur a little now as well. "I thought you might draw it that way, and I'd look . . . cowardly."

Remington laughed, shaking his big belly. "If I wanted you to look weak, I could make you look weak. In fact," he shook his finger. "if it was in the best interest of the general for you to look weak, you'd appear as a capitulating little yellow belly in my drawings of the scene and your career would be over."

Remington sat back on his chair and reached over to the stone pipe he had taken from the top of The Stronghold. "Like this pipe, Lieutenant Casey, you are a prop . . . a prop in support of the general." He turned it around in his hands. "And an important one, I may add." He set the pipe down carefully. "No, Lieutenant Casey, you won't look like a coward. You will appear as a brave and strong leader willing to fight when fighting is needed and willing to commit to peace when peace is needed. You . . ." he pointed at Casey again. "You're going to be what the public thinks of when they think of General Miles, and when they think of General Miles, they're going to think of the next president of the United States."

Casey was not a drinking man. He had only consumed a fifth of what Remington had, but he was already feeling dizzy.

"Are you a rich man, Lieutenant Casey? Very few lieutenants in this man's army are rich men."

"Umm . . . no, I ran into some financial difficulties—"

"You mean like losing both your inheritance and your sister's inheritance on that idiotic cattle ranch? You mean like all of your father's hard work gone in a single poor investment? You mean like your famous brother refusing to loan you any more money? Those kinds of difficulties?"

Casey sat forward. "How did you know . . . ?"

Remington smiled. "Did you think I came to travel with you by random, Lieutenant Casey?" He leaned back on his chair. "With the Indian Wars over and the army clogged up with Civil War veterans, it isn't an easy organization to stand out for promotion in, is it, Ned?"

Casey shook his head. He had grumbled many times to his fellow officers about being stuck in limbo. The pay for a lieutenant was poor, and the prospects of promotion were dim. There was simply no way to leap over the aging Civil War veterans who were avoiding all conflicts and clogging the promotion ranks. It wasn't his fault he was born ten years too late to be in a war.

"I think the last big accommodation you received was for your scintillating report and recommendations regarding slop barrels at army posts." Remington laughed heartily, holding his belly, "Yes, I read that too. It's certain to earn you captain's stripes in no time . . . if the army ever declares war on pig slop."

Casey had heard enough. The whiskey was getting to him, too. Arguing with the pompous bastard was going to get him nowhere but in trouble. He started to rise again.

Remington pushed his chest. "Oh, sit, sit, sit for God's sake. I meant no disrespect. Come on, Ned, I was just commenting on your current state of affairs. It's difficult to get ahead in the 1891 army. It isn't your fault."

Casey was still half standing. He reached for the tent flap.

"Your pretty bride-to-be won't wait in Paris forever, will she?"

Casey paused a long moment, then sat back down.

"Yes, I know all about Mrs. Achenson." Remington said. "She seems a lady of some refinement. Will you marry soon?"

Casey had not told any of his fellow officers of his engagement. He didn't think anyone knew, but Nellie must have told someone. "When I have sufficient capital, we will wed," he said stiffly.

"Will the lovely Mrs. Achenson and her daughters be living at Fort Keough, Montana?" Remington shook his head. "Obviously not . . . but what should an ambitious lieutenant do?"

Remington sat back and extended his stomach in his proclamation pose. "Lieutenant Casey, I have been a poor married man, and I have been a rich married man, and I can tell you rich is better, much better. My wife left me for two years until I made my fortune, and now, as long as I have a nice house in New York for her, she loves me deeply." He smiled. "And she doesn't care what I do."

Casey set his drink down again. This subject matter was entirely too personal, and the fat man knew entirely too much about him. "Why are you telling me all of this? What do you want from me?"

Remington waved his hand. "Lieutenant Casey, I'm only saying that you're in the right place at the right time to make something of yourself. Establishing the Cheyenne troops was a masterpiece. The image of a fighting man standing for peace over war will resonate. I'll make you a hero, and General Miles will appreciate a hero when he becomes president. It's important that you remember the path out of Fort Keogh."

"I don't understand," Casey said. The whiskey and the smoky room made his head swim.

"A general can only give orders to have his wishes carried out," Remington said, his words a little slurred. "A president can only point a man in the right direction and hope things work out, sometimes orders be damned. Miles is a general now, but he will be a president soon." He waved his hand. "I think I'll take a nap before dinner. Do you think you can have someone bring me some dinner here, in . . . in an hour or so?"

Casey clenched his jaw. This wasn't a hotel. "Yes, Mr. Remington, I'll see what I can do. But what did you mean when you said—?"

Remington slid over to the cot at the same time Casey rose from it. "Very well, Lieutenant Casey, I very much appreciate it. Remember what I told you. You need to stand out as a fighting man standing for peace." He waved his hand and rolled into the bunk. "Away."

The cold, black night slapped Casey in the face immediately as he emerged from Remington's tent. The wooziness of the whisky left his head as the cold bit at his nostrils. He ambled slowly toward the tent he shared with his executive officer, thinking about what the fat man had told him. The politics discussed were nothing new. They had been in the army gossip network for months, but the way Remington was so blatant about it . . . Casey felt like a piece on a chess board—a very minor pawn. He passed by the invitation of his tent flap and made his way to where the men were eating. He was in command and needed to eat with his men.

"Did the Cheyenne interpret correctly?"

Two Strike had dropped back in line to ride next to Plenty Horses. Wrapped in his three blankets, it looked like the old man's voice was coming out of an old pile of discarded clothing.

"I-I think so," Plenty Horses said. "I couldn't hear everything very well."

The Brule head chief made a sound something like a nose blow. "Plenty Horses, I brought you with the party because you know English." The voice was quiet but had a harsh edge. "I need to know if the interpreters the *waisicus* are using are translating the words correctly."

Plenty Horses sighed. He wished he'd been asked to accompany the head chief because he was a great warrior, not just to listen to talking. "I will listen better next time."

Two Strike grunted and urged his horse back to the front of the party. Plenty Horses looked around to see if any of the other warriors in the patrol had heard the conversation. Nobody turned toward him, and the other riders were just ahead or just behind him. No warrior rode side by side with him, not since he had come back from the east.

It wasn't fair. It hadn't been his idea to travel east to the Carlisle Indian School. He'd only been fourteen at the time. When his father said to go . . . he went. For five years, he had endured the white man's school. The other Indian children and even the teachers had made fun of him because he couldn't learn to read and write. The teachers finally gave up and loaned him out to work on farms to offset the cost of being at the school. When he was nineteen and still in third grade, they finally gave up and let him go. He could never survive in a white man's world. He couldn't learn from the books and hated working on the farms.

He was so happy to return to Dakota to live as a Lakota warrior.

But the life in Dakota was not the way he had imagined. His family didn't know him. His friends thought he'd become a white Indian and avoided him. He'd forgotten how to hunt and how to ride like a warrior. He failed to become what the whites wanted, and he'd failed to be what the Lakota wanted.

Now he'd failed Two Strike again in trying to interpret. He understood some of the English words but could not put them into Lakota easily. It was like being at school all over again. Plenty Horses let his horse drop back to the end of the group. He rode alone to the camp at White Clay Creek.

Chapter Two

JANUARY 7, 1891

WHITE MOON WAS DREAMING of mountains. The sky was clear and the air was crisp and clean. It was simple. He took a deep breath . . . "Wake up, White Moon!" Someone was shaking his foot.

"I said 'wake-up,' you oaf," Lieutenant Casey said in a harsh but quiet voice. "I need you to get something to eat and be ready to ride with me in twenty minutes."

White Moon rolled over and opened his blankets to the cold. "Where are we going?" he mumbled. "Which company . . ."

"No company," Casey said. "Just the two of us and perhaps one other. Now get ready."

Twenty minutes later, White Moon found himself riding out of camp with Casey and Rock Road just as the sky started to lighten. The rest of company hadn't been roused. "Where are we going, Lieutenant Casey?" he asked.

"We are going to look at the Brule camp on White Clay Creek," Casey said, keeping his eyes to the road. "We need to know if they have rifle pits like they had on The Stronghold."

"Why are only three of us going?" White Moon asked. He was no coward, but it didn't make sense that they were riding to the hostile Brule camp in broad daylight with only the three of them. If they were going to sneak up on the Brule, they were not doing a very good job of concealing themselves. "I don't—"

"White Moon," Casey said firmly. "You're a soldier. Just follow orders."

"Yes, Lieutenant," he said dropping his voice. Casey had insulted him in front of Rock Road, who now looked over at him and smiled. It wasn't like the lieutenant to insult him, especially in front of a fellow soldier. Rock Road was four years younger than he and was always trying to impress the white officers. White Moon imagined how Rock Road would retell the story again and again. "White Moon was afraid," he'd say to the other scouts.

Casey had told the entire company they were to have no contact with the Lakota. White Moon decided the orders must have changed since they were riding directly toward them. He would not ask the lieutenant again, however. He would only obey orders.

They rode slowly along White Clay Road through the Badlands. It was comfortable riding, and the road was well worn. They made no attempt to conceal themselves. By midafternoon, they came upon a large group of Lakota passively watching a herd of cattle. Greeting the group amicably, Casey had White Moon ask where the main camp was located. The Lakota men pointed further down the road. They said it was a one-hour ride if one moved slowly.

White Moon politely thanked them for the information, and they turned back to the road. Since they had no gifts to give, the Lakota men turned away and ignored them. After Two Strike's insults at the foot of The Stronghold two days before, White Moon had wondered how the Cheyenne would be received. These Lakota men were detached but not surly. They were not in the mood to fight.

"Rock Road," Casey said. "Black Shield and Bear Foot are patrolling to the north. I need you to go back and check on them to make sure they're within sound of me, but tell them to remain unseen." White Moon had seen Casey talking to the two other Cheyenne scouts before they left but had not seen them since. He assumed Casey had ordered the scouts to shadow them but remain hidden. He was going to ask, but after his earlier humiliation, he kept his mouth shut.

After Rock Road headed off to the north, White Moon and Casey continued down White Clay Road, moving slowly. He let Casey lead the way and hung back a little. The cold winter air was quiet, and the only sounds were the slow plodding of their horses' feet along the frozen road and the lolling of cattle in the distance behind them.

Then they heard the sound of other horses on the frozen road ahead of them, coming fast. White Moon pulled closer to the lieutenant, who did not appear to be concerned. Neither of them said anything as they stopped and waited.

Two riders approached at a quick pace. They were definitely Lakota and, from what White Moon could see, looked to be painted for war. White Moon rested his hand on the stock of his rifle, still loosely sheathed in the scabbard. Casey was resting his hand on his revolver, but he remained relaxed.

"*Hau, Kola!*" (which White Moon knew meant "Hello, my friend" in Lakota) Casey said and extended his hand as the two Lakota warriors got within a few yards. These two men definitely had a different feel about them than the cattle herders they had met an hour ago. As Casey rode forward to shake hands with each of the men, White Moon hung back warily, his hand still on the stock of his rifle.

Neither of the Lakota riders appeared to be more than twenty or twenty-one years old. The leader of the two spoke to Casey in English. "I'm Plenty Horses. My uncle Two Strike asked me to watch this road for soldiers." He spoke English pretty well with a refined accent. White Moon thought he must have learned it somewhere other than the trading post at the agency.

"I come in peace," Casey said, holding his hands out wide. "It's just White Moon and I."

Plenty Horses had deeply set eyes. He looked over White Moon and then moved his horse to fall into step with Casey's. They moved slowly down the road toward the Brule camp. White Moon heard Casey speaking softly as they rode but could not make out the words, although he could tell they were in English. Plenty Horses nodded, mumbled a few replies but then shook his head emphatically. Casey gestured down the road and White Moon heard him say, ". . . for peace." Plenty Horses shook his head again. The other warrior rode far to the other side of the two, keeping Plenty Horses and Casey between him and White Moon.

Another rider approached them on the road, which White Moon surmised led to the Brule Camp. He was Lakota as well, but was not in war paint. Reigning in in front of Casey and Plenty Horses, he introduced himself to Casey in Lakota as Bear Lying Down. Casey pointed to White Moon, and the man said in Lakota that he was just visiting the camp, that he had a pass from General Miles. He reached into the blanket he wore around his shoulders, and Plenty Horses and Casey both moved their hands towards their guns. They relaxed when he brought out a crumpled paper. Bear Lying Down ignored the two Lakota warriors and spoke directly to Casey, waiting for White Moon to interpret.

Through White Moon, Casey told Bear Lying Down that he wanted to visit the Brule camp on White Clay Creek. He said General Miles wanted him to visit and that if he was really carrying a pass from the general, he should go back to the village and tell Red Cloud he was here.

Bear Lying Down looked cautiously at Plenty Horses and the other warrior. "I was just at Two Strike's camp to visit and need to get back to Pine Ridge," he said, shaking his head. "I don't want to go back."

Casey pointed at the man and gave him an order. "Go back and tell the chiefs that General Miles sent me here to talk with them. Tell Red Cloud that Bear Coat sent me. Now!"

Before White Moon could finish interpreting, Bear Lying Down reacted based upon the tone of Casey's voice. He turned his horse around and left at a gallop towards the Brule Camp.

Casey lifted the reins to continue moving down the road, but Plenty Horses pulled in front of him. "No further," he said in English. "No closer to the camp until the chiefs have spoken."

Casey looked like he was going to issue another order, but then his shoulders relaxed. "We will wait here then."

White Moon and the other Lakota warrior stared at each other while Casey and Plenty Horses talked as they waited at the side of White Clay Road. Each of them had a hand relaxing very close to the butt of their weapons. White Moon was too far away to hear what they were talking about but there was a relaxed tone. He gazed around him at the desolate plateaus of the Badlands a quarter mile in the distance. He hoped that the canyons were not filled with Lakota warriors.

Nonetheless, he was glad when they finally heard hoof beats on the road from the camp. He didn't think the Lakota would let the two of them into their camp. Why would they let them walk into the camp and spy on them? He knew enough about the proud Lakota Sioux to tell they would not be impressed with a mere lieutenant. In fact, he worried they would be insulted that General Miles thought so little of their status that he sent such a low-ranking officer to talk to them. He would have told Casey all of this if he'd asked. Casey had not asked him anything on this mission.

He was relieved to see that there were only two riders and not a full Lakota war party coming toward them. Accompanying Bear Lying Down was a rider dressed in white man's clothes, riding hard down the frozen White Clay Road.

Steam rose from their horses as they reined in and approached Plenty Horses and Casey. Casey raised his hand and said, "*Hau, Kola!*"

The man in white man's clothes rode up to Casey and shook his hand. In English he said, "I'm Pete Richards. Red Cloud is my father-in-law."

"Very good," Casey said breaking into a smile. "General Miles would very much like me to meet with Red Cloud." White Moon immediately tensed. If Casey had asked, he would have told him Red Cloud was a chief of the Oglala Lakota. There was more than a little rivalry between the Brule and Oglala. But Casey hadn't asked.

"This is not an Oglala camp," Richards said. "It's the camp of Two Strike's Brule." He looked warily at Plenty Horses and spoke in a lower tone. "Red Cloud said he would try to slip out tonight and return to the Pine Ridge Agency. He will talk with the general's person there."

Casey shook his head. "It is imperative I speak with Red Cloud now," he said. "General Miles wants me to meet with the camp leaders." Again White Moon cringed. It was Two Strike's camp of Brule at White Clay Creek. Red Cloud was not a leader there. He was only a guest.

Richards shook his head. "Red Cloud said this is no place for an army lieutenant right now. The young Lakota warriors are still angry. Let them calm down a few days, and Red Cloud will talk with you at Pine Ridge," he said. "But you need to get away from the camp now." He pointed back down the road.

Plenty Horses watched the conversation intently. White Moon didn't know if Richards was aware that Plenty Horses understood

English. Red Cloud's Oglala and Two Strike's Brule were allies but distinctly different bands of Lakota.

Casey tried again. "I just want to speak with the chiefs to bring peace. We don't want any more killing."

Richards shook his head slowly. "The young warriors were insulted by the killings at Wounded Knee. It's more difficult than ever to keep them calm. Let a few more weeks pass. That is all." He turned his horse away and put his back to Casey. His horse ambled slowly back toward the Indian camp.

Casey angrily pulled his horse around to the opposite direction. "I will come back and try talk with the chiefs again," he said.

He motioned to White Moon, who advanced to the lieutenant's side. They started back down the road away from the camp. White Moon took a deep breath and felt his muscles start to relax. He was relieved there had not been trouble. Casey's face was still tense and thoughtful. White Moon knew the lieutenant well enough to determine he was already planning what to do when they returned. He hoped he would be asked to give his opinion the next time. The situation was far too tense for an army officer to walk into the middle of an armed camp of violent young warriors without knowing what he was doing. Perhaps Casey understood that now.

"Lieutenant," he said. "I don't think that—"

Casey's head turned toward him, and in an instant it snapped forward. A spray of blood and brains filled the cold winter air as the reverberation from a shot echoed across the frozen prairie. Casey's body fell forward off his horse and plopped onto the ground face up. White Moon saw a bloody hole where Casey's right eye had been.

He moved as if underwater, withdrawing the rifle from the scabbard and wheeling around to protect himself. The other three Lakota men were staring at Plenty Horses. He was standing behind his horse, calmly sliding his rifle back into its scabbard. Without a word, he mounted his horse, turned his back on White Moon and the dead body of Lieutenant Casey and slowly ambled down the road toward the Brule village. He never looked back.

Richards immediately rode up to White Moon with his hands held up. White Moon could only think of getting to safety. He turned his horse and started to ride off to escape. Richards yelled at him to stop and come get Casey's gear to take back to the army camp. White Moon was still in shock. He'd just seen his lieutenant killed in front of him. Why hadn't they shot him too? He looked at Richards and yelled, "Why don't you shoot Plenty Horses?"

Richards turned around to look at the slowly retreating Brule warrior. He said, "Why don't you shoot him yourself?"

White Moon looked at the figure of Plenty Horses and then at Casey's dead body. The other Brule warrior, Broken Arm, had dismounted and was claiming Casey's revolver on his hip and was pulling the boot off the dead man to get another revolver he kept there. White Moon felt powerless and unable to move.

Richards watched the Brule warrior hold the weapons up with a huge smile. "Take the horse, the rest of the lieutenant's things and get out of here," he said to White Moon. "Get out of here before there's more trouble."

White Moon looked at the dead body and shook his head. He reached for the reins to Casey's horse and made his way down the road towards the army camp, leaving Lieutenant Casey's dead body on the frozen road behind him.

Chapter Three

JESUS, WHAT A MONTH!" Nelson Miles was a two-star general and commander of the army and did not appreciate it when things didn't go right. He shook his head and held up one of the papers on his big oak desk.

Fredrick Remington moved his large body in the wooden chair, causing it to creak ominously. "I do not concur, General. Challenges create opportunities."

Major Frank Baldwin felt that dizzy feeling he got when he thought his head was going to explode. "Opportunities? For the love of God, man, people are dying out in Dakota!"

"Yes, yes, Captain Baldwin," Remington said with a wave of his hand. "I'm well aware people are dying in South Dakota. While you were sitting in some hotel room drinking whiskey, I was staring the savages in the face. General, I only meant to say we'll need to carefully orchestrate your response to these events."

"Orchestrate? Do you . . ." Baldwin started to rise out of his chair.

"Captain Baldwin," the general said. "I do not need you to repeat every statement Mr. Remington makes. You will sit down, be quiet and conduct yourself like an officer of the United States Army."

"Yes, sir," Baldwin sank back into his chair. "Sorry, sir."

The fourth man in the room, John Mayberry, shifted his chair a little farther away from Baldwin, and it scraped loudly on the floor. He was a very slight man, almost the exact opposite of Remington in body type. "General, we need to be very careful in our reaction to these events. It's important to be strategic."

Captain Baldwin did everything he could to suppress his anger. Six months ago, the general had introduced Mayberry and began including him in meetings. His role wasn't defined, but rumor had it he worked for the Democratic Party.

The general leaned back in his office chair, causing it to squeak. He held the papers in front of his face so he didn't have to look at the three men in his office. "Captain Baldwin, why don't you review the situation in South Dakota for us again?"

Baldwin had briefed the general several times, and it was his report Miles was studying, so this was for the benefit the two civilians in the room. It irked Baldwin to have to deal with them, but he shifted himself and fell into his report voice. He thought the damned little chairs Miles kept in front of his desk were to keep whoever was sitting in them uncomfortable, while the general lounged in his leather office chair. Whether that was the plan or not, it was certainly working. Baldwin would much rather be on a battlefield than perched on a little chair briefing two obnoxious civilians.

"Sir, as I have indicated in my report, the Sioux are still not back at the reservations where they're supposed to be. Two Strike is still camped on the southern border on White Clay Creek where he's been since he left The Stronghold right after the Wounded Knee . . . err . . . incident. That's where Lieutenant Casey was killed."

"You mean murdered, Captain," Remington said. "He was murdered by—"

"Enough, Remington." Miles held up his hand. He nodded at Baldwin. "Go on, Captain."

"Friendly Indians have told us the man who shot Casey is a Lakota from the Brule band named Plenty Horses. He's a relative of Two Strike, but he's not considered to be very popular or influential."

"A damned coward is what he is," Remington said slapping his hand on the table.

"Remington, I know you're not a member of this man's army, but if you don't shut up, I'm going to put you in irons anyway," General Miles slammed his own hand on the table. His face had turned red above his gray whiskers. "You wanted to be here, so you are here, but you'll let Captain Baldwin finish his report. Continue, Captain Baldwin," he said waving his hand.

Captain Baldwin for his part did not understand why the commanding general of the United States Army had permitted the fat artist and the skinny political operative to appear in his Chicago office in the first place. Rumors among the officers were that Miles was going to run for president. Somehow Remington and Mayberry were supporting him. That was all fine and good, but Baldwin didn't know what it had to do with his report. He glanced over at Remington and saw a look of insolence that no army officer would ever let pass across his face in the presence of a general. He shook his head. Dealing with civilians indeed!

"Yes, sir," he said. "Plenty Horses went to Carlisle when he was fourteen but never got past the third grade. They tried to make him a farmer by hiring him out around the school, but he was a failure at that as well. When he turned nineteen two years ago, he went back to the Rosebud Reservation. The friendly Indians tell us most of the Brule didn't like or trust him much since he got back from the school. He was probably trying to make a name for himself by shooting Lieutenant Casey. I don't think it was by Two Strike's or any other chief's orders."

"If we know who did the shooting, why haven't we arrested—" Remington started to say. General Miles snapped him a hard glare stopping him cold, and he slid his chair a few inches back from the desk.

Baldwin continued, "General, you will recall that we decided to wait until we knew more about what Lieutenant Casey was doing at the Indian camp and to let the tensions from the Wounded Knee battle recede before taking action."

General Miles looked directly at Remington. "So, Captain Baldwin, what was Lieutenant Casey doing at the Indian camp?"

"We don't know, sir. He didn't have orders to go there. Strangely, he decided to approach it with only a single scout with him, serving as an interpreter. White Moon, the scout, was confused but said he was trying to contact Red Cloud to negotiate a peace."

With his eyes still on Remington, General Miles said, "Now why would he do that, Captain? Red Cloud is old and powerless, and it wasn't even his band at White Clay."

Baldwin wondered why Miles was looking at Remington but talking to him. Remington's fleshy face was impassive but was reddening around the collar.

"That's right, sir. From what we understand, Red Cloud was more of a prisoner in the Brule camp than a leader. Lieutenant Casey had not gathered much intelligence regarding the situation, apparently."

"And yet, he stumbled his way into a hostile Indian camp," the general said.

"In Lieutenant Casey's defense, General," Remington sat forward in his chair. "If he could have negotiated peace, it would have been a glorious coup. A single fighting man . . ."

General Miles leaned across the table. "I understand what a nice painting it would have made, Mr. Remington, but now a lieutenant of the United States Army is dead because he didn't follow orders." The general paused. The silence in the office was oppressive. "Continue, Captain Baldwin."

"Yes, sir. Two Strike claims Casey was spying on them and threatening to bring more soldiers to attack the camp. He will not let Plenty Horses be arrested. At the time, Captain Reynolds did not have the authority to engage the Sioux and didn't think further hostilities would be in the army's best interest, so he chose to withdraw. Plenty Horses remains in Two Strike's camp."

General Miles said, "Remington, you were with Casey a few days before he went into that camp. What do you think prompted him to violate orders?"

Remington shifted in his chair. "Ned Casey was a quality officer. I'm sure he was only doing what he thought the general wanted and what was best for mankind."

Captain Baldwin sat up straight and said, "Quality officers do not disobey orders and by doing so create a whole host of problems, not to mention putting people's lives in danger."

"When an officer's in the field facing the enemy, sometimes following orders isn't as black and white as it is when sitting behind a desk," Remington said directly to Baldwin.

Before he could respond, General Miles interrupted, "Mr. Remington, Captain Baldwin has had more field experience than any man in the army and won two Congressional Medals of Honor."

Remington's face flushed red. "I'm aware of Captain Baldwin's record, but I won't have Ned Casey's reputation besmirched!"

Baldwin spoke in a low voice. "Lieutenant Casey was a friend of mine as well, Mr. Remington, but he made a terrible error going to that camp, and Plenty Horses made a terrible error in shooting him."

General Miles held up his hand. "At this point, there's nothing to be done regarding Casey's motivations. What we have to deal with now is how to get everyone calmed down and restore peace to the area."

"And punish Lieutenant Casey's murderer," Remington said indignantly.

Ignoring Remington's remark, Baldwin switched back to his report voice and continued. "Sir, I'm afraid things have become more delicate. I received a telegraph this morning that complicates the situation even further."

This was new news for everyone in the room, including the general. Even Mayberry sat at attention.

"It seems there are now conflicting reports about the January 11th Sioux attack on the ranchers at Bear Butte. You may recall the report from our troops was that a group of Sioux warriors attacked the post office at Valleyview, South Dakota. The troops and ranchers ran them off and confiscated the items the Indians had stolen in an earlier attack on settlers in the area. One Sioux man, named Few Tails, was killed."

Mayberry interjected. "I believe I saw a story on this in the *New York World*."

"So fast?" General Miles said. "God help us, the newspapers are getting information as fast as we are."

"Two Strike now says the Sioux who was killed was hunting the area accompanied by his wife and one other family member. Her name is Clown, and she survived the fight and walked for two weeks through the snow from Bear Butte back to Pine Ridge even though she had been shot twice. General, that's a hundred miles." Baldwin shook his head.

He'd be hard pressed to make that walk himself today. "About the same time that she made it back to the agency at Pine Ridge, One Feather, the man who was with Few Tails, showed up with his wife and daughter. They lost their baby daughter on the ride back to Pine Ridge. Both of them are claiming they were peacefully and lawfully hunting at Bear Butte with a pass from the agent when they were ambushed and robbed by the white cowboys."

"Ah, Christ," Miles said shaking his head. "So now we have two Indian deaths from the incident and a brave wounded woman making a winter march. Does the agent corroborate they had a pass?"

"We have not been able to verify it yet, General, but Few Tails and One Feather were well regarded, friendly Indians. To be quite honest, given the circumstances, their story seems much more viable than the one reported by our troops and the ranchers. Sir, I believe the Indians."

Mayberry spoke directly to the general. "Coming on the heels of Wounded Knee and the Casey shooting, this will not reflect very well."

Captain Baldwin ignored the political advisor and continued with his report. "Two Strike says he won't give up Plenty Horses to be arrested unless the white men who killed Few Tails and the baby are arrested too."

"That's outrageous!" Remington said slapping the table again. "These are completely separate incidents. You can't compare the murder of an army lieutenant with the action of some white horse thieves."

Mayberry put a hand on Remington's arm, "You can if you are a newspaper."

General Miles sat silently, looking at his hands folded on his stomach in front of him.

Baldwin continued. "It seems, sir, that Clown and One Feather's story has already been presented to the *New York World*. It's probably the Goodman woman at Pine Ridge. We can expect a story in the next few days."

"Traitorous manipulation of the media," Remington said, raising his nose. He pointed a finger at Miles. "General, you need to get this Plenty Horses put under arrest and executed before this blows up any further."

General Miles studied him carefully. "Mr. Remington," he said slowly. "I'm a two-star general, and I don't 'need' to do anything. We have a very, very delicate situation here with the Indians, the public out in South Dakota, and the newspapers on the East Coast. It's especially delicate since someone," he frowned at Remington again, "saw fit to glorify the idiots at Wounded Knee in *Harper's Weekly*. The stakes have been raised considerably."

Remington sat up straight. "General, our soldiers actions at Wounded Knee were—"

"They were idiotic," the general said harshly. "Colonial Forsyth should have known better than to deploy his men amongst the Indians. It's a wonder even more of them didn't shoot each other."

Mayberry put his hands out as if to separate Remington and Miles. "I concur that the situation is indeed very delicate. The general is highly regarded for his handling of Indian affairs and these situations," he ticked them off on his small fingers, "Wounded Knee, the Casey shooting, and now this Few Tails business do not reflect well with either liberals or conservatives."

"Agreed," General Miles continued. "So now we have increased attention to that unfortunate Wounded Knee affair and even have people proposing Medals of Honor for our soldiers in that fiasco." Remington squirmed as the other three men in the room stared at him. "Combine that with an Indian killing an army lieutenant who was being stupid and a bunch of white thieves stupidly killing an Indian. How am I supposed to run an army, much less run for president, when all I'm dealing with is stupidity?" Miles slammed his fist on his desk as his voice rose.

The office was silent. Baldwin kept his eyes focused on the papers on the desk. Through the years he'd seen General Miles lose his temper a few times, and it was never a pretty sight. He glanced over at Remington, who had beads of sweat dripping down onto his suit, and at Mayberry, who had put his fingers into a steeple and appeared to be deep in thought.

Baldwin noticed the general was still angry but had quickly moved into problem-solving mode that had served him so well his entire military career. "Gentlemen, let's review our options." He arranged the papers in front of him. "We could conduct a raid on Two Strikes's camp and take Plenty Horses into custody. However, that would potentially cause more loss of life, to both Indian and Army personnel."

Mayberry interrupted the general in a very civilian-like manner. Baldwin thought it very improper for anyone to interrupt a general, particularly Miles, but Mayberry was not intimidated. "That would play very poorly in the newspapers I'm afraid, General. Your opponents already are casting you as a military dictator. You need to appear . . . more domestic." Baldwin wasn't aware the general had any opponents.

Miles glared at Mayberry but did not chastise him. "But perhaps if we took the cowboys in the Black Hills who killed the Indians into custody as well. That would calm Two Strike."

Baldwin interjected. "But sir, the military has no authority over . . ."

General Miles held up a finger. "But Captain Baldwin, the federal prosecutor does. He has federal marshals at his disposal to enforce the law and make arrests."

Mayberry moved to the edge of the desk and interjected, "You're right, General. You don't have the authority over both cases but the prosecutor does." He was bouncing a little in his chair.

General Miles nodded.

Baldwin shook his head. "I don't understand, sir."

Mayberry smiled broadly and turned towards him. "You see, Captain Baldwin, the army, i.e., the general, does not want to execute Plenty Horses. How would it appear to our liberal friends at the *New York World* if the general executed an unfortunate Indian man who'd killed an army officer in the wrong place at the wrong time? But if a South Dakota federal jury condemns him, why then it's domestic justice. The general is merely delivering a prisoner to the appropriate authorities to be tried. And another jury can regard the cowboys or thieves or whatever they are in the Black Hills on the other affair. Whatever, the outcome, the general has upheld the rule of law and let the judicial system work. It's all very presidential."

General Miles let a small smile show through his gray whiskers. "I'm not sure what you're talking about, Mr. Mayberry. I'm just thinking of what is best for justice. We will arrest Plenty Horses, and the federal prosecutor will arrest the Black Hills cowboys. That will make Two Strike happy and save lives. Everyone will have done their job."

Mayberry sat back in a satisfied manner. "Of course, General, and that will also make the *World* happy. Trials take months and months to prepare. Many small stories are far better than one big story. This timing will allow the entire situation to calm down," he said. "And as the trials will be in Deadwood, the outcomes are inevitable, and newspaper coverage is minimal. By the time the cases come to fruition, the public will have forgotten these unfortunate incidents, and we will be focused on a campaign."

"But sir . . ." Baldwin wasn't sure what had just happened, but it was unlike any experience he'd ever had in the army.

General Miles sat up and assumed command. "Captain Baldwin, prepare orders to have Plenty Horses arrested for the murder of Lieutenant Edward Casey. Also notify the federal prosecutor's office that he should arrest those idiot horse thieving cowboys in the Black Hills for killing the Indians. Make sure we can show proof of the arrest to Two Strike when we come to arrest Plenty Horses. I don't want any more dead bodies, Indian or white." General Miles cleared his throat. "And Captain Baldwin, it would probably be best if it were an 'informal' request."

Baldwin was scribbling on a piece of paper. "Yes, sir." He wasn't exactly sure what had just happened, but it seemed to him like the army was ceding its authority to civilians. "Sir, if we turn over Plenty Horses to the State, won't we be giving up our authority?"

Mayberry answered, "No, Captain Baldwin, the general will be a leader in administering domestic justice. This isn't the Wild West anymore. It's 1891, and we can't have a presidential candidate persecuting a poor Indian for killing an officer who was not following orders. The judiciary can address it. Meanwhile, we don't want to have the westerners criticizing a candidate for prosecuting white men for killing Indians or easterners criticizing him for not. A judge and jury can do it and take the heat either way. And by the time it all gets sorted out, the Wounded Knee incident will be a distant memory. And I agree that the direct involvement by the general should be . . . cloudy."

"And there will be no more articles in *Harper's Weekly*, isn't that correct, Mr. Remington," Miles said, pointing a finger at the fat man.

Captain Baldwin looked up from his notes. "General, about my report on Wounded Knee—I'd like to point out there were some very troubling actions that took place out there. You may note . . ."

"Forsyth should have never deployed his men intermixed with the Sioux."

"Yes, sir, but there was also . . ."

General Miles looked steadily into Baldwin's eyes. "Captain Baldwin, don't you have some arrests to coordinate? I'll deal with your report on Wounded Knee at an appropriate time."

"Yes, sir." He rose, saluted and walked out of the room. He wished he hadn't left the general alone in the room with Reynolds and Mayberry.

Chapter Four

I'M SORRY MRS. BOWMAN, you'll have to stay in South Dakota for another eight weeks, minimum." George Abbot, the fat little lawyer, adjusted his wire-rimmed glasses. "I thought I made that very clear when you were here last week."

Laura Bowman leaned forward and brushed a strand of her long dark hair from her face. "But Mr. Abbot, it's imperative I get back to New York."

"Mrs. Bowman, as I told you before, you have to remain in South Dakota for ninety days in order to establish residency or there will be no divorce." Attorney Abbot took off his glasses and polished them with a handkerchief. They were a useful prop in these situations. "I'm afraid the precedents are very well established on this point. Otherwise, what would be the point of coming to South Dakota?"

Indeed, what would be the point, she thought. The only reason she had moved to this dreadful little town on the edge of the prairie was to get free of Jonathon T. Bowman. Or, more accurately, get free of him and still have enough money to live.

"So you're saying, Mr. Abbot, that if I leave South Dakota, my divorce will not go through?"

"I'm afraid so, Mrs. Bowman. You'd have to start all over. South Dakota law establishes that ninety days of occupation is required to achieve residency." He placed his glasses back on his nose purposefully. "I'm very sure Mr. Bowman would be made aware if you left the state."

Laura sighed and sat back. She had gotten her way most of the time in her twenty-nine years of life, and she wasn't happy about not getting it now. The plan had appeared so simple. All she had to do was live in South Dakota for ninety days, and Judge Aikens would give her a favorable divorce. He was famous for it. Then she would be free of Jonathon Bowman and his philandering forever. But she never dreamed that ninety days would be so long.

"Doesn't the Cataract Hotel meet your needs?" he asked. He received a kickback from each of his clients who chose to spend their ninety days of residency in the hotel, so it damned well better serve her needs. There were many ways to make money from divorce.

"Yes, I suppose it does," she said in a quiet voice. "They do try very hard, but it simply isn't what I expected." Laura lifted her fan and started to rise. "I'm just very bored, Mr. Abbot. It's only been a week and it seems like I've been here forever."

Abbot rose and came around his desk. He shook her gloved hand gently. "Perhaps you can take in one of the symphony performances or attend the weekly dance in the second-floor ballroom?"

"Yes, perhaps," she said pulling her hand out of his grip as quickly as she could and remain polite. She'd been told the divorce lawyers and other professional men of Sioux Falls prowled the weekly dances at the Cataract for vulnerable soon-to-be divorcées. She did not consider herself vulnerable and was not miserable enough to dance with George Abbot.

The waiting room for the Abbot and Becker Law Office carried an unpleasant stench, and Laura tried not to wrinkle her nose as she walked through. A large man in ill-fitting overalls and his wife had been just about to enter Abbot's office when she'd arrived that morning. The elderly secretary had made them sit back down and had taken Laura by the arm to escort her immediately into Abbot's office. Now they were frowning at her. She raised her eyes to avoid their looks. She'd paid good money to have Abbot available when she wanted him. She thought he'd probably make more money from her divorce than ten of his farmer clients would pay him.

As she swung away from the disgruntled farmers, she almost tripped over two Indian men squatting next to the door. They stared blankly at her with cold, black eyes. Both of them had long black hair flowing down to buckskin jackets. She lowered her gaze to the floor immediately and noticed they were both wearing moccasins. Her hands fumbled with the door knob before she was able to get a grip on it and slide out into the hallway.

As the door closed behind her, she moved as quickly as she could in her long skirt. As if putting up with an insolent attorney and angry farmers wasn't enough, she'd been face-to-face with savages. She'd seen Indians in Cody's Wild West show but having them right in front of her face was quite disconcerting. It was like running into a wild animal from the zoo in the middle of Central Park.

Laura hurried down the stairs of the Edmision-Jamison Building, hoping not to meet any other undesirables. Many of the divorce lawyers in Sioux Falls kept offices in the six-story brick monstrosity. Across the street, the luxury of the Cataract Hotel was a comforting relief. It was white with dark trim and showed at least some sense of style. Crossing Phillips Avenue, she looked to the right and left and saw Sioux Falls revealed for the backward country settlement it was. If you went three blocks from the Cataract in either direction, Sioux Falls became a little rural town. Attorney Abbot and his friends could try to recreate urban life in the Cataract Hotel, but it would always be an island in the middle of desolation.

She nodded to the doorman, really a farmer dressed in a doorman's uniform, and made her way into the lobby. In the far corner, the "Witches of the Cataract" sat. They were always at the same table, and when she checked in, she'd been told that Haddie McKenna monitored all the goings on of the "divorce colonists."

For the first two days she lived at the Cataract, Laura had done nothing but sulked about her divorce. She knew coming to South Dakota was the right thing to do. Jonathon's string of mistresses had finally driven her over the top. But she was so lonely. To get out of her room, she endured sitting at the table with the likes of Haddie McKenna and her friends. Back in New York, she would have never put up with them and would have tactfully left for gayer company, but company was rare in Sioux Falls. She had resolved that wallowing in her own self-pity was preferable to the "witches of the Cataract." She'd avoided the table the last few days by just staying out of the lobby.

Haddie McKenna waved as she entered. "Mrs. Bowman, over here." She had a frightfully annoying habit of raising her voice at the end of each sentence. Laura thought it was probably supposed to portray a sense of authority, but it just came across as condescension. She paused and considered going back up to her room. Why hadn't she taken the advice of Mrs. Blaine and just purchased a house? The people of her class usually purchased or rented a house in Sioux Falls, but the thought of complete isolation repelled her. Besides, it just seemed down right wasteful to spend money on a home to stay for ninety days when there was a perfectly good hotel to stay in. However, now she felt isolated in this box of a hotel with pretentious Haddie McKenna and the other witches. Maybe if she just ignored her . . .

"Mrs. Bowman," a very soft voice said, and Laura felt a light touch on her elbow. Mrs. McKenna had sent poor mousey Elnora Flatt over to retrieve her.

Laura faced the little bowling ball of a woman and smiled. "Well good morning, Mrs. Flatt. That is a lovely dress," she said brightly. "How are you?"

Mrs.Flatt smiled broadly as she always did when receiving a compliment. In reality the dress was dreadful, made of a floral print that hung off Mrs. Flatt's ample body like a drape over a barrel. However, Laura always made a point of complementing Elnora Flatt, because nobody else ever did. "Mrs. McKenna invites you over to join her," she said in a voice so soft it could barely be heard. For all of the bluster Mrs. McKenna's diction held, or perhaps because of it, Mrs. Flatt always sounded like she was asking permission to speak.

She let Mrs. Flatt's light grip on her elbow guide her to the "witches table." As usual Haddie McKenna occupied her position in the corner that allowed her to watch both the street out the window as well as the comings and goings of everyone through the lobby. It was impossible to get in or out of the Cataract Hotel between the hours of seven thirty and ten thirty in the morning without being under the gaze of Haddie McKenna. Laura knew because she'd already tried a few times. She suspected Haddie reported potential opportunities to one or more of the divorce lawyers with offices across the street.

"Visiting your lawyer this morning, Mrs. Bowman?" Mrs. McKenna slurped her tea a little. She always drank it with her pinkie extended in an exaggerated fashion as if that were the way elegant people did it. Laura knew she was dead wrong.

"Umm, yes," she said. She stood across the table as the ladies watched her expectantly. She really didn't need to explain herself to them, but . . . Laura was never really very good at confrontation.

"Well, sit down, have a cup of tea and tell us all about it," said Mrs. Johnson, who always took the position just to Mrs. McKenna's right. The quick side-glance and frown she received from Mrs. McKenna made it clear she'd expected Laura to ask permission to join them.

Sitting at the table was the absolute last thing Laura wanted to do. However, she enjoyed Mrs. McKenna's anger so much she made herself comfortable in the open chair.

"Well, thank you, Mrs. Johnson," she said with her best winning smile. "I'd be happy to join you."

Mrs. McKenna recovered nicely. "That's wonderful, Mrs. Bowman. Elnora, could you be a dear and have the boy bring us another pot of tea?" Elnora Flatt lowered her eyes, slid away from the table and made her way to the kitchen.

"So . . . what did Mr. Abbot have to say today?" Mrs. McKenna said. "Were there any developments on your action against Mr. Bowman?"

"Umm, no, nothing new, I'm afraid," she said. "I was just checking on some things."

Haddie McKenna stared across the table, waiting for more information, and then her small yellow teeth made a brief appearance as she broke into a condescending grin. "It's almost like clockwork. After their first week in Sioux Falls, everyone makes a trip to their lawyers to see if they can get out of the residency requirements. And the story is always the same for every one of them. No leaving South Dakota!" Her laugh was an annoying cackle.

Laura flushed a little but would not give McKenna the satisfaction of being right about her frustration about living in Sioux

Falls. She poured from the white tea pot with the blue design. "Oh, no, I was just visiting with Mr. Abbot about some technicalities." She smiled across the table. "Nothing very exciting, I'm afraid."

The corners of Mrs. McKenna's mouth slowly dropped, but she valiantly kept her smile in place. "Oh, I'm glad it was nothing to do with you hating this place." Her eyes indicated that she loved hearing about people's misfortunes.

Laura was certainly not going to give her the satisfaction. "On the contrary, Mrs. McKenna, I find the whole community positively adventurous. In fact, in Mr. Abbot's waiting room I came face to face with real Indians." In reality, Laura was terrified by the smelly Indians, but she didn't want the ladies of the table to know that. Besides, getting them focused on a subject, any subject, other than her divorce was a positive development.

The mention of the Indians certainly accomplished that. Mrs. Johnson's eyes lit up. "Oh, yes, I've seen several walking down the street." She leaned over the table, almost dipping her ample bosom into her tea cup. "It's like being in the middle of a real life Wild West show!" Abigail Johnson had come from Buffalo, New York, to get her divorce.

The wrinkles around Haddie McKenna's eyes deepened, and she could barely contain her excitement. She raised her hand and pointed across the lobby where a well-dressed man of about thirty was drinking coffee while standing at the hotel desk. "You see that man over there?" she said in a whispered tone that could be heard several feet away. "He's here to cover the Indian trial for the *New York World*. Isn't that exciting?"

Laura couldn't help but turn her head to follow Haddie McKenna's boney finger. The man with the short dark hair in the light-colored suit looked somewhat familiar, but she didn't know why. He looked up from his coffee and noticed the ladies in the corner of the lobby staring at him. The corners of his mouth raised in a small smile as he nodded to them. His expression froze for a moment as he looked at Laura Bowman's face.

At twenty-nine years old, Laura Bowman hadn't lost the fresh good looks that had put her at the center of the New York social scene a decade earlier. Since she was shy by nature, she'd never been comfortable with admiring looks from men she didn't even know. She had always lowered her dark eyes and hidden behind her long chestnut hair. Perhaps that's why she'd been so willing to move almost directly from her father's protection to the matrimonial protection of Jonathon Bowman.

She noted the man's attention and quickly broke eye contact. Her cheeks flushed at the unwanted attention. Why had she let that McKenna woman draw her out? Why didn't she listen to her resolve to stay in her room until her ninety days were up? Then she could get her divorce and return to New York. Why couldn't they all just leave her alone?

Haddie McKenna was quite pleased she had caused some commotion, and she enjoyed Laura's embarrassment. "His name is J.T. O'Day, and the *World* covers the most lurid topics. Do you know him, Mrs. Bowman, being from New York and all? Mr. O'Day seemed quite fixed on you. Of course I don't suppose you would ever read such a scandal rag, and you couldn't be in the same social circles but, still . . ."

"So do you? Do you know him?" Mrs. Johnson interrupted. "We get both the *World* and the *Journal* in Buffalo, and I find the stories intriguing. It's so good to read about real people and . . ." Her plain dark eyes grew impossibly wide. "Oh, my God! He's coming over here."

The skin around Haddie McKenna's mouth had gone so hard it looked like she'd formed a beak to peck at the insolent Mrs. Johnson for interrupting her, but even she was taken aback as J.T. O'Day himself approached their table.

"Ladies," he said in a voice entirely too high pitched to fit his tall dark form. "I'm J.T. O'Day from the *New York World,* and I couldn't help noticing you from across the lobby." When he smiled, his bright-white teeth sparkled from below his closely cropped black mustache. Everything about J.T. O'Day was perfectly in place. He glanced at the older ladies at the table, but his eyes quickly came to rest on Laura Bowman. "Mrs. Bowman, I presume?"

Laura's eyes had never left her plate as he approached. The last thing she needed was to have her divorce drug through the yellow pages of the *New York World.*

Haddie McKenna addressed the reporter directly. "So, Mr. O'Day, are you and Mrs. Bowman acquainted in New York? "

O'Day laughed and put is head back in an artificial way. "Oh, Mrs. Bowman and I certainly are not seen in the same society." He made a small insincere bow. "I only know the lovely Mrs. Bowman by reputation."

Laura was now flushed entirely red as she raised her head and gave the man a nod. "I'm pleased to meet you Mr. O'Day."

"I'm Mrs. McKenna and this is Mrs. Johnson," Haddie said in an effort to regain control of the conversation and to beat the loud, impertinent Johnson woman to the punch. When Mrs. Flatt made a movement to introduce herself, Haddie put a hand on her arm to silence her. "What in the world is the *New York World* doing in Sioux Falls?" Her hard mouth broke into a smile, and she looked around to see if anyone caught her joke.

O'Day kept his attention focused on Laura Bowman. "Oh, I'm here to cover the Indian murder trial," he said. "And what could possibly bring the lovely Mrs. Bowman out here to Dakota, the 'Divorce Capital of the World'?"

Laura felt her face flushing even redder. How dare this reporter talk to her in that manner? She had no intention of being the subject of the New York rumor mill generated by the yellow journalism of the *New York World*. She opened her mouth, but could not think of anything to say. Their plan had always been to keep the divorce as quiet as possible, but she hadn't considered using an alias. Perhaps she should have. Who would have thought she would see anyone from New York in Sioux Falls, South Dakota?

It was Mrs. Johnson to the rescue. The overweight madam from Buffalo had no intentions of being left out of the conversation. "Why is the *New York World* interested in an Indian trial, Mr. O'Day?" She batted her brown eyes at the reporter. "Don't we have enough Indians in the East?"

O'Day looked at the other women at the table as if he was seeing them for the first time. He was going to be in this backward cesspool for weeks. There would be plenty of time to root out additional divorce stories and who knows what else.

"When the newly appointed major general of the army and potential presidential candidate has an interest in the trial of an Indian, the *New York World* has an interest," he said, a bit louder than he needed to. "The Plenty Horses trial may end up being an important part of American history."

"Why is that?" Haddie McKenna said, interested in spite of herself.

"Well, you see," O'Day leaned over the table. "Only days after the Wounded Knee battle, a Lieutenant Casey took it upon himself to make peace with the Indians. He was shot just outside of their camp by a young Lakota man who is now being tried for his murder."

"Why are they in Sioux Falls?" Haddie McKenna asked. "Good Lord, it sounds like the kind of sordid affair that should be held out in Deadwood, not in a civilized place like Sioux Falls."

"They moved the trial because they didn't think an Indian could get a fair trial in Deadwood." O'Day laughed again. "As if Sioux Falls will be different. Besides that, four white cowboys will go on trial in Deadwood as soon as this trial is completed for killing an Indian family."

Mrs. McKenna had heard enough. "Indians killing army officers . . . cowboys killing Indians . . . it all sounds so primitive. I don't think that . . ."

But Mrs. Johnson was enthralled. "Why, Mrs. Bowman was face-to-face with some of the savages just this morning." She held her hand across the table. "She was just telling us how interested she was in Indians."

Laura wanted to drop her head to her arms. There had to be a way out of this and away from these people. Why did she ever leave her hotel room?

O'Day turned to face her. "Is that right, Mrs. Bowman? It's your interest in the Indians that brings you here to Sioux Falls?"

If Laura had learned anything from Jonathon Bowman's pathological lying about his mistresses, it was that, when confronted, ask questions; don't give answers. She spoke for the first time, "The Indian man is being tried for murder?"

"Exactly," he said, brushing some nonexistent lint off his suit. "As if there is a jury in Dakota that'd dare condone an Indian killing a white army officer. Nonetheless, a trial will be held." He looked down at Laura Bowman and smiled again. "In fact, I have an appointment at the jail to interview this Plenty Horses savage later this morning. I'd be honored if you'd join me, Mrs. Bowman, to . . . perhaps give me a woman's perspective."

Accompanying this pompous reporter to the jail was the last thing she wanted to do. She had never even been to a jail, much less spoken to a real Indian. She just wanted to go to her room.

"Oh, how wonderful," Mrs. Johnson gushed. "What an opportunity for you, Mrs. Bowman."

Haddie McKenna interjected with a dirty look toward Mrs. Johnson. "I'm sure Mrs. Bowman would never consent to accompany you to such a . . ."

"I'll do it," Laura said before she could think about it. "What time, Mr. O'Day?"

He smiled. He'd been told Sioux Falls was full of lonesome soon-to-be divorcées. After being here one day, he'd made contact with a member of New York society. It might make his time in Dakota interesting. "I'll meet you right here," he reached into his pocket to pull out a gold watch, "At eleven o'clock."

"Very well, Mr. O'Day," Laura said as she rose from her seat and gave the man her hand to shake. "I'll see you then. Goodbye, ladies."

As she made her way across the lobby, she could feel eyes on her back. She could only hope Haddie McKenna would wait until O'Day was out of earshot before she expressed her disgust at the scandalous nature of accompanying the reporter to the jail. From the safety of her hotel room she could come up with a plan to get out of this . . . mess.

LAURA STOOD IN FRONT of the door of her hotel room. She wore white gloves and wondered what kind of dirt she would pick up when she reached out to touch the doorknob. She lifted a hand but then stopped and looked over at the full-length mirror to her left. She adjusted her hair around her face. She thought she still looked pretty, even though Jonathon had stopped recognizing it years ago.

How does one conduct herself at the interview of a savage in jail? Why would anyone in her right mind even consent to be present? And what does one wear? All of these questions had plagued her for the last two hours. All of her upbringing, all of what she knew, all of her previous experience told her to simply lock the door to her hotel room and refuse to answer. If she ignored O'Day for long enough, he would just go away. He couldn't have possibly thought she would actually accompany him to the jail, could he?

Perhaps it was this last thought that propelled her to change into a simple but severe dress and to dig out her white gloves. Why shouldn't she go to the jail? She was here in Dakota for new experiences, wasn't she? She would soon no longer be Mrs. Jonathon Bowman, and then she could do whatever she wanted to. For the first time in her life, she didn't have to ask her father's permission, Jonathon Bowman's permission, or anyone else's permission. If she decided she wanted to see and hear a real Indian desperado up close, why shouldn't she? She'd never seen a person who had killed a man, at least that she knew of. The opportunity to be in the same room with a killer savage was just too much of an opportunity to miss. If Haddie McKenna and the others were appalled, so much the better.

She adjusted her hair one more time and opened the door. A part of her expected to see one of the savages standing in the hallway waiting for her. She locked the door behind her and walked much more quickly than usual down the hall to the grand staircase, almost running into a tall woman with red curls.

"Excuse me," she said. She looked at the woman's face and saw the greenest eyes she'd ever witnessed.

"Well, hello," the woman said in a throaty voice.

"Hello," Laura said. "I'm sorry I ran into you."

The woman held out her hand, "You're in a hurry," she said. "You must have a man waiting for you." She smiled playfully.

When she smiled, Laura was sure she'd seen her before. Before she could think about it she blurted out, "You're Tara Monroe. I saw you in *The President's Brother* on Broadway."

"Shhhh," the woman said. "I'm Terry Porter here."

"Oh, I'm so sorry," Laura said. She lowered her voice "I loved your performance."

"Thank you," she said. "I'm trying to keep the world from knowing about my divorce."

Laura smiled. "Yes, an alias is probably a good idea. I'm Laura Bowman from New York."

Tara shook her hand. "Nice to meet you, Mrs. Bowman," she said. "I take it you're here on the same type of freedom mission I am?"

"Yes," she said. "I didn't think ninety days would be such a long time."

Tara giggled and brushed her red curls from her face. "I've been here for over a month now. You just need to find local diversions, Mrs. Bowman. Perhaps we can talk sometime."

"Yes, I'd like that," she said. She shook her hand, and they parted. Tara Monroe was a well-regarded actress, and it made sense that she used an alias at the Divorce Colony. It must be effective, or Haddie and her friends would have certainly mentioned it.

Years of training had taught her never to rush down a large curved staircase. The danger of falling was one consideration, but the danger of not making an entrance was even more important. As usual, she was painfully conflicted between her natural shyness and the need to make a societal impression.

Laura was a little disappointed nobody seemed to notice her decent, but that was probably better anyway. She looked around the lobby and felt lost. A few people milled about, and of course Haddie McKenna had her usual seat in the corner, but J.T. O'Day was nowhere to be found. How dare he keep her waiting!

The sound of harsh laughter emerged from the dark "men's lounge" at the opposite corner of the lobby. J.T. O'Day emerged with his hand on the shoulder of a man in a dark suit. The two men stopped laughing as they entered the light of the main lobby, and the man in the dark suit wantonly looked Laura over. She felt like a prize cow as the man's dark eyes went from her face slowly down to her feet and then back up to her face.

"Well, Mrs. Bowman," O'Day said as he unnecessarily slicked his hair. "I wasn't sure you were going to make our little appointment."

Laura didn't like his smile. "Oh, please, let me introduce you to Mr. Waldo Elliot, one of the most eminent citizens of this fair city."

Mr. Elliot reached for her hand. Laura gave it to him limply, pleased she'd chosen to wear gloves. "It's nice to meet you, Mr. Elliot." He was dressed in a dark, well-worn suit. Laura had overseen the purchase of enough suits to determine this was a very cheap product that hung awkwardly off his shoulders. Elliot carried himself as if he was in the height of fashion.

"I hope you're finding our little community hospitable, Mrs. Bowman," he said holding her hand a little longer than necessary. His teeth emerged from his thick brown beard. "We certainly don't have the range of entertainment you're used to in New York, but there are diversions that can be found to help while away the time."

"I'm sure there are, Mr. Elliot," Laura said as she retracted her hand. "Mr. O'Day, don't we have an appointment to get to?"

"Yes, yes," he said. "It isn't like that savage is going to be going anywhere, today or any other time."

"I don't know why we have to waste all of this time on a trial," Elliot said, shaking his head. "I've been in the Territory since '85 and have never heard of such a thing. A trial for an Indian? Indeed."

"Why, Mr. Elliot," Laura said. "Don't you think this Indian man deserves justice?"

He laughed. "I don't know how you do things back east, but we've been dealing with the Sioux ever since we settled this place. The Indian shot that lieutenant right into the back of his head. He's a cowardly killer, and he'll hang within the week. Anyone can tell you so." Elliot looked around to see if anyone was listening to him.

"If the outcome is predetermined, why is there to be a trial?" Laura said. She was feeling especially contrary today.

O'Day chuckled and unnecessarily smoothed his suit. "General Nelson Miles is getting ready to run for president. With the messy business of the Wounded Knee battle already calling his ability to settle the West into question, he can't have his big money supporters thinking Indians and soldiers are just shooting each other randomly. He needs to show he's making progress civilizing the savages."

Elliot shook his head. "As I said, we do things a little different out here in Dakota. If by any chance the court should let this Indian go, he might see a whole new side of civilization. No matter what the idiot easterners think, we can't have Indians going around shooting white men." He paused and lifted the corner of his mouth up in a smile. Laura identified a bit of egg lodged in his beard. "The trial will serve as a nice diversion for our lovely guests, however." He bowed formally. "Good day, Mrs. Bowman. I do hope to see you again, perhaps at one of the dances held in the second-floor ballroom on Saturdays. If you attend, be sure and save dance for me."

Laura thought dancing with Waldo Elliot and his obnoxious beard might be worse than dancing with George Abbot. But she smiled and nodded as he waved at O'Day and returned to the dark corner.

O'Day reached for her elbow and escorted her toward the front door. "A charmer, that Elliot is," he said.

She scoffed, "Humpf, what a disgusting man!"

"He does remarkably well here, I'm told," O'Day said as he led her out the door and onto the street. "It seems a large number of the women in town looking for a new start practice by succumbing to the charms of the likes of Mr. Elliot."

Laura looked back over her shoulder toward the front of the hotel, "You can't be serious. With him?"

O'Day laughed, deep and throaty. "You have only been here a few days, Mrs. Bowman. Three months plus can be a long time for a woman in a strange place. A diversion with someone like Elliot is probably just what the doctor ordered for a soon-to-be divorced woman."

Laura felt her face flushing. O'Day's forwardness was not something she was used to hearing. It didn't seem proper to indulge it with a reply, but she'd decided she was going to stop being intimidated. However, when it came to it, she couldn't think of anything witty to say, so she just shook her head. O'Day laughed again.

She needed to change the subject. "So tell me about this Indian we're going to see. Will he be executed?"

"Certainly," he said. "There doesn't seem to be any dispute of the facts of the case. He admits to standing out on the prairie talking to the brave lieutenant for an hour as he waited for permission to enter the Indian camp. When they told him he couldn't enter, he started back toward the army camp. Before he could get thirty feet away, Plenty Horses shot him in the back of the head. It's pretty much an open-and-shut case."

"Why did he shoot the lieutenant?"

"That, my lovely Mrs. Bowman, is what we're going to try to find out," he said as he led her up the steps of a pink granite building. "I'm told the jail is in an annex in the rear."

The two jailers appeared to be competing to see who could sport the most elaborate facial hair. One had thick bushy sideburns and another had an elaborately waxed mustache. They were very impressed with J.T. O'Day's credentials, so much that they didn't question having a well-dressed lady accompany him. The jailor with the sideburns told them, "I kin let you talk wit him through the door, but ya can't go inside his cell." He nodded to Laura, "'specially wit the lady."

"That's fine, my good man, I'm certain I can get all the information I need through the cell door," O'Day said.

A scholarly looking man in a gray suit shook O'Day's hand. "I'm George Nock, one of Plenty Horses's lawyers." He pointed at Laura, "Who is this woman?"

"Mrs. Bowman is helping me research this story. She'll be accompanying me to the interview."

Nock did not appear to be thrilled with the prospect, but he just shrugged. "Just so we're clear, you can ask the questions, but if I tell my client not to answer, he will not."

"Look," O'Day said turning to face Nock directly and moving a step towards him. "I know you never would have consented to let me talk to the Indian if you weren't desperate to get the public on your side. My readers are fascinated by killers, and your client has admitted that he killed the brave Lieutenant Casey. So let's just cut the posturing and get on with the interview." Nock stepped back, but did not respond.

A short fat man came forward and put out his hand. O'Day looked at him but never took the hand. "Who is this?" he said to Nock.

Without waiting for Nock to answer, the fat man spoke up. "Mr. O'Day, I'm C.C. Arends. Mr. Nock here said you'd need an interpreter." Arends had thick well-oiled, salt-and-pepper hair, and his white shirt looked like it must have been brand new, as it was still creased. Nonetheless, Arends was already sweating through it, and half-moon sweat stains appeared under each of his arms.

"So, you speak Sioux?" O'Day said.

"Been trading just south of the Pine Ridge for fifteen years. Got me a cute little Oglala squaw too," he said with a smile. His eyes roamed over Laura. She felt herself flush.

O'Day turned to Nock. "Doesn't the Indian speak English? I understood he had been at the Carlisle School for Indians."

Nock stepped forward. "He was there for five years, but he doesn't speak or understand English very well. I want the interpreter here to make sure his responses are clear."

"How do I know he'll interpret the Indian correctly?" O'Day said nodding at Arends.

"Why wouldn't he?" Nock replied spreading his hands.

Arends pushed forward, "I speak it just fine. Ya see all Sioux ain't the same. Mostly I trade with Oglala Sioux like my squaw, but this here Plenty Horses is a Brule Sioux. But I trade with them too. They ain't so different."

O'Day looked at the little man for an instant and then turned away from him like he never existed. His eyes were intense, but not focused on anything in particular. He looked like he was going into a trance.

Laura couldn't help but be impressed with the aura of professionalism O'Day displayed as the time for the interview drew closer. However pompous he was at the hotel, when it came to his work, he was serious. He turned to Laura, his eyes hard beneath his groomed black eyebrows, "You'll sit behind me and say absolutely nothing—not a word—not one."

She nodded, wondering what she'd gotten herself into. As the door to the cell block opened, an odor engulfed them. It reminded her of the smell of the old cellar of her father's rarely used house in the Hamptons, only with an overriding smell of ammonia. With a horrified thought, she recognized it as the smell of stale urine.

There was only one other man in the cell block besides the young Indian. He rose immediately and came to the door of his cell. She could feel him staring at her as she went by and jumped when the jailer walking with them slammed his hand against the door and ordered the man to sit back down in his cell.

Plenty Horses was in last of the six cells in the block. The jailers had put four chairs in a semi-circle in front of the door. The jailer drew an invisible line with his foot two feet in front of the barred door and said that nobody could go closer than that. O'Day sat down in one of the chairs and moved another a few feet behind him, pointing at it for Laura to sit. The jailer with the bright red sideburns stood behind her and just to her side. She thought she could feel him looking at her, but she ignored the feeling and focused on the Indian man behind the bars of the cell door.

The young Indian man appeared tall and strong; Laura thought he was at least five foot ten. He stood and came to the door of the cell. He wore leather leggings and moccasins and was wrapped in a blue blanket. His shoulders were broad, although he hunched them under the blanket. He looked younger than she'd pictured, late teens or early twenties.

Nock was explaining to him who O'Day was and that Arends would be interpreting as he had in their previous conversations. Plenty Horses stared from Nock to O'Day as Arends translated the lawyer's words into a rough guttural dialect with an uneven cadence. The words didn't sound like they should be coming out of the little fat man's mouth. Plenty Horses made no comment about the instructions and didn't even nod in affirmation that he understood what he was being asked to do. Indeed, he made no move whatsoever other than to shift his gaze from Nock to O'Day.

Laura was reminded of when Jonathon had taken her to the Bronx Zoo to see the gorilla exhibit. At the other exhibits, the monkeys and other animals had squealed and begged for food to be thrown to them, but the old gorilla had just stared. Jonathon had been incensed that the animal did nothing entertaining and had demanded zoo keepers provoke some sort of response from him. When he refused, Jonathon cut the visit short and made the entire party leave. He yelled at the zookeeper that there would be no more contributions to the zoo from the Bowmans.

Plenty Horses's dark eyes moved over O'Day's left shoulder and fell on Laura. She felt her heart freeze as their eyes met. Nock had not introduced her or provided any information about why she might be in the cellblock. She thought she detected a slight nod toward her from the young Indian man, and then he turned his attention back to Nock and O'Day.

Once the introductions were over, Plenty Horses sat on a small stool, and O'Day started the questions, his voice hard and direct. Laura immediately felt sorry for the Indian.

"Why did you shoot Lieutenant Casey?" O'Day appeared annoyed that waiting for Arends to interpret slowed his delivery.

Nock started to say something, but then reconsidered and sat back as the question was interpreted by Arends.

Plenty Horses showed no emotion either from the English or the translated version. He absorbed the question for what seemed like a very long time, his arms moving underneath the blue blanket. When he finally spoke, the words came out of his mouth weakly like a person who has remained silent for a long time. In English, he said, "The soldier was . . ." He struggled with the words for a time and then started speaking rapidly in Lakota to Arends.

"He says Casey was a spy. The Lakota were at war, and the lieutenant was observing their camp. He's very proud to be a Brule warrior and to be charged with guarding the camp. He said he was fighting to save the Lakota women and children from the army."

O'Day held up his hand. "But Casey wasn't there in an act of war. He was there to bring peace."

Plenty Horses did not wait for Arends to interpret, but started speaking to him immediately in Lakota. "The soldiers killed women and children at Wounded Knee. I fought them at Mission Ridge. They killed hundreds of Lakota. I was only acting as a warrior should act when an enemy is near the camp. I did what any other warrior would do to protect women and children. But now I'm in this jail."

He rose and took a small step back, looking around the small cell. It was about six by eight feet and was cold and spare. As he peered at the ceiling, Laura thought he looked like he was completely alone in the world.

O'Day let the silence hold for a few beats. "Do you hate the white man?"

Before Arends could interpret, Nock said, "What kind of a question is that?"

Plenty Horses again declined to wait for the interpreter and spoke in Lakota directly to Arends. "The white man has taken everything from us. They put us on small reservations, tell us when we can eat, where we can go, how we must live. They killed our people, our women and children. When the army sends spies to our camp, we act like warriors, and for this act they put me in jail."

"But you shot him in the back of the head," O'Day said.

"No man can say we Lakota are not fair fighters. We did not lay ambush to slaughter soldiers but met them in an open field to battle man-to-man. The white man came to us long ago and told us he was our friend until we could not stand his ways. My forefathers have told this story in council and by the fireside. The Lakota are fighters and the white man has driven us to fight. We are at war, and I was put in this jail."

Laura stopped listening to the questions and answers. They all seemed to blend in together. O'Day was trying to get Plenty Horses to admit he hated the white man, and Plenty Horses was trying to say he was a brave warrior and was only protecting his people. He spoke well, if haltingly, in English for short answers and more forcefully in Lakota for longer answers. She had the impression he understood English better than he spoke it. For his part, O'Day was very professional in how he asked the questions, and Laura could actually see his story being written by the responses he received. He did not focus on collecting the facts. He seemed to be mostly focused on painting a picture of Plenty Horses as a ruthless killer. The responses from Plenty Horses did not come across as a passionate firebrand. Laura thought he was simply stating facts, not pounding war drums.

The young Indian looked directly at O'Day and Nock as he answered the questions and appeared to be frustrated that O'Day didn't understand his position. As it became clear they wouldn't understand, his answers came even more slowly. Once he looked up at Laura, his dark eyes meeting hers. She felt as if he were asking her to be the one person in the room to understand him, the one person to care about what he was saying. She desperately wanted to get up and leave, but she was rooted to her chair. Rather than maintaining his gaze, she let her eyes drop to O'Day's sleeve. She saw him writing in his pad, "Lost and pensive. Alone in a strange country with no friends."

She jumped as O'Day stood up, his chair scraping against the floor. "I think we are done here," he said to Nock. "Thank you for the interview." He nodded at Plenty Horses and gestured toward the guard to lead them out. He looked down at Laura like he'd almost forgotten about her and paused to take her elbow to help her up. Laura was still somewhat dazed as he escorted her out of the cell block.

She was aware of O'Day walking her through the courthouse, but it all went by in a blur. He said nothing, just steered her by her elbow. She didn't know what she had expected from the interview, perhaps the speeches she'd seen on stage at one of the Wild West shows that came through New York periodically, but it was nothing like that. Plenty Horses didn't appear to be a savage at all. He didn't act like a barbarian, and she sensed intelligence behind his eyes. O'Day was playing some sort of game, but Plenty Horses's answers felt sincere to her. She didn't fully understand what he'd been trying to get across, but she certainly felt his frustration and his loneliness.

As they reached the double doors of the courthouse, they walked into the bright sun and the familiar Phillips Avenue; the interview became less of a memory than an image. "Well, that was about what I expected," O'Day said. He'd lost the crisp professionalism in his voice, reverting to a more conversational tone.

She looked up at him, but he kept his eyes focused down the street as if he was talking to himself. "He doesn't accept responsibility because he has no idea of what's going on here. He has a different sense of right and wrong." He turned to Laura, still holding her by the elbow. "He's the first one of his band brought before a tribunal on a charge so serious. There was something pathetic about it."

"Pathetic" wasn't the word she would have used, but she felt what he had said was basically correct. Plenty Horses didn't seem so much a man on trial as a confused visitor from another world.

A short, thin man in a faded blue army jacket stood against the wall on the sidewalk. He'd overheard their conversation. "Pathetic? You don't know anything about it." He slurred his words and had several days' growth of a beard. As he came closer, Laura noted he smelled horrible. "Wha' gives you to the righ' ta judge?"

Laura moved a little closer to O'Day and felt his hand tighten around her elbow. "Just ignore him," he whispered and he steered her to the other side of the walkway.

The obviously drunk man started to say something else and then just waved in disgust muttering, ". . . don't know . . . don't care . . . don't give a damn. Ain't nobody gives a damn."

Laura looked back over her shoulder at the inebriated man. She'd seen her share of drunks and panhandlers in New York, but this man seemed different somehow as if he was really feeling pain. He wasn't just ranting or begging.

"Is that a friend of yours?" O'Day smirked. "I suppose the frontier's full of drunks like that—just like everywhere else."

She just shook her head and focused on the walkway in front of her. "I was told that Sioux Falls is a Prohibition town."

O'Day laughed. "You can get whiskey in every drug store here for medicinal purposes." He swept a hand down Phillips Avenue. "You know, it isn't just women here for divorces. There are men who are forced to spend time here as well. They need masculine diversions like gambling, drinking and err . . . other forms of recreation."

Laura felt her face flush, and she tried to pretend she didn't hear him. The last thing she wanted to hear about is how men occupied their free time.

"So what did you think of our little interview?" he asked. "Have you had your fill of frontier adventure now that you've seen a real live savage?"

"He didn't seem a savage at all," she said, her voice carrying very softly. "He just seemed like a very scared, young stranger in a very different world."

He looked over at her, still holding her elbow. "You have to remember, he's not exactly a stranger to the white man's world. He spent over five years at the Carlisle Indian School in Pennsylvania."

"He did?" Laura was surprised. She'd heard O'Day saying something to that effect to Nock, but it hadn't registered. From the way Plenty Horses carried himself, she would have sworn he had been in the strange world of the West all of his life.

"Yeah, he was there from the time he was fourteen and went back to the reservation when he was nineteen, a couple of years ago."

"Didn't he learn English when he was there? I was told the school was making new citizens out of the students." She was pretty sure the Bowmans had contributed to the school or one like it, but Jonathon handled all of that type of thing.

O'Day laughed. "Not everyone is Charles Eastman. Let me guess, your husband saw a lecture by Eastman or some other 'Indian success story' and sent money to the school."

That was exactly how it happened, but Laura was not about to give O'Day the benefit of being correct.

"I saw records that Plenty Horses was there all right, but he spent three of the five years in the 'outing' program learning to work in the surrounding farms. When he was released, he was in third grade but had done three years of farm work." O'Day smirked again. "And we all thought slavery was abolished."

They were nearing the entrance of the Cataract Hotel. Laura would really have liked to have talked with O'Day a little more to understand the interview, but he said, "I was glad you got to act as my assistant today, Mrs. Bowman." He moved his grip on her elbow so he could shake her hand. "As much as I enjoy your company, I have to get this story written while it's still fresh. Good day."

Laura found herself suddenly alone as O'Day walked quickly toward the next street corner. She looked up and down Phillips Avenue. In the week she had been here, she'd spent as little of her time on the street as she could, confining herself to the comfort of the Cataract Hotel and the lawyer's offices across the street. She took a deep breath and entered the lobby. It would be another lonely night in her room replaying the events resulting in her divorce. She knew she was right to leave but couldn't help but feel guilty.

Chapter Five

Laura awoke with her nightclothes soaked in sweat. She slipped out from under the thick comforter and let the cool morning air find her body. She'd been dreaming. In her dream she'd been in the jail at the interview of Plenty Horses. He'd raised his head and his eyes had caught hers. In the next instant, she'd been looking out of the cell, looking at O'Day and Nock and . . . Sitting behind O'Day, where she had been standing, was only a faint image, like a ghost. They'd been questioning her, but instead of words she'd only heard a buzzing. No matter how hard she'd tried, she couldn't understand what they were saying. The men had been getting angrier and angrier, and the buzzing had kept getting louder. She'd tried to tell them she didn't understand, but the words coming out her mouth were gibberish. She'd dropped her gaze from the men on the other side of the bars to the door itself. The door had been locked, and she knew it wouldn't open; it would never open.

She shuddered in the cool air and looked out of her third floor window without noticing anything in the gray morning light. The cold penetrated her thin nightclothes and tortured her skin. Somehow, she felt like she deserved it, deserved to be punished. The wave of cold came in the window and wrapped around her, holding her prisoner. She shook her head and actually looked out the window for the first time. The dawn brought the sun and warmth. She deserved to be warm. She turned and crawled back under the comforter, letting it restore warmth to her body.

Today she would attend the first day of Plenty Horses's trial. It had been on her mind all night since the interview. No matter how many times she shook her head and reminded herself it was not her problem, that she had enough issues of her own, the blank stare of the young Lakota warrior came back to her. She'd been prepared to see the wild eyes of a killer consumed with evil, or the dead eyes of a young man not aware what he had done. She'd even prepared herself to see the hard eyes of a professional solider who obeyed orders to kill for a living.

Instead she saw the eyes of a sincere young man, slightly bewildered. When O'Day had asked him the obvious question of why he'd shot Casey, he'd said a-matter-of-factly that he was protecting his tribe. Then he'd launched into a long diatribe about the evils the white man had inflicted on the Lakota, a speech he was obviously repeating from what others had told him. It was a political speech. But before he let the obvious answers flow from his mouth, she'd seen vulnerability in his eyes with a touch of bewilderment and a sense of inevitability. In that instant, she saw he had shot Casey because he thought he had to, because he couldn't do anything else. And now he was alone, and they were going to hang him.

She took a deep breath. She would go to the trial.

Laura wasn't sure which dress to take out. What did one wear to a murder trial? She decided to be as sedate as possible. The last thing she wanted was call attention to herself. She just needed to witness the drama.

She didn't care to face Haddie McKenna at her perch at the edge of the lobby of the Cataract. She rang for room service and had her breakfast brought up to her room. She made plans to sneak out a side door without going through the lobby.

O'Day had told her that the trial was scheduled to start at 9:45 a.m. Since it was a Friday she assumed that most of the citizenry of Sioux Falls would be at work, but as she left the Cataract she heard a commotion the three blocks down Phillips Avenue to the Masonic Building that was serving as the courthouse. A crowd had gathered, spilling out into the street. A number of the people in the street were rough frontiersmen with formless slouch hats and their thumbs hooked in their gun belts. They almost all had long, unkempt beards with the remnants of tobacco juice spilling out the corner of their mouths.

"That damned Indian needs to hang!" one of them hollered from Laura's left side. When he swung his arm in the air, she was afraid he would hit her. Beside him, a farm woman of Dakota, identifiable by her homespun dress and quaint bonnet, stood close to her man. Her face was hard, and her plump cheeks rose red with agitation.

Laura made her way along the sidewalk toward Masonic Building. O'Day had told her it was to serve as the temporary courthouse as they expected a crowd far too large for the regular courtroom. The building included a drug store (doing great business, especially the therapeutic alcohol) and a real estate office on the first floor. The courtroom was to be on the second floor. There were over two hundred people standing in front of the building, and she didn't see how they could all possibly fit in the upstairs ballroom, now courtroom. Ahead, she spotted Abigail Johnson and Elnora Flatt and two other residents of the Cataract Hotel pushing their way through the crowd. The locals were slowly giving way, but the hard looks on their faces made it clear they were not happy about giving the wealthy "divorce colonists" preferred access to the courtroom. Laura moved quickly to fall into their wake, letting her desire to see the trial overcome her reluctance to throw class into the faces of the locals.

As the women were still thirty feet from the Masonic Building steps, the voice of the police chief could be heard over the throng. "I'm sorry, folks, but all the seats in the courtroom are occupied. There's no more room."

"Let us into the balcony then," a voice from behind Laura said. "We want to see the murdering Injun on trial." Laura felt drops of spit hit the back of her head. It took all her will power to not run her hand over her hair.

The chief shook his head. "I'm telling you, every public seat is taken on the floor and in the balcony. You're just going to have to go home."

"There sure as hell better be more seating at the hanging, that's for damn sure," the man behind her shouted to a chorus of cheers from the other locals.

"Goddamn it," a quieter voice to her left said. "Only God-damned excitement in a year and they won't let us in."

There was an unsettling movement from the rear of the crowd. A wave of silence started at the edge and moved toward the middle.

Locals pushed aside to make room for a U.S. marshal leading a contingent of Lakota men. The five men were all dressed uncomfortably in new suits. One man's hair was cut awkwardly just above his ears and pulled across the top of his head in a low side part. The other four wore their hair long in traditional Indian style, flowing to their shoulders and parted in the middle. Their faces showed no emotion as they took in the silent crowd of rowdy settlers. They simply made their way behind the marshal who was pushing people out of the way. When the group went by Laura, she was pushed and stumbled into the person to her left.

"Why do the Indians get to sit in the courtroom and we don't?" a rough voice from the back carried over the crowd.

"They're part of the trial," the chief of police said. "I'm telling you one more time that you need to break this up and go home before I start putting people in jail."

"You ain't got room for all of us in your jail, Homer. You gonna put my wife in with me?"

Another voice piped up, "You can lock her up with me instead. She'd have a hell of a lot more fun."

After some good natured laughs, and the tension began to lift. The tightness of the mob at the front of the steps started to loosen as the locals moved to find a place to sit on the side of the street.

"Thank goodness," Abigail Johnson said as she worked her way to the chief. "I didn't think you'd ever get this rabble to disburse. We'll need to save a seat for Mrs. McKenna as she will be a little late."

"I'm sorry, ma'am. The courtroom is full," the chief said his hands held out wide. "There just isn't any more room."

"No room?" she said. "I'm afraid I don't understand. We are going to the Plenty Horses trial and we need to save a seat for Mrs. McKenna."

"No, ma'am, you are not going to the trial and not saving a seat for anyone," he said. "The seats were all filled up hours ago. You're just going to have to go back to the Cataract."

"But Mrs. McKenna, told us—" Abigail Johnson stammered.

"I'm sorry, ma'am, there's just no room."

The women looked at each other, stunned. Mrs. Johnson shrugged. She didn't look like she was looking forward to telling Haddie

McKenna they'd been turned away. The ladies put their backs to the insolent public official and noticed Laura behind them. "Why, Mrs. Bowman, I didn't even see you there behind us," Mrs. Flatt said. "Can you believe they won't let us into the trial?"

Laura felt a strange sense of relief. Last night she'd debated with herself about attending the trial. Her natural inclination was to avoid conflict, take the easy way out and stay in her room. But her presence at the interview had drawn her in and piqued her curiosity. The dream this morning . . . She shook her head to clear the frightening image. Over breakfast she'd convinced herself to be brave and attend. Now she could relax, knowing she had made the attempt to do the brave thing, but just couldn't get in. She'd been brave all by herself with no one else pushing her. Yes, she'd been brave.

"I guess they just have too large of a crowd," she said trying not to smile. "I'm sure we'll hear all about it through the newspapers."

"Not if I don't get through this infernal mass," a firm voice behind her said. She felt a hand grip her arm just above the elbow and turned to see J.T. O'Day in a stylish tan suit. He waved at the chief. "As you know, I'm from the *New York World*, my good man. I need to get by." He strode forward his hand still holding Laura's arm.

"Yes, Mr. O'Day, a seat has been reserved for you," the chief said opening room for him to walk up the courthouse steps. "But who is—"

"This is my assistant, Mrs. Bowman," O'Day said, pulling Laura forward. "We absolutely need to make certain Mrs. Bowman has a seat in the courtroom next to me or I won't be able to file my stories in an expedited manner."

Laura opened her mouth to say something, but O'Day continued to pull her forward. She felt a wave of animosity from the Cataract Hotel coven behind her but just kept her eyes forward and let O'Day pull her along.

The rowdy crowd that stretched into the street behind her, rumbled. A rough voice called out; "I wonder what she assists him with," followed by chortles of laughter. "I bet she expedites reeeaaaal good!" another voice said, getting even more laughs. O'Day tightened his grip on her arm and pulled her straight to the steps, never turning his head.

Once they were well past the chief and at the top of the stairs, she whispered at O'Day, "Just what do you think you're doing?"

"You wanted to get into the trial didn't you?"

"Yes . . . no . . . I mean . . . I think so."

"Well, that's hardly an appropriate way of thanking me. You can't go back now," he said peering back over his shoulder with a smile.

"What that man said . . ."

"What do you care about what a dirty farmer or those old biddies from the hotel lobby say. At least they have something to talk about other than stringing up that poor Indian."

Laura walked a little faster down the hallway towards the courtroom. "Do you really think they'll hang him?"

O'Day's white teeth appeared from behind his black mustache. "Did you hear what they were saying out there? If the jury doesn't hang him, they'll have a major riot on their hands. The fact of the matter is, they'd never get him out of the jail alive. Do you think anyone in this town could vote to let an Indian who admitted to killing an army officer to go free? Or anyone in the whole damned state for that matter?"

"He didn't seem like a killer when we interviewed him yesterday. He looked like a frightened, confused young man."

"He blew off the back of that army lieutenant's head. That is a fact. Indians don't kill soldiers and then peacefully return to their tipis."

O'Day was still dragging Laura along as he strode purposefully down the hallway toward the courtroom. The hall was filled with people who'd made it past the chief but still didn't have a place to sit. "But why a trial, and why here? Don't the army and the Indians usually just work these things out by themselves?"

"That was in the old world, Mrs. Bowman," he whispered as they entered the door of the courtroom. "We are in a crazy world of politics now, even out on the frontier. It's a new age."

She had more questions for him, but the scene of the courtroom captured all of her senses.

As the police chief had said, the courtroom was packed. The seats on the floor were mostly filled with women in brightly colored dresses. Laura recognized a number of other soon-to-be divorcées who must have had the foresight to arrive early enough to get a seat. There were also a number of townswomen, identifiable by the more home-style fashion sense. The edges of the courtroom were filled with men, most of which appeared to be local merchants. There was a smattering of frontiersmen and farmers, all dressed in their Sunday best, but most of their class had been relegated to standing in the streets.

One of the officers ordered into usher duty led Laura and O'Day to the third row seats on the left side designated for press. The men who operated the one-person editor/reporter/advertising executive/printer/delivery boy duties at the little weekly South Dakota newspapers frowned when they were pushed even closer together to make room for the famous J.T. O'Day and his "assistant." Laura ignored their stares and squeezed herself next to a rough-looking man in a worn suit and a bushy blonde-gray beard. He mumbled a name she didn't understand and said he was from the *Yankton Free Press*. She wondered how often they bathed in Yankton, as his scent made the cramped seating arrangements even more claustrophobic. She leaned as much as she could towards the smiling J.T. O'Day, who smelled of soap and hair oil.

In the front two rows of seats, the Indian men who had walked by earlier sat stoically. She noticed the man right in front of her with his hair parted to the side wore dangling metal earrings. She'd never seen a man wear earrings before.

In front of them, two white men sat at a table stacked with papers. She recognized defense attorney George Nock from the interview session the previous day. Both he and the other man at the table, whom she took to be the other defense attorney David Edward Powers, wore their hair short but sported long drooping mustaches. They wore identical conservative suits with frock coats extending to the floor when they sat. Laura thought they looked like the pair of walrus at the Bronx Zoo.

The rumblings of the crowd quieted as two uniformed guards brought Plenty Horses into the courtroom. He seemed much taller and thinner than he did in the dark of his cell during the interview the previous day. He had on a worn shirt and slacks and still wrapped himself in the blue blanket he'd kept draped around himself during the interview session. He was the least dapper of all of the Indians present. As he shook hands with his defense lawyers, the blue blanket slipped and Laura noticed that the left hand he used to grip the blanket was missing some fingers. He quickly wrapped his malformed hand back into the worn blue blanket.

He looked back over his shoulder and nodded at the other Lakota men in attendance. He shook hands with a dour-looking older Indian sitting directly behind him wearing striped pants, a dark jacket and vest and beaded moccasins. The big reporter from Yankton next to her whispered to nobody in particular, "That's his father, Living Bear."

Prosecutor William Sterling sat at the other table and watched Plenty Horses get settled. Sterling had a round face with a prominent nose and sloping chin that made him appear to be constantly trying to follow a smell. Unlike most of the men in the courtroom, he was clean shaven and combed his hair straight back. Laura thought he groomed himself more like the men she knew in New York than any other Dakotan she'd seen. His assistant at the prosecution table, J.G. Balance, had the exact opposite look with thin, receding hair and a long, full beard.

Laura turned to ask O'Day a question, but he was furiously scribbling on a pad he'd pulled from his pocket. When she started to say something, he paused long enough to give her a fierce look and continued scribbling. Apparently being J.T. O'Day's assistant consisted primarily of making an entrance and then sitting quietly.

The courtroom quieted and everyone rose as the judges were announced. There were two seats at the elevated platform. Alonzo J. Edgerton was the first to enter. The big man beside Laura whispered to her that he was from South Dakota and had presided at the grand jury hearing. The second judge, Oliver Shiras, took the other seat, and Laura's guide told her he was from Iowa. She was grateful for the information from the smelly giant as O'Day continued to ignore her while he made notes.

Judge Edgerton welcomed everyone and proceeded to blandly recount a series of legal statements that meant nothing to Laura. From the way the men were reacting, she took it that they were working on selecting a jury. A series of men came into the courtroom and submitted to questions by the defense and prosecution. Laura pretty much ignored the activity and spent her time watching the Indian men in front of her. She'd never seen Indians up close before coming to Dakota. Plenty Horses watched the activities impassively, as if he were looking out of a window at the passing countryside. She remembered the expression on his face during the interview the previous day when he'd said that he was only protecting the women and children in his camp when he shot Casey. There'd been a spark of emotion in his eyes then, but today he looked like a statue.

Before she realized it, the judge announced that jury selection would continue after lunch. The participants all rose, and the judges left the chamber. As the people slowly made their way out of the courtroom, she thought the sense of excitement that had filled the room when they'd entered was lost. Most of the audience in the courtroom appeared as bored as she was.

"Did you enjoy yourself?" O'Day asked as they slowly shuffled out the courtroom.

"I'm afraid I didn't understand much of what was going on," she admitted.

"You've learned the first rule of being a good reporter. Don't be afraid to admit you don't know something." O'Day laughed and touched her arm just above the elbow. "Let's have lunch, and I'll tell you what you saw."

They got a table at Dickerson's Diner across the street, the best place to eat close to the courthouse according to O'Day. As they'd crossed the street, they overheard some locals in front of the store complaining that prices had increased dramatically as soon as the trial started. Laura remarked that there were no locals in the diner and repeated what she'd heard on the street. O'Day laughed and said that the prices were still well below what he paid for lunches in New York. Laura had never really considered what the prices were in either place. Things just got paid for.

"You see," O'Day said between bites of a roast beef sandwich, "the defense is trying to get eastern-focused men on the jury while the prosecution wants western-focused. And the prosecution wants jurors with the least amount of education possible. Their perfect juror is a dumb, mean man who thinks the Indians are just savages." He waved his sandwich. "It seems like there are quite a number of them available."

Laura nodded as she picked at her pile of food. She had not gotten used to the huge platefuls served at every meal in South Dakota.

If she had to stay in Sioux Falls much longer than ninety days, she'd need all new clothes.

"The defense is thinking an eastern, educated jury might be more progressive about the plight of the Indians. The prosecution wants the traditional Dakotans who think the only good Indian is a dead Indian."

"Oh, they can't think that."

O'Day shrugged. "Based on what we saw in the street this morning, it sure looks that way."

O'Day cut his remarks off quickly as a figure loomed over their table. "Are you finding anything to interest your readers, Mr. O'Day?" George Nock stood over them with a smile on his face and a piece of mashed potatoes lodged in the corner of his drooping mustache. Laura hoped it wouldn't drop onto their table.

"There is always something interesting to write about, Mr. Nock," O'Day said putting his silverware down. "How do you think it's going?"

"Oh, no comment, of course," Nock said holding up a finger. "I'm sure we'll find a very fair jury." He didn't sound very convinced. "And you still want to talk with our witnesses tonight?"

O'Day nodded. "Yes, and you'll have an interpreter present?"

Nock nodded and turned to Laura. "I'm glad to see your continued interest in the proceedings, Mrs. Bowman. It's always good to see such an interest in civic affairs, especially from such a beautiful, prominent woman." He was playing the public opinion angle as much as he could.

"Thank you, Mr. Nock," she said with a smile, trying to repress the blush she felt blooming towards her neck. "I'm learning a great deal."

Nock made a quick bow and worked his way out of the diner without depositing his mashed potato blob on their table. O'Day scoffed. "Don't get too enthused about his interest in you, Mrs. Bowman. He's probably trying to figure out if he can get you to contribute financially to the defense fund."

"What do you mean?"

"The last I heard, Powers and Nock thought some group from back east would be paying for the defense of the Indian, but the funding hasn't come through yet. I doubt either one of them will get a dime out of this whole fiasco."

"Who are you seeing tonight?" she asked.

"Nock wants me to interview his Lakota witnesses. The more sentiment I can create for the plight of the Indian, the stronger his case. It's still a terrible case, however. Everyone knows that Indian is going to hang. It's just a matter of how sensational it's going to be." O'Day smiled. "Sensation sells newspapers, though, and sensational is what I do best."

Laura said nothing. They returned that afternoon to watch the trial. Now that she knew what to look for, she could see that Nock and Powers were pushing hard to get educated men onto the jury and were not very successful. All the while, she kept her eyes focused on the Lakota men in front of her. She was intrigued not only by Plenty Horses but also with the other four Indian men quietly observing the proceedings. She thought they must be even more lost in the proceedings than she, but they didn't show any interest or boredom or nervousness. They didn't show any emotion at all.

As had been the case in the morning, O'Day had made a big production of escorting her into the courtroom after lunch, but then ignored her once they sat down. As the activities of the jury selection washed over her, she daydreamed about how she might do something to help the Indians. She'd never "done" anything, at least not by herself . . . at least not before coming to Sioux Falls to get a divorce.

At four o'clock Judge Edgerton pounded the gavel and declared they were done for the day. Again, O'Day made a production of escorting her out of the courtroom. He seemed to delight in showing Laura on his arm in public but then ignored her afterward. When he'd first offered to let her attend the interview of Plenty Horses, she'd been concerned he was using it to mask nefarious intentions. Now she was beginning to suspect her appearance on his arm might be the mask.

As they made their way out onto the street, she found herself with her arm linked in his. She was aware of people staring at them, but it bothered her less all the time. She asked him, "Just what am I supposed to be doing . . . as your 'assistant,' I mean?"

O'Day put his hand to his chest. "Why Mrs. Bowman, I can assure you that I have nothing but the most honorable intentions."

She looked up at him and smiled. "It appears to me, Mr. O'Day, that you are more interested in having a woman on your arm in public than anything else."

O'Day's head snapped around. It was the first time the confident O'Day was caught off guard in her presence. For a moment he was quiet. Then he smiled and said, "Your training in the society circles of New York has honed your intuitive qualities well, Mrs. Bowman. Do you object to being my escort?"

"Not at all, Mr. O'Day," she said. "I just wanted to clarify our arrangement." Laura was pleased with herself. "However, you don't have to be so rude to me when I ask you questions. When I ask you something, I'm not just making conversation. I want to know what's happening."

"Mrs. Bowman, I have a job to do and . . ."

"I know that," she said holding up a hand. "And I can help. I really can." As they neared the Cataract Hotel, she gripped his arm with more confidence. "I want to know more about the Indians."

"Well," he said. "As you know and are no doubt hinting at, I'm going over to the Merchants Hotel tonight to have dinner with Plenty Horses's father, Jack Red Cloud and the other Lakota witnesses. Would you like to . . ." he held his arm out from his body a little with her hand still on it, "accompany me?"

Laura did not hesitate. "Yes, so nice of you to ask. What time?"

O'Day pulled a watch from his front vest pocket. "It is nearly five now. I told Nock I'd meet them at 6:30, so I'll meet you in the lobby at 6:15."

Laura gave him a smile and squeezed his elbow. "Very well, Mr. O'Day, I'll be your assistant again tonight for dinner."

She slipped her hand from his arm and made her way toward the main staircase of the Cataract. She was sure the entire lobby was watching her, but she ignored them. Out of the corner of her eye she saw O'Day go to the dark corner where the men lounged. Part of her wanted to go scandalize Haddie McKenna at her table in the other far corner, but she decided she'd probably already done as much as she could for the day. Any more would just be overkill. It was kind of fun not caring. A great deal had changed in twenty-four hours.

Laura and O'Day met precisely at 6:15 p.m., as promised. After seeing him head toward the other men, she'd expected him to be intoxicated, but he didn't appear to be. Whatever J.T. O'Day's faults were, he was serious about his work. She was also relieved he was not in the company of the obnoxious Waldo Elliot.

As they strolled down Phillips Avenue, she noticed what a pleasant late spring evening it was. There was activity on the street but there wasn't the hustle and bustle of the city streets she was used to.

"Why are you talking with the Indians today?" she asked.

"Nock plans on calling them as witnesses to set the stage for his defense," he said. "He figures if I can get a good story or two about the plight of the Lakota, it will soften up the jury." He shook his head. "Nobody in this two-bit town reads the *New York World* anyway, so I doubt it'll have much impact. The Sioux Falls and other Dakota papers already have plenty of opinions on Indians. They remember all too well what this country was like when they got here. The Indians are still considered dangerous creatures—like the bears and wolves they killed to settle this place." He paused. "The bears and wolves are almost all dead now."

"Oh, how could they think that," she said in a harsh voice. "Mr. O'Day you have entirely too active an imagination."

"You were out on the street this morning. Do you really think any of those people screaming for blood would hesitate to shoot Plenty Horses, if they got the chance? Do you think they'd hesitate to shoot one of the men we'll be talking with tonight?"

"I have far too much confidence in human nature to believe you." She could never tell when O'Day was exaggerating to make a fool of her or telling the truth. "So what are you going to ask the Indians?"

"Background mostly. Nock said he didn't want me to ask about the events leading up to the shooting until after they testified. He promised access afterward, so I agreed. Tonight we'll just try to get an idea of Sioux history from the mouths of the Indians."

"I get mixed up about what Sioux is, what Lakota is, or Brule or Oglala. Are they all tribe names?"

O'Day sighed deeply as if he was talking to a child. "I'm going to regret taking you along, I can tell. Sioux is the name of the whole nation and includes Indians from Northern Minnesota all the way through the Dakotas, Nebraska, and Montana. It's what whites and other tribes call them, not what they call themselves. The Sioux that stayed in Minnesota are called Dakota, and the ones who went further west across the Missouri are the Lakota. Dakota and Lakota are also the names of the dialects of the same Sioux language. The Lakota are split into smaller bands, one of which is Oglala and another is Brule. Their reservations are quite close to each other in Western South Dakota, but they are kind of friendly rivals. Plenty Horses and his father are Brule. He Dog and Jack Red Cloud are Oglala. Now, no more questions."

"Yes but . . ."

O'Day gave her a sharp look as he held the door open for her.

The Merchants Hotel was a nice, comfortable facility. It probably would have been considered elegant in most prairie cities of this size, but it paled in comparison to the Cataract. Laura had heard of a few less wealthy residents of the Sioux Falls Divorce Colony coming here to stay, but it was mostly a hotel for the business community. Laura realized she didn't know where O'Day was staying. She'd just assumed he was at the Cataract but had never seen him anywhere but in the lobby. "Where do you stay in Sioux Falls, Mr. O'Day?" she asked.

He smiled. "Why, Mrs. Bowman, how forward of you."

She felt herself flush. "I . . . I was just asking because . . ."

"Because you are becoming increasingly nosey, I know. I think I prefer the scared, quiet New York wife. Or soon-to-be ex-wife, I should say."

She felt a little guilty about her interest. She had absolutely no romantic interest in O'Day and she felt nothing of that sort emanating from him either. That fact alone made her very curious. As their eyes adjusted to the dark lobby of the Merchants, she realized O'Day had distracted her so he didn't have to answer her question.

The little fat man who had interpreted for them at the Plenty Horses interview sprang to his feet and shook hands with O'Day as soon as they entered the lobby. "Mr. O'Day, C.C. Arends at your service again, sir," he said pumping O'Day's hand. Laura smiled at the obvious tightness in O'Day's neck as he smiled at Arends while his hand was being accosted.

Arends exited the handshake immediately when he noticed Laura, and she saw O'Day furiously wipe his hand on his tan coat. "And I see you have brought the lovely Mrs. Bowman to join us again." He gripped Laura's hand in both of his fleshy paws. She tried not to cringe.

O'Day interrupted the greeting. "Is Mr. Nock joining us this evening?"

Arends was still very obviously ogling Laura, holding her hand in his two. He was so gross that Laura almost thought him comical.

"Mr. Arends," O'Day leaned over his shoulder. "I said, is Attorney Nock joining us?"

"Umm . . . no sir," he said. Laura used the distraction to extract her hand and move to the other side of O'Day. "He said he's busy preparing the case but trusted you would abide by your agreement with him."

O'Day waved his hand "Yes, yes, now lead the way to our guests."

While Arends scurried forward, O'Day leaned over toward Laura. "You seem to have an ardent admirer."

Laura smiled prettily, "I'm hoping he'll ask me accompany him back to Pine Ridge to share his bed with him . . . and the squaw he bragged so much about."

O'Day face went blank with shock for a moment and then laughed. "Mrs. Bowman I do believe you are coming out of your shell."

Three Indians were at the table in the far back corner of the hotel restaurant. The tables around them were all vacant.

Laura quickly moved to O'Day's right as he placed his hand on the back of the vacant seat next to the largest of the Indian men. He had no choice but to pull the chair out for her and then take the next seat. A disappointed Arends had to take the empty seat across the table from them. Laura had instinctively decided to sit anywhere but next to Arends.

The fat interpreter introduced the older man sitting next to him as Living Bear, Plenty Horses's father, the big man sitting next to her as He Dog, and the other man at the end of the table as Jack Red Cloud. The Indians all shook hands with O'Day in a very formal manner and nodded politely at Laura.

Jack Red Cloud had established himself at the head of the table and looked to be very much in charge of the Lakota delegation. His black hair was shorter than the other two men's and parted on the side. He was still wearing the vested suit with a gold watch prominently displayed in his front pocket. Laura initially took him to be the leader of the Indian group until she saw He Dog give him a condescending look and a smile. He Dog and Living Bear had changed into cheap slacks and loose fitting shirts. It quickly became obvious to Laura that Jack Red Cloud may have considered himself the leader, but He Dog held the respect of both Living Bear and Arends without saying or doing anything. She couldn't help but think of how her husband, Jonathon Bowman, could command the attention of a room the same way. It was one of the things that had attracted her to him. Well, that, and the fact that her father suggested she should be attracted to him. The economic panic of 1883 had created some strange partnerships. Bowman knew presence meant power, and he had mastered the art of it. He Dog also carried a presence of power.

Arends ordered steaks for all of them a without asking anyone what they wanted. The Indian men watched the little fat interpreter without emotion.

As he had the previous day, O'Day asked his questions through Arends. Once again Laura was taken by how foreign both the Sioux language and English seemed in Arends's mouth. When he spoke in Sioux, or as O'Day had told her the correct name for it, "Lakota," the language sounded harsh and guttural. But when the Indian men spoke, the guttural words flowed naturally and effortlessly from them. The men themselves did not show much emotion in their faces, but the way the words flowed seemed to convey as much meaning as the utterances themselves. She found that, most of the time, she understood the basics of what was being said well before Arends translated for them.

"How is life on the reservation?" O'Day asked through Arends.

Living Bear shook his head. "The Lakota don't have enough to eat. We can't go anywhere without permission from the agent, we can't do anything without permission from some white man. How would you think it is?" Laura was shocked at the directness of his response.

O'Day continued to ask about living conditions on the reserva-tion. It was clear he was trying to paint a picture of destitution for his

New York readers. The answers from the stoic Living Bear were short and abrupt. He was a man of few words and displayed little emotion. Laura had a feeling the only reason he was talking with them was because Nock told him it would help his son.

In contrast, Jack Red Cloud spoke forcefully and expounded on every question. He reminded Laura of the local politicians that spoke at the fundraisers she'd attended with Jonathon. O'Day had told her earlier that Jack's father, Red Cloud, was one of the greatest leaders of the Sioux and was much respected. He said that way back in 1870, just two weeks after riding in a train for the first time and seeing his first two-story building, the senior Red Cloud had mesmerized thousands of people with a speech at the Cooper Institute in New York City.

Jack was very aware of his father's celebrity and wanted to show he was as powerful and eloquent. As Jonathon Bowman had whispered to her once when he still took her to a political gathering, "If you have to tell people how important you are, you just aren't very important." She thought Bowman's comments fit Jack Red Cloud perfectly.

He Dog was another matter. He was very relaxed in delivering his answers, and they had the most impact. He came across as a man who had seen and done a great deal and was by far the most confident person at the table. Laura found herself watching his muted facial expressions no matter which of the three Indians was speaking.

Finally, he looked at O'Day and commanded the floor. "You'll never know what it's like on the reservation because you've never been there and you don't know us. The Lakota were the greatest warriors in this country. No tribe could stand against us, not the Crow, not the Pawnee, not the Utes. Not even the U.S. Army could stand against us. Now we are treated like children. The men we fought in the Powder River basin, the soldiers like Miles and Crook, they respected us and they earned our respect. I stood and talked with the Great Father himself several times and other great leaders of the government in Washington sat and listened to us. They were afraid of the Lakota and did not want to fight us anymore, so they listened. But that was years ago, and they are all gone now. Even Bear Coat Miles doesn't talk with us now. Every few years, a new white agent shows up and gives the Lakota orders. These agents have never known Indians. If we don't do what they say, they take our food away like we are children. Men who have never fought the Lakota don't know the Lakota."

The spell of the speech was broken when the waiter brought plates of steaks. Laura was served first, then O'Day and then Arends. The little interpreter tore right into his meat while Laura and O'Day waited for the remaining plates to be put on the table. The servings that were set in front of the Indians had smaller, thinner cuts of meat. Without thinking, Laura motioned to He Dog that she would like to switch steaks with him. "This is too large for me," she said switching the plates. He nodded without saying anything and cut into the thick meat.

O'Day attempted to lighten the tone while they ate. "Ask them if they have seen any of the sights of Sioux Falls," he told Arends who looked a little peeved at having his eating interrupted. Before he could start interpreting O'Day continued. "I heard they went to the park to see the buffalo."

At the word "buffalo" all three Indian men perked up. Living Bear smiled uncharacteristically and said "*Tatonka*! Yes, *Tatonka*!"

After hearing Arends's translation, Jack Red Cloud said, "It has been a long time since we have seen buffalo. There were seventeen of them fenced in the pen here at Sioux Falls."

He Dog's voice was deep and emotional. "I haven't seen any buffalo in years and years. When I was a young man, they covered the plains as far as the eye could see. They fed and clothed the Lakota." He shook his head slowly. "And now we see them in a little pen. They are like the Lakota; they don't look so fierce when they are confined to a pen." He turned to Laura and said, "You should have seen them when they were free." He smiled for the first time of the evening.

They finished their steaks and the waiter collected the dishes, glaring a little at Laura for switching plates with He Dog. Arends suggested apple pie for everyone, but O'Day said he and Laura didn't have time and would have to get back to the Cataract. Arends made little effort to hide his disappointment since O'Day was picking up the bill.

They rose from the table, and O'Day thanked the Indians and shook their hands. The Lakota men only nodded at Laura but it was in a much more relaxed and friendly manner than they had greeted her.

She managed to keep O'Day between her and Arends and, thus, avoided the sweaty two-handed goodbye shake. She thought the little fat man must have been distracted by the lack of dessert.

Laura slipped her arm through O'Day's arm as they exited the Merchants onto the sidewalk. "So, what did we learn?" she asked.

Usually when O'Day replied to her questions it was with a smirk. This time he was more thoughtful. "More than anything else, I'm impressed by the differences between the men. Living Bear wanted to be anyplace else in the world than having dinner with us. He's a devoted father willing to be tortured by dining with white reporters if that's what it takes to save his son."

Laura laughed. "I agree he was only there because he had to be. I hardly thought your questions were torture, though."

O'Day continued without responding. "Jack Red Cloud wants to be a big shot in the worst way. The problem is, neither the Sioux nor the whites think he's nearly as important as he does."

Laura agreed and told him about how she'd thought about what Jonathon Bowman had said about people trying to look powerful, but really weren't. O'Day stopped on the street corner, stared at her for a few steps. "I do think you have hit on something, Mrs. Bowman. That's a very good observation."

"But I didn't know what to think about He Dog," he continued. "His whole attitude was—"

"That's because you ain't never seen a real Lakota warrior," a rough voice came from behind them. A short man in the blue army coat emerged from the corner of the building. Laura recognized him as the inebriated man who had stopped them the day before. He wasn't nearly as drunk now, but still looked and smelled terrible.

O'Day cleared his throat. "Umm . . . well, thank you for your input." He looked up the street to see if there was any help available should he need it. "You seem quite adept at jumping into our conversations, sir."

The man stayed several feet away from them. "I don't mean to scare you or nothin', Mr. Famous Newspaperman. I was just saying that you can't understand the Lakota unless you know them, know their history, know their story."

"And you know them, Mr . . . umm"

"Morgan, my name's Morgan. I know that five months ago these men had to deal with over three hundred men, women, and children being slaughtered at Wounded Knee. Think about what an impact that must've had on 'em, on the bands, I mean. It'd be like wiping out an entire U.S. city, like New York or Boston or something. Don't you think it'd have an effect on the rest of the country . . . on you?"

Laura and O'Day stood in silence. They had expected some drunken ramblings, but the little man spoke very well.

"Do you know about the Lakota and Wounded Knee?" Laura asked.

"I know enough," he said. As he looked up, the streetlight exposed his face from beneath his slouch hat. He hadn't shaved in a long time, and there were dirt patches on his face. His eyes were bloodshot, but there was intensity to his look. "I've seen you talking to the Indians. You must be finding the truth," he said. "Don't let them kill that Indian boy. Don't let them hang him."

"Mr. . . . ah Morgan is it?" O'Day said more confidently. "I'm just a reporter in search of the truth. The truth is Plenty Horses shot Lieutenant Casey. Whether he is executed or not depends on the jury."

The words seemed to physically hurt the little cowboy. Laura thought she could see pain register in his face. Then he lowered his head back into the shadow of his hat. "I suppose you're right," he muttered. He shook his head and staggered back up the dark side street.

"What a queer little man," O'Day said. "At least Plenty Horses has one advocate among the locals."

Laura agreed with him although she didn't say it. The pleading look in his blue eyes was imprinted in her mind. She'd never seen a person crumble as the little man had done from O'Day's words. "I wonder what it is that makes him care so much?"

O'Day started walking back across the street. "Perhaps all the whiskey exposed a bad memory. When he sobers up in the morning he probably won't even remember talking with us." He laughed a little. "And then he can start on his new bottle and find a new cloud to ruin his next day."

"He thought you could save Plenty Horses," Laura said. "Can you?"

O'Day looked like he was going to give her one of his glib answers with a smirk, but after looking at her face, he paused a moment and said, "I'm a reporter, and I only report the truth. To the extent I raise considerations that otherwise would not have been raised, perhaps I can help him. But that's not my job. It's my job to report the truth and entertain my readers. If readers know about these Indians, it might help Plenty Horses." He laughed a little again. "But then again, knowledge is a frightening thing. The truth may set you free, but it may also put a rope around your neck."

"So you'll help him?" She squeezed his arm.

"I never said that. I said I'd write the truth and entertain my readers. That's my responsibility."

Laura walked with him in silence, their footsteps echoing against the brick buildings. "When we first met, you said your readers would be interested in hearing about me. Are you going to write about me?"

The street was well lit the last half block to the Cataract and was mostly empty. O'Day seemed to be framing his answer carefully. "Mrs. Bowman, I've never represented myself as anything but the humble reporter I am. You, on the other hand . . . or should I say your husband, is quite prominent. My readers may be quite interested about your time in Sioux Falls, the scandalous divorce capitol of the world."

"You wouldn't," she said stomping her foot. "Why, I don't want people reading about . . . Why would you do that?"

O'Day stopped at the street corner thirty feet in front of the ornate front door of the Cataract. "The truth, Mrs. Bowman, shall set you free." He turned and walked back in the opposite direction leaving her to enter the Cataract alone.

———————————————

"Damn you for getting me into this!" General Miles pointed at Mayberry and shook his head. His face flushed bright red against his white whiskers as he put his reading glasses back on to review the introductory story to the Plenty Horses trial in the *New York World*.

Mayberry leaned against the back wall of Miles's office in Chicago. "General, I didn't expect them to move the trial out of Deadwood."

"Damn right you didn't." Miles thundered. "But they did, didn't they?"

Baldwin was getting tired of these strategy sessions with Mayberry. He sat back in his chair, "Yes, sir, but won't Plenty Horses get a fairer trial in Sioux Falls? It seems to be more . . . civilized than Deadwood would have been."

Miles took off his reading glasses and pushed the newspaper over to Mayberry. "No, Captain Baldwin, I sense this is even more of a problem." When Mayberry looked up he pointed at him. "Do you concur that this will be an issue, Mr. Political Advisor?"

Mayberry set the newspaper carefully on the desk. "In Deadwood, they would have had a quick trial for Plenty Horses and then one for the Culbertsons and be done in a few days. We then could put these . . . issues behind us. However, the situation might play out a little longer in Sioux Falls. The *World* will no doubt play this circus out for weeks and months since they sent a reporter out there." He looked up at the general. "This was not anticipated."

"Damn right it wasn't." Miles got up and started pacing.

Baldwin broke the silence. "General, how do you think the change of venue for the Plenty Horses trial from Deadwood to Sioux Falls will change things?"

Miles sat back down and nodded toward Mayberry. He sighed and spoke to Baldwin as if he was a young private. "If the trial was in Deadwood, it would be perceived as another 'westerner' issue, and the coverage would be minimal. Even though Sioux Falls is just on the other end of the state, it has become quite the little metropolis and considers itself to be a city. They have railroads coming and going from every direction. I'm afraid the newspapers will have no problem going out and covering the trial."

"And we don't want newspaper coverage?" Baldwin still considered himself a soldier. The political strategies and actions over the last year were confusing and more than a little troubling.

Miles interjected, pointing across the desk at Mayberry, "You and Remington and those other suits are supposed to control the coverage." He turned an exasperated face towards Baldwin. "That's how you get votes, Captain Baldwin, or so they tell me. Who knows what will come out if there's a long trial in Sioux Falls?"

"Yes, General," Mayberry said. "There are steps we can take to err . . . monitor coverage. It is true Sioux Falls will be a challenge, I'm afraid. Not only is it more cosmopolitan than Deadwood, but there's the whole divorce colony issue."

General Miles turned toward him. "What divorce colony issue are you talking about, Mayberry, and how does it impact the Plenty Horses case?"

Mayberry leaned back in his chair and crossed his legs. Baldwin thought he seemed to enjoy lecturing the general, "You see, South Dakota has very liberal residency requirements, and Sioux Falls in particular has a reputation for favorable divorce judges. Many people looking for a divorce who have the money to pay for it move to Sioux Falls for three months and get a favorable settlement. It's my understanding there are so many in fact it's become quite an industry there. They've built one of the nicer hotels in the Midwest just to provide shelter for these people, mostly women, as they serve their residency time."

"Oh, Christ," Miles said. "That's just what we need. A bunch of rich people walking out on their marriage vows with nothing to do. Mayberry, how could you let this spin so out of control? What the hell are you good for?"

Mayberry squirmed in his chair and uncrossed his thin legs. "General, this will complicate the situation, it's true. We'll have to monitor the situation carefully."

"Perhaps you can get your little butt out to Dakota and handle it for me," General Miles said in a very controlled voice. "I do not want this to blow up on me. Do you understand?"

Mayberry stood quickly. "Yes, General. I'll handle it." He lowered his head and made his way out of the office. He appeared very happy to be out of the general's gaze.

"I'd like you to keep an eye on this situation as well, Frank."

"Yes, sir," Baldwin said. He wondered if it was time for him to go. General Miles rarely called him by his first name even in private.

Miles sat back and shook his head. "Frank, things were so much simpler when we were out there in Montana under two feet of snow, weren't they? All we had to worry about was whether Crazy Horse would send a raiding party when we weren't paying attention, or if Sitting Bull would cut off our supply lines. Those were real dangers, things we could see . . . could react to. We could send out brave and loyal men to fight an honorable enemy. We didn't have to worry about all of this . . ." he said, waving his hands over the papers covering his desk, "politics."

Captain Baldwin nodded and said, "Yes, sir." He thought about all the tirades Miles had thrown in the officer's tent in Montana, complaining about how General Crook was "stealing his Indians" when he'd convinced Crazy Horse to surrender to him in Pine Ridge rather than to Miles in Montana. Nelson A. Miles had always been keenly aware of public opinion and politics. They were just on a different stage now. But he certainly wasn't going to remind the general of that.

"And, Captain Baldwin," the general said. "Keep a close eye on this please. I know I can trust you. I need men around me I can trust."

"Yes, sir. Thank you, sir," he said and left the office.

Chapter Six

THE NEXT MORNING, Laura wondered if O'Day would still want her sitting with him in court. She'd had another restless night with the image of Morgan's pleading face joining Plenty Horses's face full of bewilderment and dismay clouding her thoughts. The images of the two faces and her inability to do anything about either one of them haunted her sleep. She didn't remember any dreams this time, but she also didn't think she slept much.

She was also plagued by worries about how O'Day had evaded her question regarding what was being written about her. At first she was terrified. Having the entire city of New York read about her personal business was so . . . uncouth. However, after she thought about it, she realized her divorce was going to be news at some time or another. One does not leave a relationship with Jonathon Bowman and not make a public clamor.

She'd been in the eye of the public before. Her coming-out party had been well covered in all the newspapers, and, a few years later, her marriage to Jonathon had also generated considerable interest. In those instances, however, she'd had her father and Jonathon to shelter her. She didn't have the same level of confidence that shelter would be there for her after the divorce. The little games around this Indian trial would pale in comparison to what was realistically waiting for her when she got back to New York and . . .

She shook her head, throwing her hair around her face. Her focus was the trial now. She couldn't go back to sitting around with Haddie McKenna and the other ladies drinking tea. This wasn't like the diversions she'd been involved with in New York, raising money for charities and attending art shows. They were just playful excursions. The trial was real. The Indian men and the loss of their way of life were real. The boy who'd shot Lieutenant Casey was real, and the prospect he would be executed was very real. Laura Bowman really cared.

She dressed quickly and skipped down the main stairway of the Cataract. If O'Day wouldn't take her into court, she'd try to get to the courthouse early enough to get one of the public seats. And if they wouldn't let her in, she'd wait in the street. She needed to know what was going on!

O'Day was standing at the bottom of the stairs holding a coffee cup. His face brightened when he saw her, and he set the cup on one of the side tables. He strode forward and offered his arm. "Since we neglected to set a time to meet this morning, I thought I should come over early to catch you," he said showing his dazzling smile. "I'm glad we'll have time to get situated today. It'll be quite an exciting day in court."

Laura took his arm in as formal and elegant a manner as she knew how. She was aware she was putting on a show for the Haddie McKenna table but couldn't resist. Out of the corner of her eye, she could see the look on Haddie's face. The old lady was as shocked as she would have been if Laura had come down the stairs in the disarray of an early morning tryst.

"I declare, Mr. O'Day," Laura said in a mock (and not very convincing) southern drawl. "I do believe you're making a shambles of my reputation."

He made a short bow. "I'm always at the service of a beautiful lady, ma'am."

The doorman held the big front doors open, and they made their way down Phillips Avenue towards the courthouse. Laura was anxious to know what was going to happen in court, and O'Day seemed happy to answer her questions, for once. He said that now that the jury was seated, the State would make its opening statements and then would probably have time to start calling witnesses. She said the trial seemed to be going very quickly. "Out here in Dakota, they don't go for much useless formality," he said. "I'd be surprised if the whole thing wasn't wrapped up in two or three days."

They walked on in silence for a few steps, the sun now starting to feel warm on their faces. "And the hanging will be within two or three weeks," he added.

Laura didn't want to think about that. "What will the defense be?" she asked.

"My guess is they'll present Plenty Horses as being crazed by the Ghost Dance, that the whole thing was just a horrible mistake. If they're successful, they may get a manslaughter charge out of it, and he'll only have to spend a few years in prison instead being executed."

"Do you think he could survive living in a prison?" she said. The image of the little jail cell and Plenty Horses's eyes when he looked around it plagued her.

"A young Indian shoots a white army officer in the back of the head . . . I'm sure any prison time will be a challenge for him, even if he was mentally adjusted for it." He shook his head. "It's going to be tough on him no matter what."

Laura kept picturing the image of Plenty Horses's face in the prison cell. He didn't look like a crazed murderer, but then again she didn't know what a crazed murder might look like. "He didn't appear to be a killer."

O'Day shook his head. "Do you know those nice Indian gentlemen we had dinner with last night?" She nodded. "They didn't look much like killers either. I was told they have each taken more than ten scalps. He Dog, the big old lunk who took such a liking to you . . . He's taken more than fifty by himself."

Laura's eyes widened. "Oh, that can't be. That's just racist local talk."

"No, I think it's a legitimate story," he said. He gave her an evil smile. "So when you saw him cutting into the steak you traded to him, he cut into it the same way he'd cut into a man's . . . or woman's skull when taking a scalp."

Laura pushed him aside. "I will not have you talking that way around me . . ."

O'Day shrugged. "So ask him. My understanding is the Lakota bear those deeds with distinction."

The scene outside the courtroom was just as chaotic as the previous day. Laura kept her hand in O'Day's arm and her eyes focused straight ahead as a path was made for them to the steps and into the courthouse. The comments from the rough crowd were just noise, and she successfully ignored them.

They occupied the same seats in the third row behind the defense team. A few minutes after they sat down, the Indian men, wearing the same suits as the previous day, filed into the seats in front of them. Living Bear gave them a stony stare and Jack Red Cloud aimed a condescending nod toward them. However, He Dog turned and reached a big hand over for O'Day to shake. He smiled at Laura and said something like, "Good morning." She returned a small smile but could not help but stare at the large hand that had shot out towards O'Day. She pictured it holding a large knife and taking a scalp. Her face drained of color, and she shuddered when he turned to sit down.

Plenty Horses looked much the same as he was led into court for the second day. He had the blue blanket wrapped around himself just as he had the first day and during the interview. Laura thought it must give him a sense of security and also provided a useful prop to hide his deformed left hand. If O'Day was right and the Lakota culture put such a high stake in the number of scalps taken in battle, a deformity like missing fingers on a hand must have been a difficult stigma for him to deal with. There was nothing to read in his face when he shook hands with the Lakota men sitting in front of them and his gaze fell on Laura. She wondered if the spark of meaning she'd felt when their eyes met during the interview had been just her imagination. She guessed the look of pain on the little cowboy's face might have been the same. Perhaps she was just getting too emotional and reading too much into things.

The judges called the courtroom to order and went through a bunch of procedures Laura didn't understand or care about. From the tension level of the courtroom, she could tell the real trial was about to start. Across the room, to the right of the prosecutor's table, the jury sat. They all appeared to be farmers or small businessmen. Some of them had their best Sunday suits on, clean but worn, while others wore what appeared to be new work clothes complete with fold creases. All of the men had some sort of facial hair. It appeared to Laura that the defense must have been successful in keeping the most rabid of the local population off the jury. She didn't see any of the hatred in the eyes of the jury members that she noted in the crowd waiting on the street. On the other hand, she didn't see much compassion for the young Indian man, either.

William Sterling rose solemnly to give the opening statement for the State. He ran a hand over his heavily oiled hair, unnecessarily pushing it back. Laura had the impression he was lowering himself to appear in this prairie courtroom and felt he should be in front of the U.S. Supreme Court. O'Day had said there were rumors he would eventually run as a Republican for the U.S. Senate.

Sterling described how the brave Lieutenant Casey was making his way to the Lakota camp to establish peace in the region. Plenty Horses had waited with Lieutenant Casey for over an hour while another man went to seek permission for Casey to enter.

He turned and dramatically pointed at Plenty Horses, "This man shook Lieutenant Casey's hand and chatted away in friendly conversation with him for over an hour. Then the other guard returned and told Casey he would have to leave. As the officer turned to ride back to the army camp, this man . . ." He pointed again at Plenty Horses. "This man pulled out a rifle and in a most cowardly manner, shot and killed Lieutenant Edward Wanton Casey. After speaking with him as a friend for well over an hour, the defendant, Plenty Horses, calmly and deliberately murdered Lieutenant Casey."

A chill ran through the courtroom. Like the other observers, Laura's attention went from being riveted on Sterling to Plenty Horses. His face was completely impassive as if he had no idea Sterling had called him the worst kind of coward. The faces of the jury had changed as well. Like everyone else in Dakota, they were aware of the basic facts of the case, but hearing Sterling describe the cold-blooded murder impacted the looks on their faces. Laura thought they now resembled their neighbors out in the street. She felt herself wondering how any jury in its right mind could do anything but punish the cold-blooded killer with death.

Having achieved his moment, Sterling quickly outlined the case the State would make and said they would prove without a doubt that Plenty Horses was a murderer and should be hung pursuant to the laws of the United States of America, the State of South Dakota and the inherent laws of man.

When Sterling sat down, Laura could not imagine a white person in the room who didn't feel Plenty Horses should not be executed. She turned to look at the faces of the people behind her and saw hard, cold determination. She was surprised to not see the hatred and emotion the "lynch mob-like" crowd in the streets had demonstrated. The farmers, their wives, and the businessmen in the room did not appear to be inflamed by passion. They looked determined to punish a deadly killer. Even the other divorce colonists gave Plenty Horses a hard look. Although some of them had lost the color in their faces, they were ready to see the Indian hang for his crime.

The judges recessed the court for lunch and said the State would begin presenting its case in the afternoon. Laura again filed out of the courtroom with O'Day and went with him across the street for lunch. She didn't feel much compulsion to ask many questions today and O'Day demonstrated even less intention to answer. He quietly made notes in his pad and only grunted his order when the waitress showed up. The diner was considerably less occupied than it was the day before as the key players in the trial were not present. Platefuls of food were carried out the door and across the street. They were no doubt working through their lunches.

Laura ate about half her sandwich but wasn't hungry. O'Day never even looked up from his pad as he wolfed his down. It seemed everyone was working on the case—doing something—but her. She rose and told O'Day she was going to get some air. He grunted and waved his hand.

The full midday sun hit her as she left the diner. On their walk to the courthouse that morning and across the street to lunch she'd hardly noticed the weather. Now, it felt sparklingly clear and warm. A slight breeze had cleared the stockyard smells from the air. In short, it was the most beautiful day she'd seen since coming to South Dakota.

She walked along Phillips Avenue away from the Cataract Hotel and the courthouse. In the weeks she'd been in Sioux Falls, she'd never ventured more than a block or two from her home base. The sound of flowing water encouraged her to take a left and walk the side street toward the Big Sioux River that flowed through town.

The street continued a few hundred feet to the river, and a small bridge connected Sioux Falls with the road to East Sioux Falls. It was about six miles away and supported the rock quarry industry. Two women, dressed like hotel maids were crossing the little bridge toward her. The land across the river looked quite different than the prosperous downtown side. The bright sunlight and flow of people on the street behind her created a safe feeling. Laura hitched up her dress so it wouldn't drag on the road and made her way toward the bridge. When she met the women coming from the other side, she recognized one of them as the maid who cleaned her room at the Cataract in the afternoon, but she couldn't remember her name. She smiled and said hello, but the woman just gave her a polite nod and smile. The other maid didn't smile at all. They showed no interest in conversing with her.

Laura walked to the middle of the little bridge and leaned over the railing. While the banks of the Big Sioux River was picturesque along the little green area on the downtown side, the other side was overgrown in a tangle of trees and vines. Downstream she could make out the large structures of the flour mills that drove the economy of the region. The roar of falling water came from that direction in the distance if she listened very carefully. As the dark water flowed beneath her in swirls topped by white foam, she considered how far removed it was from the life at the Cataract or in the courtroom.

A stick snapped on the opposite side of the bridge. Emerging from the overgrown area just downstream of her she saw the figure of a man. He'd climbed up the bank and now was making his way toward the bridge.

Laura quickly turned and started to walk back toward downtown. She stopped when the man spoke. "Aren't you the lady that met with the Indians last night?"

She recognized the voice of the drunk man she and O'Day had encountered on their way back from the Merchants, the man whose face that had showed so much pain. His voice sounded calmer and less dramatic in the light of day. Just before the edge of the bridge she paused and turned. "Yes, I am," she said. "Can I help you with something?" She knew that talking with the man was probably not the safest thing to do, but in the bright light of this spring day she didn't fear him.

He walked slowly across the bridge toward her, limping slightly on his left leg. He wore dirty dungarees and a light blue shirt. The union coat he'd worn the previous day was gone. A large, formless, black slouch hat made him seem even smaller than he actually was. When he was a few steps from Laura, he stopped and leaned against the railing. She saw he was barely an inch or two taller than she was.

"Ah, umm . . . I'm sorry to bother you again, ma'am," he said.

She leaned against the railing of the bridge just a foot or so from his side. It was only a step or so to get off the bridge and run down the street to safety. "Yes, what can I do for you?"

"I saw you were in the courtroom . . . that you can get into the trial . . ." he said. "The Indian's trial, I mean. I just wanted to know how it went today."

Laura wasn't sure what it was, but she felt the little man's intensity about the trial again, as she had last night. His hat was pulled low again, but she could see his blue eyes peering out intently from the shade. "The prosecutor said he was a killer, that he murdered that officer in cold blood."

The little cowboy nodded and looked upstream, putting his face into the sunlight. She saw he wasn't as old as she thought, maybe in his early forties. "Yeah, I supposed he did."

She continued. "I think he was pretty effective. The audience . . . and the jury looked like they believed him."

He shook his head. "Are you going to help him?"

"Me?" she said. "What can I do to help him . . . even if I wanted to?"

"I suppose you're right," he said, wiping the mud on the top of his worn boot against the railing. "It's just that you and that O'Day are parading around in the middle of it all."

Laura felt her face redden as she recalled the vulgar comments from the men in the street. "I'm assisting Mr. O'Day with his reporting of the case. I can assure you there is nothing inappropriate about my accompanying him to confer—"

Morgan laughed. "You don't have to convince me, ma'am. It's pretty clear he needs a nice lady like you to . . . well, to make him appropriate."

"I help Mr. O'Day—What do you mean make him appropriate?"

Morgan looked up at the sky. "What a man does or doesn't do ain't none of my business, ma'am. You don't have to worry about O'Day acting inappropriate with you. It ain't no woman he goes running off with after he drops you off."

Laura felt her face flush. She wasn't sure what Morgan was talking about . . . except she was *exactly* sure what he was talking about. In an instant it all fit, but she didn't want to let on to this man. She changed the subject quickly.

"I'm sure Plenty Horses has a fine defense team. Don't you think Nock and Powers are doing what they can?"

"They're doing what the system says they can, I guess," he said. "But there's things they can't get across. Things they don't know. Things they can't know unless they were there."

Laura was suddenly aware of the roar of the water far downstream. When she'd run into the cowboy before in the street, he spoke with a slur and sounded plaintive. Today, he spoke calmly and directly. The way he formed his words sounded like they should be coming from someone else.

"What do you mean unless they were there?"

"It's a different world out in Dakota, out in the Badlands, I mean. Things that make sense here in these fancy courtrooms coming out the mouths of fancy men in fancy suits . . . they make no sense out there."

"Is that where you're from . . . the Badlands?"

"I'm not from anywhere . . . not anymore," he said. He looked up from under his hat. "I'd appreciate it if you'd let me know if you see anything that could be done for that Indian boy . . . anything to help him, I mean."

"I'm sure if there was anything to be done, Attorney Nock or Powers would be—"

The man interrupted, "I tried to talk to them, and they had no time to speak to someone like me." He opened his arms as if putting his dirty clothes on display. "They ignored me. A lot of people ignore me these days, so I'm able to see . . . things . . . to hear things."

Laura spoke without thinking first, "Well, if you cleaned yourself up and tried to talk to them when you weren't half passed out from drinking whiskey—"

He snapped around sharply, then relaxed and shook his head. "You're probably right, ma'am. I don't like it much, but you're probably right." He moved away from the railing to stand in the middle of the bridge. "What I'm saying is, I may be able to help. I'm not sure how, but I may be able to."

Laura nodded. She felt bad for insulting him. "That's all very well, but I'm not in a position to . . ."

He held up his hand. "Look, I'm sorry if I offended you, ma'am. My name's Morgan, and if you see anything I can do to help, you just let me know. I'll be around. I'm staying just across the bridge there on the way to East Sioux Falls."

He nodded at her and walked back towards the other side, his boots knocking hard against the wood slats across the bridge.

"All right, Mr. Morgan," she called after him. "I'll let you know if I hear anything." Laura wasn't sure why she said anything. Perhaps because he was the only white person she'd spoken with who wanted Plenty Horses saved.

Halfway across, he stopped and turned back to her and tipped his hat. "Thank you, ma'am. I appreciate it."

Laura nodded and then hurried down the side street towards downtown. Once her feet felt the paved street of Phillips Avenue and she met people on the walkway, she felt safe again. Well, "safe" really wasn't the right word, more like "comfortable." The cowboy made her feel uncomfortable, as if he had put expectations on her. She didn't want to feel responsible.

By now the officials at the courthouse had accepted her "role" as O'Day's assistant, and she breezed by the officer at the bottom of the steps of the courthouse after making her way through by the group on the street. She slid into her seat next to O'Day just before the judges entered. O'Day was still making notes and only grunted as she slipped in. He evidently didn't give a damn where she went after lunch.

Judge Edgerton called the court to order and gave Sterling permission to make his case. The first witness was Dr. B.L. Ten Eyck, an assistant army surgeon. He ascertained that Casey was killed by a bullet that "entered the back of his head and came out under the right eye." Laura felt the blood drain from her face as description of how the bullet entered the army officer's body was described so nonchalantly. She ascertained no emotion from what she could see of Plenty Horses or the other Lakota men sitting in front of her. The defense made no attempt to contradict the facts of the shooting.

After a couple of hours of testimony from other witnesses laying out the details, Laura found herself becoming jaded about the facts of the shooting. What had seemed like a horrific act a few hours ago was now just a fact and lesson of geometry regarding where Plenty Horses was, where Casey was, and which direction Casey was facing.

The most intriguing witness was a Cheyenne Indian named White Moon. He wore a blue uniform with red-and-white trouser stripes and a white chevron on either arm indicating his rank of corporal. His long hair was braided down his back and tied with strips of mink skin. He strode up to the stand with a ridged, military bearing. Laura was reminded of visiting Buckingham Palace on her honeymoon and seeing the king's guard march. He was very much a soldier, a very proud Cheyenne soldier.

For the first time in the trial, she noted a change in emotion from the Lakota men setting in front her. He Dog leaned over and said something to Jack Red Cloud, who scowled and shook his head. When the big man turned his head away in disgust, she saw a hard tenseness in his eyes. If she'd ever doubted He Dog had killed and scalped fifty people, his look convinced her otherwise. He looked capable of scalping the Cheyenne soldier on the spot.

White Moon's testimony was translated by a white mustached interpreter from Fort Keogh. She whispered to O'Day, asking why they had a different interpreter. Surprisingly, he whispered back that

Cheyenne and Lakota spoke different languages. It made sense, but somehow Laura had always thought all Indians spoke . . . well, Indian.

Sterling led him through a series of questions establishing that he was Casey's chief of scouts. Like the other witnesses, he responded in a very factual way but paused periodically to give Plenty Horses a fierce look. His hatred of the Lakota man on trial for shooting his lieutenant was very obvious. When Sterling asked who shot Lieutenant Casey he replied, "Plenty Horses!" The defendant gazed back at him without a flicker of emotion, although Laura noted He Dog had moved to the edge of his seat.

Sterling then asked White Moon what he did after the shooting. "I started back to camp," he said. "I could do nothing else."

Sterling then asked what he took with him. He said, "I took Lieutenant Casey's horse and led him home, led him to the camp." Upon further questioning, he said he had not spent any time with Casey's dead body. "I went right away," he said.

Looking around the room, Laura saw several faces frowning at this conduct, including some of the jurors. Leaving a dead comrade in the middle of the road while you calmly led his horse away did not sound like very brave behavior. Laura wondered why Sterling had even brought this up. She made a mental note to ask O'Day about it.

On cross-examination, Nock asked him to describe the purpose of Lieutenant Casey's mission. He asked specifically if Casey was trying to set up peace talks. "No," White Moon said. "He only wanted to see the camp." From Sterling's body language at the prosecutor's table, it was obviously not the answer he had expected.

Laura was physically drained by the time Judge Edgerton finally recessed court for the day. She had to admit Sterling had made a strong case.

O'Day paused as they made their way out of the crowded courtroom. "Well, I'll be damned," he muttered, his attention focused well ahead of them. He increased his pace through the crowd, leaving Laura in his wake.

When she finally got to the top of the courthouse steps she saw that O'Day was already a half a block ahead, pushing through the crowd. He was yelling something across the throng of people on the street. Laura followed the direction where he was yelling and identified a thin, dark-haired man in a black suit. The man glanced back at O'Day, waved and then moved quickly around the corner.

O'Day had stopped pushing his way through the crowd. He looked back and waited for Laura. When she finally made her way next to him and slipped her hand through his arm, she scolded him, "You are not a very polite gentleman."

He laughed at her, and his body relaxed, "A gentleman sometimes, polite only when I have to be. Did the damsel have to navigate her way all by herself?"

Laura had to admit that her comment sounded pretty foolish. It was easy to forget she was not in upper crust New York anymore. She changed the subject as quickly as possible. "As you know, I'm more than capable of taking care of myself without your escort," she said. "Why were you rushing out so fast?"

He looked to the side street where the man in the dark suit had left them. "It appears there are more forces at play in this trial than I had originally thought."

She waited for him to continue, but he appeared lost in thought. "Well," she said, "aren't you going to elaborate?"

He turned his head towards her, "Ummm . . . yes. I noticed a man here I didn't expect, or at least I thought I didn't. I haven't quite figured out how he fits into the mix, if it was him."

He offered nothing more. She considered telling him about the encounter she'd had with Morgan on the bridge, but held back at the last minute. For one thing, O'Day was too preoccupied to give her an answer, and secondly, telling him more about the little cowboy felt like a betrayal of some kind, but she wasn't sure why.

"So do you want to give me an expert analysis of what I saw today?" she said. One sure way to get O'Day to open up was to tell him how smart he was.

"I have an interview with White Moon and Rock Road tonight, the prosecution's Indian witnesses."

"An interview!" she said. "Where are we meeting with them?"

"The way you ran out at lunch, I didn't think you were interested," he said.

"Of course I'm interested. I'm your assistant, remember."

"Well, I'll admit the Indians seem to like having a beautiful lady present, and they talk more when you're there. I'll stop back here at 6:15. Sterling's assistant set up a private room in the back of the Merchants. He obviously has a great deal more pull than Nock and Powers do."

"You're writing and writing all the time, why don't I ever see any of your articles?" she said as they neared the door.

"You aren't a subscriber to the *World*?"

"Do you want to help Plenty Horses?" she said.

"I don't want to help anyone. I'm a reporter. I report the facts, remember."

"But you said yourself he was sure to hang."

"That's what the law says. If he murdered Lieutenant Casey, he should hang. It isn't up to me to decide if he committed murder or not. That's the jury's job."

"But you know he's just a scared kid."

"Reporters can't get caught up in the case. We report the facts."

"Well, I don't care. I'm not a reporter. I think Plenty Horses needs help, and I'm going to try to help him."

O'Day smiled and patted her arm. "You do that, Mrs. Bowman. I'm certain your help will be greatly appreciated." It occurred to her that if she were on Plenty Horses's side, O'Day might not let her go with him as his "assistant." However, he didn't seem too concerned. She was partially relieved, as accompanying O'Day was the only way she could even monitor the trial, and partially insulted he considered her interest as merely a mindless female diversion. That Morgan man at the bridge hadn't treated her that way. He'd actually asked her questions and sought her help.

She smiled sweetly, "Well, thank you for your kind escort, Mr. O'Day. I'll see you at six fifteen, then?"

"At your service, my lady," he said with an exaggerated bow.

As O'Day made his way to the dark corner, Laura walked toward the central staircase. On impulse she turned quickly to the right and, before she changed her mind, walked over to Haddie McKenna's table. Her direct assault startled the little group.

"Hello, ladies," she said in a breezy manner. "I haven't had a chance to speak with you in a few days."

Abigail Johnson was squirming with anticipation. "Mrs. Bowman, I see you've utilized your connection with Mr. O'Day to get a front-row seat at the big trial. You must tell us all about it." Haddie McKenna loudly put her cup down. She made it very clear the tawdry details of the trial were well beneath her interest especially since she was not able to attend.

"I'm afraid it's rather boring, with a great deal of legal rambling," Laura said. "But Mr. O'Day is very kind to instruct me as to what it all means."

Haddie saw her opening. "I see you and the reporter have been spending quite a bit of time together. Is there romance in the air?"

This was exactly the question Laura had been hoping for. "Oh, certainly not. Mr. O'Day is a perfect gentleman and has made no advances. I believe he sees my presence as a way of relaxing the people he interviews."

Abigail Johnson interceded again. "Oh, but Mrs. Bowman, you are soon to be a single woman. Wouldn't a reporter like Mr. O'Day be an exciting catch?"

Laura laughed. "Certainly not, Mrs. Johnson. Mr. O'Day and I are nothing more than colleagues with an interest in the trial of this Indian boy. Have you been following it?"

"It would be unseemly to get involved in such a rough matter," Mrs. McKenna said.

"Well, I think it's a wonderful adventure, and I'm very fortunate I get to see it unfold," Laura said as she stood back up. She'd made her little speech to throw "the coven" off any rumors of a relationship between her and O'Day, for a few minutes anyway. "Good day, ladies," she said. "I have to prepare for this evening's meeting."

"Mrs. Bowman," Abigail Johnson said, "are you going to be attending the dance on Friday? Mr. Waldo Elliot was inquiring." The ballroom on the second floor of the Cataract was the scene of the weekly dance. Many of the soon-to-be divorcées attended, as well as a number of lawyers and notable locals. Laura had assumed it was the source of many of the tawdry rumors that filled the Sioux Falls divorce colony. Mrs. Johnson continued, "As elegantly as Mr. O'Day carries himself, I bet he is quite a dancer."

"I haven't thought about it, Mrs. Johnson," Laura said. "I'm not sure I'd have time for dancing." With that she waved one more time at the ladies and walked towards the central staircase.

She made quick work of getting herself ready for the meeting with White Moon, Rock Road, and the Cheyenne interpreter. She was struck by their military bearing in the courtroom and how different they were from the Lakota men she'd met the previous night. She had also noted the animosity White Moon seemed to have for Plenty Horses and that He Dog had for White Moon. She decided she would not want to have He Dog that angry with her. She wondered if the Cheyenne would act differently at dinner as well.

Knowing what to expect and what her role would be made preparing for dinner much easier. She knew she was to look desirable, yet completely unattainable, elegant yet womanly. O'Day wanted the men to open up in the interview, but not disrespect her. Playing a role as a distraction felt a little demeaning, yet when she thought about it, that's exactly what she'd done since her coming out party nearly fifteen years ago. She'd played the role of the successful business tycoon's daughter, the role of the excited fiancé, the role of the newlywed in love, the role of the dedicated wife and now the role of the jilted, soon-to-be divorcée. She wondered if she'd ever get to play herself.

O'Day was waiting for her at the bottom of the stairs and escorted her down the street to the Merchants. They were met by the same waiter as the night before but were escorted upstairs to a private room on the second floor.

On the walk over, she asked if he'd seen the man he'd been looking for at the end of the trial again. He evaded her question with a series of mumbles.

Meeting them at the table were White Moon and Rock Road from the Cheyenne, along with the interpreter William Rowland. Sterling's assistant, J.G. Ballance, had also joined them at the prosecutor's insistence.

White Moon and Rock Road were still in their military uniforms. Although both wore their hair in long braids, they carried themselves as soldiers. The thin interpreter seemed to spend most of his time smoothing his long white mustache. He spoke in a low voice and O'Day had to ask him to speak up several times. Unlike the Lakota delegation from the previous night, none of the men looked as if they wanted to be there. White Moon, in particular, was very uncomfortable.

Laura worked her smile and charm on the men, but it had little effect. White Moon appeared almost in pain every time O'Day asked him a question. Rock Road perked up perceptibly when dinner was brought to them, but White Moon ate little, kept his eyes low, and pushed his food around the plate.

It was pretty clear, even to Laura, that the Cheyenne had been well coached on what they could and could not say to O'Day. After every question, one or the other would glance toward Ballance before they answered, and as soon as they finished, they'd look back at him. For his part, he kept his attention on the dishes in front of him, merely nodded his head from time to time almost imperceptibly. His full beard almost touched his plate several times.

The only time either of the Cheyenne conveyed much emotion was in their expression of the greatest amount of affection and respect for Lieutenant Casey. White Moon said, "Lieutenant Casey told us, told everyone, that we were soldiers, not Indian scouts. He was our friend and our commander." Without being prompted Rock Road told a story about how three of the Cheyenne scouts were accused of killing a white rancher. Casey had raised the money for their defense himself. He'd traveled three hundred miles to force the authorities to conduct an investigation. "Most army officers would have given up on the Indians, but Casey supported us."

O'Day asked them about their relations with the Lakota. "The Cheyenne and Lakota were allies for generations," the reporter said. "Was it difficult riding against them with Lieutenant Casey?"

The Cheyenne men looked at each other. White Moon spoke for them, "Lieutenant Casey made us soldiers, good soldiers. Soldiers follow orders, and we followed the orders of Lieutenant Casey."

"Yes, but—"

White Moon showed the first bit of emotion that Laura had seen from him as he turned sharply toward O'Day, and said in English, "We are soldiers!"

There was an uneasy silence at the table. When O'Day asked particulars regarding the events of the day Casey had been shot, both Cheyenne men carefully recounted exactly the same testimony they had given in court. Ballance would not permit any follow-up questions from O'Day, interrupting him by holding up his hand and saying, "This was all covered in court today, Mr. O'Day. Weren't you paying attention?"

"Yes, but my readers would be interested in knowing more details."

Ballance shook his head. "I think we are about through here," and pulled away from the table. The Cheyenne men stood at the same time, towering over O'Day and Laura. As they rose, Laura thought she could see a look of relief in White Moon's face.

As they left the Merchants Hotel to walk home, she felt the need to be more than just a pretty bauble on O'Day's arm. "Why did Sterling ask White Moon the questions about what he did after the shooting? It didn't put him in a very good light."

"Exactly," O'Day said. "Sterling knew that and wanted to be the one to bring it out rather than let Nock and Powers do it."

"They're lying you know," she said.

"Who's lying?"

"The Cheyenne," she said. "White Moon, in particular. Every time he had to speak, I saw him carefully phrasing each word and then looking to see if Ballance reacted. They're afraid of something."

"Oh, they were just nervous about talking to a world famous reporter and all," O'Day said waving his hand. "And Sterling and Ballance were probably just trying to make sure they didn't contradict their testimony from court. It was a boring interview. I doubt I'll even get a story out of it, but it was truthful."

"I've been lied to enough to tell when a man's hiding something," she said. "I'm telling you, there's something White Moon isn't saying."

"Your women's intuition may be useful in navigating the social scene, but—"

"You were just too wrapped up in getting all the details of how wonderful Casey was to see their reactions."

"Mrs. Bowman, I've been a reporter for over fifteen years. I think I can tell when people are hiding something."

By this time they were just in front of the Cataract Hotel. Laura was growing tired of O'Day's arrogance. "Mr. O'Day, you may discount my 'intuition' all you want, but it tells me a great deal about whom you will be meeting about fifteen minutes after you deposit me here at the Cataract." She felt his arm tighten through the sleeve of his coat. She slipped her arm out of his and took a step back. In a very low voice she said, "And I know it's not one of the women of the town. You should respect me more." She desperately wanted to see the expression on his face, but just turned and walked the rest of the way to the big doors alone.

Just before she entered the Cataract she noticed a familiar dark figure standing at the far corner of the street. Without thinking about it, Laura told the doorman she would be right back and hurried toward him.

Morgan stood just around the corner in the dark shadows cast by the lights on Phillips Avenue. He nodded when she came closer but did not step into the lighted street.

"Are you spying on me?" she said. She'd about had enough of these men and their silly games.

His voice was low but clear. She didn't detect a slur form alcohol or any smell it. "I said I would be available to help . . . if I could."

"I want to ask you about something. Can you step into the hotel for a moment?"

The shadows of his hat shook. "I don't think they'd like me in that place," he said. "Can you come down behind, at the laundry door in a few minutes?"

"Yes," she said nodding. "Five minutes." He melted back into the shadows, and she walked across the front of the Cataract, noting Haddie McKenna's table was empty in the front window.

Laura knew that meeting the little cowboy was not the proper thing to do, but she was tired of being a bauble on the arm of O'Day. Morgan had said he wanted to do something, and she wanted to know things.

She made sure she was seen in the lobby of the Cataract and then slipped up to her room. As soon as she closed the door, she opened it again and slipped into the hallway. She'd been aware of the narrow little service stairs at either end of the hallways. In her first days at the Cataract, Abigail Johnson had whispered the narrow little stairs were often used for "assignations." She'd cackled bawdily and put her hand on Laura's shoulder. Laura couldn't think of anything more revolting than the overweight Abigail Johnson taking part in any kind of "assignation" and had just given her a blank stare and cold shoulder. It had done the trick, as Mrs. Johnson always acted like the little comment had never been made.

As she opened the door and made her way down the dark stairway, it was like passing through a cultural divide to another world. The Cataract was all about warmly lit wood tones offset by colorful textures of carpets and draperies. Once she passed through the door to the stairs, it was either bright, stark light or darkness, either black or white.

She hurried down the stairs. At the ground floor, hallways to the left and right looked worn and well-traveled by the hotel staff. Straight ahead was a large door. She found it unlocked, opened it and slipped out on to a wooden dock. It smelled musty and creaked. This was where supplies were loaded for the hotel.

To her left the dark figure stepped out of the shadows again. This time she moved toward him without a second thought.

"Mr. Morgan," she said to the half-covered face. "You said you wanted to help. I have two things you can help me with." He'd been right about the information he gave her about O'Day. The reporter's reaction made that clear enough. She sensed the dynamic between Laura and O'Day was changed now, changed forever, and she had the little cowboy to thank for that.

Morgan nodded and waited silently for her to make her request.

"There was a man at the trial today, a man that had not been here before who I think must play an important role. When O'Day saw him, he really wanted to speak with him, but the man disappeared. It was as if he didn't want O'Day or anyone to know he was at the trial. Can you find out who it is?"

The black hat nodded. Laura went on, "And at dinner tonight it was very obvious White Moon was lying about something . . . something about the shooting. Can you find out what he's covering up?"

Morgan's voice rumbled from deep in the darkness. "I can find out about the man, I reckon. This town ain't that big. It'll take some time to find out about White Moon."

"Just find out what you can," she said. "And don't let him know we're looking for him. That means you shouldn't drink."

"Me drinkin' has nothing to do with you one way or another," he said.

She chose to ignore his comment. She'd made her point. "Can you meet me at the bridge again tomorrow at noon? Do you think you'll know anything by then? The trial's in its third day and may be over soon. If we don't do something, that Indian man is going to hang."

Morgan nodded, and his boots scraped the ground as he faded into the darkness. Laura looked around and saw no one. She backed slowly to the door and slipped inside. Hurrying up the stairs, she nearly ran over one of the upstairs maids she had a nodding acquaintance with. "Excuse me," she said. "I was . . . just getting some air."

"Of course, ma'am," the young maid said, moving to the side to let Laura by. The look she gave her indicated that she suspected there was more to it.

From behind her, lower on the stairs, came another voice. "Yeah, out getting air. That's a fine way to put it." Tara Monroe was following her up the stairway.

"Excuse me," Laura said. "I was just . . ."

"I saw you out on the loading dock with that little cowboy, Mrs. . . . Bowman, was it?" Tara's laugher filled the stairway. In spite of herself, Laura couldn't help but smile.

"He's looking into some things for me . . . is it Mrs. . . . Porter or Monroe?"

"Call me Tara, please. Yeah, I've seen him spooking around," Tara said. "My compliments. He's a good little spy."

"I'm Laura," she said. "You seem to be well acquainted with the area."

They opened the door to the stairway and made their way down the hallway. Tara gave Laura her famous smile. "There are men in the divorce colony as well as women. They spend their time drinking and gambling. I find it quite fun. You should come out and join me sometime."

"Oh, I don't quite think I—"

"Yeah, yeah, I understand. Just let me know if you want to explore the wild side at Sandy's sometime. It is the best place, other than the whore house of course."

Laura couldn't hide her surprise.

"Oh, come now, did you think that actresses just sat around drinking tea? Live a little, Mrs. Bowman." Tara Monroe blew her a kiss and skipped up the next flight of stairs.

Laura opened the door to her room and slipped inside. She locked it and turned the deadbolt and then leaned back and sighed. Her heart was pounding, and she felt a sheen of sweat across her chest. As she wiped an errant strand of hair from her forehead, she saw that her hand was shaking. She couldn't remember a more exciting time in her life. She'd confronted the normally suave and confident O'Day with information that silenced him. She'd talked with a crazy, famous actress. She'd snuck out of the hotel in a clandestine manner to meet with a strange, silent man in the darkness and given him instructions to gather intelligence for her. All of her activity was to try to keep an Indian man from execution. She wondered what Haddie McKenna and her coven would have thought, or even her friends from New York. They never cared about anything but themselves or perhaps what scandals were currently underway and being reported in the *World*. Laura felt morally superior.

Chapter Seven

S HE SLEPT LITTLE that night, wondering what Morgan was doing to collect information for her. She'd never had anyone actually working for her, especially not a rough-and-tumble man like Morgan. Oh, sure, the servants in her father's house and her husband's house had done what she asked, but they were serving her, not working for her. For a moment she pictured Morgan threatening to kill someone if he didn't tell him what he wanted to know.

Coming down the stairs in the morning, she was a little surprised O'Day was not in the lobby. She assumed he must not have liked the confrontation they'd had when they parted the previous night. She resolved she'd go to the courthouse alone, boldly walk by the guard at the door and take her normal place in the third row in the courtroom. Against all of her natural tendencies of shyness, she briefly pictured herself walking through the crowd in the street with her head held high.

Seconds later, O'Day came through the door a little out of breath. "Sorry I'm late, Mrs. Bowman. I was unavoidably detained."

Laura considered making a smart remark about where he might have been, then thought better of it. She'd made her point. There was no reason to overstress it. O'Day immediately started talking about what they would see in the trial that day. It was clear the evening conversation in front of the Cataract had not happened as far as he was concerned. That was all right with Laura. She did not want to go into sensitive issues again. She felt a new level of respect from O'Day. *Or perhaps fear*, she thought.

"Did you find the man you were looking for at the end of the trial yesterday?" she asked.

"No, I never saw him again. I didn't get a good enough look at him to be sure, but it could be other factors are in place in this trial."

"What do you mean 'other' factors?"

"I'll explain if I figure out who it was," he said.

She thought about telling him about asking Morgan to find out who the man was, but decided to keep that activity to herself.

Plenty Horses appeared much more aware of his surroundings on the morning of the third day of the trial. He was still pale and thin but came out of his trance long enough to study the jury closely. It was as if he was trying to read their minds and now understood they held his life in their hands. The first two days of the trial he attended with a mindset that the white people were just going through a series of formalities before they executed him. Perhaps the aggressive questioning Nock had pursued with White Moon and the other Cheyenne had convinced him he might have a chance.

In their first interview, O'Day had asked him if he would be able to understand English well enough to understand the arguments his lawyers were making on his behalf. He replied that "Indians all like good speakers and enjoy listening to debates whether they understand all the words or not." Laura noted that he now seemed to be following Sterling's speeches more closely.

Bear Lying Down was the Lakota man who had been leaving the Lakota camp just as Casey started his conversation with Plenty Horses. Casey had sent him back to the camp with the message that he wanted to talk with the chiefs, preferably Red Cloud. Sterling had him explain the events, and he added nothing new to the facts that other witnesses had presented. As Nock was cross-examining him, he asked him to describe the condition of the Lakota camp. Sterling immediately objected that the condition of the camp was irrelevant.

Nock said, "I want to show by this man what the condition of the average Sioux in these camps was at the time: that they were in a state of torment bordering on frenzy, quite enough to unsettle any man's mind. This we will present in order to make plain the fact that the defendant was not responsible for the crime alleged against him, which I will now state is to form part of our defense."

O'Day whispered to Laura, "That's the first shot across the bow to prove that the agitation made Plenty Horses crazy."

Sterling responded, "Your honor, this commentary has nothing to do with the murder the defendant committed. I would request all testimony of this nature be stricken from the record."

The two judges briefly conferred and then overruled the objection. Ever the professional, Sterling kept his face impassive as he returned to his seat, but Laura saw his hands shaking under the table. The ruling was a blow to the prosecution.

Nock gleefully led Bear Lying Down through a line of questioning indicating that the camp was fortified because the Lakota thought of themselves as combatants. So many Indians had been killed at Wounded Knee that the Lakota were gathering at the White Clay Creek encampment to protect themselves. "We had a battle one day and thought there might be another fight," he said. "All were armed in some way with guns, revolvers, and knives."

As Bear Lying Down returned to his seat after Nock's cross-examination, a buzz through the audience prompted an angry gavel by Judge Edgerton. For the first time in the trial, the body language of the lawyers at the defense table showed some aspects of positivity. As they broke for lunch, Laura thought Plenty Horses might have a chance to live. She wanted to do anything she could to give him that chance.

She hurried through lunch with O'Day. As usual, he spent most of the time scribbling in his notebook and shoveling food into his mouth. He hardly noticed when she said, "It's such a nice day again. I think I'll go for another walk."

She made her way across the front of the courthouse and to the little side street, at a much faster pace than she was used to. Her feet ached with the increased activity, and she found herself breathing hard. As she came to the bridge, she consciously forced her body to slow down and reminded herself that she was supposed to be on a leisurely stroll.

She was disappointed Morgan had not appeared at the bridge. The exciting plans, the jolt of adrenalin from the activity, the long sleepless night . . . it was all for naught. She kicked at the post of the railing, stubbing her toe. She should've known better than to count on some drunken little cowboy. She was just another silly little woman passing time trying to—"

"You're gonna hurt your foot kickin' posts like that." A voice rose from beneath her. She tilted her head and looked into the shadows beneath the bridge. "Maybe you should just stay right there enjoying the day, and I'll let you know what I found out."

Standing at the edge of the bridge looking at the river flowing, she felt ridiculous. She'd stood there alone yesterday actually looking at the trees, but that had felt natural. Now she felt she was some sort of a statue looking for a place to put her arms. "So," she said into the air above the passing stream. "Did you find out anything?"

"White Moon is one troubled Indian. I don't know what it is that's haunting him, but he don't sleep much, and he paces around his room like he's in a cage."

"What's he hiding?"

"Don't know, at least not yet. I know the Lakota hate him and he hates them, but there's something else. I might have to go back to the reservation to find out."

"There's no time for that," she snapped looking down under the bridge. "The trial will be over in a day or two."

"Well, then there ain't a hell of a lot I can do about it, is there?"

Laura tapped her foot on the bridge impatiently. "What else did you find out?"

"That man you were lookin' for, the new one in town," the voice from beneath the bridge said. "I think his name is John Mayberry. He's some sort of a big-shot politician back east."

"John Mayberry," she said thinking the name sounded familiar, but she wasn't sure why.

"That's the name," Morgan said. "I don't know much about what he is or was, but I know he ain't too keen on people knowing he's here in Dakota."

"Where's he staying? Where can we find him?"

"You can find him about a quarter of the way to Chicago or some place, I guess," the voice from beneath the bridge said. "He got on the morning train headed east."

"He's already gone?"

"Ain't that what I just said," the voice said. "You know everything I do now, I suspect."

"Well," she paused. "Thank you Mr. . . . umm, Morgan."

"I hope it helped. I'll keep my eyes open."

"Is there a better place for us to meet where you can tell me anything else you find?" There was a silence. "Mr. Morgan, is the reason you're down there under the bridge because you've been drinking?" His words were more slurred than they had been the previous night.

"You got what you wanted."

"Mr. Morgan, thank you for finding out who that man was. I'd like to be able to talk with you again . . . to look you in the eye."

"It's been a long night. It wouldn't be good for a lady like you to be seen with . . . me."

"Well," she said. "There probably are advantages for us to be discrete. There must be some place where we can meet in public. I feel like I'm talking to a troll under the bridge."

"There's an all night diner over on Third Street, but it ain't much of a place for a lady."

"Let's meet for coffee there tonight at nine o'clock, then."

"All right," he said. "I'll see you there at nine."

"And, Mr. Morgan," she said. "Don't be drunk, or I'll go right back to the Cataract."

Laura waited to see if there was any response from beneath the bridge. After several seconds of awkward silence she simply turned and walked back towards downtown. Just before she got to Phillips, she looked back. A small, dark, dirty figure was walking with a slow stumble across the bridge.

The afternoon session was almost ready to start when Laura made her way to her seat next to O'Day. The hubbub of the afternoon crowd was just starting to quiet when she whispered to him, "There is no use looking for Mayberry anymore, he's already on a train east."

O'Day's mouth dropped open. He started to stammer a response when the bailiff announced the judges. As she rose to her feet, Laura felt his eyes on her and made a point to keep her gaze forward. She knew it was childish and pompous to create the drama, but she couldn't help it. Today, this minute, for the first time since she'd come to Sioux Falls, she felt like she had some control.

Sterling wrapped up his case in the afternoon with the other witnesses at the shooting. Pete Richards, Red Cloud's half-white son-in-law held the courtroom in rapt attention as he described the shooting of Lieutenant Casey in lurid detail. He provided no new information, but hearing the details of the shooting directly in English from an eye witness was chilling and brought the horror of the act home.

Then the Lakota Broken Arm recalled, through the translator, how he stripped Casey's body of its pistols. The nature of a Lakota warrior came through by his actions. "Casey had a pistol shoved down along side of his leg, down in the boot. He had two belts on. One of them had a pistol, the other was a cartridge belt. He was lying on his face. He had one leg drawn up and one leg stretched. I took him by the arm and pulled him over on his back so I could take his belt off. His hat was off a little ways from him. I went and picked the hat up and laid it close to his head. Then I jumped on my horse and started off. One pistol I gave to Red Cloud's son and told him to give it to his father. The other I gave to Little Wound."

Laura thought that Sterling had made a mistake in having Broken Arm convey this testimony. She could sense he had wanted to horrify the jury by the callousness of the act of shooting, but it came across as more of a part of the culture of being a Lakota Warrior protecting their camp. Stripping a body of weapons was a completely rational and logical thing to do if your camp was in danger.

In this atmosphere, David Powers rose to give the opening statements for the defense. He started slowly, attempting to match the firmness of resolve Sterling had created. In an effort to humanize Plenty Horses, he described how he had been sent to Carlisle Indian School at fourteen. He described how he was there for five years and never got past the third grade. When Plenty Horses was released from the school, he had rejoined the Lakota. In the two years he'd been back, he'd worked to regain the trust of his Lakota family. Powers described the Ghost Dance and the impact it had on the Lakota people and upon the impressionable Plenty Horses especially. He was a troubled young man, searching for the identity that had been robbed from him in that school in Pennsylvania. Powers pointed to the Ghost Dance and the hatred of whites it was based upon as the spark that drove Plenty Horses to distraction.

"When the U.S. Army killed 300 of his kinsmen at Wounded Knee, Plenty Horses stood with his fellow warriors and fought the soldiers at Drexel Mission. When he encountered Lieutenant Casey spying on his camp, he did what any good warrior would do. He did what any U.S. Army solider would do if they had encountered an Indian spy in their camp. When there was an enemy threat to his camp, he protected the women and children there by shooting the intruder."

"Ladies and gentlemen, this is not a murder. The unfortunate shooting of Lieutenant Casey was an act of war, and Plenty Horses was just acting like any soldier would."

All eyes again went from the speaker to Plenty Horses still wrapped in his blue blanket at the defense table. Laura thought Powers had done an admirable job of presenting Plenty Horses's case in a reasonable manner, but didn't get a feeling that the audience, or, more important, the jury, was swayed. There may have been a few nods of assent from the audience, but there were none from the jury.

Laura was not schooled in the rules of war. Indeed she'd never thought about it. War was something she had learned about in history books. The killing that took place in war was an abstract fact, just numbers. Each side had a certain number of casualties and eventually one side would win. She'd never thought about what separated a good war killing from a bad war killing, nor did she want to.

Nock and Powers called their first witness, Philip Wells. He'd been doing the translation for the Lakota witnesses so the spectators in the court room were used to seeing him, but now that he was a witness in his own right, nobody could take their eyes off of him. It was well known he'd been in the middle of the heaviest fighting at Wounded Knee. A Lakota warrior had sliced his nose from bridge to lip, leaving it hanging by only by skin. Wells had shot the warrior and left the battle to find a doctor. In no time, the doctor had sewn his nose back on and he'd returned to the battle. Now, five months later, his nose was still barely attached. The scars of the wound were emphasized even further by his short hair and his mustache that was waxed to hold it straight out past his jaw line. Laura thought the long mustache was like two arrows pointing to the horror of his scarred nose.

Powers established Wells' familiarity with the Lakota and his participation in the Wounded Knee battle, and then asked a simple question, "Who was the battle fought between?"

Sterling jumped up. "I object to the introduction of any testimony for the purpose of showing that a state of war existed between the Sioux Indians and the government of the United States." He went on to explain that the government did not concede there was a war at the time Casey was killed. He sought to keep any sense of war out of the case.

Powers was not intimidated and countered Sterling in a spirited manner. He said the United States government recognized the Sioux tribes as a nation and one of the powers of a nation was the power to declare war. Plenty Horses was simply acting as a soldier defending his nation. "In this case the act of the defendant in killing Casey was the act of a belligerent in the prosecution of a war, and inasmuch as his act in killing Casey has been endorsed by the Sioux Nation, the civil authorities of this government have no jurisdiction to try him for murder."

As he finished his speech, there was a hush through the courtroom. It was very clear now what the defense was based upon and the court's ruling on this issue would impact heavily on the outcome of the trial. The prosecution responded vigorously. Sterling's assistant, Ballance, pointed out that all treaties with the Lakota referred to them as a tribe, not a nation.

The arguments went back and forth for the rest of the afternoon. Laura quickly found herself bored as the lawyers argued the wording of court rulings, treaties, and other legal documents. The simple question evidently had no easy answers. The Lakota men in front of her watched the flow of the argument with rapt attention. She supposed that not knowing English was probably a benefit in this instance as they were only reacting to the emotion demonstrated by the legal teams. Since she didn't understand much of the legalese being bandied about, she felt like she was in the same situation as her Lakota friends for once. They were much better at following the activity based upon tone and body language than she was.

The judges indicated they wanted to consider the question overnight. As the spectators filed out of the courtroom, for the first time, there was a sense that this was actually a trial and not just a formality to Plenty Horses's execution. Laura heard one of the men in front of her say, "I'm not sure what all of the legal mumbo jumbo meant. It doesn't seem to me an Indian can go around shooting army officers no matter if they're a nation or a tribe or a bunch of loafers." A woman next to him, obviously his wife, said, "If there wasn't a war, what happened at Wounded Knee?"

Laura hadn't thought about the issue in those terms. If Plenty Horses was considered a criminal, she wondered if the Army's Seventh Cavalry would be considered criminals. She was about to ask O'Day about it as they got to the sidewalk when he pulled her off to the side and into the doorway of the hardware store. "How do you know that was Mayberry?" he said.

She'd gotten so wrapped up in the testimony at the trial she'd forgotten about dropping the bomb on O'Day at the start of the afternoon session. The intense look in his face took some of the pleasure away from torturing him. "I have my sources," she said coyly.

"This isn't a damn game, woman!" he said sharply. "Tell me why you think it was Mayberry and why you think he's gone."

"I . . . um, I . . ." she stammered. She had no idea he was going to react in such a manner. "A man told me who he was and that he saw him get on the train."

"What man?"

"Just a man I met," she said. She immediately decided she was not going to give Morgan's name to O'Day. She wasn't sure why.

He turned and started walking down the sidewalk, not waiting for her to take his arm. Laura hurried to catch up. "Was Mayberry the man you thought you saw?"

It frustrated her that she wasn't in control any longer, but she wanted to know why this was important.

"Yes, that's who I thought it was," he said without turning to look at her.

"Who is he?"

He stopped and turned to look at her. "This isn't a game. If you don't know what you're doing, don't get involved."

An inspiration hit her. She knew that name! It had been at one of the boring political functions Jonathon had forced her to attend. It was considered good form in New York political circles to bring your wife to functions and then abandon her. She hated trying to talk to the other wives. "I know Mayberry works in the New York political world," she said. "I've met him!"

She desperately hoped O'Day wouldn't question her on this fact. She assumed she'd shaken his hand and then he'd gone with Jonathon to the library to smoke and get away from the women. But then again, she never was a very good liar. "I'm afraid I don't remember much about him," she admitted. "I remember his name from a political gathering of some kind Jonathon took me to. Why is he important?"

O'Day smiled. "Ah, I could see that. Mayberry would've been trying to get your soon-to-be ex-husband to contribute to the party." The fact that Laura had admitted not knowing anything about the man had put O'Day back in charge as the expert. "One has to ask why he would have an interest in the trial of an Indian man in Sioux Falls, South Dakota."

"I'm not sure," she said. "Why?"

O'Day looked like he had an answer to his question, but he wasn't going to tell Laura. He shook his head. "I have an interview with the old Injun fighter Wells tonight. Would you like to attend?"

"Of course," she said. "At the Merchants again?"

"Are these interviews boring you, Mrs. Bowman?"

"Not at all," she said. "What will be the focus of this talk?"

"Sterling and Ballance approved the interview as long as it was background. Wells doesn't know anything about the legal arguments on the status of the Lakota, but he does know the Lakota. The readers will be bored silly with the wrangling going on by the lawyers, but they like hearing about Indians. And frankly, Wells can express more about the Lakota than they can themselves."

O'Day may have been frustrated with her for giving him the Mayberry information, but he was definitely paying more attention to her. Maybe he even respected what she had to say. "Be ready at six fifteen," he said. "And wear something nice. Wells has been out in the frontier a long time and with that nose of his, he isn't going to get much female attention that he doesn't pay for."

Before Laura could say anything, he quickly walked towards the telegraph office to file his report on the third day of the trial. She was fuming, but there was nothing to be done about it.

Their routine of O'Day picking her up at the Cataract and escorting her to the Merchants was now well established. They were led upstairs to the private room on the second floor again, and Phillip Wells was the only other person at the table.

Laura found it difficult to not look at the scarred nose on the old Indian fighter. The angry-looking scar started just at the bridge of his nose and followed a jagged line on the right side and then curved around to his lip. He wore a bandage across the top of his nose, but the cut and scar was open for all to see.

"What did you think about the discussion this afternoon while you were on the stand about whether the Indians were at war?" O'Day asked. Laura thought that this first question directly violated the promise he'd made to the prosecutors.

"Oh, hell, I don't know," Wells said, pulling at one of his mustaches. He had so much wax on them that Laura expected to hear them squeak. "All that crap is for the lawyers to figure out. War or not, I couldn't tell you what to call it. As far as I'm concerned, shootin' is shootin'."

Laura couldn't help herself. "Well, yes, Mr. Wells, but it makes a significant difference if Plenty Horses committed a crime or not."

Wells looked her up and down. He wasn't used to being in the company of a beautiful woman and certainly wasn't used to answering questions from one. He said nothing but made a show of turning and facing O'Day. It was clear he didn't want to hear any more from Laura on the subject.

"It's a sorry thing to think about," he said. "The fact of the matter is, that boy, Plenty Horses, is the last of the Lakota warriors. No matter what they decide in this case, the Indian Wars are now over for sure. Any Lakota man that acts like a warrior is gonna be considered a criminal from now on."

O'Day was writing on his pad furiously. This was exactly the kind of quote he was looking for from the old Indian fighter.

"It's a damn shame the last of the Lakota warriors happened to be a scared kid trying to prove himself by blowing off the back of a man's head when he wasn't looking."

Laura tried again. "Are the Lakota a warlike people?"

Since O'Day was writing in his pad, Wells answered Laura's question this time. "I don't know if you'd call them warlike. I'd call them warrior-focused.

"You see," he said. "When the white man started to settle these parts forty years ago, the Lakota controlled about everything from the Missouri River to the Rocky Mountains and from the Canadian Border all the way to Kansas. They'd pretty much run out all the other tribes.

"They were a nomadic people, picking up every few days or weeks and moving to the next spot, following the buffalo mostly. The buffalo herds, at that time, stretched as far as the eye could see, so food was relatively easy to come by. Now it wouldn't make sense for a man to acquire things to show he was superior to everyone else since he'd have to move them all the time.

"For a man to gain status, he had to show what a great hunter or warrior he was. All the best Lakota leaders were great warriors. Spotted Tail, Red Cloud, Sitting Bull, all of the greatest head chiefs, were great warriors when they were young. You had to be a great warrior or none of the Lakota would follow you. They don't like being told what do to so they don't take to strong leaders.

"Greatest warrior of them all was Crazy Horse, of course. He was a lousy leader, but he could fight like crazy, was as brave as the day is long and instinctively knew how to deploy fighters. With him organizing Lakota fighters, they kicked the army all over in the mid-seventies. He made a damned fool of Custer.

"But Crazy Horse was a good example of what happens when a warrior doesn't have a place to fight. When they got him on the reservation, he about went nuts, kinda like putting a wild wolf in a cage. A wolf will either submit and lay down to die or throw itself against the bars until it kills itself. Crazy Horse got so paranoid he turned all the other Lakota against him, and they finally killed him. A warrior just ain't any good in the time of peace.

"Well the rest of these Lakota are a whole lot like Crazy Horse, only not so obvious. Their culture is based on traveling around the country hunting and raiding other Indians. When they got put on the reservation and told to stay in one spot, they didn't know what to do with themselves. They wouldn't let them fight, there wasn't anything to hunt, so they had to give 'em food. What the hell was a warrior to do? They're still trying to figure that out.

"He Dog—you met him. He was Crazy Horse's best friend. He saw what happened to him when they caged him on the reservation. Ain't none of them know what to do.

"There's a big difference between a 'warrior' and a 'soldier.' The strength of a soldier is that he follows orders no matter what. A warrior follows his heart."

Wells had talked for most of an hour, right through their steaks. O'Day was scribbling the entire time while Wells talked to Laura. She thought she understood more about why He Dog and the other Lakota men acted the way they did. She pictured them as warriors, taking scalps and hunting buffalo only a few years before. Now they were walking around in white man's suits. They were like a piece of history that time forgot.

O'Day was in a very good mood as he walked her home. "That was exactly what I wanted to hear from Wells," he said. "Regardless of what the law says, the Lakota are killers and have always been killers. That's what my readers need to hear."

"I'm not so sure that's what he was saying," Laura said. "He said their culture was based upon customs of war. I could say the same thing about many of our customs of business."

O'Day gave her an exasperated look. "Well, regardless of what your expert analysis is," he said, "this whole thing will be over in a day or two, and I can go back to New York. And you can concentrate on extracting yourself from your marriage to Jonathon Bowman."

She hadn't really thought about it that way. When the trial was over she would be left with the boring life interacting with the other colonists at the Cataract. And who knows what O'Day would be writing about her?

"Do you really think it will be over so quickly?"

"Sure," he said. "Once the judges make a ruling on whether the government was at war with the Indians, it's just about wrapped up. I can't believe Nock and Powers can have more than a few witnesses. After all, nobody disputes what actually happened. The whole case is about the why."

"Yes," she said. "I suppose you're right." They were more than a block away from the Cataract, and she stopped. "You can let me off here and hurry off to wherever it is you go. I want to get some night air."

O'Day stared at her carefully. "I'll be working on my story and getting it filed before morning," he said. "You have to be careful walking around at night."

"Oh, it's barely dark," she said, waving her arms to the gray dusk sky. "Summer is coming soon."

"Very well," he said. "I don't seem to be able to talk you out of much of anything these days." He turned to the left and walked slowly up the side street.

Laura was happy to be rid of him. She looked forward to telling Morgan what Wells had said and not being second-guessed like she was by O'Day. The diner was only a block off Phillips Avenue, and she saw by the clock in the window of the drug store that she would be there easily by nine.

The diner was small but clean. A counter had room for six stools, and there were five tables spread in the remaining space. She smelled the grease on the hot grill, but there was nothing currently cooking. The two men sitting at the counter immediately turned when she entered. A woman in a homespun dress sat at the first table with a man in overalls. They fell silent as well.

The only other table occupied was in the back corner. A small man in a black hat was sipping a glass of water. When he looked up she recognized Morgan's blue eyes. He had on a light-blue shirt that he must have purchased that afternoon because the creases were still in it. He immediately stood and tipped his hat for her. She made her way past the other tables and took the empty chair he'd slid out for her.

Laura drew her sweater around her, now very conscious of how overdressed she was. "I'm glad you could make it, Mr. Morgan," she said.

"I don't got much else to do, ma'am," he said, but she could tell he was pleased to be there. It was obvious he had made an effort to be clean and sober for their meeting.

"Have you eaten yet?" she asked. "I had a bite earlier, but I could certainly use some food." She was not the least bit hungry but assumed Morgan was.

He nodded, and they both ordered steak, eggs, and coffee. While they sipped their coffee, she told them what Wells had told them about the Lakota at dinner.

"There's fightin' and then there's fightin'. That damned fool Wells was always looking for a fight, whether there needed to be one or not," Morgan said in a low voice.

"He said that . . . Do you know Phillip Wells?" she said.

"Yeah, I know him. He scouted for the Seventh."

"You were . . . were you in the army, Mr. Morgan?"

"I was."

"You served with Mr. Wells?"

"Yeah." He shifted in his chair. "Anything new on Mayberry?"

"Oh, yes, I almost forgot. I know him, or knew him, anyway. He was raising funds for politics at a function my . . . um, husband . . . hosted."

"What would a New York politician be doing in Sioux Falls at the trial of a Lakota man?"

"That's what I asked O'Day. He just smiled and shook his head."

"Well, it seems like you'd be the person to find out." Morgan sipped his coffee as the cook came around the counter with their steak and eggs.

"Me? I thought you were the one who could find out things."

"I can nose around out here in Dakota, but New York is a completely different world." He cut a bite of his steak and coated it in bright yellow egg yolk. "It's your world."

"Yes, I suppose it is." Laura moved her food around her plate.

They ate in silence, conscious of the scraping sound of their utensils against the plates. Morgan raised his head, the knife poised in his right hand. Laura noticed a drop of egg yolk on it, slowly dropping. "Just what are we supposed to be accomplishing with this 'looking into' stuff?"

"Umm . . ." she stammered. "I want to help Plenty Horses. I want to do something."

"They're gonna convict him in a day or two. How's any of what we're doing gonna help him?"

Laura shook her head. "I know, I can't explain it. Those Lakota men, what they've lost . . . I want to do something to help them . . . to help Plenty Horses."

"Have you talked to his lawyers?"

"And say what? That I'm a New York woman here for a divorce who wants to help? I want to bring them something that'll help Plenty Horses, to free him. Then they might listen."

Morgan gave a short laugh. "It ain't likely they'll be listening to either of us unless they see something that can really help. A broke-down soldier and a New York divorced lady—they probably wouldn't see much help coming from us."

Laura raised her coffee cup, making a toast. "Mr. Morgan, here's to surprises." He smiled and matched her toast.

Morgan finished all of the food on his plate. "What do we do from here?"

"I'll try to find out more about Mayberry, and you figure out what White Moon's lying about," she said. "I guess we'll see what the trial brings tomorrow."

There was an uncomfortable silence when the cook took their plates and said, "That will be two dollars." Morgan stood and worked his hand into his pocket. He brought out a worn dollar bill and counted out five quarters. Laura noticed there was only a handful of coins still in his pocket. She'd brought no money. She rarely directly paid for anything.

"Will I see you on the bridge tomorrow, then?" she said, a little embarrassed about Morgan paying for her meal.

"I'll be on the street in front of the courthouse," he said. "If you have any news, you can tell me there."

She rose, and he escorted her to the door. For some reason she didn't want to have him walk her to the Cataract. She nodded and thanked him for meeting her, then quickly turned and made her way down the shadowy half block to the main street.

There was nobody on the street, and she didn't look back until she got to Phillips Avenue. When she looked back, the street behind her was empty.

She walked quickly, the soles of her shoes clicking on the walkway. She told herself she didn't want to be seen with Morgan because he would be embarrassed. Or that she didn't want anyone to know the New York divorcée was researching a murder. However, she knew the real reason.

She didn't want anyone to see her with him.

Chapter Eight

APRIL 28, 1891

EACH DAY THE SIZE OF THE CROWD outside the courthouse had grown. It was no longer just divorce colonists with nothing better to do or rough, out-of-work frontiersmen. It seemed everyone who wasn't required to work was dressed in their Sunday best and standing outside of the courthouse.

Laura and O'Day made their way through the throng with no incident. If people were still saying things about her as they passed, Laura didn't hear them, or she chose not to hear them.

O'Day was strangely quiet, even more preoccupied than usual. As they walked down the hallway, Laura tried to get information from him. "Why do you think Mayberry was here?"

"Well, if I had to guess, I think it may have something to do with General Nelson Miles," he said. "The outcome of this case could have some implications should he choose to run for president."

"What would this trial have to do with a presidential election?" she said quietly so the people walking down the hallway wouldn't hear her.

"If Miles runs for president, he has to maintain a careful balance. If he appears too warlike, he'll get no support from the East Coast liberals. They already think he's been hard on the Indians and someone will eventually have to pay the political price for the string of broken treaties. After all the effort the abolitionists went through to free the slaves, it seems silly to persecute another race of people. However, if Miles is perceived as too soft, he may lose his western and business support. Indians are an impediment to development regardless of the social implications."

"What does this trial have to do with all of that?"

"Casey's shooting is part of the Wounded Knee campaign whether the prosecution wants it to be or not. Thus far, the army hasn't paid a gross political price for killing all those Lakota. But if it's presented in the wrong light, the public may turn on Miles, the president, and anybody else who had anything to do with it."

"But how . . ."

He shushed her as they took their seats.

The judges had considered the question posed to them by Powers and Nock the previous day. The spectators in the court were unusually quiet as the room filled. Every one of them knew that the ruling on the admissibility of evidence of a state of war was key to the outcome of the case. The defense table looked as upbeat and positive as Laura had seen them. Nock patted Plenty Horses on the back as he took his seat. He Dog and the rest of the Lakota contingent sitting in front of them was smiling at some inside joke.

As the judges entered, the courtroom went dead silent for the first time since the trial started. Judge Shiras cleared his throat and launched into the explanation of their ruling. "Judge Edgerton and I have considered the motions put forth by both of the State and the defense regarding the admissibility of testimony regarding a state of war between the Sioux and the government. We do not hold that Sioux can be considered an independent nation. They are part of the United States of America pursuant to statute, treaty, and custom." Laura saw Nock's shoulders sag. Powers was writing something down and grinding his teeth so loudly that Laura could hear it from the third row.

"However," the judge continued, setting off a collective intake of air, "We do hold that an Indian can be considered a belligerent in a war." Laura looked over at Sterling and noticed him break the pencil he held under the table. The judge went on to explain the ruling in legalese terms, but the ruling was made. Nock and Powers could try to show how the events occurring around the killing, including the battle at Wounded Knee, had preyed on and distorted their client's mind. They would seek to prove that Plenty Horses had been driven to killing Casey by the passions of war.

Nock and Powers gleefully recalled Phillip Wells to the stand. The rough looking frontiersman was only too happy to paint a picture of violence and wild, crazy Indians. He was a character straight out of dime novels as he testified that it was only through the efforts of gallant warriors like himself that the Indians were held in check. Indians like Plenty Horses were poised for war.

The defense followed Wells with Living Bear, who testified regarding the state of affairs inside the Lakota camp at White Clay Creek. The slaughter at Wounded Knee had frightened them. He said the Indians had dug rifle pits and were preparing to fight the army to the bitter end in order to protect their women and children. He also said the government had suspended rations, there was no game available, and the camp was hungry.

Sterling tried to get Living Bear to admit that the Brule at White Clay Creek had been preparing to surrender before Casey was killed. But the Lakota man was adamant in his claim the Lakota were entrenched and expecting to fight. He Dog followed up Living Bear's testimony with the same assessment of the state of affairs at the camp, although he did admit that some of the men were preparing to go to Pine Ridge to avoid being in the fight when the shooting occurred. Sterling salvaged at least a small victory in this line of questioning.

The judges called a recess for lunch, and the spectators in the courtroom let out a collective sigh. The morning testimony had been riveting, full of exciting descriptions of battle fortifications and grim, armed Lakota men swearing to defend their women and children against another vicious attack by the U.S. Army. This was exactly what the spectators, particularly the easterners staying at the Cataract, had been waiting for. The body language at the defense table was as positive again.

The Lakota men sitting in front of her were proud of their testimony. After countless days of watching speakers parry back and forth about issues they didn't understand or care about, they had finally gotten to stand up and talk. They told the white people they had been men . . . men ready to fight. Anyone who looked into He Dog's eyes as he testified understood his sincerity in declaring his willingness to lay down his life to save the women and children in his camp. It was clear that he'd done it before and had been willing to do it again.

At lunch, Laura wanted to ask O'Day more about the riveting testimony of the morning, but he held up his hand and said he was working on his story and could not be disturbed. The readers in New York would get to hear a full and picturesque account of how the Lakota were preparing for war. It was like seeing a Wild West show with real people.

Laura finished her small meal quickly and left O'Day at the diner. She looked up and down the streets, but didn't see Morgan. She wandered down the block and looked toward the bridge. It was empty. Reluctantly, she turned back to and went into the courtroom.

The spectators were still buzzing about the morning's testimony. She heard one man behind her say, "I don't know what the difference is if there was a war or not. The Indian killed the officer, shot him in the back of the head. How can he get away with that?"

"But if it was part of a war . . ." a female voice said.

"Hell, what do you know about war, woman." the rough voice said. "The Indian shot an officer."

Nock and Powers strode into court confidently. They couldn't have asked for much more from the morning of testimony. They were ready for a strong finish.

O'Day just made it back to his seat as court came back to order.

Judge Silas addressed the defense table. "You may call your next witness."

Powers stood and said, "Your Honor, we call Plenty Horses to the stand."

A wave of murmurs spread through the spectators, and Judge Silas pounded the gavel and demanded order. Laura hadn't expected Plenty Horses to take the stand in his own defense. "Did you know he was going to take the stand?" she whispered to O'Day.

"Shtttttt," he said.

Plenty Horses had more color to him than he'd had at the start of the trial. He stood and pulled his blue blanket up over his shoulders, keeping his deformed left hand hidden. He walked confidently to the stand, his face as impassive as it had been the entire proceedings. Philip Wells walked across the front of the courtroom to take his customary translator seat next to the witness stand where he'd sat for every Lakota witness.

Sterling rose and said, "You Honor, I object to using Mr. Wells to interpret." He pointed at Plenty Horses who had just sat down in the witness chair. "This man has had an education and can get along without an interpreter."

Nock sprang to his feet, "But, Your Honor, I know that he cannot speak English well enough to testify intelligently. I say an interpreter is absolutely necessary."

The judges briefly conferred. Judge Edgerton asked Plenty Horses several questions in English. The young Lakota man provided responses in English in a quiet, heavily accented voice.

Judge Edgerton again conferred briefly with Judge Silva and said, "It is the ruling of this court that Plenty Horses does not need to use an interpreter unless he does not understand what is wanted of him."

Nock's face turned beet red. "Your Honor," he almost screeched. "I have been with the man almost daily, and we have always had an interpreter to conduct our conversations. In fact I never tried to talk any length of time with him after the first futile attempt without the aid of Philip Wells. The defendant understands some English, but he is unable to articulate what is necessary to describe on the stand. In trying to do so, he may prejudice his case beyond repair."

Nock was on the verge of grabbing the front of the bench separating him from the judges. "We ask for an interpreter, because it is absolutely essential for the proper presentation of his evidence, and if that be refused," he dramatically took two steps back toward the middle of the courtroom, "you will force us to close our case without a word from the defendant on his behalf."

A murmur swept through the courtroom. Judge Shiras pounded the gavel forcefully. "I will not have any disturbance in this court," he snapped. He leaned toward Nock. "It is not necessary to make a threat," he said in an icy voice.

Nock squared his shoulders. "We are not threatening, Your Honor, but presenting the case in its true light," he said.

Judges Edgerton and Shiras briefly put their heads together and Shiras said, "The court has ruled on this matter. No interpreter is needed." He slammed the gavel.

Nock stood at attention and then spread his arms away from his body. "Then, Your Honor, we refuse to permit Plenty Horses to testify," he said in a loud voice. "And we also close our case." He dropped his hands to his side and lowered his head.

The courtroom was absolutely silent. Laura felt she could hear her own heart beating. Then court erupted as everyone started talking at once. Laura watched Plenty Horses. Head erect, his eyes turned to the open window, perhaps looking at a free sky that he may never see again, he kept his arms folded in front of him under the blue blanket. He showed no emotion except for a sense of sadness and of loneliness.

He turned to look at the judges, one of which was pounding the gavel, trying to regain control of the court. Laura thought his brown eyes didn't show hate or even bewilderment as he looked at the judges who might have just made a ruling that would cost him his life. He merely stared at the judge as if he had expected the ruling to go against him. He was in a strange land with strange customs.

The judge excused Plenty Horses and then, sensing it was useless to try to regain order, immediately recessed the entire courtroom. The Lakota man walked slowly to the defense table where Powers whispered something in his ear. He nodded and then slowly began to make his way out of the courtroom with his usual escort of two marshals, followed by his father.

Uncharacteristic of O'Day, he raised his voice above the clamor of the other reporters, "Plenty Horses, are you disappointed you didn't get to testify?"

He stood behind the defense table and the crowd quieted momentarily. In a clear voice he said in English, "I wanted to tell them all," he nodded toward the now empty jury box, "that I am not guilty of murder. If they do not care to hear me, I am satisfied. Probably it is better that way."

He then turned away from O'Day and the other reporters who were shouting more questions to him and slowly followed the marshals out of the court, his stoic father walking slowly behind him as if it were a funeral procession.

Laura found herself barely able to move. She expected O'Day to follow Plenty Horses out of the building along with the other reporters, but he was leaning over the railing, furiously talking with Powers. He nodded and then conferred with Nock. They talked back for several minutes while the spectators made their way out of the courtroom. Then Nock put his hand on Powers's shoulder and nodded. O'Day pointed at Laura, and they nodded again.

The reporter grabbed her by the arm and pushed his way through the spectators still filing out in the wake of Plenty Horses. "Come on, come on," he said.

Laura wanted to ask him what was happening, but he was clearly too preoccupied to answer. As they reached the hallway, he pulled out his watch. "We have only a few minutes. I've got to get a brief story filed and then . . ." He looked up at her and smiled. "We have the coup of the day. Nock and Powers have agreed to let me interview Plenty Horses today, in just an hour. I need to have you there. He's been much more forthcoming when he sees you in the room, the comfort of a woman or something. You'll be at the jail in forty-five minutes. Do not talk to anyone. Do not do anything. During the interview you won't say anything . . . is that clear?"

"Umm… yes," she said. "But why is he . . ."

"The jury may not get to hear his testimony but America will, or at least the readers of the *New York World*. Do not let anyone know. I'm going right to the telegraph office and get a quick story filed." O'Day smile broadly, "Damn, this is what it's all about!"

"Can I help?" she asked. "Do you want some notes or questions or . . ."

"Just get to the jail, don't tell anyone you're there and prepare to look good." With that statement, O'Day slipped out of a side door. Laura followed him as far as the door and then witnessed him running down the street anxious to get his story filed.

O'Day's excitement was contagious. Energy pulsed through her body, but she had no place to put it. She desperately wanted to do . . . something . . . something to make a difference. The spectators in the street were milling around, all talking and clogging Phillips Avenue.

The abrupt closing of the case had shocked everyone. Opinions varied about how much value Plenty Horses's testimony would have had on his case, but by refusing to allow an interpreter, the judges had given even more credence to the position that the whole trial was merely a formality to his execution. However, even the roughest of the group agreed there was definitely a war of some kind on between the Indians and the army. "You still can't go around just shooting officers. Hell, if they let him off, every Indian in the country will feel like they can shoot any damned white person they run into," a large man with a full, unkempt beard said.

Out of the corner of her eye, she noticed a small, dark figure peering around the corner of the Jefferson building, watching the crowd in the street. Laura hurried down the steps to Phillips Avenue and made her way toward the figure. As she reached the corner, Morgan stepped out.

"Looks like things are wrapping up," he said nodding to the people loitering around the street.

"Oh, Mr. Morgan, it was so exciting!" she said. "The defense called the Indians and Phillip Wells, and they told how tense everything was because of the battle." She gestured frantically with her hands. Morgan leaned against the building but kept his attention on her. "And then they were going to have Plenty Horses testify but the judges wouldn't let them use an interpreter, and Nock just said, 'Fine, then we'll close the case.'"

"Seems like quite a gamble to me," Morgan drawled.

"And the best part is Mr. O'Day got permission to interview Plenty Horses so he can tell his side of the story in the *New York World*, and no other paper will have it."

"That's probably a good deal for the *New York World*, but the jury's here in Sioux Falls, not in New York. They ain't gonna see it."

"Yes," she said a little breathlessly. "I suppose that's true, but it will get his story out there. Maybe they'll be able to do something."

"So it goes to the jury tomorrow?"

"Yes, the judges said both sides will make final arguments and then it goes to the jury. Do you think they'll deliberate a long time?"

Morgan shook his head and scratched his shoulder against the stone wall of the building. "I do not. I don't think it'll take them very long to decide to hang that boy."

Laura had been so caught up in the excitement of the day that she'd forgotten the prospect of an execution. "Oh, do you think so?"

Morgan nodded. "We ain't been much help to them I'm afraid. I did find out White Moon might have told the soldiers at the army camp a different story than he told here. And I found out Miles has had one of his staff people pokin' around at what happened at Wounded Knee and Casey's shooting. Somebody knows something."

Laura took a few minutes to absorb what Morgan told her. She'd almost forgotten that they had agreed to do what they could to help Plenty Horses. "What does that mean?"

"Well, without going out to the reservation, I don't know what it means. Nobody's saying very much. Since the case is already going to the jury, I don't reckon anything I found would do any good."

"Maybe Mr. O'Day can print something about it and they can overturn the trial or something."

Morgan laughed and shook his head. "Once that jury decides to hang the Indian boy, your friend O'Day will be long gone and on to another story."

All the elation Laura had felt minutes ago left her. The reality of the situation and the certainty of the outcome emptied her.

"It's been nice meeting you, Mrs. Bowman." Morgan nodded at her curtly.

She noticed his face and arms were washed and the light-blue shirt was clean. His blue eyes were clear and when she looked into them, they touched her. "You aren't giving up, Mr. Morgan?"

"Oh, I reckon I'll run down the information out on the reservation, not that it'll do any good," he said. "It ain't like I have anything else to do."

"Will you tell me what you find? When will you go?"

"I'll be here until the trial is over. But, like I said, there ain't much that we can do before tomorrow."

"Please Mr. Morgan, I'd like to . . . I'd like to meet you again . . . and compare notes . . . on the trial I mean . . . even when it's over."

Morgan squinted one eye. "I don't mean to bother you with—"

"Mr. Morgan, how about if we meet tomorrow after the trial at the same diner, say at seven? We can compare notes on what we found," she said.

"Well, it ain't going to do much good, but I guess I can do that," he said.

"Very well," she said smiling brightly. "I'll see you at the diner at seven tomorrow. And Mr. Morgan . . ." He looked up, his blue eyes very clear and sparkling beneath the brim of his hat, "This time I'm buying."

She turned and walked down the street toward the jail. She wanted to turn around to see if he was watching her but thought that would be obvious. She decided she would assume he was.

Nock was already at the jail when she arrived. He looked completely drained and slumped in the chair with his arms dangling at his side. He started to rise when Laura walked in, but she waved him down and took the seat next to him.

"Congratulations on an exciting performance today, Mr. Nock," she said.

He smiled, lifting the edges of his walrus-shaped mustache. "Thank you Mrs. Bowman. We shall soon see if the jury understood."

"And you're making a final statement tomorrow?"

"Yes," he said. "Mr. Powers and I will split the final statement."

Laura wondered if she should tell him about the information she and Morgan were collecting, but she couldn't see how it would help at this late date. Just then O'Day came in with the fat little interpreter that made the question moot.

As they had in the prior interview, they made their way down the hallway between the cells to the rear of the jail. It seemed like such a long time ago that Laura had been in this same place. So much had changed. Again, she could not help but selfishly wonder what would happen once the trial was over and she was just another soon-to-be divorcée waiting out her time in Sioux Falls.

Plenty Horses looked much more alert and alive than he had the first day they were there. His posture was erect and eyes were filled with life. He'd changed from the shirt and slacks to an older work shirt, but still wrapped the blue blanket around him, hiding his left hand.

Nock reintroduced O'Day and Laura and explained they represented a newspaper in New York that wanted to hear the testimony he would have given if the judges would have allowed it. He said the jury would not hear it, but at least other white people would hear and appreciate what he had to say.

He nodded and seemed eager to start talking. Throughout the first interview and all through the trial, Laura had not heard him utter more than a few words at a time. Today, he moved to the edge of the stool and spoke enthusiastically. He'd pause periodically to let the interpreter translate. As soon as the last word was out, he'd launch into another series of sentences.

Plenty Horses's words sounded foriegn coming out of the mouth of the fat little interpreter, but Laura found that if she concentrated on Plenty Horses's eyes, it was easy to link the words to what he'd said. She also noticed O'Day had been right to suggest she be there as many of his comments were directed at her. It was as if she was representing all the white people in New York.

"I came back from the Carlisle School with nothing. They taught me how to work in the fields of the farmers but nothing else. When Carlisle let me go, nobody wanted me. Farmers around Carlisle had other students to work for them, so they did not want to pay me, an Indian. I had no chance of employment living with the whites, nothing I could do to earn my board and clothes. I came back to Pine Ridge. There are no farms there, and I didn't like working farms anyway. The Indians at Pine Ridge and Rosebud didn't like me because I had been away living with the whites for five years. Some of them said bad things about me, and I was in many fights. I was living in Pine Ridge with my father that winter that the army troops were brought in. Then came the killing of Big Foot's band. I heard the shooting and ran out to help." He shook his head and paused for Arends to catch up.

"It was an awful sight. The survivors told such a pitiful tale that we all went into camp not far away, and it was said there would be war. Everyone felt the government had injured too many Lakota to give in. In the camp there was much Ghost Dancing and much excitement.

"The day Casey was killed, I was out from the camp watching so that no troops came to harm my father and relatives. Of course, I was in a bad frame of mind. Our home was destroyed, our family separated and all hope of good times were gone. There was nothing to live for.

"Along came Casey on horseback with a Cheyenne scout who was now an enemy Indian who'd sided with the whites against the Lakota. The Cheyenne were friends of the Lakota in my grandfather's and my father's time, but they had turned against us and now wore army uniforms. Casey got angry when he was told he could not examine the Indian camp. He said he would 'go away then but would return with soldiers enough to capture our chief.'"

Plenty Horses stood and gripped his blanket tightly around him as these last sentences were translated. "I understood him to say that his object was to kill them . . . to kill our chiefs. You can understand my state of mind at hearing we were to suffer still more because we arose to demand the food and clothing the government owed us. All this passed before my mind, and then I thought that . . . right at my side rode a spy from our enemy who was boldly announcing his determination to come back and do us further injury."

He sat back on his stool, still wrapped tightly in the blue blanket. While the words were being interpreted, he stared at Laura. When the final word was translated he shrugged his shoulders and said in English, "He turned to go and a moment later fell dead with a bullet from my gun in his brain."

The cell block was silent. Even O'Day's scribbling had stopped. Nock broke the silence. "That will be all for this evening. I have a closing presentation to practice."

Laura had been mesmerized by Plenty Horses's testimony. Once Nock stood, she snapped out of her trance and rose as well. She let him lead her out through the jail. Laura was together enough to decline Arend's invitation to walk her back to the Cataract, and she left with O'Day.

"If he could have made that testimony this afternoon, he would have had the court in the palm of his hand," she said.

"Don't over-read it," he said. "You have to give Nock credit. He prepared him well."

"What do you mean?"

"Tell me, where did a third-grade dropout come up with words like 'frame of mind' and 'sense of determination'? Do you think there are Lakota words for those terms? He schooled not only Plenty Horses but also the interpreter. Plenty Horses could have never delivered that testimony in English."

"I don't think that's correct," she said.

"And by delivering the testimony to me rather than in court, he avoids dealing with cross-examination. Sterling would have taken him apart. No, Nock and Powers knew exactly what they doing by demanding the interpreter and then closing the case when they couldn't have him. It might give them some grounds for appeal, although I doubt there'll be time before the execution."

"So, is that what you'll write?"

O'Day laughed. "Are you kidding me? His testimony is pure gold, and the readers of the *New York World* will eat it up. Especially since we, Mrs. Bowman, are the only ones who have it."

She shook her head. "I don't think I like reporting."

O'Day laughed again.

"What do you think will happen tomorrow?"

He stopped just outside of the Cataract. "They put up a good fight, but I don't think it's enough to convince that jury. No matter what, we're still in Dakota and an Indian shot a white man. He can't be set free."

"So all of this," she waved her hand at the people moving down the street. "All this did nothing to save that Indian boy's life."

"Mrs. Bowman, it's my job to report the news and entertain my readers. This story will do so. I'll see you tomorrow for the last day of the trial."

Laura entered the lobby. She heard one of the women from Haddie McKenna's table call out to her, but she was in no mood. She acted like she hadn't heard anything and rushed up the stairs.

She thought about how empty her life was going to be in two days when the trial was all over.

Chapter Nine

JUDGING FROM THE STRENGTH of the sun streaming into her hotel room, the last day of the trial was going to be a warm one. Laura hurried to get dressed and into the lobby. O'Day had told her they were expecting a large crowd for the last day, so tickets were being issued, and they needed to get to the courtroom early. The lobby was buzzing with women dressed in their finest. Haddie McKenna sat alone at her table, looking as if the trial were beneath her, but Abigail Johnson and Elnora Flatt were standing near the front door waiting for her.

"Oh, Mrs. Bowman, we are so excited," Mrs. Johnson said clapping her hands like a little girl. "Mrs. Flatt and I both got tickets to see the last day of the trial. Now we'll be able to participate just like you do."

The women were clutching their gloves and chattering like they were going to a Broadway musical, not the possible end of a man's life. Nonetheless, Laura smiled politely, "Wonderful," she said. "The last day of the trial should provide you a good summary." The thought that their attendance was anything similar to hers was revolting.

"Oh, I know. Mr. Sterling always dresses so stylishly, and the Indian men have their hair braided. It's just like going to a Wild West show, but in real life," Mrs. Johnson said.

Laura was about to address her comments when she felt a firm hand on her elbow. "Good morning, ladies," O'Day said with a polite bow. "There seems to be significant activity this morning."

"Yes, Mr. O'Day," Mrs. Johnson said with a girlish giggle. "Since they're issuing tickets to the trial today, we can go without standing in the street and waiting in line. I was just telling Mrs. Bowman I'm so excited to experience this trial like she's been."

"Of course, Mrs. . . . ummm . . . Johnson, isn't it?" O'Day said. "Mrs. Bowman's been a great spectator." He smiled at Laura, "We should probably go."

"Well, Mr. O'Day, if you need any help from me, reaction to the proceedings and such, I mean, I'll be back here this evening." Mrs. Johnson batted her large brown eyes. Laura thought she looked like a lonely cow.

"Thank you, Mrs. Johnson. I'll certainly keep that in mind."

The heat of the street hit them as they exited the big double doors of the Cataract. "The nerve of that woman," Laura said. "She's giddy as a schoolgirl going to her first musical."

"Are you jealous you may be losing your status as 'the leading divorce-colonist observer'?"

"What do you mean?" she said. "These women know nothing of what's going on in this trial and have no appreciation for the consequences."

"Ahhh, I see," he nodded. "In three days you've become a legal expert."

"No, it's not that," she said. "It's just . . ." She looked up at him, "This is more than just a spectacle. This is a man's life."

"That it is, Mrs. Bowman. But I suspect the spectacle will be the primary focus today."

"The thought of the opinion of that woman mattering is revolting! Why, she doesn't even know what's going on. Why would you ever put her into your coverage of the trial?"

O'Day laughed, "On the contrary, Mrs. Bowman. I think Mrs. Johnson would be a fine interviewee regarding the proceedings. Her opinion is exactly what my readers will want to hear. I hadn't thought about it, but I'll most certainly seek her opinion of the trial today."

Laura glowered but had to admit O'Day was right. If she were back in New York reading an account of the trial she would no doubt be more interested in who was in attendance and what people like Mrs. Johnson thought, than the legal doctrine. It just didn't seem right that people like Abigail Johnson, who had no idea about what the Lakota had gone through, would form public opinion.

As they neared the courthouse, the crowd on the sidewalk was double what it had been in previous days. The midmorning sun was already making it uncomfortable, and Laura dreaded how warm the courtroom would be. O'Day was able to push his way through the crowd with her in tow.

Even though it was still an hour before the trial was to start, Plenty Horses was already at the defense table. Despite the heat, he was wrapped in his blue blanket. The courtroom was filling up quickly, and Laura was thankful she had a seat beside O'Day. She was surprised the audience was two-thirds women, at least a hundred of them.

The chattering rose to an even higher level than usual as the spectators passed time waiting for the judges to enter. Plenty Horses had nodded to her when she first came in but now sat as in a trance, staring at the front wall of the courtroom. Nock and Powers had papers spread out across the table and were studying them, periodically whispering short comments to each other. He Dog, Living Bear, and another Lakota man she didn't recognize sat stoically, seemingly oblivious to the commotion. He Dog had nodded politely to O'Day and smiled at her when they came in but then scowled at the throng behind them. He put his back to them to face the front of the courtroom. Laura wondered what he must be thinking of the white man's customs and at the chattering white women watching the spectacle.

At last, the judges and jury entered. The judges took the packed house in stride, but the jury members appeared transfixed by the larger and more feminine audience. Laura saw two of the men of the jury run their hand over their heads to put stray hairs back into place.

Judge Edgerton slammed the gavel down and called the court to order. He explained that the defense would make their final arguments, followed by the prosecution, and then the case would be turned over to the jury. Like most of the audience, Laura found herself staring at the twelve men on the jury who would determine if Plenty Horses would live or die.

Powers and Nock traded off different parts of the final presentation. Powers matter-of-factly described the state of affairs on the Pine Ridge Reservation the previous winter. Laura felt O'Day squirm with delight as he quoted *New York World* news stories regarding how General Nelson Miles had fortified the Pine Ridge Agency. Powers said Miles had cut off all rations to the Lakota through most of the winter and had turned the distribution center into an armed camp. "There was no question the entire reservation was in a state of war," he said. "What was this poor savage to think?" He pointed dramatically at Plenty Horses, who was staring at the floor in front of the table. "He was a warrior in the middle of a war zone."

From behind Laura an audible sigh came when Plenty Horses was called a poor savage. Glancing back, she noted that the ladies in the row behind her were glaring at Sterling.

It was up to Nock to make the emotional plea. He spoke of the maltreatment of the Indians at the hands of whites for years and years. In a low, deep voice he described the Lakota way of life before the whites came to the plains and then outlined treaty violation after treaty violation. Laura thought she saw He Dog nod a little as Nock pointed at them and said they were the most persecuted race in America.

He used that argument to outline the high state of excitement the Ghost Dance religion brought to Pine Ridge. "These savages now saw hope, hope of a return to a way of life the white man took from them," he said dramatically.

"Then when Sitting Bull was killed and the army ruthlessly attacked Big Foot's band at Wounded Knee, how would you expect the proud Lakota warriors to react? They saw soldiers pouring into Pine Ridge and fortifications going up. The Lakota saw war, and they needed to protect themselves."

Nock's voice had started as a low rumble but now was increasing in both pitch and volume. Beads of sweat appeared on his forehead. The warm, stuffy courtroom served to emphasize the claustrophobic emotions as Nock portrayed the Lakota as trapped in a war against the army, a war of survival. Casey's actions, he maintained, were part of an escalation of hostilities.

"The army was out to finish the job they had started at Wounded Knee!" he said. "How did Casey leave his camp? Did he leave it as though peace was lingering on every side? No!" He slammed his fist into his palm. "Nor as a peace-going citizen. He starts to the Lakota camp armed . . . armed for battle.

"And with him he took his Cheyenne scout, White Moon," he pointed across the room at the Cheyenne man in his blue uniform. "You heard his testimony that he and Casey didn't go to the Lakota camp at White Clay for peace, they went there as spies. They were preparing for an attack!

"Gentlemen of the jury, how do you think the army sentries would have reacted if they had encountered Lakota spies reconnoitering their camp?" His voice rose an octave, "They would have shot them . . . shot them dead!"

Nock paused to let his words resound through the courtroom. In a much lower and calmer voice, he appealed to the jury for a fair trial. He said the Lakota only wanted justice. He pointed at Living Bear and said "It would be wrong to kill this man's son, a troubled Lakota warrior, for only doing what warriors do . . . for only doing what any warrior would do."

He wiped the sweat off his forehead and returned to his seat. The courtroom was like a furnace. Judge Edgerton said court would break for lunch and would resume at two o'clock to hear the prosecution's closing arguments.

The chattering of the room started the instant the judge slammed down the gavel. The women in the room were taken by Nock's testimony. "My God," O'Day said in a low voice. "If these women sat on the jury, the Indian might have a chance of living." The crowded courtroom was emptying quickly as people were hurrying to get a breath of fresh air. He slid by Laura into the aisle. "I'm going to get some quotes over lunch. I bet the diner will be full anyway. You're on your own, Mrs. Bowman."

She nodded and then noted that he was headed for Abigail Johnson who was furiously fanning herself.

Laura let the flow of spectators carry her out into the street. The sun was now beating down on them and heating up the city even more. From the talk she was hearing around her, Nock had been very convincing. She couldn't help but think it sounded like the ladies were discussing the performance at the intermission of a play. In her opinion,

Nock had hit the emotional buttons but had failed to do much with the facts. She knew Sterling would come at the case portraying Casey as a hero. These gadflies would probably change their opinion once they heard different emotional pleas.

She wanted to discuss the case, but there was nobody around who understood it. She felt very alone in the crowded street. She watched the corners of the buildings but didn't see any dark figure peering. She found herself wandering down to the side street that led to the bridge and was surprised to see one of the maids from the Cataract standing on the crest of it.

She joined the woman on the bridge and leaned against the railing to watch the water flow beneath them. "Have you heard about the testimony this morning?" she asked.

In the bright sunlight, lines on the woman's face were more pronounced, adding five years to her appearance. She was probably about Laura's age but looked more . . . worn. "I haven't followed it much," the woman said. "I've got better things to do with my free time."

Laura kept her focus on the river. "What do you like to do in your free time?"

The woman laughed. "As if I had much. Between working at the Cataract and taking care of my two kids and husband, there just ain't much free time."

"But surely you must be following the Plenty Horses trial. They may hang that man."

"Ma'am, what goes on between the Indians and the army is no concern of mine." She pushed back a mop of curly hair. "Getting my kids fed, that's a concern of mine. Making sure my husband keeps his job, that's a concern of mine. Makin' sure he don't spend his pay getting drunk all the time, that's a concern of mine."

She spit once into the river and kicked a piece of mud off the bridge. Her shoes clunked on the deck as she made her way down the bridge past Laura. "I reckon I better get to work cleaning your room."

Laura watched her make her way down the side street toward downtown. She'd never wondered where her next meal was going to come from. She kicked a small piece of mud off the bridge and watched it hit the water. She looked to the left and then the right, took a deep breath and spit as far as she could into the river. She smiled, nodded, and made her way off the bridge back towards the courthouse.

As Laura filed her way through the bodies clogging Phillips Avenue, her stomach growled. As she looked around at the ladies making their way back into the courtroom, she was glad she'd missed lunch.

"Did you get some quotes," she asked O'Day when he slid into the seat beside her.

"Oh yeah, this'll be a great story," he said, patting his notebook. "If it was up to the ladies, the Indian would go free." He laughed a little. "Well, as long as he promised to stay on the reservation and never bother them. I get the impression they look at him more as a lion in the zoo, one that killed an errant zookeeper. Savages do what savages do. It's the zookeeper's fault if he wasn't careful."

"That is a disgusting thing to say," she said.

O'Day tilted his head. "It may be disgusting, but it's how they see it."

Before he could say more, the judges were announced and the court was called back to order.

Laura had been so focused on the women behind her she'd forgotten to look at jury during Nock's emotional appeal. Now as they waited for Sterling's closing, they didn't appear to have been overly impressed. She noticed fewer ladies sat in the audience than during the morning.

Sterling was younger than either Nock or Powers, but he carried himself as a much older and experienced man. With his clean-shaven face and impeccably groomed hair, he appeared confident and official. In a high, clear voice he appealed directly to the jury that they needed to deal with facts, not emotional pandering. Moving slowly in front of the prosecution table, he pronounced that there was no state of war with the Indians. He looked directly at two of the older jury members. "There are those of you who served in the Civil War, who know what a war looks like. Don't let the theatrics of the defense sway you. The belligerent Indians were not at war with the United States. They were merely breaking the laws. They were just belligerent."

As he spoke, Laura found herself watching for reactions on the jury. The two older men obviously nodded. Sterling had scored an important point with the Civil War veterans.

"And even if there was a state of war, which there was not," he continued holding up a hand. "Even if there was a state of war, what kind of a solider shoots a man in the back?" He shook his head. "What would have happened if one of the Confederate soldiers would have shot General Grant in the back at Appomattox?" He slapped his hand for effect. "That man would have been considered a traitor and a criminal."

He turned and gestured towards the Lakota men sitting behind the defense table. "The defense wants you to believe the condition of Indian society should have an impact on this cowardly act of murder. Gentlemen of the jury, the act of murder is a punishable offense regardless of whether you are an Indian or a white man. If a white man cowardly shoots a man in the back, he is guilty of murder. I ask you to treat this defendant as a white man.

"There is testimony that the defendant, Plenty Horses, took no part in the Ghost Dance, and by his own statement said he did not believe in the Messiah. An hour before the murder was committed, Plenty Horses was as cool and deliberate as he was at the time he shot his gallant victim.

"Lieutenant Casey was a brave young soldier trying to make peace, trying to avoid any further bloodshed." Sterling dramatically gestured toward Plenty Horses. "Here is a man who shook hands with Lieutenant Casey as a friend, and a minute later, when his back was turned, he deliberately drew his gun and put a bullet through his victim's head. This is one of the most inexcusable, one of the most unprovoked, one of the most cowardly murders in the history of the United States."

Sterling paused for effect. The heat of the courtroom did not seem to impact him. He was as cool and official as ever. "Something has been said about the sympathy for the defendant and sorrow for his old father." He gestured towards Living Bear. "I ask you not to forget that while Edward Casey, like the prisoner, had neither wife nor children, he had a mother. Today his mother, who lives by the side of yonder sea, yearns for her son with a mother's love, which never dies, yearns for her soldier boy who will never return to her."

O'Day quietly snickered. He whispered, "Especially since she died thirty years ago."

Laura turned her head to look at him, but Sterling commanded the attention of the court again.

"I plead not only for the broken-hearted mother, not only for that young life of Edward Casey so sadly and cruelly blotted out, but I plead for justice. I plead for the sanctity of human life. I plead for the honor and for the safety of the people of the state and the district of Dakota."

Sterling had effectively slipped out of his official mode and into the emotional mode. He made these final pleas directly at the men of the jury. Laura had the feeling Nock had been addressing the audience and general public, while Sterling was directing all of his emotion at the jury.

When he finished and sat down, the court took a collective breath.

Judge Shiras spent half an hour outlining the case for the jurors, telling them the Indians had no status as an independent nation and so could not declare war. Nevertheless he said, they could engage in a war against the government, declared or otherwise. "Consequently," the Judge said, "the jury can come to three conclusions in this case. One is that Lieutenant Casey was shot while the Sioux and the United States were at war, in which case, you must acquit the defendant. Two, if there was not a war, and the defendant shot Lieutenant Casey with deliberation and malice, you must find him guilty of murder. Three, if the defendant fired at Lieutenant Casey in a state of great mental excitement, without deliberation and premeditation, even if there were no state of war, you must find him guilty of the lesser crime of manslaughter." Judge Shiras held up three fingers, "Three options: acquit, murder, or manslaughter." He slammed the gavel and recessed the court. None of the jurors looked at Plenty Horses as they filed out of the jury box.

O'Day pulled out his watch and whispered, "It's 3:40. And now we wait."

They made their way through the crowd. Laura had the distinct feeling that people in the audience, the women in particular, did not care for Sterling. "I can't believe he called the poor Indian boy a 'cold blooded murderer," the lady in a green-print dress said. "It's one thing to discuss the case, but he didn't need to be so brutal. I expect better from a refined man like Mr. Sterling."

O'Day hurried them through the crowd exiting the courtroom. "When will the jury come back?" Laura asked as she struggled to keep up.

"It could be anytime," he said. "I'd suspect they'll at least deliberate a few hours."

"Are you going to wait here for the jury to come back?" she said.

He was looking over the top of the people filing out of the courthouse. He waved and pulled Laura behind him towards the side street. A redheaded boy of about twelve in overalls was standing there nervously.

"Okay, Billy, you know what to do?" O'Day reached into his pocket and brought out a coin.

"I think so, Mr. O'Day," he said nodding his head. "I stay right here on the front steps of the courthouse. If they call the jury back . . . I run like hell . . . ahh . . . pardon ma'am, heck I mean . . . I run down to the telegraph office and get you."

"That's right, Billy," O'Day said patting his hand. "Now this is important, I'm giving you half now and half when you come get me."

"Thanks Mr. O'Day, I'll make sure I stay right here until they come back."

Laura dug into her purse and pulled out a coin, "And after you get Mr. O'Day, come find me at the Cataract." She was glad she'd brought some money that day.

"Gee, thanks, ma'am," the boy smiled but then his face clouded. "Ma'am, they don't let me into the front of the Cataract much. I can only go to the loading dock." He started to hand the coin back.

"Nonsense," she said. "I'll speak to the doorman. You'll just need to speak to him." She patted his outstretched hand.

O'Day started striding back down the street toward the telegraph office. Laura hurried to keep up with him as he hadn't extended his arm. "Well, Mrs. Bowman, I believe we have a plan. By this time tomorrow, everyone will be gone, and you'll be able to get back to life at the Cataract."

"Do you . . . um . . . need anything from me?" she said.

"I just need to get my stories filed and then be here for the jury's verdict."

Laura let O'Day go on ahead. He didn't even look back to say good evening. She slowed and put her back against the hardware store window. Billy was now standing at attention just outside the open door of the courthouse. Many of the spectators were milling around the street, afraid to leave lest they miss something.

Laura made her way down to the Cataract. She let the doorman know she'd be in her room and asked to have someone sent up if Billy appeared. She thought about ordering something to eat, but remembered she'd told Morgan she would meet him at the little diner at seven. She wondered where he'd been all day, or any day for that matter. The first couple of times she had seen him, he had been so drunk he could hardly talk, however the last few times they had conversed, he had been very coherent. He certainly was different than any other man she'd ever met.

She lay down and took a nap and was surprised when she awoke at 6:30 p.m. There was still no word from the jury. Laura hurried to get herself together to meet Morgan for dinner.

Laura had never been one to worry much about punctuality, but it felt important to not be late for her dinner with Morgan. On her way out the front door, she instructed the doorman that if Billy arrived with news about the jury, he should be sent down to Mable's Diner. He gave her a questioning look, but nodded and said he would.

She'd selected her clothing very carefully. Her goal was to look attractive but not unattainable. The idea sounded kind of silly to her when she put it that way, but that was how she felt. She wasn't sure what she wanted from or with Morgan, but it was something . . . something different from other men she'd known.

Laura arrived at the little diner with two minutes to spare according to the clock on the back wall. Morgan was already at the same table they'd been at before, but he looked like a different man. She'd never seen him without his hat. His blonde hair was freshly washed and oiled into place. He had a large, ugly looking scar the size of a fifty cent piece on his right temple.

"My, Mr. Morgan, don't you look nice," she said. He stood up and pulled her chair out for her.

"Thank you, ma'am," he said. "It was about time, I guess."

"And that looks like a brand new shirt and tie as well."

He fingered the tie. "It's been awhile since I wore a tie."

"I didn't see you outside the courthouse today," she said. "The final arguments were quite engaging."

"I was loading some lumber . . . I needed to make some money."

"Well, you wear it very nicely."

"Thank you, ma'am."

"Could you just call me, Laura? And what can I call you besides, Mr. Morgan?"

He smiled and ran a hand over his hair. "Just Morgan is fine, ma . . . Laura." He leaned forward across the table. "So tell me about the final day of court."

"The courtroom was packed. They issued tickets to get in, and most of them apparently went to divorce colonists. They had no idea what was going on in the courtroom." She shook her head.

"Nock and Powers made an emotional appeal for the Lakota and said there was a state of war present. They said Casey was a spy and Plenty Horses needed to shoot him."

Morgan nodded. "How did that go over?"

"With the spectators, it went well. The jury didn't look so impressed, though."

"What did Sterling say?"

"He presented Plenty Horses as a cold-blooded murderer."

"What do you think?"

"Casey was wrong to be there; Plenty Horses was wrong to shoot him. But I don't think he should die for it." Laura shook her head. "The look on the faces of the jury members . . . by the time Sterling was done, they looked like they hated him."

They ordered dinner and talked about the weather. The food was plain but good.

"Morgan, can you tell me what it was like out there . . . out on the reservation last winter?"

He looked down at his plate and scrapped at a bit of gravy with is fork. "It was cold . . . and dangerous."

He kept his eyes on his plate, but the words still came out of his mouth slowly, "I don't know what the lawyers, or the law, or the ladies know or think about war, but it isn't like anything you can imagine if you haven't been there. It isn't as simple as it is on paper. Killing does things to a man, things that can't be undone." He shook his head. "I don't think I have the right words in me to describe it . . ."

"How did you injure your forehead?"

Morgan put his fingertips to the scar. "It's just one of those things you pick up in a battle, in a war."

"You left the army after Wounded Knee."

"I wasn't doing much good for the army after that . . . and they weren't doing much good for me. Yeah, when my hitch was up . . . I left."

"What have you been doing since you left the army? Did you have a trade before you went in?"

He looked up, his blue eyes impossibly clear. "When I was a kid I helped on my folk's farm in Ohio and then worked in a store. I wanted some adventure, so I joined the army."

"Will you go back to Ohio?"

"Ain't nothing there anymore for me. Ain't nothing anywhere," he muttered as he moved his silverware around on the table.

"Morgan, what will you do with yourself . . . I mean after the trial is over?"

"You mean will I go back to livin' in that whiskey bottle?"

"I didn't say that . . ."

"I know what you said." He shook his head and looked at the ceiling. "I've wallowed enough I guess. I think I'm going to go back out to Pine Ridge. Maybe I can do something."

"Do something for Plenty Horses?"

"Nahh, his fate is in the hands of the jury. Maybe I can do something for the Lakota, though." He rubbed at the scar on his forehead. "I owe them that."

He moved his chair and focused on Laura like he was eager to change the subject. "What about you, Mrs. Bowman . . . err, Laura? What will you do when you're not being an expert on an Indian trial?"

"I suppose I'll finish getting divorced and go back to New York," she said. "I still have to be here in South Dakota for two more months."

"What do you do in New York . . . besides being married?"

"You know, Morgan . . . I'm not sure what it is I do."

He laughed. "Seems like that—"

The boy named Billy burst into the diner. "Mrs. Bowman, I have information from Mr. O'Day!" He was breathing hard and his face was red with exertion.

"Is the jury back in?" she asked.

"No, ma'am. I mean yes, ma'am, I mean, they sent a note to the judges but are still talking."

"So they aren't ready to make a decision."

"No, ma'am. Mr. O'Day just said to let you know."

"Thank you, Billy," she said reaching in her bag for a coin. "This is for you."

"Thank you, ma'am. Mr. O'Day said they probably won't come back in now until tomorrow morning."

"Very good, Billy. Have a nice evening."

The boy left. Morgan chuckled. "So, tomorrow the trial will be all over, and you can go back to getting unmarried."

"Yes . . ." They both moved silverware around. When the cook brought the bill over, Laura placed some money on the tray.

"Thank you," he mumbled. "It doesn't seem right, letting a woman pay for my dinner."

She smiled. "It was my pleasure, Mr. Morgan, and a thank you for all the help you've given me the last few days."

"I don't recall doing much to help anyone."

"I enjoy your company."

They left the diner and walked slowly down the side street toward Phillips Avenue. The night had cooled the hot sticky air of the day, and a light breeze cut across Laura's face. "I suppose I should walk you back to the Cataract," he said.

Laura instantly had the image of Haddie McKenna and the other ladies peering out the window to see her walking with the little cowboy. He'd put his hat back on and pulled it over the scar on his forehead. Even dressed up as much as possible, he still looked like an uneducated yokel.

"That's all right, Mr. Morgan. I think I can make it on my own." She reached out a hand and tried to shake his. He looked down at her outstretched hand and slowly raised his hand to meet it. "Thank you very much for dining with me, Mr. Morgan. I've enjoyed getting to know you."

Before he could stay anything, she turned and walked down the darkened sidewalk toward the lights on Phillips Avenue. She felt terrible. It had been easy to identify the hurt in his blue eyes even as they peered out from the black hat. She wasn't sure what he'd expected. Well, she had to admit, she wasn't sure what she had expected either. She immediately regretted leaving so soon. Going to the little diner with him had felt partly like a charity case, to see if he would show up drunk or otherwise, but he'd cleaned himself up well. She'd found the conversation interesting. When you got through the rough exterior, as she had about half way through dinner, he was a witty and interesting partner. Surely he would understand she couldn't show up at the Cataract with him. She was only protecting him so he wouldn't feel out of place.

Her heels were clicking on the sidewalk. She knew she wasn't protecting him. She was protecting herself, her reputation. She was becoming as bad as Haddie Mc—

A figure stepped out of the shadows and grabbed her arm. A body moved in front of her and bent her back. Someone was kissing her fiercely. A mustache scraped across her nose and lips covering hers prevented her from screaming. She pushed back on the man's chest has hard as she could and kicked at his shins, connecting solidly with the toe of her shoe.

"Ouch," he yelled and let go of her, hopping on one foot. When he looked up a beam of light hit his face.

"Randolph!" she exclaimed. "What are you . . . ?"

Before she could finish the sentence a dark figure flew across her line of sight and into the man hopping on one foot. The two men tumbled to the ground and a black cowboy hat flew across the street.

"No!" she cried. She heard three distinct splats of skin on skin in rapid succession. She jumped on the back of the man on top. "No, Morgan, stop it. I know him." She gripped his right arm with both of hers before it smacked the man on the ground again.

"Morgan, no, I know him," she said. "Don't hit him anymore."

He stood and wiped his hands on pants. He leaned over and picked up his hat. "Who is he, and why did he attack you?"

"Who is this oaf?" the man on the ground was moaning. "Call the police. He hit me."

"Randolph, shut up," she said harshly. "Why did you grab me like that?"

"Ohhh God, my nose hurts," he moaned. "I wanted to surprise you."

Morgan took another step forward and spoke slowly. "Who is this?"

"He's . . . he's a friend. A friend from New York," she said. She walked toward Morgan two steps.

Morgan stared at her starting to comprehend. "I suppose I'll leave you and your friend to get reacquainted." He turned back and walked up the dark street. He turned and mumbled, "I'm . . . I'm sorry."

"Oh God, my nose. Call the police," Randolph Hiller said.

"You're fine," she said kneeling down to help him up. "You're lucky to be alive. In this part of the country, you don't just jump out and grab a woman on the street."

"Who . . . was that man and why did he beat me?" he said struggling to get up.

"He's a friend who's been working with me on the trial."

"What trial?" Hiller put his nose in the air, trying to stop the bleeding.

"Why, the Plenty Horses's trial of course," she said. "What are you doing here?"

"I thought I'd surprise you. I wanted to make sure you were being taken care of."

Laura sighed heavily. "You said it would be best if we didn't see each other again until I got back to New York after my divorce."

"I know, I know, that's what I said. But I was reading about you in the *New York World*. 'Laura Bowman, the gay soon-to-be divorcée enjoying Sioux Falls.'"

"What are you talking about?"

"Don't you get newspapers in this Godforsaken place?"

"I haven't had time to read one in several days. What are you talking about?"

"There was an article in the *World* about how you live in the only luxury hotel within two hundred miles with all sorts of other divorcées in a colony, just passing time."

"And you thought it would be a good idea to come and check on me?" she said.

"I came to keep you company, Laura." Hiller pulled out a handkerchief and wiped the blood from his nose. "I didn't come out here to get my face beaten."

"Do you really think it's a good idea for you to be seen here with me? How will you explain being out here?"

"I don't know," he said. "I love you, Laura. I thought the three months would go quickly, but they aren't. I wanted to see you."

Laura looked up and down the street. There were a few people strolling along Phillips Avenue, but nobody had paid them much attention. "Where are you staying?"

"I have a room at the Merchants Hotel, but I thought I'd stay at the Cataract with you tonight."

She shook her head. "You are not staying with me at the Cataract tonight or any other night. I'll take you back to the Merchants and you can get yourself cleaned up. We can have lunch tomorrow."

She didn't even want to be seen walking by the bleeding man. They made their way down to Phillips Avenue, and she stayed near the buildings so she wouldn't be recognized. For his part, Hiller stumbled a little while holding his bloody handkerchief to his nose, but had stopped moaning. Laura suspected he was looking for sympathy more than actually enduring pain. "Why did that man hit me so many times?"

"He hit you three times. If someone had rushed into a dark street in New York and grabbed me, I hope you'd have reacted the same way."

"He's lucky I didn't see him coming, or I would have given him what for." With the handkerchief to his nose, Heller's voice had a nasal quality to it that made Laura want to laugh, but she maintained control.

"I'm sure," she said as they got within a block of the Merchants, "you can make it the rest of the way from here. I'll see you tomorrow."

"You're going to leave me here, wounded in front of the hotel? After I came all this way to see you?"

"Randolph, I never asked you to come out here. I need to sort things out." Against her better judgment, she kissed him on the cheek and walked away from him.

She didn't look back as she quickly walked towards the Cataract. Now things were in a fine fix. Randolph probably had grounds to assume there was more to their relationship than there actually was. She'd decided to address the situation when she was divorced and got back to New York. She certainly hadn't expected him to show up here in Sioux Falls.

Laura had enough to worry about. She didn't need to be thinking about him. Or Morgan either for that matter.

Chapter Ten

EVERY TIME LAURA FELL ASLEEP, unfocused images swirled around her mind: Plenty Horses's face, pleading for justice, Hiller's face full of desire, Morgan's face full of contempt. Sweat covered her body, and she shivered in the morning light.

She hadn't thought about Randolph Hiller in a week. He may have been the one most responsible for deciding to not ignore Jonathon's indiscretions any longer, but she was past that decision point. She'd come to Dakota for a fresh start, not just to transfer her dependence from Jonathon to Randolph.

Laura contemplated not going to the trial this morning. Lying in bed behind a closed door, she could shut out all the problems. If she waited long enough, perhaps they would all go away. But that was the old Laura. She decided that, since the trial was almost over anyway, her absence would raise more questions than it would conceal. She'd come too far to hide from reality now.

She ordered a small breakfast brought up. The maid carrying the tray looked familiar, but it wasn't until she left that Laura realized she was the woman she'd spoken to at the bridge. The maid had said nothing to her and had demonstrated no familiarity.

By 8:30 she was downstairs in the lobby. At the table in the corner, Haddie sipped coffee and carefully took in the face of each person in the room. Laura knew that, within a day or two, Randolph Hiller's name and face would be among the most talked about at the gossip table.

O'Day came into the room and motioned for her to follow. He walked so quickly toward the courthouse that Laura could barely keep up.

"You're certainly in a hurry this morning, Mr. O'Day," she said between breaths.

"This trial will be over in a few hours, and I'll be on my way back to New York," he said. "It can't be too soon. I've had enough of the prairie life."

"How did your stories yesterday go?"

"Of course they'll be award winning," he laughed. "I think they went well."

"What do you think the outcome will be . . . of the jury, I mean?"

"That's the question of the day. The word at Sandy's was that it was three to one they would convict him of murder, two to one for manslaughter and ten to one to acquit."

"What do you think, though?"

"I'm not much of a betting man," he said. "It doesn't really matter much. Either murder or manslaughter, I guess. That boy will hang if it's murder or will soon die in prison if it's manslaughter. We'll sell papers either way."

They continued up the courthouse steps and into the courtroom. Laura decided she didn't care much for the newspaper business and didn't care much for O'Day either. The process was getting routine now, and the crowd was buzzing with excitement but complied with what the police told them to do.

At the stroke of 9:00 a.m., the jury filed into the room. The judges entered afterward and called the court to order. The room went immediately silent. Laura was conscious of the waving of fans from the women sitting behind them. The level of silence was almost oppressive.

Judge Shiras pounded the gavel. "Foreman of the jury, have you reached a verdict?"

The jury foreman rose, fingering the lapel of his Sunday-best coat. He stood with his eyes lowered. "No, Your Honor, we have not."

A collective gasp went through the room. The judges asked the foreman if there was any chance of the jury coming to a verdict. "No, Your Honor, we're at a complete impasse. We cannot issue a verdict."

The judges briefly conferred, and then Shiras slammed the gavel. "We declare this to be a mistrial. The jury is dismissed."

A buzz broke through the crowd. "What does this mean?" Laura whispered and then pulled on O'Day's arm. "What will happen now?"

"There'll be another trial," he said through clenched teeth. "We'll go through the whole process again."

Judge Shivas pounded the gavel to bring the court to order. "The next session of this court will be held in Deadwood beginning May 25."

"Your Honor," Nock stood up, his voice rising above the din of the courtroom. "Your Honor, neither Mr. Powers or myself are being paid for our services. Moving the trial to Deadwood would cause a great financial burden on the defense and limit the defendant's chance at a fair trial."

Judge Shivas and Edgerton conferred again and then Edgerton pounded the gavel, "Very well, unless the prosecution opposes, we will hold the new trial back here in Sioux Falls on May 25. Court is adjourned."

O'Day was out of his seat at the sound of the gavel and ran across the front of the court to where the jury was filing out. He caught up to the foreman and grabbed him by the arm.

Inspired, Laura followed as closely behind him as possible. She wanted to hear what had happened.

"Well," the jury foreman said. "The first ballot came out six for murder and six for manslaughter. After a while it was eight for murder and four for manslaughter, but never got no closer than that. The last ballot was six and six again. We could have remained out for four days and never come any closer to an agreement."

"There were no votes to acquit?" O'Day asked holding his pad high. "Did anyone at any time vote to acquit?"

The jury foreman laughed. "No, sir. Twenty-three ballots and there was never any votes to acquit from nobody. The question was whether it was to be murder or manslaughter."

Laura turned around and watched Living Bear lean over the railing and grip Nock with trembling hands, tears streaming down his face. Throughout the trial, Living Bear had worn the stoic face of a worried father. Now he was smiling and crying and shaking hands with everyone within arm's reach.

Plenty Horses was still sitting stone-faced at the table facing to the front. It was as if he didn't understand what was happening, and for the moment, nobody was explaining much to him. Laura heard one of the other reporters ask him how he felt. He looked up but made no response.

While O'Day continued to question the jury foreman, the other jury members stood at in the jury box and watched the flow of people through the court. They were disappointed. The spectators had come to see resolution, and they got only a month delay. Laura clearly heard one of the jurors say to nobody in particular, "I have lived on the border too long to look upon the outrages of those savages as permitting of any mitigating circumstances."

Laura looked at him in horror. Standing in the middle of the court room, Powers heard him as well and quickly responded, "Then you are not without prejudice, although you swore you had none before becoming a juror."

The cocky smile was replaced immediately with a look of utter panic on the face of the juror. The defense lawyer took a step closer to him. "Perjury is a serious offense," he said. The man immediately pushed by the other jurors and worked his way out of the courtroom. Powers winked at Laura.

"It seems that man is a little concerned about you throwing him in jail for perjury," she said.

Powers laughed. "I have to admit, I quite enjoyed that." He nodded to where O'Day was still interviewing the foreman. "From the sounds of what the foreman's telling your employer, we might just be delaying the inevitable."

Laura shook her head. "I don't work for Mr. O'Day. I've just been watching the trial closely, and he has provided me escort."

Powers shrugged. "I see," he said, sweeping his arm over where the spectators had been sitting. "I suppose there's no end to the amount of interest out there."

It just struck Laura that the trial was not over. She would not return to drinking tea waiting for her divorce to clear. She was going to be doing things!

On impulse she took a step closer to Powers and grabbed him by the arm. "Mr. Powers, we would like to do something to help you with the defense of that Indian man. Would you be willing to let us help?"

Powers took a step back and nodded toward O'Day. "Ma'am, I'm sure that the *New York World* cannot be in the business of directly helping . . ."

"Oh, no," she said. "Not Mr. O'Day, he would certainly not compromise his newspaper. I mean another person, a person who was out on the reservation when this all happened. We could help."

Powers looked her up and down. "Umm . . . well, Mrs., um . . ."

"Bowman," she said. "Laura Bowman. I'm staying at the Cataract Hotel."

"Ah, I see," he said. As soon as Laura mentioned the Cataract he seemed to lose interest. "Well, Mrs. Bowman, I'm sure Mr. Nock and I will be more than capable . . ."

"Mr. Powers," she said. "If we could just meet with you and Mr. Nock . . ."

"Yes, yes, that'll be fine," he said walking back towards the defense table. Just set up an appointment with our girl."

Living Bear was still making the rounds, shaking hands with anyone who would talk with him, his face streaked with tears. Laura wondered if he had any idea that his son would be tried again.

The reporter from the *Sioux Falls Argus Leader* was still trying to get a response from Plenty Horses. Finally, he looked up at the reporter and said, "I thought last night they would hang me sure. But now I feel it will not be so. My father is glad once more."

Laura made her way out of the courtroom, which was still buzzing with activity. The ladies from the Divorce Colony were very pleased with the result. "Oh, we will have much to talk about for the next month," she heard one of them remark.

As she entered the street, the feeling was different. The locals had expected a hanging, not a hung jury. The news of the split vote between manslaughter and murder had made it to the street quickly. "I can't believe they aren't hanging that Injun," one man with a heavy beard said. "I heard every one of the war vets voted for manslaughter. Can you imagine them not supporting the army?"

"Well, at least it'll be good for business," another man said. "Another month of all these people here has got to bring in some money."

"You damned fool, you think the folks here for the trial are gonna stay all month? They'll all be outta here by noon tomorrow, you just watch."

Laura picked her way through the people on the street, watching for Morgan. With a sinking feeling in her stomach, she remembered that he might not be interested in seeing her again. She needed to find him and explain . . . explain about meeting with Nock and Powers, explain about Hiller, explain about . . . well, everything. She watched around the corners of the buildings but saw nothing.

The lobby of the Cataract was buzzing with people. "Oh, Mrs. Bowman," Abigail Johnson gushed at her before she could make it to the stairway. "Can you believe it? The trial will go on in another month."

"Yes," she said looking for a reason to move away from the overweight woman.

"I suppose you and Mr. O'Day will have a great deal to do for the next month," she said. "Please tell Mr. O'Day if he needs another assistant in writing his stories, I'm very well versed in journalism."

"Yes, I'll tell him," she said. She wondered what exactly Mrs. Johnson thought she did for O'Day. She started to drift toward the stairway when a porter from the front desk tapped her on the shoulder.

"A note for Mrs. Bowman," he said, pausing to wait for a tip. She was flustered enough and so anxious to extract herself from Abigail Johnson that she ignored the man's tip expectation and took the note toward the stairway.

As soon as she reached her room, she tore the note open. As she had expected and feared, the note was from Randolph Hiller requesting her company at 12:30 for lunch at the Merchant's Hotel. The absolute last thing she wanted to do was have lunch with Randolph Hiller, especially today.

But she knew she had to go. After all, wasn't Randolph the reason she was here in Sioux Falls in the first place? When everyone else had assumed she would just live with Jonathon Bowman's string of mistresses, he'd told her she shouldn't have to. He was the one who had given her solid proof that her husband had been keeping at least two, if not more, mistresses in the City. He was the one who'd told her she didn't have to live that way. He was the one who'd told her how she could get a nice, quiet divorce in South Dakota. He was the one who'd said there would be life after a divorce.

But she didn't feel like the woman in New York who'd agreed to his plans. She didn't feel the need to ask a man what she should do . . . to seek permission. She was part of trying to save a man's life.

Nonetheless, she needed to go see him, and as it was already 12:40, it would appear she would be late. Laura looked in the mirror and moved her hair back over her ears the way Randolph liked it. Then she shook her head and pushed it back into place.

The lobby of the Cataract was so filled with people she was able to slip out the front door without having to stop and talk with anyone. She made her way down the sidewalk towards the Merchants along the shaded side of the street. It was still intolerably hot, and Phillips Avenue was buzzing with the news of the trial. She watched the street corners again for Morgan but saw no sign. She wondered if she would ever see him again.

The lobby of the Merchants was filled with people carrying bags and porters wheeling trunks. Living Bear and He Dog were dressed in buckskins, looking very picturesque as they carried cheap leather bags through the crowd. Fat, little C.C. Arends was waddling behind them with a heavy bag in each hand. He Dog smiled and walked towards her. He said, "We go."

Laura directed her comments toward Arends for interpretation. "They are going back to Pine Ridge, Mr. Arends?"

"Yes, Mrs. Bowman," the little fat man said, wiping the sweat already beading up on his forehead. "Mr. Powers and Nock said that there is no more money to house witnesses here in Sioux Falls, so they are going home until the trial starts again next month."

She smiled and nodded at the Lakota men. "Tell them I hope they have safe journeys and enjoy seeing their families again."

Arends translated, and He Dog replied in Lakota. "He said it will be good to get back to civilization."

They laughed, and the men moved to the door, the Lakota leading the way and Arends struggling with his bags. She thought that, to them, their life on the reservation was probably much more civilized than what they saw here in Sioux Falls. She could only imagine how different they would find New York if they ever got there.

Speaking of New York, she thought to herself, she'd better get to the dining room on the second floor and Randolph Hiller. She sighed, thinking she'd rather be going to Pine Ridge—or anywhere else in the world, for that matter.

In the dining room, he'd taken a seat next to the window and was sipping coffee. His nose looked painfully swollen.

"Ahh, Mrs. Bowman, late as ever, I see," he said, standing and bowing to her. "I see a month in the hinterlands has not changed your sense of punctuality." He reached for her hand to kiss it, but she avoided his attempt and slid into the chair across from him. Hiller's theatrics had been romantic in New York, but here in Sioux Falls they seemed contrived. She had no desire to draw attention to herself or Hiller.

"Randolph, what are you doing here?" she said before he launched into another dramatic display. He frowned.

"This is hardly the reception I expected, Laura. After all, I came all the way across the country to visit you."

"I know," she said. "I'm sorry, it's just that I have a great deal to do, and you surprised me."

"What is it you are 'doing'?" he said. "It appears to the people here you just squire around Mr. O'Day in public—and God knows what in private." He poured some cream into his coffee and stirred it. "I was actually somewhat jealous when I heard about it, but have been informed that Mr. O'Day is known for using beautiful women as . . . cover I guess you'd say."

"Mr. O'Day has been nothing but a complete gentleman, unlike you, I may add," she said. "And whom I chose to 'squire around with,' as you put it, is definitely none of your business."

Hiller laughed. "Well, I don't doubt Mr. O'Day's intentions are honorable, in that regard anyway. I was just making conversation about your 'work' here." He shook his head. "Honestly, Laura, you've become so sensitive."

"Randolph, why don't you just go back to New York, and I'll see you in the fall," she said. "We can sort things out then, after my divorce is final."

"Laura, I don't understand. We can enjoy this time out here . . ." he waved his hands. "here in the 'Heartland of America.' You won't have to spend your time with this Indian thing."

Laura dropped her fork on her plate, creating much louder clamor than she intended. The conversations at the surrounding tables quieted, and the other customers turned toward them. She picked her napkin off her lap and threw it on the table. "I have things to do this afternoon." She stood and walked out of the room.

"Laura . . . Laura," he said. "What am I supposed to do?"

There was a considerable disturbance in General Miles's outer office. He looked up at Baldwin over the papers covering his desk and shook his head.

John Mayberry burst through the door, barking behind him at the corporal serving as the general's clerk. "The general will see me, for God's sake. What the hell is wrong with you?"

General Miles waved at the clerk, "It's fine, Corporal, Captain Baldwin and I are just finishing up."

As the clerk was still pulling the door shut, Mayberry threw a telegraph message on the general's desk on top of Baldwin's carefully constructed report.

"It's the worst outcome possible, General. This is an utter catastrophe." Mayberry stomped around the room, almost tripping over Baldwin's outstretched boots. He made no effort to move them.

"Mr. Mayberry," General Miles said calmly, "would you please tell us what you are so excited about?"

"It's the Plenty Horses trial, General. It was a hung jury." Mayberry pointed at the telegraph message. Baldwin put his hand forward and looked at the general, who nodded. He picked up the message and studied it. Generals did not pick up messages thrown on their desks like trash.

"It looks like they'll hold another trial on May 25, General." Baldwin said. "They had a hung jury, six for murder and six for manslaughter."

"That's exactly what I said," Mayberry almost spit across the table. "They're going to have a brand new trial. It'll be in the newspapers for months now. God, when will this all go away?"

General Miles leaned back on his chair and mumbled as if to himself, "Can't believe they want to hang that boy."

Mayberry slapped his hand on the table. "Whether they hang him, let him go, or send him to prison doesn't really matter. What matters is that every day this is in the newspapers, it's bad for you, General. It does nothing to help your campaign and makes it very difficult to raise money."

Captain Baldwin cleared his throat. "It would seem justice should be the prime motivator here, Mr. Mayberry."

Mayberry turned on him. "Don't give me any of your condescending attitude, Captain Baldwin. Your report on Wounded Knee could still get the general's campaign killed. Without my edits we would already be . . ."

"What edits?" Baldwin said, sitting up straight in his chair. "What edits to my report, Mr. Mayberry?"

Mayberry looked at the general. "In the interest of, umm . . ."

General Miles frowned across the desk. "Stand down, Captain Baldwin." This was the voice that had commanded men on the battlefield. In a softer tone he said, "Mr. Mayberry and I decided some portions of your Wounded Knee report would not be included in the public version submitted to Congress."

"What portions, General?" Baldwin was working very hard to stay restrained. His voice shook a little.

"The primary focus of the report was that the damned fool Forsyth disobeyed orders and mixed his men with the Indians. We lost at least twenty good soldiers because of his blundering. His mismanagement—"

"General . . . sir." Baldwin had never interrupted the general before. "Excuse me, General, but what part of my report was edited?"

"Not really edited, Captain," the General said. "Certain elements were de-emphasized . . ."

Mayberry shook his head. "Oh, for God's sake, Baldwin, how could you be so goddamned stupid to say those idiot soldiers of yours chased women and children down for a mile and then executed them?"

Baldwin's dark eyes drilled into Mayberry. "I put it in the report, because it's the truth, Mr. Mayberry."

"Captain," General Miles said, holding up a hand as if to separate the two men. "Captain, I made the decision on what material was relevant to include in the Wounded Knee report."

Baldwin seethed as an uncomfortable silence filled the room. When General Miles made a decision, he was not likely to override it. "Yes, sir, General Miles," he said with a nod.

"Now that we have that settled," Mayberry said. "What are we going to do about this trial? The longer it goes on, the more exposure we have to potential . . . harmful revelations. General, I'm already having a difficult time raising sufficient money to adequately fund . . ."

General Miles held up a hand. "Mr. Mayberry, justice will be served one way or another. I'll take this under consideration." He picked up the telegraph Baldwin had thrown across the desk. "In the meantime, I suggest we all get back to doing our jobs. That will be all, Mr. Mayberry."

With a dirty look toward Baldwin, Mayberry left the room, loudly pulling the door shut behind him. It was not loud enough to constitute a slam but forceful enough to record his displeasure. *He's always a politician*, Baldwin thought.

"He's right, you know, Captain Baldwin," the general said in a much more friendly tone than he had used earlier. "We're going to need to watch this trial very closely." He leaned forward across his desk, "And I don't want Mayberry involved any further. Captain Baldwin, I'm going to need you to monitor these proceedings, in person if you must."

"General, I can't be party to . . ."

"Captain Baldwin, you will follow orders with the honor and integrity you have always conveyed." He pushed together the papers covering his desk. "This report is fine. Pass it off to someone else to complete. I want you to concentrate on the Plenty Horses trial."

The tone of General Miles's voice made it very clear there was not going to be a discussion regarding Baldwin's assignment. "Yes, sir," he said standing and saluting. "I'll review the information available and keep you informed, sir."

"I think you'd better get out there, to Dakota. You need to make sure you are, mmm . . . a party to all aspects of the information on the second Plenty Horses trial. I also think you need to insure that the Culbertson Trial in Deadwood is prosecuted appropriately."

"Yes, sir. Are you concerned about the Deadwood trial?"

"Look, it appears the Indian boy is going to be guilty. If he's sentenced for killing a white man and the white men in Deadwood are found not guilty of killing Indians, we're going to have a situation that will drive Mayberry even crazier than he already is."

"Have you spoken to him about the second case?"

General Miles shook his head. "The less Mayberry's involved in military affairs, the better." He shook his head and put a hand through his full head of curly gray hair. "Captain Baldwin, politics are going to drive me to distraction."

"Yes, sir," Baldwin said. "I suppose it's the price you pay."

"It's the price *we* pay, Captain Baldwin. It's about time we get some leadership in Washington. We can make a difference, Captain."

"Yes, sir." Baldwin rose. "I'll catch the next train to Dakota. Thank you, sir."

Laura threw her bag across the hotel room. Damn that Randolph Hiller. What was he doing here, anyway? She had no desire to spend the next two months listening to his pompous utterings. She wondered what she'd been thinking when she had seen him in New York.

She shook her head. The one good thing he'd done was convince her to get the divorce. She would have never had the courage to do it herself, would have never known to go to South Dakota, would never have changed her life. For that she was grateful for him.

Now that she'd started the process, she had no desire to get into any kind of a relationship, especially with Hiller. She'd taken orders from men all of her life, first from her father and then Jonathon Bowman. She didn't need to take orders from Randolph Hiller too.

Laura took a deep breath and looked in the mirror. She had something to offer, something besides a pretty face. She wanted to do something. She straightened her dress and made her way out of the Cataract to the Edmison-Jamison building across the street where most of the Sioux Falls lawyers had offices.

Nock and Powers had their offices on the third floor. The lawyers focused on divorces occupied the second floor, where Laura's lawyer, George Abbot, had his nicely furnished office. The third floor required another flight of stairs and had much darker and less cared-for furnishings.

The elderly lady sitting at the front desk looked surprised to see her. "Mr. Powers told me this morning to just to stop in and meet with them," she said. "I'm going to help research their case."

"I don't see anything on either Mr. Nock's or Mr. Powers's calendars."

"Could you please check with Mr. Powers?" Laura had not come all the way up here to be shut out.

The lady gave Laura a dirty look and slowly rose. She knocked on the door to the left and entered. A minute later, Powers came out, now dressed in a loose-fitting shirt and shook her hand. "Come in, come in," he said. "Now, what can we do for you?"

"I'm Laura Bowman. I spoke with you earlier, Mr. Powers . . . about helping on the Plenty Horses trial," she said.

It was clear he had been expecting a paying client. "Oh, I see Miss, err, Mrs. Bowman is it?" He gestured to the wall between the offices. "My partner and I, well, we need to rebuild our practice, you see, with paying clients. We won't have much time for the . . . case."

"It's Mrs. Bowman," she said. "But I can help you. I can help you get Plenty Horses acquitted."

"That's very nice of you, Mrs. Bowman," he said. "But we just won't have that much time . . ."

"If you knew you'd be handling my divorce work after the trial was over, would it help give you more time to work on the Plenty

Horses case?" she said. "Currently Mr. Abbot has started preparations, but I don't think he has actually done very much."

Powers eyebrows rose. "Well, we don't usually participate in the divorce proceedings, but that would certainly be a help to our practice."

"Very well," she said. "I'll have paperwork sent up this afternoon. Do you think it'll cause problems with Mr. Abbot and the other lawyers?"

Powers laughed. "By taking on the Plenty Horses case, our office has become somewhat of a pariah in the legal community anyway."

"Then you can use our help . . . on the case?" she said.

Powers rose and went out his door. Laura heard him knock on the door in the next office and then a murmur of conversation. In a minute he returned with George Nock walking in behind him. Nock took the other chair in front of Powers's desk.

"Nice to see you again, Mrs. Bowman," Nock said. "I understand we'll be working with you both as a client and as a . . . helper."

"Yes, that's what Mr. Powers and I discussed."

"So, Mrs. Bowman, what do you plan on doing to help us?"

"I know about the case. I was with Mr. O'Day when he interviewed a number of people. We can help run down some of the leads to help get Plenty Horses acquitted."

"When you say 'we,' Mrs. Bowman . . ."

"Oh, I have an associate who was at Wounded Knee and knows the reservation. He can help get you the information you need."

"But he isn't here?"

"I'll make connection with him once we understand what types of information you'll need."

Nock looked across at Powers and sighed. "As you are no doubt aware, all twelve members of the jury at Plenty Horses's first trial voted him guilty, guilty of either murder or manslaughter. The only question was the punishment they wanted to extract."

"What do you need to do to get an acquittal?" she said.

"We need to show a state of war to more forcefully demonstrate that Plenty Horses was a soldier and Casey was a spy."

Powers broke in, "I just got a telegram from General Miles's office. He's sending Captain Baldwin out to monitor the case. Baldwin was the one who did the Wounded Knee investigation. He wants to talk with Plenty Horses tomorrow."

"Can I sit in on the interview?" she said. "I've been at two interviews with Plenty Horses with O'Day." She nodded to Nock. "He likes me."

Nock smiled. "She's right. Plenty Horses was more comfortable talking with O'Day when she was around. Very well, Mrs. Bowman, you're hired. Although, like Mr. Powers and myself, you won't be paid." He smiled. "We're meeting Captain Baldwin at nine o'clock in the morning tomorrow, at the jail."

Nock nodded at Powers, and they both stood. On the way out the door, Nock stopped to speak to the elderly secretary. "Mrs. Frazier, Mrs. Bowman here is going to be working with us. Please give her all the assistance you can."

Mrs. Frazier gave them a forced smile. "Of course, Mr. Nock."

Laura thought Mrs. Frazier would be less than pleased about taking any orders from her, but she smiled at her anyway. "I'll have the file from Mr. Abbot's office sent right up then," she said. "Thank you, Mr. Nock. I hope I can be of some assistance."

"I'm sure you will, Mrs. Bowman," he said none too convincingly.

Laura let herself out of office and tripped down the stairs to the second floor. She went down the hall to Abbot's office. There was nobody in the waiting room except the secretary, who was in her early twenties and very attractive. Laura considered just leaving a message with the secretary but decided she needed to start taking more responsibility. She could not avoid confrontations all of her life. She asked to see Mr. Abbot.

The secretary knocked on his door and slipped in. After a few minutes, she reemerged followed by George Abbot. His hair was in a slight state of disarray and he was struggling into his coat. As Laura followed him into the office she looked at the leather couch in the back wall of the office and decided she was probably interrupting a nap.

"Mrs. Bowman, as I told you last week, there's nothing for you to do but stay in place until August when you will be a full resident of South Dakota. My associates at the Cataract are gathering the information we'll need to prove your continued residency."

"Yes, Mr. Abbot, I understand. However, that's not what I'm here for today. I'm afraid I've had a change of heart in utilizing your services."

"What? Mrs. Bowman, if you've changed your mind about getting a divorce, I assure you that . . ."

"No, Mr. Abbot. I've decided to utilize another law firm to represent my interests. Please send me an itemized bill for your work thus far and send my file up to Powers and Nock."

"Powers and Nock? They don't handle divorce proceedings. I was assured that . . ."

"Assured by whom, Mr. Abbot?"

"Well, by the referral of . . . Mrs. Bowman, surely . . ."

"Mr. Abbot, please see that my file is sent to Powers and Nock." She rose and nodded at him. "Thank you, Mr. Abbot."

She turned and walked out of the office. Laura had always been one to avoid conflict at all costs. Her stomach ached, her heart was beating wildly, and her breath was short. But she'd done it. She'd taken control.

Laura's knees were weak, but she ran down the stairs and into the street. Crossing into the Cataract, she felt better and stronger than she had in . . . she didn't know when. She found herself looking along the street corners. No dark figure lurked there.

Chapter Eleven

MAY 1, 1891

LAURA FELT A HIGHER SENSE of purpose than she had . . . well . . . in forever. She was going to have an impact, not just as window dressing for a reporter or as the wife of a banker or the daughter of a businessman. She was going to be doing actual work to free an innocent man. Sure, she'd purchased her way in, but she was going to make a difference.

She had a quick breakfast in her room and descended to the lobby. Haddie McKenna and the other ladies were back to their usual spot. Before she could slip out, she saw Elenora Flatt being dispatched to come over and get her. She decided to just grit her teeth and bear it and made her way across the room before poor Mrs. Flatt got there.

"Will you have a cup of coffee with us, Mrs. Bowman?" Haddie McKenna said pointing to the empty chair Mrs. Flatt had vacated.

Laura smiled and took a different vacant chair. "I can only stay a minute as I have errands to run."

"Surely with the trial over, you'll have more time," Haddie said. "I do believe you were with Mr. O'Day almost every instant this past week."

"Yes, it certainly was busy," she said. For some reason she did not want to tell these ladies she was now working with Nock and Powers. "Now there are just so many things to get caught up with."

Abigail Johnson poured coffee into her cup. "When I spoke with Mr. O'Day yesterday, I didn't see you," she said. "It was so much fun speaking for the public. I can't wait to read my name in the *New York World*." She put a hand on Laura's arm, "Of course, I suppose that's old hat for you."

Laura smiled. "I don't really read the newspapers much," she said. "I really must be going."

Haddie held up a hand. "I understand you terminated your relationship with Mr. Abbot's legal firm yesterday."

The unspoken question, "why?" hung in the air, but Laura had no intention of discussing it. "Yes, I did," she said with a quick smile. "Good day, ladies."

She now knew where at least some of the referral fees Abbot had mentioned were going. It made sense that since Haddie monitored the comings and goings at the Cataract, she would provide information to entrepreneurial lawyers like Abbot. She recalled she'd barely been checked into her room fifteen minutes before a message arrived with Abbot's card and a bouquet of flowers.

She wondered where O'Day was and if he'd already taken the train back to New York. She hadn't had time to speak with him since the verdict was read. She also kept her eyes on the side streets, but Morgan was nowhere in sight. She didn't think she was going to be of much help to Nock and Powers unless she found him.

Nock was already in the waiting room to the jail. He'd gone back to wearing a suit, although this one was older and more worn than his courtroom attire. He looked older and tired. The trial had taken a toll.

She greeted him, and he blinked a couple of times as if trying to remember why she was here. "I'm excited to be able to work with you," she said. He smiled, and they sat back down.

A tall, middle aged man with gray-tinged dark hair strode into the room. Even if he had not been dressed in a captain's uniform, it would have been obvious he was military. Some people have the ability to take command of a room just by walking into it. Laura's father was that way, and in the right element, her husband Jonathon was as well. Nock immediately lost the sleep in his eyes and stood to shake hands, "You must be Captain Baldwin. How nice to meet you."

Baldwin's eyes were dark, almost black, and framed by his dark eyebrows that seemed to attack a person when he stared at them. He smiled, showing sparkling white teeth. He wore no facial hair to cover his jutting chin. At almost fifty, Baldwin had not lost his ability to command a room. "You must be Mr. Nock. Thank you for arranging for this interview."

"Anything we can do to promote justice, Captain. This is Mrs. Bowman, our . . . she's helping us with the case."

Baldwin nodded, "Mrs. Bowman, you are an attorney?"

She stumbled on her words, as Baldwin had flustered her. "Oh, no, nothing like that, I'm afraid. I'm just doing what I can to help."

Baldwin nodded. His appearance was so dramatic, they had not noticed Phillip Wells come in behind him. Wells also had the ability to command a presence himself, but in Baldwin's shadow, he was easily overlooked. "Is there anyone else we are waiting for? I want to get on the afternoon train to Deadwood," Captain Baldwin said in a deep voice.

Nock gestured to the jailor with the thick red sideburns who led them through the jail cells. As she had in her previous trips through the cells, Laura kept her eyes focused forward. She had no desire to make eye contact with criminals.

Chairs were set up in a semi-circle around Plenty Horses's cell door, as they had been for the previous interviews. As before, Plenty Horses sat on a stool with his blue blanket wrapped around him. The euphoria of the hung jury had worn off. He was still in jail and looked paler and more drawn than ever. He nodded to each of the men as they were announced and smiled at Laura. Baldwin looked sideways at her when she received the smile but made no comment.

Captain Baldwin asked a series of questions regarding what Plenty Horses was doing on the day in question and how he came to shoot Casey. His questions were short and to the point, as if he was used to people responding to him. His dark, hard eyes never left the Indian man, even as the conversation went back and forth through Wells's interpretation. Laura thought Plenty Horses conducted himself well, but he didn't say anything to Baldwin that hadn't come out in the first trial or the interviews with O'Day.

Abruptly, Baldwin slapped his knees and said, "That's all I need. Thank you, Mr. Plenty Horses and Mr. Nock. I'm now finished."

He was the first person to stand, making his height advantage even more pronounced. Laura smiled again at Plenty Horses, and he lifted the corner of his mouth shyly. The chairs scraped on the concrete floor, and the jailor led the way between the blocks. Laura looked over to her left and stopped dead still.

Sitting in the back of the cell block was a familiar figure. "Mr. Morgan," she said, "what are you doing here?"

The jailor was still walking ahead of them and had to stop and retreat two steps. Baldwin almost ran over her.

"There ain't much to do here in jail but sit," he said. "An' listen to you guys talk with Plenty Horses."

Laura turned to the jailor, "What's he doing here?"

Before the jailor could respond, Morgan came to his feet and said, "They said it was public drunkenness and creating a disturbance, I guess." He rubbed his chin. "At least that's what I remember."

She tried to look around Baldwin to talk to Nock, "Mr. Nock, we need to get Mr. Morgan out of here, he . . ."

Baldwin's voice fairly boomed through the jail cell even though he didn't speak very loudly. "Hell of a way for a Medal of Honor winner to act . . . Corporal . . . err . . . *Mr.* Morgan."

The prisoner shook his head slowly. "There's honor, and then there's honor, Captain Baldwin. You think your medals make you act honorably?"

Baldwin maintained his focus on Morgan. "Mr. Nock, can you please find out if Mr. Morgan has been assigned a bail amount? I will write a check before I leave today."

Laura was conscious that her mouth was hanging open. Baldwin gently took her arm and steered her forward. "Good day, Mr. Morgan." He turned his head back toward the jail cell. "I suspect you will be out within the hour."

Morgan coughed. "Thank you, Captain," he said as he settled back into his bunk.

"Can you meet me at the diner?" Laura said around Baldwin's body. "When you get out, I mean?"

Morgan didn't respond. Baldwin ushered her out into the waiting room.

"How do you know Morgan?" she said to Baldwin once they were in the room.

Baldwin turned to look at Wells, "Did you know he was here?"
Wells shook his head. "No, sir. I haven't seen him in months."

"Captain Baldwin," Laura persisted. "How do you know Mr. Morgan?"

"Morgan was a soldier, and a pretty good one," he said. "He's had some problems since . . . last winter."

"You mean Wounded Knee," she said. "I know he was there."

"Yes," he said. He turned to Nock. "Mr. Nock, I'll be checking out of the Merchants Hotel within the hour. Please send a messenger for Mr. Morgan's bail check. If he needs an attorney, I'd appreciate it if your firm would handle it. I will cover all expenses, of course."

"Gentlemen, and ma'am," he said nodding to Laura. "I have to pack. It was nice meeting you." He strode out of jail with Wells following a step behind him. As the door closed behind him, the energy level of the room dropped.

Laura turned to Nock. "What was all that about the Medal of Honor?"

He put his hands up. "I don't have any idea what that entire exchange was about. Frank Baldwin is one of the few people in history to have won two Congressional Medals of Honor, one in the Civil War and one in the Indian Wars. He's General Miles's man."

"And I," he said brushing the front of his ill-fitting suit. "Have no intention of not following his orders." He turned to the jailor, "When can Mr. Morgan be released?"

"I don't know, sir," the jailor said. "I'm not sure if . . ."

"Look," Nock said holding up his hand. "You heard the Captain. I'd suggest you find whoever has the authority to set bail for Mr. Morgan and get it done as quickly as possible, presumably before Captain Baldwin leaves on the afternoon train."

"Yes, sir," the man said, pulling at his sideburns. He wrote a note and gave it to one of the younger police officers in the room.

"Thank you," Nock said. "Please send someone to my office when things are arranged." He motioned to the door, and Laura accompanied him out.

"I had no idea an army captain had so much authority," Laura said. Nock led her over to a bench next to the courthouse steps.

"Captain Baldwin isn't just another officer, obviously," Nock said. "With his Medal of Honor credentials and close association with the most powerful man in the army, perhaps the country, he can feel confident issuing orders." Nock laughed a little. "I have to admit, I quite enjoyed issuing a few orders on his behalf. Usually nobody listens to me."

Laura smiled. She liked Nock's self-deprecating sense of humor now that she had met him outside of the courtroom. "Will Captain Baldwin's interest in the case help or hurt Plenty Horses?" she said.

Nock shook his head. "I'm not certain. It depends on where he comes down on some key elements. It's interesting he's going to Deadwood to evaluate to the indictment of the Culbertsons."

"Who are the Culbertsons?" she said. "It's in Deadwood? That's in Dakota as well?"

"South Dakota," he said. "Yes, it seems a few weeks after Wounded Knee and the Casey shooting, a Lakota man was killed on the slopes of Bear Butte. Four white cattlemen have been charged. Rumor has it General Miles refused to turn Plenty Horses over until the Culbertsons were charged, but I haven't seen any proof of this."

Nock shook his head. "I don't envy Sterling. After prosecuting this case of an Indian killing a white man, he has to go to Deadwood and oversee the prosecution of some white men for killing an Indian. The cases shouldn't have anything to do with one another, but in the right circumstances, they could be put side by side in the public eye as a measure of racial justice."

"I'm not sure I understand, Mr. Nock."

"Well, how would it look if Sterling wins his case here in Sioux Falls and Plenty Horses is convicted but then loses his case in Deadwood and the white cowboys go free? Or even more inflammatory, what if the reverse happened and an Indian goes free but the whites are convicted?"

"But the cases aren't related?"

"You're right, they aren't, and the one should not impact the other, but that doesn't mean they won't." Nock shook his head. "I wish I had the time or funds to monitor that case in Deadwood."

"I'll go!" she said.

Nock laughed. "You . . . go to Deadwood?" Nock shook his head. "I'm afraid that would not be . . . appropriate, Mrs. Bowman." He put out his hand on her arm, "Although I appreciate your enthusiasm."

"You said I could help. All I'd need to do is evaluate what's happening, listen to what's being said and report back to you," she moved to the edge of the bench, almost falling off. "I can pay my own way out. I'd still be in South Dakota so I wouldn't impede my residency. Please, Mr. Nock. I truly do want to help."

He studied her and moved his head from side to side. "Well I suppose . . . if you really wanted to. Let me get some more information on when the Grand Jury indictment is scheduled and if the witnesses would be willing to talk to you."

"Thank you, thank you, Mr. Nock. You'll find I will be very helpful."

She rose and started walking back towards the Cataract, almost skipping, and then stopped. "And Mr. Nock, will you let me know when Mr. Morgan's released? I want to . . . err . . . coordinate efforts with him."

Nock waved his hand. "Certainly, Mrs. Bowman. Orders, orders, everyone gives orders," he said, but he was smiling and waved her off.

LAURA SAT AT THE SAME TABLE at the back of the little diner. She worked on her second cup of coffee, alternating drinks from a glass of water. Morgan was late. She'd said to meet her there at 3:00 and it was now almost 4:00. Between the lunch and dinner crowd, the diner was empty except for the cook.

She'd been watching people walk by, evaluating their silhouettes, their shadows cast in the window, trying to determine if one of them was Morgan. Twice she'd felt her heart stop when a likely looking candidate crossed the window but then felt it drop when it passed the door. She looked at the clock on the wall behind her again. She'd give him another five minutes and then—

He opened the door and walked into the diner, blinking to get his eyes used to the darkness after the bright sun on the street. When he saw her, he nodded and slowly made his way to the table, sliding out and sitting in the chair across from her.

"I'm glad you made it, Mr. Morgan," she said.

"Why did you want to see me?" he said, his voice croaking like it hadn't been used in a while.

"I thought you might like something to eat," she said. "The food in that jail cannot be very good."

He nodded and muttered, "Thanks."

"Two specials and another cup of coffee please," she said to the cook. He nodded and brought over a fresh pot along with a semi clean cup. She poured a cup and slid it towards him.

"Thank you for protecting me the other night," she said in a soft voice.

He made a small laughing noise. "I guess you weren't really looking to be protected."

"Randolph Hiller is . . . *was* a friend of mine from New York. A friend . . . who helped me," she said. "He just surprised me at the wrong time."

"I saw what kind of friend he is," he said.

"What's that supposed to mean, Mr. Morgan? Who are you to . . . ?" she paused to calm herself and took a deep breath. "Anyway, I have news. We're going to work with Nock and Powers to help Plenty Horses."

"You and this Hiller guy?"

"Of course not. Randolph has nothing to do with it," she said. "He has no skills whatsoever. You and I are going to help him."

Morgan raised the brim of his hat. She could make out a little bit of the scar on his forehead. "What the hell are you talking about?"

"I spoke with Nock and Powers. They have no time or money to gather any more information regarding the Plenty Horses case. Since he was going to be convicted on every jury vote, they need something else to get him acquitted. You and I are going to find it."

"Just how do you see us doing that?"

"As we've discussed, there are some things that didn't look right at the trial: White Moon lying about something, about Wounded Knee, I don't know, anything that might make a stronger case. I'm going to go to Deadwood and attend the Grand Jury for the Culbertson's trial. And then—"

"You're what?" He slid his chair back.

"I'm going to Deadwood."

"Alone?"

"Well, I don't know. It can't be that far. It's still in Dakota. And I thought you could go back to the reservation and see what was missed in the first trial."

Morgan sat back as their food was delivered—roast beef and mashed potatoes. He hesitated but then dug in, eating with a relish. Laura watched him as he hunched over and shoveled food to his mouth, wiping a bit of gravy from his mustache, and thought about how different he was from Randolph Hiller. Exact opposite, almost. Hiller was tall and was developing a paunch, where Morgan was short and lean. Hiller was eloquent and his voice was clear and pleasing. Morgan said little, and when he did, it was more like a low growl. She also thought Hiller treated her like a pretty accessory, and Morgan treated her like an intelligent woman.

"So, what about it Mr. Morgan? Will you help me with Plenty Horses?"

"His lawyers know you're doing this?"

"Of course, they look forward to our input," she said as she thought, *and the fee for handling my divorce.*

"I don't have any money . . . money to travel . . ."

"Don't worry about that, Mr. Morgan. I'll cover your expenses," she said. She lowered her eyes. "Umm as long as it doesn't go for . . ."

Morgan looked up, his blue eyes hard under his heavy blond eyebrows. "You mean so I don't drink it all up," he said. He held his knife above his plate, a drop of gravy slowly made it down the length of the blade and hung on the tip. "A man does what he does, and sometimes he ain't very proud of it. But he's always got to own up to it. I get too drunk sometimes and get to fightin'. I wish I didn't, but I do. If you can't live with that, just leave me alone."

Laura thought that a week ago, she would have avoided confrontation, changed the subject or left the room. "Mr. Morgan, did you drink so much before you were at Wounded Knee?"

Morgan watched her, his face as stoic as the Lakota. When she didn't drop her gaze, he finally did and resumed cutting his roast beef. "I don't know," he said. "Not that it matters so much one way or the other."

Her voice was soft, and she put a hand on his arm. "Let's get this Indian boy acquitted, Mr. Morgan, and then see what tomorrow brings."

He didn't move his arm, but stopped mid-bite, frozen. Then he nodded and brought another spoonful of mashed potatoes to his lips. "So what do we need to do?" he finally said in a low voice.

She removed her hand and started picking at her food. "Did you get a chance to speak with Mr. Nock during your . . . umm . . . release?"

"Not really."

"I'd suggest we stop by their office and tell them our plans so they're aware specifically of what we're doing."

"I need to talk to Baldwin first."

"I'm afraid he is already gone, Mr. Morgan. I heard him say he was going to be on the afternoon train to Deadwood."

"Not much of a man to let grass grow beneath his feet is he?" he said.

"Was he at Wounded Knee too?"

"No, he's a staff officer for General Miles."

"Mr. Nock said he won two Medals of Honor, one in the Civil War and one in the Indian Wars. How do you know him?"

"I don't. After Wounded Knee, he was investigating, and he talked to me."

"What did you tell him?"

Morgan paused and took a deep breath. "I told him the truth, Mrs. Bowman."

"At the jail, he said something about your Medal of Honor."

"I don't have a Medal of Honor. I don't know how you get a medal for killing people."

"But he said . . ."

"Don't we have something to do or someplace to go?"

Laura put her silverware down and signaled to the cook. "Very well," she said. "Let's go visit Nock and Powers."

They made their way down the street and to the Cataract, walking side by side. Laura started to slide her arm through his, but thought better of it when he moved away from her on the sidewalk. The movement was subtle, and he made no expression, but she felt a screen of tension between them, and sensed putting her arm through that screen would not be good for either of them.

They made their way up the stairs to Powers's and Nock's office. Mrs. Frazier gave Laura a pasted-on smile but lost even that when she saw Morgan. "We would like to see Mr. Nock and Mr. Powers, please," Laura said. She wished they would have had time to make Morgan bathe.

Mrs. Frazier put her pasted-on smile back on. "Mrs. Bowman, without an appointment . . ."

Nock came out of his office and looked surprised to see them. "Mrs. Bowman and Mr. . . . . Morgan, isn't it? Is there anything wrong?"

Laura rose and started walking into Nock's office. "I want to update you on the activities Mr. Morgan and I are going to undertake to help you with the Plenty Horses case," she said. She turned and motioned for Morgan to follow her. He slowly made his way in her wake.

Nock shook his head and followed them into his office. "So, Mrs. Bowman, what is it you want?"

"I've decided I'm going to go to the Grand Jury hearing in Deadwood. It'll only be for a few days, and I'm sure the experience will be helpful. Have you made arrangements yet?"

"Well, it was only a few hours ago . . . I'll have Mrs. Frazier get the address and scheduled time . . ."

"Fine," she said. "I'll work with her. Is there anything specific I should be watching for?"

"Well," Nock said, "anything we can do to promote the idea that there was a state of war between the Indians and the citizens would be beneficial." He stroked his mustache thoughtfully. "You won't be able to attend the actual Grand Jury proceedings, of course, but I may be able to get you a meeting with the primary witnesses. I have a friend out there who'd help. I'd like to know exactly what interest General Miles and

Captain Baldwin have in that trial. I'd also be interested in what kind of a chance Sterling has in getting a conviction out there if the Grand Jury does indict them. If he gets Plenty Horses hung and then the Culbertson's get off, he'll have some serious questions to answer."

"Very well, Mr. Nock," she said. "That will be very exciting. I thought Mr. Morgan could return to the reservation. Is there anything specific he should see?"

Nock observed Morgan, who kept his eyes to the floor. "You're familiar with the area, Mr. Morgan?"

"He was at Wounded Knee," she said before he could answer.

Morgan gave her a deadly stare but said nothing.

Nock sat back in his chair. "Really, Mr. Morgan? I suppose that might explain the interest Captain Baldwin took in your . . . err . . . situation. You're a member of the Seventh Cavalry?"

"Was. Ain't no more," he grunted.

"Have you read Captain Baldwin's report on Wounded Knee? Do you agree with his evaluation?"

"I don't know about it."

"I'll have it provided to you before you go. I'd be interested if there was anything left out. Umm . . . Mr. Morgan, you do read?"

Morgan ignored his last comment, "What did it say?"

Nock picked at his mustache and pushed some papers around his desk. "It was very critical of Colonel Forsyth's tactics. It said he violated orders by mixing the soldiers with the Indians."

"He's right. That was damn stupid," Morgan said in a flat voice. "What else?"

"Mmm . . . that it was regrettable . . . etc. . . . etc. The newspapers have covered the story, but it hasn't generated much public interest. Nobody wants to hear very much about Indians being killed."

"I'll look at it and then talk to some people at Pine Ridge."

Nock shuffled some of the papers on his desk. "Even though he was our witness, Mr. Wells seemed to avoid talking in detail about Wounded Knee with us. I don't know if it was the injury to his nose or something else. I believe he'll be returning to Pine Ridge very soon. Perhaps you can coordinate with him."

"Wells is a pretty good man," Morgan said. "I'll talk to him."

"You'll need to find . . . err . . . expenses . . ."

Laura perked up. "I told Mr. Morgan I would finance his endeavor. And I'd also wonder about what White Moon testified. He's lying about something."

Nock put his fingers into a steeple and nodded. "I see . . . hmmm . . . very well. Mr. Morgan, you need to be sure to be back here by May twenty-eighth or the bail supplied by Captain Baldwin will be forfeit and a warrant will be issued for your arrest."

"Don't worry about that, Mr. Nock," Laura said. "Mr. Morgan will be back in time. You can have Mrs. Frazier send over the copy of Baldwin's report to my room at the Cataract. I'll get it to Mr. Morgan." Abruptly, she rose, nodded to Nock and made her way to the door. Morgan shook his head and followed in her wake.

As they went down the stairs, he said, "You sure are full of spit and hellfire on this."

"Mr. Morgan, I've not felt like I've been in charge of anything in a long time. I'm going to get Plenty Horses acquitted." He mumbled and shuffled his feet. "Where are you staying Mr. Morgan?"

"I don't . . ."

She reached in her bag and pulled out a handful of bills. "You will take this and get yourself a room at the Merchants Hotel. We can study Baldwin's Wounded Knee Report there. I'll send you a note when I've received the report." She wrinkled her nose. "And perhaps you could bathe, Mr. Morgan."

Morgan held the money up in front of his face for a moment and then slid it into his pocket. Laura marched across the street to the Cataract. "Good day, Mr. Morgan. Once we review the report, you can make your travel arrangements." Just before she got to the doorman, she stopped and turned back to face him, "And, Mr. Morgan, I'm depending on you . . . depending on you to . . ." She decided she shouldn't tell him not to drink whiskey. "Well, good day," she said and entered the Cataract.

As Laura made her way up the stairs, Tara Monroe fell into step with her. "You seem to be very busy, Laura," she said.

"The Plenty Horses trial has me running all over the place," Laura said. "You heard they had a hung jury."

Tara shook her red curls. "Oh, yes, it was the talk of Sandy's. I think they were angrier about not being able to pay off the bets than they were anything else."

"So . . . you spend a great deal of time . . . at the drinking and gambling parlors."

"Well, tea drinking at the Cateract just isn't my style, I'm afraid."

"It sounds dangerous."

"Men are only as dangerous as you let them be. As long as you don't let them control you, the power is in your hands."

"Well, Mrs. . . . I mean Tara, I appreciate what you do. I don't know if I can control men the way you do."

"Laura, you're a good woman," Tara said. "I'd suggest you be careful about that Hiller man. He seems to think he has your future planned and is celebrating."

"You know Randolph?"

"He's a regular at Sandy's and probably other places," she said. "Dump him, Laura. You can do better. But now I have to go."

Laura was so startled she could not respond. By the time she formulated a response, the actress was gone down the hallway.

Chapter Twelve

May 3, 1891

IT APPEARS TO ME Mr. Nock's evaluation was correct and Baldwin's primary concern was that Colonial Forsyth disobeyed orders." Laura had several pages of the report spread over the breakfast table in the dining room of the Merchants. "They interviewed some of the junior officers, who said the smoke and confusion led to the killing of the women and children. It just says that the deaths of the noncombatants was 'unavoidable and unfortunate.'"

She leaned across the table. "Does that compare to what you remember, Mr. Morgan?" she said.

Morgan sat quietly, holding one of the papers with his right hand. Laura noticed the paper was trembling like a leaf in a light breeze.

"Mr. Morgan, are you all right?" she said, reaching a hand toward him, but not making contact. It occurred to her that presenting the report to Morgan was not very sensitive to what he'd been through. In fact, it was incredibly insensitive. "I'm sorry, Morgan," she said. "I should have thought . . ."

"It's all right," he said quietly as he set the paper down. "Smoke and confusion . . . that's true."

"Do you know the men they interviewed?"

"Some of them . . . but they don't sound right." He pushed the paper aside and took another drink of coffee. "Maybe you sound different when you talk to another officer, especially someone like Baldwin."

Laura set back in her chair and said nothing. Then she straightened her back and spoke very quickly. "Morgan, at the end of the report . . ." she put her finger on one of the pages. "It recommends you for the Medal of Honor."

He dropped his silverware on the table and slid his chair back. It was as if a wall had just gone up between them. "Well, I think I have what I need," he said in a low voice. "I'll be leaving on the afternoon train."

"Morgan . . ." she said as she reached across the table again. He acted as if he never heard her.

"You stay and finish breakfast. I'll get out to Pine Ridge. Then you can get some time with your . . . friend," he said.

The urge to throw a glass of water into his face was tremendous. She was angry, and she was hurt. "Very well," she said gathering the papers. "We both have things to do to help Plenty Horses."

"Why are you doing all . . ." he spread his hands out over the table, "this?"

"I want to make a difference," she said. "What about you? Why do you care?"

His voice rumbled. "Sometimes a man has to try to help."

"You didn't do anything wrong . . . at Wounded Knee, I mean," she said.

"How do you know what I did or didn't do?"

"I read the report," she said.

"Reports say whatever the army wants them to say."

"I can tell, Mr. Morgan. I know you. I know you'd never do anything . . . inappropriate."

"You can't tell what a man does in war, Mrs. Bowman." He stood and set his napkin down. "Thank you for breakfast . . . and everything."

She handed him an envelope. "There's some cash in there. If you need more, write to me at the Cataract."

He took the envelope and put it in his vest pocket without looking inside.

"Laura, how nice to see you," a friendly voice came from behind him. Randolph Hiller was making his way across the room. When he saw Morgan, he froze.

Morgan looked at him and then back to Laura. He squared his shoulders to Hiller and took a step toward him. "It seems like I should apologize for smacking you in the face," he said leaning even closer to the taller man.

The conversation at the adjacent tables quieted. Laura was acutely aware of a man in the far corner scraping his knife across his plate.

Morgan shrugged, and the corner of his mouth rose in a small smile. "Don't think I will, though." He turned and tipped his hat to Laura. "Goodbye, ma'am." He walked by Hiller and out of the restaurant.

"What are you doing with that dirty little cowboy?" Hiller said as he slid into the seat across from her.

"Mr. Morgan and I are working together," she said as she gathered the papers in front of her. "I thought you were going back to New York."

"I'm quite enjoying myself here," he said. "Besides, New York just isn't the same without you. I want to spend some time with you Laura, only you."

"It wouldn't be advisable for us to be seen together," she said.

"You mean until after the divorce," he said. "Oh, don't worry about that. We're a long way from New York. Once you're free, we can go back to the way we were and not need to sneak around. "

Laura dipped her head. Why did his voice have to be so loud . . . and so obnoxious? She didn't want everyone in the restaurant to hear him. The fact of the matter was, she'd decided she'd made a mistake ever taking up with him in the first place.

"I'm sorry, I have work to do," she said. "Perhaps we can talk later."

Laura rose, turned her back on him and walked out of the restaurant.

Chapter Thirteen

May 10, 1891

LAURA WONDERED IF SHE'D made the right decision as the train made its way through plains of Dakota. The car was just a row of wooden seats, nothing like the luxury sleeper she'd taken from New York. The sound of the tracks was pulsating all day as she struggled to find a comfortable position on the unforgiving wooden seat.

Alex Winters, the little hardware salesman, had finally shut up. Over her objections, Nock had given the little man a few dollars and asked him to watch over her on the train trip to Deadwood. His little green eyes had lit up at the prospect, and for the first hour he had engaged her in what she assumed was courting patter, at least in the hardware salesman world. She had firmly asserted she was a married woman and hadn't the least intention of straying, even with such an attractive man as Alex Winters. He finally admitted that, yes, there was a Mrs. Winters back in St. Peter, Minnesota, and, yes, she was very lucky to have him, indeed.

Without the pressure of a romantic interlude, he put his focus on describing his great success as a business man. She now knew what a prosperous place Deadwood was. He evidently made three or four trips a year from Minnesota out to the still-booming Deadwood to unload excess inventory from his Saint Peter store at a substantial profit and great personal risk. He said that it was no place for a lady as beautiful as she, "Unless, of course, you count the ladies of the evening." The little man had rubbed his chubby hands together in a manner that led her to conclude that a good share of the profits of the trip would soon be reinvested with said ladies of the evening.

Laura had grown up with the boasting of men who somehow always related money and power to sex. Why would he think she would find the fact he used the profits from the trip on prostitutes instead of his family attractive in some manner? She wondered if Mrs. Winters was rubbing her hands together at the prospect of little Alex being out of town so she could engage in some extra activity with the saloon owner down the street. She shook her head. Tara Monroe was influencing her thinking.

Despite his objections, she'd managed to see Morgan off the day before in the company of Phillip Wells. He'd remained skeptical about her trip to Deadwood but didn't argue with her. She'd prepared herself mentally for a knockdown drag-out fight like she would have had with Jonathon or her father if she'd decided to do something they were opposed to. Morgan just shook his head, sighed and wished her well.

She'd done everything she could to avoid Randolph Hiller. She was aware she was being incredibly rude and issue-avoidant by not talking with him, but she just wasn't ready to deal with him. The woman who had the affair with Hiller didn't exist anymore. The woman who had needed someone . . . anyone to find her desirable was left back with the dark memories of New York. She didn't need Randolph, didn't need Jonathon, and didn't need her father to tell her what to do anymore. But she still hadn't found the courage to confront Hiller directly. Laura shook her head. She needed to take the next step.

The further west they went, the more the plains of Dakota appeared desolate. Laura watched them pass, mile after mile, green rolling fields of natural grass. The railroad had established ambitious little towns that supported a railroad venture across the state, but for the most part, they were only little train stations with one or two little wooden buildings and a house or two. For several miles on either side of the towns, there would be fields of corn and a few farmsteads gathered around a sod hut.

Laura had traveled through upstate New York, New England, and, on her honeymoon, even to Europe. She'd seen rural areas, but the plains of Dakota shocked her. They were so isolated, so desolate, like another planet. She found it shocking she could look out for what seemed like a thousand of miles, and see not one sign of a human being.

Crossing the wide Missouri River at Chamberlin was a welcome break, but then the landscape became even more rugged and more remote. The fields became less green and the breaks between settlements even more pronounced. Winters told her she was lucky to see the area in the spring. In a very few months, the oppressive heat of midsummer would turn the area into a gray dessert. "Some years, they get some rain and it won't look too bad, but if a drought hits, this area is barely suitable for Indians."

"Are the reservations near here?" she asked.

"Naw, they didn't want them too close to the railroads so they cut the reservation up to make this pathway through the middle of the state. The Pine Ridge and Rosebud are to the south, Crow Creek, Standing Rock, and Lower Brule to the north." Winters quite liked the fact that Laura was talking to him again.

"Will we see any Indians out the window?"

"I doubt it. It's miles and miles down to the reservation and since the events last winter, the Injuns are keeping a pretty low profile." He looked like he hoped what he said was true. "At least that's what they tell me. We finally got those bastards out of the way for good."

Laura started to open her mouth but decided against it. Arguing appropriate Indian policy or any politics would mean listening to Alex Winters for longer than she could bear.

At the end of the second day, they finally made out the dark shapes of the Black Hills in the distance. The mood on the train picked up perceptibly as people moved to the windows to watch the distant black lumps on the horizon become rolling hills of pine. The train stopped at Rapid City, where Laura and her baggage transferred to another train that wound through the mountains to Deadwood.

Nock had arranged for a lawyer friend of his to meet Laura at the train station, and Alex Winters was more than happy to turn her over. His hopes of a sensuous trip across the state had evaporated quickly. "You must be Mr. Bacus," he said shaking hands with the man in the gray suit standing on the platform. "Mr. Nock told me to watch for you. This is Mrs. Bowman."

G. Winston Bacus shook hands with Winters and politely grasped Laura's hand. When she turned her head away, she saw him slip

Winters a bill, no doubt the second installment for the fee Nock agreed to in order to watch over her. She was more than a little put out that Nock had paid Winters to chaperone her, especially since he was totally worthless, but sights and sounds of Deadwood grabbed her attention.

"Mrs. Bowman, I've made a reservation for you at the Martin-Mason Hotel, just two blocks from here," Bacus said. "While it doesn't live up to your New York standards or even those of the Cataract, I'm sure it'll meet your needs for the short time you'll be here."

"Thank you, Mr. Bacus," she said. "Deadwood certainly has an energy about it."

He smiled and stroked his thick black beard. He wore a gray suit but no vest, and his tie was slightly askew. "You should have seen the place ten years ago, Mrs. Bowman. We were full of 'energy' then. However, we're quickly becoming civilized." He pointed out a large six-story brick structure across the street from the station. "Don't you think our new town hall is impressive?"

"Yes," she said. "It's very admirable." Laura thought the structure was impressive for this part of the country. It would be a small office building in the outskirts of New York. She was much more interested in the buildings along the famous main street, two blocks in the other direction. She was disappointed when Bacus led her away from the downtown toward the other side of the city hall.

"You'll be just a block away from the courthouse," he said.

"Will we have time to investigate the rest of Deadwood?" she said pointing towards the main street.

He laughed. "Mrs. Bowman, I think most of Deadwood may be a little uncouth for such a fine lady."

Laura heard some of the raucous noise from the main street of Deadwood, but followed Bacus in the opposite direction to the Martin-Mason Hotel. A part of her wanted to experience the famous street life of Deadwood, but she was there for a purpose and was incredibly tired from the ride across South Dakota.

"As per George's direction, I've arranged for you to sit down with the primary witnesses in the Culbertson case tomorrow morning. The Grand Jury is in two days."

"Mr. Bacus, is there a chance Sterling will get a conviction?" she asked as they entered the small hotel.

He ran his hand over his flowing hair, then stroked his beard. "A year or two ago, they wouldn't have gotten an indictment on them. You just couldn't put a white man on trial for killing an Indian. But the Cultertsons aren't very popular out here. Everybody knows they're horse thieves. Most of the town knows they're guilty. Still . . . you don't prosecute white men for killing Indians."

THE NEXT MORNING, Laura got up early and took a stroll. Deadwood was crammed into a deep valley. The surrounding high, rolling hills were mostly clear of timber. There were a few black tree trunks bearing evidence of fire. The town itself was nestled into the floor of the valley, which was no more than a half a mile wide. Houses or, more accurately, shacks clung to the sides of the hills.

But for all of the reputation of a Wild West town, the main business district appeared rather tame to Laura, at least at seven o'clock in the morning. Two-, three- and even four-story brick buildings lined the streets and sported a full array of domestic businesses. She stopped for coffee at a small diner. The cook behind the grill said it was at the far end of the street where the famous, nefarious Deadwood thrived. He called it the "Badlands" and said it probably wasn't the place for an unescorted lady to stroll, even in the morning light.

Laura thanked him and made her way back to the second floor of the building across the street to Bacus's office. He'd set up a small room for her to talk to the witnesses of the alleged Few Tails murder.

Bacus met her at the door and introduced her to an Indian woman called Clown and strong-looking Indian man named One Feather. Bacus then introduced her to a small white man in an ill-fitting suit named Chancery who would provide translation both for their meeting and the Grand Jury hearing the next day. He had a high, squeaky voice and offered nothing in the way of conversation not related to the translation.

Clown looked uncomfortable in a simple blue dress and wrapped a blanket around herself. Laura thought she was probably in her late twenties or early thirties. She spoke slowly, with little emotion, patiently waiting while Chancery translated. The athletic-looking man named One Feather had more energy and inserted some commentary, but let Clown carry the narrative for the most part. It was clear they had told their story several times and didn't expect to be believed. Clown in particular appeared to be going through the motions.

The men, One Feather and Clown's husband, Few Tails, had obtained permission from the Pine Ridge agent to hunt the area around the sacred Bear Butte and to visit the Crow across the border in Montana. Clown was not sure what they had done to obtain this permission, but she was very grateful they had. She was proud that Few Tails was a close relative of Oglala Chief Young Man Afraid of his Horses and he was considered one of the leading Oglala at Pine Ridge. He'd brought her along on the trip, and One Feather brought his wife, Red Owl, their baby and their daughter Otter Skin Robe to help with the processing. The men hunted, the women processed.

Nonetheless, it had been a wondrous two months away from the drudgery of Pine Ridge. The weather had held through the late fall and the hunt had been very successful. They had all the meat they could carry to take back to the reservation. The trip to visit the Crows had also been very successful. Because Few Tails was regarded as a future leader of the Oglala Lakota, the Crow were very generous with the gifts they gave them to be distributed at Pine Ridge. Clown could not help but wonder if another one of the reasons they had received so many wonderful gifts was the interest the Crow boys had in thirteen-year-old Otter Skin Robe. One Feather and Red Owl had watched their daughter carefully, but she still drew considerable attention. Clown joked with Red Owl that they would have to establish an armed guard around Otter Skin Robe if she got any more beautiful as she became a woman. Red Owl said if any of those randy Crow boys showed up in Pine Ridge, One Feather would run them off with a switch.

On the way home, they stopped where the Alkali Creek flowed into the Belle Fourche River. Clown was looking forward to getting back to Pine Ridge. They were only a hundred miles away, so there would only be a few more days of travel. Seeing different country every day was invigorating, but setting up and tearing down camp was getting tiresome. Looking at Bear Butte looming in the distance, Clown couldn't help but wonder how her ancestors did it, dragging all of their equipment on a travois behind a horse. Putting everything into a wagon was trouble enough.

That evening, a soldier boldly rode into their camp. He had sergeant's stripes on his coat and a long mustache. "What are you doing here?" he said without greeting. "Why aren't you on the reservation?"

Few Tails stepped forward with his hands outstretched to his sides. "We have a permission slip from the Pine Ridge agent," he said. He slowly reached into the front of his blanket and retrieved the paper. It was dirty and smudged from a number of white men's fingers. They'd been stopped and asked for it several times in the last two months but usually in a much friendlier manner than this sergeant portrayed.

He took the paper and squinted at it in the fading light. He handed the paper back to Few Tails with a grunt. "Looks in order," he said. "I don't know why they'd give you permission to travel out here given everything that's happened."

"We left the reservation weeks ago, far before the Ghost Dancing," Few Tails said. "Even if we'd been there, we wouldn't have participated. The agent will tell you that my cousin, Chief Young Man Afraid of his Horses and I do not support the ways of the past." Few Tails had learned English at the agency and was very proud of his ability to talk with the whites.

"Even so," the sergeant said. "After that trouble at Wounded Knee, things are a mite tense in this part of the country. You'd best get back on the reservation soon."

"That's where we're headed, Sergeant," Few Tails said. "We should be there in in a few days. Would you like to stay to eat?"

"Naw, I need to get to the ranch, seven mile yonder still before dark," he said. "Get straight back to the reservation, though, as quick as you can." The sergeant waved and rode off into the dying light.

They'd heard rumors the whites were afraid of the Ghost Dance and had sent soldiers to Pine Ridge. Few Tails had never participated in the ceremonies to return to the old ways. Young Man Afraid of his Horses had been dealing with the whites since they put the Lakota on the reservation. He said it was no use pining for days that would never return. Lakota men should learn to adapt to the whites' way of living. Few Tails had adopted his cousin's attitude that the whites called "progressive" and it had served him well. Now almost forty, Few Tails saw no use in dreaming of old days that would never come back.

"We will have to be careful," he said to One Feather. "The sooner we get back to Pine Ridge with all this meat and the gifts from the Crow, the better."

They had just finished eating and were putting the food away when they had another visitor. A short man dressed like a cowboy, not a soldier, rode into their camp. He accepted a drink of water and took it upon himself to walk around their camp peering into the tipis like he owned them. Clown did not like how the short man with the light colored mustache had no respect for their privacy, but Indians do not confront white men. Few Tails and One Feather followed the man closely, and Clown saw that her husband had a revolver stuck in his pants under his blanket.

Finally, the white man rode out of the camp, barely mumbling a good-bye. Few Tails and One Feather conferred and decided one of them should stay on watch through the night. Few Tails stood the first watch, and Clown felt him crawl back into the tipi in the middle of the night.

As soon as it was light, they packed the camp. Clown was just rolling the skin of their tipi up when she heard another rider approach the camp. She recognized the cowboy from the night before, only now he was dressed in a fur hat and a coat like the ones the soldiers wore in the winter. Again, he nosed around the camp, and with a few words, he left.

Few Tails and One Feather went out to gather the ten riding horses they had used for hunting and the two teams to pull the wagons while the women packed the camp as quickly as they could. They did not have to state their uneasiness. Even the baby seemed quiet. As soon as the men returned, the final items were thrown onto the two wagons and the teams were harnessed. They were going to waste no time in getting away from this spot and under the protective cover of Bear Butte.

Few Tails jumped up into the wagon seat next to Clown. He patted at the rifle sitting between them and took the reins. He turned and looked back at One Feather. Otter Skin Robe was sitting close next to him and Red Owl was close on the other side of her, holding their baby daughter. The wagons lurched heavily with the loads as the teams labored to get into a rhythm. Clown thought it was really good to get away from the camp site. She looked forward to getting to the other side of Bear Butte that day.

Gunfire erupted from a sage-covered knoll ahead and to their right. Clown felt her husband reach over for the rifle just before something slammed into her chest like someone had punched her. The impact threw her back against the seat. As her body bounced back forward, another punch slammed into her leg, spinning her around. She felt herself falling off the wagon and weakly reached for the seat before tumbling to the ground. The horses spooked and started running. The wheels of the wagon narrowly missed running her over and then stopped.

Clown rolled onto her side next to the wagon. She heard One Feather's wagon thunder past on the other side, turning off the road and heading back the way they had come. Out of the corner of her eye, she saw two men in fur coats riding toward her on black horses. She closed her eyes and remained completely still. The sound of One Feather's wagon was receding into the distance. The men on the horses circled the wagon and stopped at the back. "These ones are dead. Andrew, climb up there and take the wagon back to the ranch. I don't think you hit none of the other sons of bitches. I thought I told you to wait until they were all the way to the dry bed."

"Aw, hell, we got these, didn't we?" another voice said. "An' they ain't gonna run far with a full wagon."

"All right, then, Andrew, take this 'un back to the ranch. The rest of you follow me. Maybe we can get them between us and Valleyview."

"What about the dead Injuns and those saddle horses?"

"I ain't carryin no dead Injuns. You want them, you take them. We can come back and round up the horses after we get that other wagon. Let's get goin' before it gets too far ahead."

"Ah, hell," the first voice said, and the wagon lurched forward.

Clown remained motionless with her eyes closed. The pain from the gunshot wounds in her chest and leg was starting to throb, but she held her breath and remained still. She felt the wagon wheels pass within inches of her foot, but it missed her. She heard the men on horseback ride off in the other direction toward where One Feather had driven his wagon across the prairie.

She slowly opened her eye. There was no sound now but the cold wind blowing. Raising her head, she saw the body of Few Tails on the other side of the road where he'd fallen on his side facing away from her. She pulled herself across the frozen road until she could reach his arm. His body flopped back towards her, and she jumped when she looked into her husband's dead eyes. He had bright red spots across his chest and one bullet had taken part of his face.

Clown rolled back away from Few Tails's body and lay on her back in the middle of the road.

Laura noticed Clown kept her gaze on the table through the entire narrative and spoke in a monotone. She looked up and pointed to her chest where one of the bullets had pierced her and moved her chair back to point to her leg where the other wound was. Laura had been transfixed by the story and was surprised that there was not a tear in Clown's eye. She had merely delivered the information.

One Feather took up the story.

Urging the horses pulling his wagon on, he saw the rock in the middle of the road and tried to miss it, but the wagon hit it so hard it almost launched Red Owl and the baby off the seat. She screamed and grabbed for Otter Skin Robe. The team of four horses was on the verge of out-of-control now, running as fast as he could get them to move toward the Belle Fourche River. He'd seen three men on horseback and one on foot firing at them from the sage-covered hill. Most of the fire had been directed at Few Tails, and his friend had fallen almost immediately. As he turned the wagon to backtrack, there'd been a few long distance shots that hit the wagon, but his family was not hit.

Just before they got to the bluffs above where the road crossed the Belle Fourche River, three mounted men emerged and fired at them. One Feather pulled the wagon in a wide turn to avoid them and yelled at Red Owl to get the girls into the wagon box behind them and under a blanket. They were now trapped between the men who had ambushed them and the riders coming directly at them. He lurched the horses aside and headed off the road, across the prairie. The wagon creaked and bounced wildly. Otter Skin Robe screamed, and the baby wailed as they were thrown around the back of the wagon with the equipment and the meat. As they passed the sage-covered hillside, the man hiding there sniped at them. He yelled at Red Owl to keep her head down as he tried to get more speed out of the excited but tiring horses. She screamed as one of the bullets hit her. He put an arm out to try to cover her on the seat next to him as he urged the horses to get out of range of the sniper on the hillside.

Looking back over his shoulder, he saw that the horsemen had met with the original ambushers and were now keeping pace with the wagon, but not trying to overtake it. However, he knew it was only a matter of time before his team gave out or the wagon came apart as they rumbled through the untracked prairie. One Feather decided he needed to buy some time for them to find a road and get to where someone would help them.

One of the saddle horses was still running alongside the wagon. One Feather yelled at Red Owl over the screaming from his daughters behind him, "You are going to have to drive the wagon. I'm going to try to slow them down." Her eyes were large and fearful, but she nodded. The shot had hit her in the arm. Although she was bleeding, she was fully conscious. "Just keep it heading towards Bear Butte," he said.

One Feather handed the reins over to Red Owl and grabbed a rope from the wagon box. He moved to the edge of the seat and stood precariously balanced as the wagon bounced across the prairie. When the horse came back closer to the wagon again, he launched himself off the seat and onto the horse, keeping his rifle in his other hand. He grabbed the horse's mane and got it slowed down well enough to put a rope around it.

Laura pictured the feats of riding at the Wild West shows in New York and thought that One Feather's jump would have been even more impressive than anything she had ever seen, especially since it was life-and-death. The room felt warm, and she found herself breathing hard as she waited for each block of translation.

One Feather said he rode hard directly toward the three men following them. When they were in range, he stopped and fired from the back of his horse. The three men shot wildly at him a couple of times and then dismounted. Two of them got down on the ground and began to snipe at him. He kept moving back and forth to draw their fire. After several ineffectual shots and hearing the bullets whizzing by his head a few times, One Feather wheeled his horse around and rode to catch up with Red Owl and the wagon.

He looped the rope around the saddle horse to the wagon and jumped back on the wagon, taking back the reins. There was a ford at Elk Creek and a passable road he knew about from when they had hunted this area. He urged the tired team toward the ford and told Red Owl to check on their children, who were still cowering under a blanket in the back.

As the wagon approached the crossing, three new gunmen came out of the bluffs by the river, firing at the wagon. He heard the bullets thump into the wagon box. Turning away from the men, he paralleled the road, still pushing the horses at full speed. He drove the team hard, putting as much prairie between the gunmen and his family as he could.

In the distance he saw a white house. If they could get the wagon there, they could get some help, he thought, but he needed to slow the gunmen down. He pointed the house out to Red Owl and handed her the reins. The saddle horse was still running alongside the wagon. He untied the rope and had Red Owl slow the team down enough that he could remount. "Go, go to that white house," he yelled as he reloaded his rifle. He rode back along their trail until he was in rifle range of the men still chasing them. Again, he fired from horseback, moving back and forth across the trail. From a moving horse, his aim was not very good, but he only needed to slow them down until they could get to help. Looking over his shoulder, he saw the wagon was nearing the house and he turned to gallop to it.

Just as the wagon neared the house, which carried a sign that said "VALLEYVIEW POST OFFICE," gunfire erupted from it. Red Owl struggled to turn the wagon away from the little structure and toward the road past it. Bullets thumped into the box of the wagon as Red Owl screamed and urged the horses on. One Feather started firing from his horse as he approached the post office to provide cover for his wife and family. They thundered down the road until they were out of range.

Red Owl was crying from pain and frustration but still kept the wagon moving along. One Feather saw the men who had been following them only pause at the post office and continue their pursuit. It was pretty clear his team would give out soon. They had run for eighteen miles from the gunmen. He saw that another of their saddle horses was following the wagon. He used his rope to capture it and yelled to Red Owl to stop the wagon.

"Get my daughters" he hollered as he approached. Otter Skin Robe had stopped screaming, but the baby still wailed. "Wrap yourself in the blanket, Otter Skin Robe, and get on this horse." She mounted the horse he'd caught and he handed her the baby wrapped in a blanket. "Your mother is wounded and can't carry the child. You just head down the road as fast as you can, and we'll follow. "The young girl's eyes were wide with fright. "You can do this, I know you can," One Feather yelled. "Now go."

One Feather climbed back on his horse. He reached down and pulled his wife up behind him. "We'll cover them," he said. "Hold on as tightly as you can." She nodded and wrapped her arms around his belly. Looking down he saw blood running over his stomach from the wound on her arm.

He urged his horse down the same road Otter Skin Robe had gone. When they were out of rifle range of the wagon, he turned back. The men who had been following them stopped at the wagon. They dismounted and were turning the wagon around. He turned back and caught up to Otter Skin Robe to slow her down.

"They've stopped," he said. "We're safe for now."

He looked over to the left at the looming presence of Bear Butte. They had no food, no water, only a little ammunition, a frightened girl, a wounded woman, a crying baby, two worn-out horses and a hundred miles to go to get to Pine Ridge. He couldn't trust any white men. He didn't feel very safe.

One Feather had become more emotional as he told the story. "It took us three weeks to make it back to Pine Ridge, hiding during the day and riding at night," he said. "It was too cold and we had too little food." He looked up with his eyes full of tears. "Our baby died just east of the Cheyenne River," he said quietly.

Laura felt her stomach drop.

He looked over at Clown who picked up the narrative. "When I came to, everything was gone, everything but Few Tail's body and one horse that had not been killed."

"I rode to a house on Elk Creek, and I knew the people living there. They opened the door for me. But then two men inside got their guns. One loaded his gun and the white girl inside said something. A man motioned for me to go away. I ran before they could shoot me and couldn't catch my horse again."

"I walked to a store at the mouth of Rapid Creek. I was afraid I would cause trouble again, so I did not go into the store, but took shelter in the barn. For four weeks I walked at night and hid during the day until I made it back to Pine Ridge."

Laura was dumbfounded both by the outrage of the robbery and murder by the white men and by the courage of Clown and One Feather and his family. She turned to Attorney Bacus, "Are the white men being brought to justice?"

"Well, that's what the Grand Jury is all about, Mrs. Bowman," he said. "The Culbertsons claim that a band of over a hundred Lakota had attacked them and they fought them off and took their wagons."

"Surely nobody believes that," Laura said. She couldn't take her eyes of the Lakota man and woman who were sitting quietly now in the warm room. "A number of men chased them. Why were only the four Culbertsons indicted?"

Bacus stroked his beard. "Everybody pretty much knows the Cultertsons are horse thieves and highwaymen. They were the obvious choice if they were going to indict someone, but there isn't much appetite to have a trial. If the army didn't pressure the county officials, I'm sure we wouldn't be messing around with it."

"What sort of pressure do you mean Mr. Bacus?" she said.

"Only rumor and conjecture," he said shaking his head. "Nothing that can be proven. There's a chance some of the soliders were involved in the shooting. Certainly they were aware of it. Are we done here?"

"Is there any record of the army's involvement with getting this case prosecuted?" Laura said. "It would be very helpful for . . ."

"Mrs. Bowman, I'm only relating to you courthouse gossip," Bacus said. "Certainly nothing could be admissible in court." He rose from the table.

Laura couldn't take her eyes off the Lakota man and woman staring blankly at her. She'd thought of herself as a victim when she found out about Jonathon's philandering and decided to divorce him. Her petty trials and tribulations paled in comparison to what these brave people had lived through. "Will the men who did this be convicted and punished, Mr. Bacus?"

He appeared anxious to get the interview over. "I couldn't say, Mrs. Bowman. I can tell you that five years ago, they never even would have been arrested, but who knows what will happen with the Grand Jury and, if they are indicted, in court. Now, I would like you all to leave so I can get some work done. Work I get paid for."

Laura rose and left the room. The Lakota man and woman followed her, but just as she got to the street, they slipped back through an alley before she could speak to them. The interpreter, Mr. Chancery, spoke in a low voice. "They took a risk talking with you, Mrs. Bowman. They need to stay hidden until the Grand Jury."

"Are they in danger?" she said.

"Being a Lakota in Deadwood is always a danger, but the last few months have been particularly tense. Besides the trial, there's a renegade in the area breaking into buildings and attacking people. It sounds like he is looking for whiskey more than blood, but it still makes people nervous."

"A renegade . . . you mean a Lakota man?"

"Yes," he said. "A man named Stone Eagle, who had something to do with Wounded Knee."

Laura began walking back toward the hotel, Chancery keeping stride. "Wounded Knee keeps coming up," she said.

"Mrs. Bowman," he said. "What you said about proof the army pushed for the prosecution of the Cultertsons case . . . why do you need it?"

Laura sighed. She had much more important things to do than talk with the mousey little interpreter. "Oh, I'm working with the defense lawyers in the Plenty Horses trial. If we can show the army's involvement linking the two, the lawyers think it might help prove a state of war."

As they approached the entrance to the Martin-Madison, she shook Chancery's hand before he could suggest they talk further. He nodded without saying anything and made his way up the street.

She pulled the drapes of her hotel room and lay down on the bed. As she napped, she dreamed of the cold and of horsemen chasing her, chasing her across the prairie.

When she awoke, there was an envelope under her door. In small neat lettering was a note, "I hope this helps," and it was signed "Mrs. C."

Laura opened the envelope and pulled out several pieces of paper. They were the original notes for what looked to be a meeting between the county commissioners and the county attorney. Even just scanning the rough documents, Laura could see they referenced correspondence between General Miles's office and the County Attorney's office. Her heart raced. With this information, Nock and Powers could prove the letters existed and request copies. Miles had intervened.

The papers shook in Laura's hand. "Mrs. C" must be Mrs. Chancery. She felt guilty now that she had been so dismissive of the interpreter. But she could give proof to Nock and Powers that the army had linked the cases. After hearing the story of what the Culbertsons had done to Clown and One Feather, she had no doubt any jury would understand the plight of the Lakota.

Chapter Fourteen

A<small>ND THE</small> G<small>RAND</small> J<small>URY VOTED</small> to indict?"

Laura felt more alive than she had in a long time. "Yes," she said. "The trial will be held after the Plenty Horses trial is complete."

George Nock smoothed his drooping mustache. "Well, I have to say, Mrs. Bowman, I didn't think you'd come back with anything like this." He was paging through the papers that had been secretly given to her in Deadwood. "We should be able to get into court the fact that General Miles held Plenty Horses from the State until the Culbertsons were charged. I hope they'll allow it, anyway. That'll give us the opportunity to tie the two cases together."

"Based upon what you learned in Deadwood, what do you think the chances are they'll be convicted, Mrs. Bowman? The Culbertsons, I mean," Nock said.

She was very pleased to be asked her opinion. "Well, if they give Clown and One Feather the opportunity to tell the story they told me, I think the chances are very good," she said. "They were compelling witnesses, and the Culbertsons are cold-blooded killers."

"What does Bacus think?"

She took a deep breath. "He's not so certain. In fact, he was quite surprised by the Grand Jury indictment. He said if Plenty Horses is set free, he's sure that the Culbertsons will be set free as well."

"Interesting, isn't it?" Nock said, putting the papers down. "If we tie the cases together and get Plenty Horses acquitted, the murderers of Few Tails and that baby may be set free." He shook his head. "But based on the results of the first trial, if we don't tie them together, Plenty

Horses will be found guilty, and the Culbertsons will still probably go free."

"Perhaps Mr. Morgan will bring back some information we can use, Mr. Nock. I expect him back from Pine Ridge soon," she said.

Nock shook his head. "I admire your confidence in him, Mrs. Bowman, but you shouldn't get your hopes up. I'll be pleased if he doesn't void his bail."

Laura opened her mouth to comment, but thought better of it. She hadn't heard anything from Morgan and Wells since they left. Not a single word. Nock and Powers were still working on the case, but they were also busy with paying clients. The secretary, Mrs. Frazier, was more reluctant to interrupt them for her every time she came to their office.

On her way back to her room, she checked the mail at the front desk of the Cataract, just as she had every day since she got back from Deadwood. She was thrilled to see there was finally a letter for her. The handwriting was small and the letters very stilted. There were several smudge marks in the margins, as if several corrections had been made.

May 18, 1891

Dear Mrs. Bowman,

I am pleased to report I have been successful in getting statements regarding White Moon and Wounded Knee that may help our efforts. The same information was made available to the army several months ago but was not included in the report we reviewed.

I look forward to seeing you when I return.

Sincerely

Mr. A.P. Morgan

Laura read through the letter several times. The news was exciting, but a little anticlimactic. Did she really think Morgan would express his undying devotion and sign the letter "Love, Morgan"? For that matter, did she even want him to?

Chapter Fifteen

May 21, 1891

LAURA OPENED THE DOOR. She didn't remember ordering anything from the service, but that was not to say she didn't. Between waiting to see Morgan again and the anticipation of the trial in two days, she'd been very distracted.

It wasn't the maids. A short man dressed all in black stepped into the opening of the door and pushed his way into the hotel room. Laura was so surprised she took a step back as he pushed a leather satchel at her.

"What's this?" she said, her fingers involuntarily grasping the satchel.

"Open it, Mrs. Bowman. Take your time and study it. My name is J.T. Sateract, and we have some business to discuss." Sateract walked across her room to the tea table, his high, shiny black boots thumping on the floor. "I'll wait right here." He searched the table top. "Don't you keep any whiskey in here, Mrs. Bowman? For the entertainment of your gentlemen callers, I mean."

Laura was so shocked by his behavior that she didn't even try to stop him. She already felt violated. With her hands shaking, she opened the satchel and pulled out several papers. The print was small and official-looking. The title on the first page said something about an affidavit from "Randolph Hiller." Laura felt her stomach churn. Anything with Randolph Hiller's name on it could not be good.

"I'll save you the time of reading the whole document, Mrs. Bowman." Sateract plopped down in the little chair next to the table and took a deep gulp of tea, holding the cup like a whiskey glass. "God, how do you drink this stuff?" He pointed at the satchel. "It's all there. Every illicit meeting between you and Randolph Hiller, itemized and detailed, all of your transgressions against the sanctity of marriage." He sat back and put his head back as if he was making a proclamation to the world: "The Cuckolding of One of the most Powerful Men in New York."

"Where did you get this . . . this filth?"

"Why, Mrs. Bowman, don't you recognize the name Randolph Hiller there? Or did you get him mixed up with all of the other men you had affairs with?" Sateract smiled and lifted his eyebrows. With his greased back hair and dark coat, he could have been a villain in a vaudeville play.

"I never had affairs . . . he was the . . ."

"The only one? Well, he was enough. By the time the yellow rag of a newspaper your friend O'Day writes for gets through with you, the world will think you're the biggest harlot since Tara Monroe."

"This is . . . this is . . . trash. You can't . . ." She dropped the satchel on the floor as if the touch of it defiled her fingers.

"Don't demean yourself by denying it, Mrs. Bowman. Besides Mr. Hiller's sworn testimony, the package includes hotel receipts and gifts to him." He rose and walked across the room, stopping uncomfortably close to her. "And Hiller will talk to the newspapers. He'll give personal interviews . . . very personal."

She shook her head. "We were in love . . ."

Sateract laughed. "Maybe you were. But how is it going to look? Lustful adultery and deceit committed by the beautiful, innocent daughter of Walter Schultz. And it was all done under the nose of the powerful Jonathon Bowman, who was dutifully building the American economy. Can you imagine that? A wife who cuckolds a great man while he's trying to finance the economy to keep this country strong? For shame, Mrs. Bowman, the scandalous things you did to that poor man."

"You can't . . . you can't tell them. It would kill my father . . . my friends."

"I can do anything I want, Mrs. Bowman," he leaned in even closer. She backed to the wall as he advanced . . . his face only inches from hers. "In fact, I'd be willing to extract a little extra payment, just to see if the beautiful Laura Bowman is as lusty in bed as Hiller describes." Laura could smell the musk oil on his skin, the hint of whiskey on his breath.

Abruptly, he pulled back and walked back across the room, "But my employers were quite specific on that count, I'm afraid." He smoothed his long black mustache. "Unfortunately for me."

"I don't have much money . . ."

Sateract laughed. "Oh, you have money, Mrs. Bowman. You have Daddy's money, and you'll have a good chunk of ol' Bowman's money once this divorce charade is done." He waved his hand. "That is, of course, if what is in the satchel remains private. If it's released in the *New York World*, I expect the terms of your divorce will change pretty dramatically, as well as your relationship with good old Daddy."

Sateract sat back down at the little tea table and crossed his legs. He absently rubbed at a spot on his shiny black boots. "It isn't money I want either, although it would be almost as sweet as having you. But again, my employer was rather specific about that issue as well." He sighed deeply and shook his head.

"So here's the deal, Mrs. Bowman," Sateract looked up his dark eyes hard on her. "If you and the little cowboy give the package of information to the lawyers or the newspapers, our package gets to the newspapers and your husband's lawyers too."

"Package?" she said. "I don't have any package."

"The package the drunk cowboy named Morgan is going to give you this afternoon. The Wounded Knee package, Mrs. Bowman."

"How did you know . . ."

"Never mind how we know, but we do. How that drunk stayed sober long enough to collect the information is a surprise to all of us. But he's got nothing we can deal with . . . nothing but his life, and that ain't much. If it were up to me, he'd already be dead, and we would be done with this crap. But, I'm just the courier."

"Morgan! You can't kill him!"

"Nah, there ain't gonna be no killin'. And he doesn't have anything else. He's pretty much lost everything he's ever had. But you, my beautiful Mrs. Bowman, you have everything to lose. That is why you are going to give me that package and keep your mouth shut, or you'll lose everything."

"I won't . . . you can't . . . nobody will believe this . . ." She kicked at the satchel with her foot.

Sateract sighed and shook his head. "Feisty and beautiful . . . oh, the fun we could have had, Mrs. Bowman." He stood and walked across the room to the door and opened it. "Get in here, you dumb son of a bitch." He reached through the door and jerked Randolph Hiller in by the shoulder of his coat. He stumbled and then stood in the middle of the room with his eyes to the floor. "Tell your pretty mistress you're willing to be the poster boy—the kept man who cuckolded the famous Jonathon Bowman. That you ran off with his pretty young wife."

"Laura," he stammered. "Laura, I'm sorry, they said . . ."

Sateract jerked him by the shoulder of his coat again. "Tell her."

Hiller's face rose. She looked into the warm brown eyes that had held her future, that had convinced her there was more to life than the abuse heaped on her by Jonathon Bowman. That convinced her there was truly love in the world. That convinced her she loved him. "Do what he says, Laura. It's the best for all of us. You'll see . . ."

"Get out!" she shouted rushing across the room. She pounded Hiller's chest with the back of her fist . . . pounded him through his upraised hands.

Sateract was laughing. "Mrs. Bowman, Mrs. Bowman, don't hurt our star witness." He pushed Hiller towards the door and put himself between them. With is right hand he pulled the satchel and loose papers from Laura's hand. "Of course these are not the originals, but I'll take them anyway." He held the papers and satchel out and away from Laura like an adult playing keep away with a child and laughed when she reached for them. "You are a feisty one. Maybe once this is all over, we can meet again. You need a real man!"

He backed toward the door, keeping Hiller behind him and the satchel held high. "But until then, Mrs. Bowman, you just wait for your drunk cowboy to bring you the Wounded Knee information. You just hold on to it, and I'll contact you." He had backed all the way into the hallway and waved the satchel at her.

Sateract tipped his black hat and winked. "It was nice to see you, Mrs. Bowman. I hope we can visit again real soon."

Laura slammed the door shut with all her strength. She felt dirty. She wiped her hands on her dress, thinking about the papers in the satchel. It was only a few hours ago she'd been so excited to hear that Morgan would be back . . . back with the information that could get Plenty Horses acquitted. They could save that Indian boy's life.

Then she had a thought. How would she tell him? How could she tell anyone?

―――――――――――――――

THE KNOCK ON HER DOOR came at four o'clock. She'd calculated that if Morgan's train was on time and he didn't hurry to the Cataract, four o'clock would be about right. Laura had no idea what she'd say to him.

She couldn't wait to open the door and also dreaded it. *You're a woman now*, she thought. *Be responsible.*

Laura held her foot in front of the door jam and opened it only an inch, just in case Sateract had returned. Relief flowed from the pit of her stomach and out to her limbs when she saw Morgan. He had his hat off, wore clean clothes and stood well back from the door, looking very uncomfortable.

She pulled the door open and jumped at him, enveloping him in a hug. He stumbled back in surprise. She leaned her head back to see the shocked look on his face and planted a kiss firmly on his lips. His mouth was hard, and she was afraid he was going to yell, but then she felt his body relax and he returned her kiss.

Laura stepped back and motioned him to come into her room, checking up and down the hallway of the Cataract.

"Morgan, I'm so glad to see you . . . to see you're all right," she said.

The tension returned to his body. "Umm . . . yes, it is nice to see you too . . . Mrs. Bow . . . Laura . . . Nice to see you."

She tried to restrain the laugh emerging from her mouth making it come out like a giggle. She hadn't giggled like a school girl in . . . well, far too long. Remembering her promise to herself to take issues head-on, she said, "I've been wanting to kiss you. Do you mind?"

She thought she could identify a blush under his beard and mustache. "Umm . . . no . . . of course not . . ." He took a deep breath. "I haven't wanted to kiss a woman, a real woman, in a long time." He looked toward the window. "I'm glad you did. Sorry if I'm not so good at . . ."

"Mr. Morgan," she said. "You are wonderful. Now that we got that . . . umm . . . out of the way, tell me about your trip to Pine Ridge. But we will come back to . . . you know."

"I've never met a woman like you," he shook his head.

"What did you find in Pine Ridge?" she said.

The tone in the room changed as Morgan pulled a stack of papers out of his bag. "Well, first of all, you were right about White Moon lying. What he told the court was probably the truth, but when he got back to the camp after the shooting, he lied like crazy. He said there were shots fired and he had to take cover, all sorts of things. He told everyone that he fought them off and feared for his life."

Laura made notes on the pad on the desk. "How does that help?"

"Nock suspected as much and asked me to look into it. He'll completely discredit White Moon's testimony by showing him to be inconsistent and a liar. By the time Nock's done, the jury won't know what to believe from him."

Laura thought about the strict military posture White Moon projected. "He'll look like a fool in front of everyone. This will devastate him."

Morgan nodded. "It will. Nock and Powers will force him to either admit on the stand that he lied to the other scouts or to deny it, in which case he's lying under oath. I've got a white trader who heard him in camp and is willing to testify. Either way, his credibility will be shot with the jury."

"He won't like being called a liar."

Morgan shook his head. "Yeah, he puts great store in being an honorable soldier. I can see where he'd have been embarrassed to tell the other scouts he'd just walked away, but he shouldn't have lied to them. The Lakota already hate his guts. Want me to save his embarrassment and not tell Nock?"

Laura shook her head. "I didn't think this was going to be so hard," she said. "I thought what we were doing was right, but . . ."

"Doing what's right ain't always easy," he said.

"We can't let them hang that Indian boy," she said and took a deep breath. "Nock will only use it if he thinks it will help, I guess."

"The next part's worse," Morgan said. "By retracing the trail Baldwin used when he investigated Wounded Knee, I found out that three of our guys from the Seventh rode down a woman and three kids. They had lit out from Wounded Knee during the battle and nobody saw them through the smoke. A patrol from the Seventh saw their tracks and followed them. About a mile away from the battlefield they found the woman and kids hiding behind some bushes. The bastards pulled them out of the bushes and executed them one by one."

"Oh, my God!" she said.

"It was no accidental shooting. They pulled them out of the bushes and shot them dead. There was no doubt. The tracks in the snow and shell casings prove it. They murdered that woman and those children, sure as hell."

"I've never heard anything about this."

Morgan stood and walked over by the window, absently running his fingertips against the glass. "Baldwin must have known. It was in the notes he took for his report."

"But I didn't see it in the report they gave us? What happened?"

Morgan turned to face her. "I don't know. I don't know why Baldwin didn't report it."

"Nock could use that as leverage. If they find Plenty Horses guilty, the army will have to go back after those soldiers."

"But General Miles sure wouldn't look too good in the whole deal, especially when people find out someone in the army covered it up. It's not the kind of thing they want to talk about during a presidential campaign."

Laura sat back in the chair and took a deep breath. "The Wounded Knee battle is bad enough as it is, but if the story of the Seventh Calvary murdering women and children becomes public on the witness stand, the newspapers will crucify Miles."

"Yep," Morgan said. "And it might be just enough to sway a jury and save Plenty Horses."

"That's why," she said staring at the floor. "That's why they don't want Nock and Powers to know."

"Who?" he said. She'd never heard such a sharp tone in Morgan's voice. "What are you talking about?"

"This morning," she said, keeping her eyes focused on her feet. "A man came here this morning and said if you gave your information to Nock and Powers . . . he said they'd give information to the newspapers . . . information about me."

The room was silent. A wagon rumbled along the street below them.

Laura looked up at Morgan, but he didn't meet her eyes. "Don't you want to know . . . Don't you want to know what they'll say about me?"

Morgan slowly walked across the room and took the chair across the table from her. "What they accuse you of doing . . . what you did do or didn't do . . . it doesn't matter," he said. "We've all done things that we aren't proud of."

She ran her fingertips across the tablecloth. "They have proof I had an affair with Randolph Hiller . . . that I was sleeping with him." She saw the hurt in his eyes but just kept talking. "Morgan, my husband flaunted mistresses in front of me for years. He humiliated me in public, in private, in front of friends . . . even family. He did it because he could and nobody would say anything. He took great delight in it. Randolph . . . well . . . he said he cared for me . . . that he loved me."

"Mrs. Bowman, what you did or didn't do—"

"Morgan, that's why I'm here getting a divorce, don't you see? I had to get away from him . . . from Jonathon. I wanted to live . . . to start over."

Morgan took a deep breath. "I suppose newspapers will eat it up."

"Yes," she said drawing out the s. "A man can have affairs, but a woman cannot . . ."

Morgan leaned back in his chair. "And they're blackmailing you?" He shook his head. Laura told him about Sateract. As she told him the things that were said, his face grew tighter and tighter.

"I don't care," she saidn taking a deep breath. "Not anymore. I've admitted it to you. Let them do it."

Morgan stood abruptly. "Just hold on to the Wounded Knee documents," he said poking a finger on the table. "Don't give them to Nock and Powers or anybody else . . . not just yet."

He made his way quickly to the door. As he turned the knob Laura said, "Morgan . . . don't . . . don't do anything . . ."

Without looking back, he pulled open the door and strode into the hallway, letting the door close quietly behind him.

Laura lowered her head to the table and cried.

BALDWIN'S HEAD ACHED. The words on the paper in front of him moved on the page, randomly dancing. He removed his glasses and rubbed his eyes. God, he was sick of these reports, sick of these cases and sick of Dakota. He was an army officer, born to command. Investigations, political wrangling, public relations—those were all duties for civilians and politicians. He was a man of war. Captain Frank Baldwin ached to command again . . . to command real men.

There was a sharp rap on the door of the hotel room. He was so tired he couldn't remember if he'd asked the staff at the Merchants to send up a pot of coffee or not. He set his glasses down and slowly made his way across the room to open the door.

As soon as the latch cleared the jam, the door slammed back into his face, delivering a blow to his nose. Pain exploded through his face, sending waves of stars across his eyes and making his ears ring. Military training kicked in. He broke into a roll toward where he knew his service revolver was hanging in its holster on the back of the desk chair. Before he could get there, however, a boot kicked into his stomach, taking the wind from him. Writhing on the floor, he heard the hammer of a revolver being drawn back. He was aware that the door to the room had slammed shut.

"Jest sit still, Captain." The voice was low and quiet.

His ears were still ringing and he covered his nose with his hand to stop the bleeding. A towel hit him in the face softly. "Bleed into this."

Pulling himself into a sitting position on the floor, Baldwin wiped his face with the towel and leaned back against the bed. He gazed over the top of the increasingly blood-soaked towel.

"Goddamn it, Morgan, what the hell are you doing?" he said in a nasal voice.

The little cowboy pushed his hat up with the barrel of Baldwin's service revolver, exposing the scar on his forehead. "You've been spending way too much time behind a desk, Captain," he said. "If you spent a little more time in the field, you'd still be able to take a punch."

"You're going to prison a long time, Mr. Morgan," Baldwin said. His sinuses were on fire, and his eyes were watering so bad he could barely see.

"Could be, Captain," Morgan said in a quiet voice. "But with all due respect, sir, you deserved it . . . maybe worse. You still might just get it, too."

Baldwin pulled the towel from his face and looked at the blood soaked into it. His nose ached but wasn't bleeding as freely. "What did I do to deserve this, and who are you to mete out punishment to an officer?"

"You sent that Sateract character to accost her. Captain, I know you're an officer and all, but I really thought better of you."

"What the hell are you talking about, Morgan?"

Morgan paused. "A man named Sateract and that New York slime Heller stopped at Mrs. Bowman's room today."

"They did what? What does Mrs. Bowman have to do with anything?"

Morgan set the revolver on the desk, hard metal on the smooth wooden surface. "You don't know anything about it?"

Baldwin shook his head slowly, his ears still ringing and eyes watering. "I don't know what you're talking about."

"Sateract and Hiller visited Mrs. Bowman and told her that if we gave the information I found about Wounded Knee to Nock and Powers, they'd release things about her and Hiller to the New York newspapers."

"Goddamn them!" Baldwin said. The sharp exhale sent a new stream of blood out of his nose. He held out an arm. "Morgan, help me up. Now!"

The cowboy held out a hand and pulled the officer to his feet. He was still a little dizzy and immediately sat down on the office chair. "Do you really think I'd resort to that level of blackmail?"

Morgan shook his head. "I'm not sure what officers are capable of, but I think I believe you now. My guess is you're not that good an actor. If you didn't send them . . . who did?"

Baldwin wiped his face again with a clean spot on the towel. "I can guess, and I don't think the general knows anything about this. If what you say is true, Morgan, I'll help you find those pieces of scum myself. I haven't been stuck behind a desk that long."

"The gallant Medal of Honor winner to the rescue, huh," Morgan said with a small smile. Then he lowered his voice, "But you're still the man who covered up what Davis, Malcomb, and Overstreet did at Wounded Knee. You know they murdered those Indians."

Baldwin shook his head. "I didn't cover up anything. It was in my report."

"I read your Goddamned report. Your name is on it, and there's nothing in there about them tracking down that woman and those kids. You knew those bastards trailed them more than a mile from the battlefield and then executed them. There was no confusion, no mistake, no smoke . . . They just murdered them and you know it."

Baldwin leaned his head back to stop the blood dripping from his nose. "You know I did the interviews. You know what I put it into the report."

"I can read, Captain, and I know there ain't nothing in your report. You might have put something in there orginally, but you also know someone took it out. All I know is it ain't there now." There were a few beats of silence in the room. "And you know I have the same proof."

"You don't understand, Morgan . . . you don't understand politics. There's nothing to be gained by telling the public about what those idiots did. People don't understand what war's like. A lot of innocent people were killed that day. You know that better than anyone."

Morgan walked across the room and looked out the window. He didn't seem concerned that his back was to Baldwin who was sitting at the desk besides the revolver. "You're right, a lot of bad things happened that day, things that . . . that we have to live with." He turned to face Baldwin. "But if telling people about them can save that Indian boy from hanging, it does make a difference! If they find him guilty of murder they'll have to find those three bastards guilty too . . . and the Culbertsons guilty . . . and probably me guilty too for that matter."

"Who do you think 'They' is? 'They' don't have to do anything. It's up to the jury. Morgan, it was war, people get shot . . . people get killed . . . some who are supposed to and some who aren't," Baldwin said.

"If it was war, then the jury has to find that Indian boy innocent."

"How do you know they won't? How do you know they won't acquit Plenty Horses without those . . . shootings at Wounded Knee made public?"

Morgan shook his head. "Come on, Captain. You know how the first trial turned out. We're in Dakota, for Christ-sake. An Indian kills a white man, he's got to . . ."

Baldwin settled back into his chair and moved some papers around the desk, "Morgan, the general can be president . . . president of the United States of America. You know how good he would be as president, how good for the army it would be, how good for the country. He's a good man, Morgan. General Miles will make a great president."

Morgan shook his head. "That Indian boy ain't gonna hang . . . not if I can help it."

Baldwin stood and walked across the room, still a little unsteady on his feet. "So where does that leave us?"

Morgan stood very straight with his shoulders held back, almost at attention. "I'm gonna go kill those two bastards who tried to blackmail Mrs. Bowman, and then I'm gonna make sure the jury hears everything it needs to hear to acquit Plenty Horses."

Baldwin took a deep breath and let it out slowly. "I can't let you kill them, Morgan. You won't do yourself or anyone else any good if you're back in jail."

"I don't much give a—"

"Yeah, I know you don't care what happens to you, but there are other people who don't want to see you ruin your life." He walked over to the mirror and looked at his nose. "Besides, I can't afford to keep bailing you out of jail."

"I got no life . . . not anymore. Captain, I'm telling you that I'm going to—"

Baldwin faced him, standing tall. He was back in command. "Shut up, Mr. Morgan. Here's what's going to happen. You're going to tell Mrs. Bowman she doesn't need to worry about those two men ever again. If they ever even talk to her, I swear by everything that I hold sacred, I'll kill them myself."

"You're not my commanding officer and—"

Baldwin held up two fingers, "Second, Mr. Morgan, you will hold off making what Davis, Overstreet, and Malcomb did at Wounded Knee public. Do not give the information to Nock and Powers. You will give me a little time . . . time to make it right. If the shootings need to come out, I want control how they're presented. Let me tell the story. Let me tell them about war."

Morgan faced him. "Captain, I do believe you didn't agree to cover up those murderers. Hell, you probably didn't have anything to do with giving out those medals for . . ." He sighed and then pointed his finger at the army captain. "But listen . . . sir, I'm not going to let another Lakota boy die."

Baldwin shook his head. "Give me a little time, Morgan. Let me make this right."

"Ain't nothin' ever going to be right, Captain. What's done is done, and we can't ever bring those people back to life. You're right, there were a lot of innocent people that died that day." Morgan nodded at the bloody towel on the floor. "Between that . . . and bailing me out of jail, I guess I owe you something. But Plenty Horses has to go free." His voice became very quiet. "That much . . . that much we can do."

"Mr. Morgan, I give you my word. I'll tell the world about the murders myself if it'll save that boy. But you and Mrs. Bowman can't give the information to Nock and Powers or anyone else unless I tell you to. I need to do it my way."

Morgan nodded. Their eyes met. For a moment Baldwin thought he might salute, but he just lowered his eyes and walked out of the room.

Baldwin rubbed the bridge of his nose. He hoped it wasn't broken. He sighed and started packing his things. It was going to be a long night.

LAURA PACED BACK AND FORTH across her room at the Cataract. She should've never told Morgan. She should have just let them do what they wanted. Damn men anyway!

There was a short knock at the door. When she opened it, Morgan slipped in. She looked both ways down the empty hallway as she closed the door behind him.

"You didn't do anything . . . regretful?" she said.

He laughed a little. "Regretful, maybe, but nothing too bad. Baldwin swears up and down he had nothing to do with Sateract and Hiller." He paced across the room. "I believe him."

"You didn't go after them?"

"Baldwin asked me to specifically tell you that if either of them ever bothers you again, he'll kill them himself." Morgan paused, "I believe him . . . for now. If there's any more contact from them, I'll handle it myself . . . I swear it."

Laura sat down in the desk chair. "What a relief. I'd still rather let them do their worst in the papers than have Plenty Horses hang."

Morgan looked around for a place to sit and ended up perching uncomfortably on the bed. Laura had to admit, she took a perverse pleasure in seeing how ill at ease he was.

"Baldwin said he put the murder of that woman and those kids in the report of his investigation, but somewhere along the line before it became public, that part vanished. It seems the murders might hurt Miles's presidential aspirations."

Laura nodded. "The newspapers will have a field day. No wonder whoever hired Sateract didn't want that to go public."

"Baldwin doesn't want it public either. His image as the 'white and pure Medal of Honor winner' will be tarnished forever if comes out that his investigation covered up the murder of a woman and kids."

"What are you going to do? We have to give this to Nock . . . don't we?"

Morgan sighed and walked across the room. "Baldwin said he was going to make it right. I don't know what that means, but he wanted a little time. I didn't say anything about the White Moon information so we can give that to Nock and Powers in the morning."

Laura absently fingered her skirt. "I wonder if any of this will be enough," she said.

"If we keep the murders quiet for a day or so, that'll keep Sateract and Hiller out of your reputation and give Baldwin some time."

"Morgan, my reputation is the least of our worries."

"It may be easy to say that now . . . here in Dakota. In a few months you'll be back in New York, doing . . . whatever people do there."

"I suppose so," she said, but she didn't want to think about it. "Thank you Morgan . . . for everything."

He hooked his thumbs into his pockets and looked at the floor. "I reckon we've been helping each other," he said in a low voice.

She took a deep breath. "Are you disgusted with me for having a relationship with Hiller?"

"It isn't for me or anybody else to judge you. We've all done things we aren't so proud of."

"I was different . . . different then. Somebody, some man, was always telling me what to do . . . who to be."

He moved back against the window and tipped up his hat, revealing the scar on his forehead in the reflection. Then he pulled it back down. "I suppose I should get back to the Merchants. Don't want the ladies of the Cataract a-talkin' about me being here."

Laura laughed, a welcome sound to both of them. "Morgan, the ladies of the Cataract talk no matter what." She chuckled and said, "It feels good to not be one of them."

They reveled in each other's smile for a moment. "Well . . ." he said and made his way across the room to the door, thumbs still hooked in his pants.

Just as he reached out for the door knob, Laura jumped up and kissed him on the cheek. "Good night, Mr. Morgan."

His face froze. "Um . . . night," he said and went out the door.

Laura put her back to the door and noticed her face in the mirror across the room. It was the first time she'd smiled, really smiled, in a long, long time.

———————————————

BALDWIN LEFT HIS BAGS at the train station and confirmed the train east was to leave at midnight. He looked at his pocket watch and confirmed it was ten thirty. *That should be just about right*, he thought.

Thirty minutes later, he was standing in front of a three-story house a mile to the east of downtown Sioux Falls. A drive led around to the back of the house where it was clear several horses and wagons sat out of sight from the road. The house was wooden framed and lights were lit at either end of the porch, even at this late hour. There was no signage on the front of the house other than the number 512, but Baldwin was certain he had found "The Paradise." The bartender at the little illegal bar had told him he was "almost sure" that Sateract had been headed for the whorehouse when he left earlier that night.

Baldwin checked to make sure his service revolver was in his holster and made his way up the steps to the porch. He briefly debated knocking on the ornate door or barging right in, but the decision was made for him as he found the door locked. He heard piano music through the door as he knocked. The curtain was pulled back and a pair of eyes peered out at him.

When the door opened a wave of music, smoke, and heat flowed out of the door. A huge man with a shaved head stood in the entry way and looked down on him, considering the captain's bars on his shoulders, They would either mean trouble or a big-paying customer. "What do you want?" he said in a low rumble.

Baldwin made a snap decision. He touched the brim of his hat and as the big man's eyes followed his hand, he took a step forward and kicked the man in the groin. In a universal look of agony, the big man crumpled to the floor, clutching himself. Baldwin grabbed the front of his shirt and said in a tight voice, "Sateract, where is he?"

"I would've expected better manners from the famous Captain Frank Baldwin," a female voice from the doorway at the other end of the room said. "Do they give Medals of Honor for kicking citizens in the balls?"

He'd seen her before, in New York, he thought. He dropped the big man who was still groaning and approached the woman. "I wasn't sure he was going to be cooperative." As he moved into a better light, he recognized her. "You're Tara Monroe."

"Why, Captain Baldwin, I'm flattered to be recognized by such a distinguished gentleman."

"I saw you in New York in *My Father's Cousin*," he said. "What are you doing in a whorehouse in Dakota?"

Tara smiled and brushed her famous red curls from her face. "Why, I'm getting divorced, Captain Baldwin. And the Paradise has the best piano player in this dreary place." When she smiled she showed her perfect teeth. "I guess I know what you're doing here . . . what all men do here. But don't get your hopes up, I don't go upstairs. That's for the working girls. I'm sure you'll be well taken care of."

Baldwin stared into her green eyes and got a scent of lavender and whiskey. He shook his head. "I'm looking for a man named Sateract."

She shook her head and stood aside to let him into the parlor. "I wouldn't have thought men were your pleasure, Captain. But who am I to judge what brings pleasure to another human being. There's another house that specializes in—"

Baldwin growled. "Is . . . Sateract . . . here?"

"My goodness, Captain, don't you know it's impolite to ask the identities of customers at the Paradise. Why, the proprietor, Mrs. Becker, will already be angry with you for incapacitating her . . . doorman. If you—"

"I know where I've seen you here in Dakota. You were talking to Mrs. Bowman the other night."

"Ah, yes, Mrs. Bowman. I'm afraid her heart is elsewhere, Captain. She probably isn't your type anyway."

"Sateract is trying to blackmail her. I need to find him."

"Blackmailing Laura?" Tara's voice lost the playful tone. "What's he done?"

"Never mind," he said. "Just tell me where he went."

Men did not give orders to Tara Monroe. However, Frank Baldwin didn't appear to be a man to be trifled with. Besides, everyone knew Sateract was scum. Tara wouldn't be surprised if he did attempt to blackmail the little New York socialite. "I heard him say he was going to Blanca's Room." She pointed at the stairs, "Second floor on the left, Number 4."

Baldwin didn't ask how she knew the room number and who it belonged to. With a final look into Tara's green eyes, he climbed the stairs. When he reached the top, he confirmed that the big man was still writhing on the floor. Tara was leaning on the railing watching him. "I love it when the hero enters during the second act," she said and pointed to the left. Then she knelt down to the big man, "Poor Bruno, let's get you some ice."

Baldwin checked that his service revolver was still in his holster as he stopped at the second door to the left. Grunting came from the first door, but all was quiet in Room 4. He slowly turned the doorknob and found it unlocked. As he quietly pushed the door open, he saw that it hadn't been chained on the inside. The girls and clients at the Paradise evidently did not need to take precautions for police raids.

The room was half lit by a candle on the desk. Baldwin drew his revolver and peeking around the corner of the door. Two naked women lay on the bed. Between them a short dark-haired man snored. A large woman with roll of fat exposed on her naked back was closest to him and had her arm across the sleeping man's chest. A young woman on the opposite side saw Baldwin and started to scream, but he raised his revolver and put his finger to his lips to silence her. She slid out of the bed and grabbed a robe on the chair on the other side of the bed. Baldwin saw she couldn't be more than eighteen or nineteen and was painfully thin. The other woman, who might have weighed twice as much, still slept with her head on Staterac's shoulder.

Baldwin made his way around the bed, past the cowering young prostitute. When he was close enough, he put his revolver right on Sateract's closed eye and said, "Time to wake up, Mr. Sateract." When the large woman with her head on his shoulder started, he put up his hand. "Quiet, ma'am. Mr. Sateract and I need to have a conversation."

The big woman rolled away and got out of the bed. Sateract's dark eye blinked open, and he started move, but Baldwin pressed the barrel of his revolver more forcefully against the closed right eye. "Don't move, Mr. Sateract,' he said. "You and I are going to be traveling companions, and I don't want to have blood all over me."

"Who are you?" Sateract said. "You will pay for—"

"Come along, Mr. Sateract," he said. "We're going to Chicago to talk with General Miles and your employer."

Baldwin glanced at the two naked women. "I'd suggest you ladies quickly dress and remove yourselves," he said. Reaching over to Sateract's wallet on desk he threw it at the larger woman. "You can split whatever money there is in there. I'll be taking care of Mr. Sateract's expenses for the next few days."

"Do you know who I am? Who I work for?" Sateract sputtered.

Baldwin pulled the revolver away from his eye and landed a right hand directly into his nose. He put the gun back to Sateract's head, "We'll have a great deal of time to discuss employers on the way to Chicago."

He looked over at the large woman who was handing a fist of bills to the younger woman. "Please be a dear and have a buggy ready for us. Mr. Sateract and I will be down shortly. We have a train to catch."

The woman tossed Sateract's now-empty wallet back on the desk. She was stuffing bills into her front pocket of her robe. "Oh, and one more thing, ma'am."

"Yes," she said.

"I'm certain Mr. Hiller is in one of the other rooms up here. Please tell him he will be joining Mr. Sateract and myself on our little trip. I'm sure he'll understand that running would not be a good option. He should wait for us in the hall."

By the time Sateract and Baldwin started down the stairs, Randolph Hiller was already dressed and standing at the bottom of the stairs. "I don't have anything to do with—"

"Never mind, Mr. Hiller," Baldwin said as he made his way down the stairs with his revolver stuck in Sateract's back. "We'll have plenty of time to discuss this matter on our journey."

"It's too bad you're leaving us, Captain Baldwin," Tara Monroe said, standing at the other end of the entry way. "You are a most amusing man." Baldwin tipped his hat to her and went out the front door with his two guests.

Chapter Sixteen

MAY 24, 1891

NOCK SCANNED THE PAPERS in front of him. "Very interesting, Mr. Morgan," he said. "And this man, Thompson, is willing to testify?"

"He said he would. There's not much love for the Cheyenne scouts at Pine Ridge." Morgan crossed his legs in front of him. "They think the Cheyenne sold the Lakota out."

Nock nodded his head. "White Moon will look like a fool."

Laura moved to the edge of her chair. "But he told the truth when he testified. What difference does it make that he tried to justify himself to the other scouts?" She couldn't get the image of the proud Cheyenne soldier out of her head.

"Once the jury sees a man exposed as a liar, they stop believing anything he says . . . he loses credibility." Nock rearranged the papers again. "A good part of Sterling's case is the image of brave Lieutenant Casey and White Moon marching toward the Lakota camp for peace. If White Moon's reputation is tarnished, their whole image is tarnished. This case is all about perceptions."

He looked up at Morgan. "This will help, but I'm not sure it's enough to get the jury to acquit. Did you find out anything else?"

Morgan looked across the desk steadily. "Nothing right now."

Nock sighed. "Well, I think Baldwin will testify there was a state of war between the army and the Lakota. Rumor has it Sterling himself went to Chicago to get Miles to say there was no war going on. Miles wouldn't back down. I'm planning on putting Baldwin on the stand, and Sterling will do everything he can to keep the war question out of it."

Laura put both hands on the desk. "Will he testify that Miles tied the Few Tails murder to the Casey shooting?"

"I told him of the documentation you brought back with you from Deadwood, Mrs. Bowman. If I ask Baldwin directly and the judges allow it, he'll confirm there was an attempt by Miles to tie them together."

"Will that help?" she said.

"Every little bit helps, Mrs. Bowman," Nock said. "But you just never know what will resonate with the jury. If we can tell the story of Clown and One Feather, it will generate some sympathy for the Lakota. We tried to do that generically in the first trial, but it didn't resonate. Maybe with these very personal stories, the jury will be swayed."

"You think Sterling will try to keep it out?" Morgan said.

"Sterling's going to object to everything we've got, I'm afraid." Nock said. "And frankly, I'm not certain what the judges are going to allow. Did you say Wells will not be coming back?"

Morgan cleared his throat. "I got the impression someone told him if he wants to stay in the army, he needs to stay out of Sioux Falls. One day he just disappeared, and I ain't seen him since." Morgan shook his head. "You better not count on his testimony."

Laura's eyes brightened. "What about Morgan? Why don't you put him on the stand to testify?"

Nock's eyes dropped to the desk. He fidgeted with the buttons on his vest. "Once a witness is on the stand, he's open to cross-examination."

There were several beats of silence. Morgan finally said, "What Mr. Nock is trying not to say is that, after Sterling tells the court how often I've been in jail the last few months, they aren't going to believe anything I say. Ain't that right, Mr. Nock?"

Laura reached towards him, but could only put her hand on the arm of his chair. "But you've changed, Morgan . . . and after everything you've seen . . ."

"Mr. Morgan is correct that Sterling would certainly attack his credibility. I think we're better off on depending on Baldwin's testimony."

"Will it be enough?" she said. "Will it be enough to get an acquittal?"

Nock rolled his chair back. "You never know what a jury will do, Mrs. Bowman. Thank you two for your help. You've given us a fighting chance. If you'll excuse me, I have to prepare for the trial tomorrow. Mr. Morgan, if you hear from Wells or if any of the other leads you were pursuing come through, please let me know."

Chapter Seventeen

PLENTY HORSES'S SECOND TRIAL was called to order at 9:30 a.m. It had been less than a month since the hung jury ended the first trial, but to Laura, it seemed a lifetime. She no longer had one of the treasured seats with the reporters next to J.T. O'Day. She sat in the back in the gallery, as quiet and out of the limelight as possible. If she could have donned a disguise, she would have.

Morgan was supposed to be sitting next to her, but late last night Nock had told her that Plenty Horses's father had not appeared in Sioux Falls for the second trial. Living Bear had been one of their more effective witnesses at the first trial. They had decided to have Morgan search for him as discreetly as possible. Laura missed seeing the stoic old man standing firmly behind his son.

She was struck by how tired and pale Plenty Horses looked as he entered the courtroom for his second trial. She hadn't seen him since the interview with Baldwin right after the first trial, and he seemed to have shrunk. Part of the difference may have been his clothing. In his first trial, he'd come to court in nondescript slacks and a shirt always hidden beneath his ever-present blue blanket. But for the second trial, he wore a bright scarlet shirt and yellow silk scarf.

The other difference she noticed was a spark in his eyes. Through most of the first trial he had the defeated look of someone waiting to die who just needed to get through the crazy white-man formalities. But today even from across the courtroom, she saw a spark of hope. Given that the hung jury had voted unanimously to convict him and disagreed only on the scale of punishment, she thought this hope may be misplaced. However, Laura felt that, through the efforts she and Morgan put forth, he might have a fighting chance. She doubted he'd been briefed on what had gone on in the last month, or if he had, that he understood it. He would probably never know they had worked for him, but she knew, and that was all that counted. In fact, Laura felt better than she had in her entire life based on what they had accomplished. She only hoped it would be enough.

Sterling's opening remarks were similar to ones he'd made at the first trial. He put significant focus on discrediting Plenty Horses's claim that he shot Casey while defending his people. Sterling said the Lakota spurned Plenty Horses as a "book Indian" because he'd been at a white school for five years. He said Plenty Horses murdered Casey because he thought it would make him appear more like a warrior. He was only trying to impress his fellow Lakota with an act of violence, not acting to protect them.

His first witness was Rock Road, the Cheyenne soldier who had accompanied Casey and White Moon at the start of their mission. He appeared in a jaunty spring suit with loud checks. The roughly dressed man next to Laura said audibly that "civilization seems to agree with the Injun. Ain't none of us could afford a suit like that."

Rock Road repeated the testimony he'd given in the first trial. On cross-examination, Nock asked the Cheyenne if he liked the prisoner, Plenty Horses. He said he did not. Nock prompted him further, "You hate him, don't you?"

"Yes," he said firmly. "If I had been with Lieutenant Casey on that road, Plenty Horses would not be sitting here in this courtroom. I would have killed him on the spot." Laura's attention focused behind the prosecution table to where White Moon sat. He had been there when Casey was shot, and he had just walked away. He face registered no visible reaction to Rock Road's testimony.

He was the next witness to the stand. White Moon sat straight and still as a toy solider as Sterling led him through the events leading up to the shooting again. His answers were crisp and delivered sharply. His face showed no emotion as he described how his friend and commanding officer was shot after shaking hands and talking in a friendly manner with Plenty Horses.

Powers took the cross-examination. Early that morning, he'd spent several hours with Morgan regarding what he'd learned in Pine Ridge so he was well prepared. "Did you tell William Thompson, on returning to camp, that you did not know who shot Casey because the man who shot him was covered in war paint?"

White Moon squirmed uncomfortably. There were several moments of painful silence before he answered. "No," he said.

Powers moved across the courtroom to stand right in front of the witness. "Did you tell Thompson or say in his presence that you fired two shots at the man who killed Casey?"

"I did not"

"Did you say in his presence that you regretted you had missed killing the party who shot Casey to the applause of the other scouts present?"

"I think not."

Laura thought that Powers had set him up beautifully. William Thompson was at this moment sitting in a room in small boarding house in Sioux Falls. Morgan had brought him back with him from Pine Ridge, and Powers wanted him kept away from the prosecution until he could be presented. His testimony would turn the stately, professional-looking White Moon into a lying braggart. From Laura's perspective, it was like watching an accident unfold. She already felt bad about how ridiculous he would look and guilty about her role in eroding his respect. She took a deep breath and reminded herself how important it was that Plenty Horses be acquitted.

When court finally adjourned for the day, Laura made her way out of the courtroom with the mass of spectators. She let the flow of bodies take her out towards the street, not really watching where she was going. As the mass of people negotiated the steps to the courthouse, she was jostled from the side and out of the stench of sweat she picked up a familiar scent of bay oil. She looked up into the face of J.T. O'Day.

"Well, hello, Mrs. Bowman," he said. "I haven't had a chance to see you since I've been back to Sioux Falls."

"Good afternoon, Mr. O'Day," she said. "Did you enjoy your time back in New York?"

His bright white teeth gleamed against his neatly trimmed black mustache. The trip to the east had restored his sense of personal style. "I certainly did. I didn't see you at the Cataract this morning. I wondered if you'd lost interest in the justice system?"

"I've been working directly with Mr. Nock and Mr. Powers since the first trial," she said a little smugly. "I was concerned that continuing to 'assist' you may compromise my position."

O'Day laughed. "Well, I certainly wouldn't want to be the one to compromise you, Mrs. Bowman. I'm sure whatever you're doing for the esteemed defense team is of incredible value."

Laura had the urge to kick him in his condescending shins as hard as she could but miraculously abstained. She forced a smile and said, "Well, we all have to do what we think is right, Mr. O'Day. Have you had a chance to reconnect with your, err . . . friends here in Sioux Falls?"

The smile never left O'Day's face, but appeared more strained. "I've made several friends here, Mrs. Bowman."

She smiled as sweetly as possible. "Of course you have, Mr. O'Day, and my associate has had a discussion with at least one of your more . . . intimate acquaintances."

O'Day's face visibly fell. "Why do you have interest in my friends?"

"Social reporting's so messy, Mr. O'Day, and privacy a treasure."

The crowd opened up, and Laura took advantage of it, leaving the reporter behind her. She hadn't planned on confronting O'Day about his social life unless he chose to print unsavory items about her in the *World*, but his condescension had angered her. She doubted her poorly veiled threat would have any impact on what he would or would not print about her in the social columns, but she felt better that she would at least make him think about it. Once again, Tara's connections and Morgan's research had proven valuable.

Laura had become so adept at avoiding the social institution in the lobby of the Cataract, they stopped even trying to engage her. She was certain they were saying all sorts of terrible things about her. It could be her imagination, but she had a sense the maids and other workers at the Cataract treated her with more respect and friendliness as Haddie McKenna had made her a target of derision.

Chapter Eighteen

STERLING OPENED THE NEXT DAY of the trial by calling the Lakota Broken Arm to recount the shooting. His story was consistent with what White Moon had said, and he also recounted how he took the pistols from Casey's body.

On cross-examination, Nock focused on where Broken Arm received his rations for food. He was successful in showing the rations came from the War Department rather than the civilian Bureau of Indian Affairs. Nock pointed out that if there were no war against the Lakota, the civilians would have been in charge. Since the War Department had taken control, he said, it was reasonable to assume they were on war footing.

Sterling called other witnesses to clarify the actions around the shooting. Nock and Powers did not dispute any of the facts of the shooting itself but used their cross-examination to determine there was a state of war. Plenty Horses's uncle testified that, in the Lacota camp, warriors were wearing war paint because they were concerned they would be attacked by the army at any time.

The final prosecution witness was Thomas Flood, a Pine Ridge interpreter. He said he had talked to Plenty Horses frequently in English. In Nock's cross-examination, he was able to establish that the defendant usually spoke Lakota. Both sides were gearing up for another battle over Plenty Horses's use of an interpreter if Nock called him to the stand again.

With the calling of Sterling's last witness, the judges called the court to recess for lunch, with the defense case to start in the afternoon.

Laura could feel the sense of anticipation in the spectators. The trial had dragged on now for weeks, and they were ready to see it end.

In giving the defense's opening remarks, Powers put more focus on the status of war than he had in the first trial. He had originally portrayed Plenty Horses as driven temporarily insane from the passion of the Ghost Dance. This time he presented him as a hero, bent on protecting his people in time of war. Powers described how the government had failed to keep its promises to the Lakota for years. He said that women and children had been starving because the government would not allocate the rations they were obligated to by treaty, but the Lakota had still not committed any outrages. Then, when the army sent soldiers to the Pine Ridge Reservation in the winter of 1890-1891, the Lakota took it as a declaration of war. Still, they took no action until Sitting Bull was killed and the army attacked and killed hundreds of innocent Lakota men, women, and children at Wounded Knee.

Powers asserted that when Casey arrived at camp threatening to bring more troops, Plenty Horses had no choice but to shoot him to protect his people. Powers told the jury, "Place the responsibility of Casey's blood where it belongs, not upon this deluded chief of the forest, but upon the damnable system of robbery and treaty violations that brought it about."

Powers and Nock kept the focus on the war as they called the prominent Lakota leader American Horse as their first witness. The big man had been a Lakota chief through the tumultuous 1870s and still had a great following. A veteran of nine different trips to Washington, D.C. to negotiate with federal officials, he was no stranger to responding to questions from white men. He'd been unavailable at the first trial, and now Powers wanted to use his presence to create a picture of the Lakota Nation as a unified and solid nation, a nation in a state of war.

American Horse marched confidently to the witness stand carrying a red fan. As he took the witness chair, he immediately turned and scowled at the jury. A veteran leader, American Horse knew how to establish a presence and intimidate white men. Powers launched right into the issue at hand, asking, "What was the condition of the Sioux before the trouble arose?"

Sterling jumped to his feet with an objection before the big Lakota chief could respond. Powers explained to the court that his line of questioning was appropriate because the condition of the Lakota led them into a state of war. To Sterling's relief, the judge upheld the objection, stating, "If such a vast field of inquiry were opened, it would open up the whole dealings of the white with the Indians since the time of Columbus. Such an investigation would be simply impossible." Laura shook her head. How could an airing of the travesties against the Indians not be appropriate to the case?

Undeterred, Powers tried again by asking American Horse about the Ghost Dance craze. Sterling immediately objected again before the Lakota man could respond. In the prep session with Nock and Powers, they had told Laura and Morgan they expected Sterling to aggressively object to any attempt to bring the state of war into the case. The prosecution had built their entire case based upon the presumption that the Lakota were not, and perhaps could not, be at war with the U.S. Army. If Nock and Powers could prove anything to the contrary, they had a chance to beat Sterling.

The judges again supported Sterling and upheld the objection. They said that questions would only be permitted if they showed Plenty Horses's state of mind specifically, not the Lakota people's state. Powers attempted to ask more about the Ghost Dance and the flight across Dakota to Wounded Knee, but all his questions were blocked by objections. Powers dismissed American Horse from the witness stand without scoring any significant points. The proud Lakota chief glowered menacingly at Sterling and then the jury.

Powers then called William Thompson to the stand. Laura squirmed in her seat. This would be the most significant contribution she and Morgan made to the case, yet. As Powers started, she silently mouthed each question. Thompson stated that when White Moon returned to the camp from the Casey shooting, he reported that he didn't recognize the shooter because of face paint. He also told the other soldiers he fired two shots at the retreating killer.

When he had been on the stand, White Moon had told a very different story; he had denied everything Thompson now asserted. The white trader's testimony revealed him as a liar. Laura couldn't see the faces of the jury members very well from her seat in the back of the courtroom, but their body language indicated that Thompson's testimony had an impact. It was very believable, and they looked from Thompson, on the witness stand to White Moon sitting behind the prosecution table. The Cheyenne soldier maintained his impassive face, but his body had visibly tensed when Thompson started his testimony. Laura thought she could see his shoulders drop as it went on.

The court went silent as Thompson left the stand. As much as she wanted to see Plenty Horses acquitted, she felt terribly sorry for White Moon. The proud soldier she and O'Day had interviewed at the first trial had completely lost his credibility. It was bad enough he had left Casey's dead body in the road and had done nothing to avenge him. Now, it was revealed he'd lied to his fellow soldiers. Looking around at the other spectators, she thought they seemed to have the same feeling. Watching the Cheyenne soldier's status evaporate was incredibly uncomfortable.

Without Living Bear or Phillip Wells available to testify, Powers was ready to put the final stamp on the war issue, and he called Captain Frank Baldwin to the stand. Laura's stomach burned as she waited for the final piece of testimony that would tear down the prosecution's case once and for all. Baldwin could provide testimony linking the Culbertson case, establishing a state of war, and the final key element, describing the execution of women and children at Wounded Knee outside the battlefield.

"Captain Frank Baldwin," the bailiff called again. Like most of the other spectators, Laura turned to look at the back doors. When the door opened, one of the policemen acting as bailiffs emerged and announced, "He's not here."

The court erupted in murmurs of confusion. The judge slammed the gavel several times. "Mr. Powers, it seems your witness is not available."

Powers looked as perplexed as everyone else. "Your Honor, I'd ask that the court be recessed so we can find our witness. His testimony is vital to our case."

Judge Edgerton pulled out his pocket watch. "It is getting late in the day anyway. Court is recessed until tomorrow morning at nine o'clock. We will continue with the defense case at that time." He slammed the gavel, and the spectators took a collective gasp.

"I wonder where the hell Baldwin is?" the man sitting next to Laura said to nobody in particular.

She felt the blood drain from her face. As the people around her rose and made their way out of the court, she sat still. What had Baldwin done? She and Morgan had not seen him in the last two days, but he'd told them he would be there to testify. He'd promised.

NOCK PACED BACK AND FORTH behind the desk in his office. Laura and Morgan had met for a quick dinner at their little diner and then made their way to Nock's office. At dinner, they'd decided Morgan had to break his promise to Baldwin and tell the lawyers about the murders at Wounded Knee and the subsequent cover up. Nock hadn't given them the chance, however.

As soon as they entered, he pointed to a telegraph on his desk. "Baldwin says he'll be on the late train tonight and will be here in time to testify," he said. "He said he doesn't need to review the questions and I should just put him on the stand and give him latitude. He'll do the rest."

Laura looked at Morgan and saw him nodding. Baldwin had been very specific about how he wanted the murders revealed. If the murders were to be presented, he wanted to put Miles in the best light possible.

"Do you think we should trust him, Mr. Morgan?" Nock asked. "If he says he'll be here, will he show up?"

Morgan said nothing and kept his focus on his boots.

Nock answered his own question. "I guess we don't have much choice. Phillip Wells will not be testifying?" Morgan shook his head.

"And you haven't found Living Bear?"

"They think he's still at Pine Ridge," Morgan said quietly. "The court sent a marshal for him, but I heard he was headed to Sioux City to gamble. They aren't working too hard to bring Living Bear back."

"Someone has been pretty effective at keeping our witnesses away from Sioux Falls. I'm not sure who it is, but there's clearly an effort to kill our case."

Laura said, "What do you think your chances will be, Mr. Nock?"

The lawyer sighed and sat back down. "We made some progress with the White Moon testimony. He looks like a fool now. Anytime we can make a prosecution witness look like a fool to the jury, it helps our case. I hope the judges give us some latitude with the Culbertsons trial and the state of war. Perhaps they'll be more lenient with the famous Captain Baldwin on the stand."

Laura said in a soft voice, "So Baldwin's going to be the key?"

Nock nodded. "Baldwin and our brilliant closing arguments," he said with a smile. "If we can get Captain Baldwin to declare a state of war and tie in the Culbertsons, maybe . . . just maybe . . ."

Nock rose to his feet and extended his hand. "Well, I had better put the finishing touches on my closing. Thank you both for everything you've done. You've given us a fighting chance."

Morgan had just taken back his hand when a redheaded boy rushed into the office, breathing hard. He looked like he must have run up all four flights of stairs. "Mr. Nock, Mr. Nock . . ."

The boy's face was red, and he was gasping for air. "Mr. Nock," he said. "It's White Moon . . . he tried to kill himself."

Laura felt the blood drain from her face. Morgan reached for her hand and squeezed it lightly.

Nock sat heavily back in his chair. "What happened?"

"After the trial, he went back to the Merchants. When American Horse and He Dog were at dinner, he went to their room and stabbed himself in the neck. He was bleeding all over their bed."

"My God," Nock said. "Is he going to be all right?"

"They took him to the doctor's office. There was blood everywhere." The boy gestured with his hands.

"I did this to him," Laura said in a monotone. "I'm responsible. I said he lied. I told you to . . ."

"He did this to himself," Morgan said, holding her hand in both of his. "We only brought out the truth."

Laura pictured the Cheyenne scout's face when they'd dined together. He had been so stiff . . . so upright . . . so proud of his uniform . . . so proud of being a soldier. She had taken it all away from him.

"Billy, do they know if he'll live?" Nock said in a quiet voice.

"He ain't dead yet, Mr. Nock. Nobody seems to know if he's gonna live or not."

Nock had gone into a quiet, dazed state, his eyes glazed. "Thank you, Billy," he said barely audibly. "I appreciate it." He opened his desk drawer, took out a coin and handed it across the desk. "Can you please stop by Mr. Powers's house and tell him? He's working from his home tonight."

The boy smiled and said, "Thank you, Mr. Nock," and left the room at a trot.

As boy's footsteps receded down the hallway, Laura collapsed against Morgan's shoulder. She buried her face in the rough cloth of his coat and sobbed. She was aware of his arms around her but not much else.

"I'll take her home now, Mr. Nock," Morgan said.

She felt Morgan's strong arms pulling her to feet.

"Mrs. Bowman, I know how bad you feel," Nock said. "This is one of the worst parts of my job. But you have to know, we only pursued the truth and only to save our client."

All Laura could do was nod. Morgan walked her down the stairs and across the street to the Cataract. She was aware of taking steps and of Morgan's arm around her, but nothing else. When the doorman asked if everything was all right, Morgan mumbled to him politely. When they finally got to her door, she fumbled to find her key, unlocked the door and they entered.

"Laura," he said. "We did what we had to do."

She looked up at him with a new torrent of tears streaming down her cheeks. "He might die."

"Yes, and Plenty Horses might live because we brought out the truth."

Laura took a deep breath. "Yes, that's right, I guess." She looked up at him. "Thank you . . . thank you for taking care of me," she said. "I want to spend some time by myself to . . . to work this out."

"I understand," he said. "I'll try to find out how White Moon is and meet you before court tomorrow."

"Thank you," she said. "I'll see you tomorrow."

Morgan nodded and walked out of the room.

Chapter Nineteen

May 29, 1891

I'M TIRED OF ALL THIS CRAP," the fat man said. "This damn thing has been going on forever. They need to hang the damned Indian and get it over with."

Laura tried to ignore the man sitting to her left. His girth took up a good share of the bench. She scooted a little closer to Morgan, but didn't want to lean on him obviously. He'd met her in the lobby of the Cataract that morning, and she'd taken his arm, ignoring the looks from Haddie McKenna's table. He told her White Moon was going to recover. She'd closed her eyes and thanked God. She wanted to help Plenty Horses, but had no desire to hurt anyone.

There was more of a sense of unease in the courtroom than any other day she'd attended. A month ago the sense of rowdiness on the streets had put a pall of inevitability to the proceedings. The courtroom arguments were just an added sideshow to the hanging everyone expected. As the first case dragged on, the defense kept pointing out uncomfortable assertions regarding the mistreatment of the Lakota. Sioux Falls spectators were aware these things were true, but nobody wanted to spend much time thinking about them. They were someone else's problem and didn't impact the stores on Phillips Avenue. The spectators wanted the trial to provide a nice, clear *guilty* or *innocent*, black or white, hang or not hang result. The trial had muddled the issues and there was too much confusion now. The *Argus Leader* had run a headline that morning: "Was it War?" Nobody wanted to think about Wounded Knee, but it continued to be forced on them.

Laura wondered what they would think when Baldwin testified about the three troopers riding down and executing women and children. Morgan had confirmed the Captain had made it to Sioux Falls, although he'd been unable to talk with him. She'd been so proud of Morgan when he brought back the proof of that incident. The strain of the last month showed in the lines on his face, or perhaps it was the strain of the last five months. He still hadn't described to her what his role had been at Wounded Knee, but she knew it had a profound impact on him. He'd been driven to wallow in drink and then driven to help Plenty Horses. He felt her staring at him, gave her a half smile and patted her arm. "It'll be over soon," he whispered. "One way or the other." She nodded and wondered if she wanted it to be.

Powers called R.O. Pugh, the issue clerk at the Pine Ridge agency when court was called to order. Pugh testified that the Indians had received no rations from November 1890 to mid-January 1891. When the members of Two Strikes's band, which included Plenty Horses's family, finally did surrender in January, they received their rations from the War Department. Over Sterling's objections, Powers told the court they were, therefore, treated as "prisoners of war."

Laura looked at the faces of the spectators. It was so clear to her there was a war on and Plenty Horses was just a soldier. She could only wonder if that meant anything to them. To the frontiersmen present, it seemed the question was only whether an Indian had killed a white man.

As Pugh sat down, a tension settled over the courtroom. Everyone knew who would testify next. Powers called Captain Frank Baldwin to the stand. All the heads of the spectators turned in unison to the back doors of the courtroom. Would he show up this time?

The doors opened, and Baldwin marched smartly down the aisle. The difference between the man she'd met and talked with informally and this person approaching the witness chair was remarkable. Captain Baldwin strode down the aisle of the courtroom with a purpose. In his dress-blue uniform and military bearing, he was the epitome of what a U.S. army officer was supposed to look like. Laura couldn't help but feel the jury would agree with anything Captain Baldwin told them.

Under Powers's questioning, Baldwin testified that he had visited the Wounded Knee battlefield. When he was asked to describe what he saw there, Sterling objected, stating that, "There is nothing to show that the Indians who fought at Wounded Knee had anything to do with or were even known by the defendant. They belonged to different tribes."

Laura held her breath. If Baldwin was not permitted to discuss Wounded Knee, he couldn't testify about the murders the troopers had inflicted and Plenty Horses would surely hang. All the work she and Morgan had put in would be for naught. Baldwin patiently waited for the judges to rule on the objection. Judge Edgerton overruled it, and Laura let a long breath out. Baldwin would testify. He smiled as if he was surprised there was any question of whether he could say anything he wanted.

Powers asked him to describe what he saw at Wounded Knee. "I saw a great many dead Indians. I saw guns, ammunition, cooking utensils, etcetera, scattered everywhere. I saw over one hundred dead bodies of Indians—men, women, and children. I saw a body which was said to be that of Big Foot. His body was at the west end of the string of bodies."

The graphic picture had silenced the courtroom. Most of the people in the room had heard of the atrocities of Wounded Knee, but to hear the Medal of Honor captain calmly and vividly describe them was heart-wrenching. Laura looked over at Morgan and saw his eyes tearing up. It was as if he was in a trance and Baldwin's words were the only thing in the world he heard.

She wished he would hurry up and describe the murders. The horror of Wounded Knee would prove a state of war was on, but nobody thought it would be enough to convince the jury to let an Indian go free. Now was the perfect time for him to describe how he found the tracks of the three troopers who had tracked the woman and children a mile from the battlefield. She bounced on the bench and thought, *Come on, come on, Captain Baldwin. Get this over with.*

Powers asked, "Was the battle, Captain, a result of war?"

Before Sterling could get in his objection, Baldwin said, "It was without a doubt. The army was equipped as they should have been at such a time. Sentinels were stationed and Pine Ridge was fortified." There was a stirring through the courtroom. This was the most impressive declaration of the state of war yet.

Sterling pounded the table, "Your Honor, I object!" His voice almost screeched with indignation.

Edgerton slammed the gavel. "Objection sustained. The jury will disregard."

"Oh, no," Laura whispered. "They have to consider it."

Powers took the defeat in stride and walked back to the defense table. He turned back to face the witness. "Where was the defendant first taken when arrested?"

Sterling jumped to his feet again. "I object!" He did not want to give Baldwin a chance to answer again before he could object. He turned to Powers and demanded, "What do you propose to prove?"

Powers replied, "That the defendant was arrested as a prisoner of war and was held as such. I will show that Plenty Horses was held by General Miles as a prisoner of war and that General Miles absolutely refused to deliver the prisoner until certain conditions were met."

Laura had not expected Powers to tie in the Few Tails murder with this line of questioning, and evidently Baldwin hadn't either. A glimmer of uneasiness appeared behind his professional exterior. The next few minutes would perhaps have a significant impact on the next presidential election.

"What do you mean?" Judge Edgerton asked with a growl. "The defendant was arrested on a warrant from this court. I'm not aware that this court has been put under conditions by General Miles."

"I have seen all the correspondence between the War Department and the attorney general in which the War Department absolutely refused to deliver over the defendant to civil authorities until certain whites who had committed outrages were arrested and dealt with." There was a collective gasp in the courtroom. Laura pictured the smug faces of Culbertsons on the way to the Grand Jury three weeks ago. She could see O'Day writing furiously. Her work in Deadwood was coming to fruition.

Judge Edgerton was not deterred. "General Miles is in no position to exact any conditions from this court."

"But . . ." Powers said holding up some of the papers Laura had brought back from Deadwood.

Edgerton cut in and slammed the gavel. "The court is absolutely through with this matter."

Laura thought she detected a look of relief on Baldwin's face. The judge had overruled Miles's demands to tie the Culbertsons to

Plenty Horses from going into a public record. Now he had to bring up the murders. It was the only way to get an acquittal.

Powers was winding down the testimony from Baldwin. Laura leaned over and whispered to Morgan, "When is he going to talk about the murders? It has to be soon."

Morgan's cheekbones stuck out prominently from his face. It was as if his face had turned to stone. "I'll kill that son of a bitch if he crosses me," he said between clenched teeth. "He isn't going to do it. He's going to let them hang that boy. I trusted him. I . . . will . . . kill him."

Laura reached across her body to put a hand on his arm. His bicep was hard, hard as a rock. She didn't know if she could hold him down, but she would try. "It's all right, Morgan," she whispered. "We'll figure out another way."

Morgan turned and looked at her face, his blue eyes flashing, "He said he'd do it. He said he'd testify to those murders and save Plenty Horses," he growled. "I believed him, Goddamn it. I trusted him. Damned officers anyway." Morgan's voice was rising, and some of the spectators around him were turning their heads.

Powers said, "I have no further questions, your Honor."

Sterling rose, "I have no questions, your Honor."

Captain Baldwin got up from the witness chair and looked at the faces of the jury. Laura thought she saw him shake his head slightly. He'd established a state of war, but nothing else. She didn't feel like it would be enough.

Morgan's hands were shaking. His face had lost all color. When she looked into his eyes she saw a combination of anger, betrayal, and sadness. She had no doubt he would kill Captain Baldwin before he could get on the train back to Chicago. She could hold him here, hold him with her, until the court recessed and then he'd be gone. Gone to her . . . gone to the world. He would kill Baldwin and would be sentenced to death . . . or Baldwin would kill him first. Either way, Morgan would die, and she would be alone. And Plenty Horses would die. She shivered. *God, please don't call a recess*, she thought. *Just a few more minutes please.*

Powers approached the bench. "Your Honor, we are ready to make our final arguments."

In a moment, the judges would recess the court to the next day. Laura gripped Morgan's arm with both hands. When the spectators filed out of the courtroom, she knew Morgan would tear away from her, find Baldwin and shoot him. Plenty Horses would die, Morgan would die, and Laura Bowman would be left alone . . . again.

Judge Edgerton took his gavel in hand and lifted it to call a recess.

"Wait a moment, gentlemen," Judge Shiras cut in. He pointed at Sterling and then at Powers and said, "If you have both concluded the presentation of testimony, I have something to say to the jury."

Laura had never in her life felt such a sense of silence. The over two hundred people in attendance held their collective breath.

Judge Shiras continued, "There is no need of going further with this case." Before anyone could react he said, "Members of the jury, I'm going to instruct you that you have only one verdict available to you. You must find the defendant . . . not guilty."

There was a stunned silence in the courtroom. Even the bailiffs looked shocked. Morgan's face lost the hard tenseness that had been there only seconds ago. Laura's stomach churned. The actions didn't seem real. Time seemed to slow down to a crawl.

Shiras continued, his voice rising over the murmurings spreading across the courtroom as the impact from his words registered. "From the entire evidence, it clearly appears that on the day when Lieutenant Casey met his death, there existed in and about the Pine Ridge Agency, a condition of actual warfare between the Army of the United States there assembled under the command of Major General Nelson Miles and the Indian troops occupying the camp.

"While the manner in which Plenty Horses killed Lieutenant Casey was such as would meet the severest condemnation, nevertheless we cannot deny the fact that Lieutenant Casey was engaged in an act of legitimate warfare against the Indian, and was in such condition that he might legitimately be killed as an act of war by a member of the hostile camp against which he was then operating."

"Under these circumstances, it is the judgment of the Court that a verdict of guilty could not be sustained and, therefore, the jury is instructed to return a verdict of . . . not guilty."

A man sitting behind Laura shouted, "That's it! It's over. It's . . . not guilty."

She felt the tension drain out of Morgan's arm, and now her fingers dug into his flesh. He turned toward her, his mouth only a few inches from her ear, "My God, you did it. He's free."

She kissed him right then and there . . . right on the mouth. She didn't care who saw them. His lips were hard and dry and hers were soft and supple. She put her hand behind his head and held it there, held him to her. He tried to pull away at first and then fell into the kiss. For the moment, she didn't care if life would ever go on. In that single moment, she was happy . . . incredibly happy.

She pulled back and placed her hands on either side of his face and studied his eyes. "*We* did it," she said. "We did it . . . you and me together." She kissed him again and this time he returned it, his lips and tongue entwined with hers. They felt the commotion in the courtroom, heard the shouts, felt the spectators moving around them, but neither of them could leave the kiss. Then together, it seemed, they broke the kiss and rejoined the real world. They'd had their moment and now they were back to reality.

The courtroom was in bedlam. Laura hadn't considered how the citizenry would react to an acquittal. There had been such a remote chance of it, she hadn't spent much time thinking about it. A couple of the rough-looking frontiersmen were shouting it was a travesty, but most of the audience was gleefully shaking hands and hugging one another. A piece of history had just occurred, and they'd witnessed it.

Plenty Horses was standing and shaking hands with Nock, Powers and the Lakota men behind them. From across the room Nock caught Laura's eye and waved triumphantly. He mouthed, "My office tomorrow," and she waved back. Sterling, ever the professional, was packing his briefcase. Laura thought it was ironic. He now had to try to get a jury in Deadwood to convict four white men for shooting a Lakota man.

Given the tone of the conversations at the start of the first trial, Laura thought the spectators would have been incensed about the directed verdict, and she would have feared for Plenty Horses's life. The angry mob that would have stormed the streets at the start of the trial never materialized. Through the weeks of proceedings, the average spectator had gained more appreciation for the state of war. There didn't appear to be any appetite for revenge. Most people were just glad it was finally over.

Morgan had his arm around Laura's back, and they took in the celebrations in the courtroom, letting the excitement wash over them.

"What about Baldwin?" she said, turning toward him.

His face clouded. "He still lied to me . . . to us."

She didn't want to think about Baldwin, or the citizenry, or even Plenty Horses. She wanted to think about Morgan. "Let's go to my room and have a glass of champagne," she said. "We can celebrate there."

———————————

Laura rose to answer the knock on her room door, and Captain Frank Baldwin strode through the threshold without being asked.

"I thought you might be here," he said, nodding at Morgan, who was sitting at the table by the window.

Laura quickly moved to the left near the desk where Morgan had set his pistol. He would have to move her in order to get to it.

"I'm sorry," Baldwin said in a strong voice. "I couldn't tell you. I wasn't sure Shiras would go through with it." He poured himself a glass of champagne and lifted it in gesture of a toast.

Laura said, "It was you . . . you who convinced him?"

Baldwin sat down in a chair across from Morgan. "We needed to come up with a way to get an acquittal without any additional fallout from Wounded Knee being exposed in open court. With the general's blessing, I had a conversation with the judge."

"So that's why you didn't say anything about the murders on the stand," she said. "You knew Shiras was going to direct a verdict."

"I was pretty sure," he said. He took another sip of champagne. "It was the only way."

Morgan hadn't moved since Baldwin entered the room. When he finally did speak, his voice was low and slow, "You took a big chance, not testifying about the murders. If Shiras would've let it go to the jury, they would have found him guilty."

"Well, we don't know that," Baldwin said. "We don't know what the jury would have done with or without the testimony about the murders . . . or anything else for that matter. Going straight to the judge was the only way to insure a Not Guilty verdict."

"General Miles approved of this posturing?" Laura asked.

"Not officially of course," Baldwin said. "The evidence of war was overwhelming. Sterling knew that when he went to Chicago and talked with the general." He smiled and pointed at Morgan, "You didn't know that, did you? Two weeks ago, Sterling approached the general face to face. General Miles wouldn't leave the Seventh Cavalry hanging by submitting that there was no war on. Politics be damned." It was clear he was proud of the stand the general had taken.

Morgan spoke again, quietly, "I'm sure that was more your doing than the general's."

Baldwin smiled. "Let's just say Mr. Mayberry and I had a little debate in front of the general behind closed doors. I won." He sipped the champagne. "I don't think Mr. Mayberry and I are ever going to be best friends. And after the general and I had a discussion with Mr. Sateract, Mayberry will no longer be working with the general on his presidential aspirations."

"Sateract has been taken care of?" Morgan said. His voice was barely above a whisper.

Baldwin nodded towards Laura, "The general made that very clear to Mr. Sateract. Mayberry was no longer associated with him and, therefore, there would be no money . . . ever. The general also made some unspecified threats and sent him back to New York, but that's not to say that Sateract and Hiller might not show up again sometime. Slimy creatures are like cockroaches. Just when you think you've stepped on all of them, they spring back to life."

"You shoulda killed them both," Morgan growled. "I would have."

"Mr. Morgan, it's 1891. You can't just go around shooting people," Baldwin said. "Hasn't there been enough killing?"

"How did you know Shiras would be open to directing a verdict?" Laura said changing the subject before it got more heated.

"Shiras wanted to do the right thing . . ." Baldwin chucked. "Besides, making friends with the man in charge of judicial appointments in future years could be a good career move."

"You took a hell of a chance," Morgan said looking over towards the desk at his gun behind Laura.

Baldwin smiled. "You were going to kill me, weren't you?" Morgan's head nodded slowly. Baldwin continued, "You thought you were, but you wouldn't have done it. Mr. Morgan, I don't think you have much killing left in you."

"I'd do what had to be done."

"Perhaps," Baldwin said. "But you knew it would be wrong. You and I both know I wanted the right thing as much as you did."

Morgan shook his head slowly. "So, Davis, Overstreet, and Malcomb get away with killing that woman and those kids, and the general avoids another public embarrassment?"

Baldwin's face darkened. "They won't be publically court marshalled, if that's what you're asking. Their careers in the army are over, and they'll have to live with what they've done."

"That's all?" Morgan said. "That's justice?"

Baldwin swirled the champagne in his glass. "It was war, Mr. Morgan," he said. "They thought they were doing the right thing in a dangerous and chaotic situation." He looked up. "I don't want to be the one to judge them . . . do you?"

Morgan shook his head slowly. "I guess most of the Seventh did things that day we're ashamed of . . . that we have to live with."

"The war is over, Mr. Morgan," Baldwin said. "Let it end. Plenty Horses was found not guilty because he was a warrior performing in a war. From now on, there are no more Indian Wars, so there will no longer be any warriors . . . there will be only criminals. That goes for both the Lakota and the army. Plenty Horses was the last Lakota warrior."

Morgan stared at his glass. Finally he said, "Just because you absolve those men . . . and me . . . from guilt, doesn't mean we're free from it."

"That's true, Mr. Morgan," Baldwin said. "Each soldier . . . and warrior . . . has to live with himself . . . with his own values . . . with his own actions. That's where true guilt or innocence lives."

He threw back the remainder of the champagne in his glass. "Well, I have a train to catch back to Chicago. I wish I could've told you more, but it was the only way." He pointed at Morgan's revolver on the other side of Laura. "If you still want to kill me, you'll either have to do it in the next hour or come to Chicago." He made a short bow to Laura and said, "It was a pleasure, Mrs. Bowman." He made his way across the room to the door and turned, "I don't expect to see either of you again. It has been a pleasure." With a final nod, he made his way out the door.

Laura stood in the middle of the room. "Morgan, we've done a great thing. We deserve to celebrate. I deserve it, and you do, too."

"I'm going to order dinner served here," she said. Walking across the room she stood directly in front of him, bent over and kissed him on the mouth. With her hands cradling his face, she said quietly, "And you are staying the night . . . here . . . with me. All night, Mr. Morgan . . . All night."

Chapter Twenty

MAY 30, 1891

WELL, WE DID IT," George Nock said, clapping David Powers on the back. They finally looked relaxed as they sat on one side of the little conference table facing Morgan and Laura.

Laura smiled. "How's Plenty Horses handling it?"

"We had a dinner at the Merchants last night and turned him over to He Dog and American Horse," Nock said. "I'm not sure he fully understands what happened yesterday, or the last three months, for that matter. He was just happy to be free."

Powers chuckled. "It was quite the sight this morning. Butterfield had everyone involved with the trial at his studio for photographs. The Indians, Nock and I, Sterling and Balance, and the marshals all posed in various combinations. You two should have been there. He'll be selling those photographs for years."

Morgan pushed up his hat. "I don't think anybody wants to see a photograph of me."

Nock laughed. "White Moon was even there. I think he's going to be fine . . . physically, anyway."

"That's a relief," Laura said. "I hope it was worth it to do that to the poor man. Do you have any idea what the jury would have done had the question gone to them?"

Powers ran his fingers along the lapels of his coat. "O'Day claims they would have voted to acquit, but the *Argus Leader* says that they would have found him guilty of either manslaughter or murder. I guess we'll never know."

"So everyone's going home now?"

"Plenty Horses said he wasn't going to take any white charity," Nock said. "It might have been nice if he would have taken enough to pay his lawyers, but he invited us to visit him back on the reservation." He shook his head. "He did agree to take some money to sign some souvenirs for some of the ladies to cover his train fare. You may see them on sale in New York, Mrs. Bowman."

Laura forced a smile. "Yes . . . New York . . . It seems like such a faraway place now."

"Well, we'll be working with you to get your divorce completed as soon as possible so you can get back there," Nock said.

"Oh, and I almost forgot, Mr. Morgan, most of the legal community turned out for the picture taking this morning. I had a conversation with our Magistrate James O'Connor. He's agreed to drop all charges against you. You're free to go, as long as there are no further… incidents in Sioux Falls."

"Thank you," Morgan said his voice very low. He ran his fingertips along the edge of the desk. "There won't be any more incidents."

"What are your plans, Mr. Morgan, now that the trial is over and your legal problems are rectified?"

Laura's face drained of color. The answer to this question had hung over them for the last several days. She'd thought about talking with him about it that morning, but she had not wanted to break the mood. The last twelve hours had been an enchantment. Her father had once told her to not ask a question if you didn't want to hear the answer. Now, the question had been asked for her.

"I'm going back to the Badlands," Morgan said in a voice that was barely audible. Laura knew that was the answer he was going to give, but she had dreaded hearing it.

"What do you plan on doing there?" Nock asked. Powers had been watching both Morgan and Laura and read Laura's face. He put a hand on Nock's arm to stop further questioning.

"Not sure," Morgan said, diverting his eyes to the window.

Powers broke in quickly. "Well, as we said earlier, your help has been greatly appreciated. Mrs. Bowman, we look forward to working with you. Mr. Morgan, if I don't see you again, it has been a pleasure."

Laura smiled and shook hands with each of the lawyers. She was unable to say anything but nodded to them again as Morgan escorted her out of the office. They walked slowly down the stairs in silence, both of them unwilling to discuss the subject on both their minds.

When they reached the street and faced the Cateract, Laura spoke. "When will you leave?"

"Soon," he said. "The longer I wait, the more difficult it'll be."

She turned to him, and they stood together on Phillips Avenue, looking into each other's eyes. "Will you stay tonight?"

He put his hands on her arms. "I'll stay tonight, but I'm going on tomorrow's train."

She turned toward the Cateract, not willing to look back into his eyes. "Will you have dinner with me . . . in the Cateract dining room . . . tonight . . . please."

"Yes, Laura." Morgan tried to pull her back to face him, but she pulled away. "Laura . . . I . . ."

She started across Phillips Avenue. "Very well, Mr. Morgan," she said over her shoulder. "I'll make a reservation for seven o'clock. Please meet me then."

She never looked back. He stood on the street and watched her until she entered the large double doors of the Cateract Hotel.

MORGAN SQUIRMED UNEASILY in the oversized frock coat. Laura had been quite surprised when he showed up for their dinner in the coat. When she'd complimented him, he mumbled that Powers had loaned it to him. The lawyer was several sizes larger than Morgan. It looked a little ridiculous over the rest of his clothes, but she was touched by the effort. She knew how difficult it must have been for him to ask Powers to loan him the coat.

After spending a good deal of the afternoon crying, Laura had resolved she would not let her sense of loss ruin their last night together.

"You look very . . . beautiful," he said. "Dressed like this . . . in a place like this . . . you're as pretty as a dream."

Laura gave him her best smile. When she made the reservation at the Cateract, she'd tipped heavily in advance in order to get the best table. She'd resolved she would not be self-conscious about walking into the elegant dining room with Morgan. It turned out to be much easier than she had imagined. They'd barely drawn a second glance from the other diners, and Morgan, although visibly nervous, had acted with perfect manners.

"You look very hansome yourself, Mr. Morgan," she said, toasting him with her glass of wine. He gave her a half-smile and toasted her back with his water glass. He had not ordered a drink.

Laura took a deep breath. "So . . . tomorrow . . . to the Badlands?"

The lines on his face deepened. "We both knew it was going to happen . . . didn't we?"

Laura smiled weakly, "I knew it, but I didn't want to admit it."

"It wasn't as if we could ever . . . you know . . . be together," he said.

She smiled, "You're right. I don't think I would be much help to you in the Badlands."

Morgan laughed out loud. "The only thing more ridiculous than you living in a sod house in the Badlands would be me trying to live in New York City."

They both smiled and toasted again. Putting the issue on the table eased the tension and they were both relieved to be past it.

"Morgan, you don't need to do it alone . . . whatever it is you think you have to do . . ." she said. "If I can't help you . . . please let someone help."

He shook his head. "I'm sorry, Laura. I have to . . ."

"I know," she said wiping a tear from the corner of her eye. "I know you are doing what you think you have to do." They became very cognizant of the background noise in the dining room. Finally, Laura smiled and squeezed his wrist.

"I did get you something to take with you," she said. She'd been carrying a bag when he met her and she'd put it under the table while they ate. "I wanted to give you something to remember . . . to remember me . . . to remember what we've done." He nodded.

She pulled a wooden box from the bag and set it on the table. "I know you feel you have to go to the Badlands to . . . that you have to go . . . but you don't have to walk away from all comforts." He ran his fingers over the top of the box, exploring the smooth service with his fingertips. "Open it, please," she said.

Prying the box open, he smiled and pulled out a pewter salt and pepper shaker set. He laughed and said, "Why, I'll be the most elegant cook on the prairies."

She returned the laugh. "I wanted you to always know that no matter what you are doing out there, no matter how isolated and desolate it is, you can still remember to add some spice to your life."

He laughed out loud again as he admired the set and carefully placed them back in the wooden box. "I'll treasure these every time I eat."

Laura reached into the bag again. "I wanted you think of me in New York when you ate, but I also wanted to give you something that was always with you . . . everyday . . . all the time."

She handed him a smaller box. With hands shaking, he opened it and pulled out a gold watch. He held it to his face and tears welled in his eyes.

"Laura, I truly wish I could stay . . ." he said in an uneven voice.

"Shhht," she said putting a hand on his arm. "I cried my eyes out all afternoon. I know it has to be this way . . . I just want . . . tonight."

He smiled and put the watch on the table. "It will be with me forever, along with the memory of you." He shook his head. "I wish I had something to give you."

Laura pulled her hair back, and her dark eyes gleamed in the candlelight of the Cateract. "Morgan, you've given me my life back. I'll never forget you."

She stood and held out her hand to him. "Come with me, Mr. Morgan. Our last night isn't over, yet."

Epilogue

June 30, 1892
Interior, South Dakota

Dear Mr. Morgan:

I was so pleased to hear from you. It is hard to believe that it has been over a year. Thank you for letting me know about Plenty Horses's upcoming marriage. He seems to have recovered from the ordeal of his trial. I know the Lakota will never recover from the loss of their way of life, but at least there are some small victories.

I'm happy that I was able to help you start your ranch. I know it will help, and please let me know if there is anything else I can do.

As I indicated in my last letter, New York seems to be a different place since I've been back, or perhaps I'm a different person. Since I don't see many of the people I formerly associated with, the article that O'Day wrote has had little importance. I will continue to work with the American Foundation and have been helping with the women's suffrage movement. It isn't much, but I feel like I'm doing something.

I was sorry to hear about the Culbertsons' trial, but not surprised. I'm glad that Clown got to tell her story in an open court, even if the jury set the murderers free. I suppose the result was inevitable. There was no coverage of the trial here in New York.

I understand that Captain Baldwin was in New York with General Miles last week. According to the newspaper, the general's presidential campaign is now dead before it really got started, even without the Wounded Knee issues being made public. Thank goodness Plenty Horses didn't have to die to protect that secret.

Morgan, I know you think you have to pay for what you consider your sins, but you don't need to do it alone. If you won't let me into your life, I hope you let someone in, someday. Man isn't meant to live solitarily.

You are a good man and have done nothing to ever be ashamed of. I wish you believed that as much as I do.

I'll never forget you.

Affectionately and Forever Yours:

Laura Schultz

New York, New York

Author's Note

The characters, settings and events included in this book are purely fictitious, but are reflective of what may have happened in 1891. The courtroom scenes in particular are based upon newspaper accounts of the Plenty Horses trial, and the conclusions reflect the actual outcome. My thanks to the staff at the Old Court House Museum in Sioux Falls, South Dakota, for allowing me access to newspaper stories regarding the trial and the South Dakota divorce colony. They have the rifle Plenty Horses used to kill Lieutenant Casey in their collection, and I was thrilled to be able to examine it.

A good historical novel encourages readers to investigate history. An excellent resource regarding the actual Plenty Horses trial is a book by Roger Di Silvestro called *In the Shadow of Wounded Knee: The Untold Final Chapter of the Indian Wars*. I also utilized Peggy & Harold Samuels's biography on Fredric Remington to speculate about what happened in the days leading up to the shooting. A good source of the information regarding the South Dakota divorce colony was a 1990 article by Connie Develder Schaffer published by the South Dakota Historical Society (Vol. 20 No. 3) called "Money versus Morality: The Divorce Industry of Sioux Falls." In order get an idea of what it was like to live in the divorce colony, I was fortunate to find in the Augustana College Center for Western Studies an original 1895 copy of *The Divorce Mill: Realistic Sketches of the South Dakota Divorce Colony* by Harry Hazel and S.L. Lewis.

History created a spell-binding plotline. I can only hope that my dramatization in this novel lives up to it.